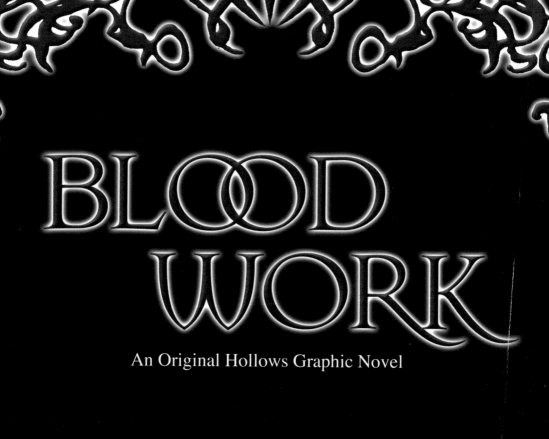

BLOOD WORK

An Original Hollows Graphic Novel

Kim Harrison

Illustrations by Pedro Maia
and Gemma Magno

Ballantine Books • New York

Blood Work is a work of fiction. Names, characters, places, and incidents are the products of the author's imagination or are used fictitiously. Any resemblance to actual events, locales, or persons, living or dead, is entirely coincidental.

Published in the United States by Del Rey, an imprint of The Random House Publishing Group, a division of Random House, Inc., New York.

Del Rey is a registered trademark and the Del Rey colophon is a trademark of Random House, Inc.

LIBRARY OF CONGRESS CATALOGING-IN-PUBLICATION DATA
Harrison, Kim.
Blood work : an original Hollows graphic novel / Kim Harrison; illustrations by Pedro Maia and Gemma Magno.
p. cm.
ISBN 978-0-345-52101-9 (hc : alk. paper) 1. Morgan, Rachel (Fictitious character)—Comic books, strips, etc. 2. Vampires—Comic books, strips, etc. 3. Cincinnati (Ohio)—Comic books, strips, etc. 4. Graphic novels. I. Maia, Pedro. II. Magno, Gemma. III. Title.
PN6727.H376B57 2011
741.5'973—dc22 2011285302

Pencils by Pedro Maia and Gemma Magno

Inks by Eman Casallos, Jan Michael T. Aldeguer, and Jezreel Rojales

Colors by P. C. Siqueira and Mae Hao

Lettering and design by Zach Matheny

Printed in the United States of America on acid-free paper.

www.delreybooks.com

2 4 6 8 9 7 5 3 1

First Edition

Introduction

Writing has always been a way for me to share the thoughts and images in my head. I've been playing with the written word for a good bit of time now, but nothing I can put on paper will surmount the simple fact that we are a visual species, highly tuned to the subtle shifts of expression and body language. It's the limits of the medium. So when the chance arose to try my hand at a visual representation of the same world I'd been playing in for the better part of a decade, I jumped at it. I had no idea what I was getting into—or how much fun it would be.

My brother was into comic books while growing up. I'll be honest with you. I looked a couple over, then went back to my science fiction and fantasy novels. But I remember the few that I read, and that's the thing. *I remember them*, whereas I couldn't possibly tell you what I dropped them for. The bold colors, the fast, smart storylines, the minimal dialogue all let me absorb the story by sight. Comic books—excuse me, graphic novels— reach into our psyche and make a more direct connection. It's all about what we see, and after nearly a decade of writing novels, I was itching to find a new way to tell a story.

So I blithely took on the task of writing my first graphic novel script, not knowing how much fun it was going to be to imagine more fully the "movie" in my head, manipulating the same images I've always been seeing, giving them structure not with words but shifts of POV, close-ups, expansive shots, trying to find the best way to tell—no, *show* the reader what was important to the story and pull them one more panel forward, one more page turned.

So here is my first graphic novel for you, *Blood Work*, written, scripted, and parceled into tiny boxes by little-old-me. I had a fabulous time learning a new way to tell a story, and I hope you enjoy it.

Kim Harrison
August 31, 2010

CHAPTER I

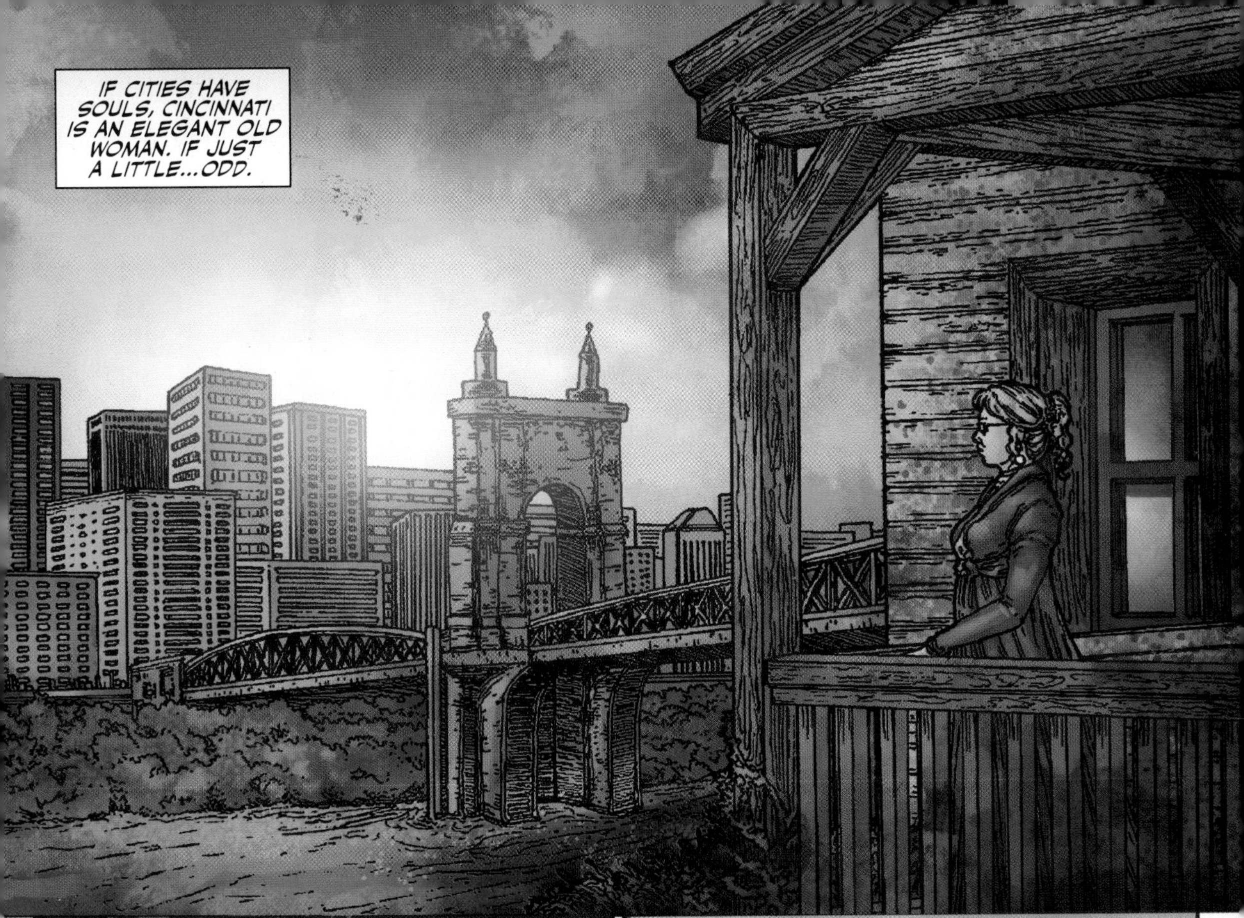
IF CITIES HAVE SOULS, CINCINNATI IS AN ELEGANT OLD WOMAN. IF JUST A LITTLE...ODD.

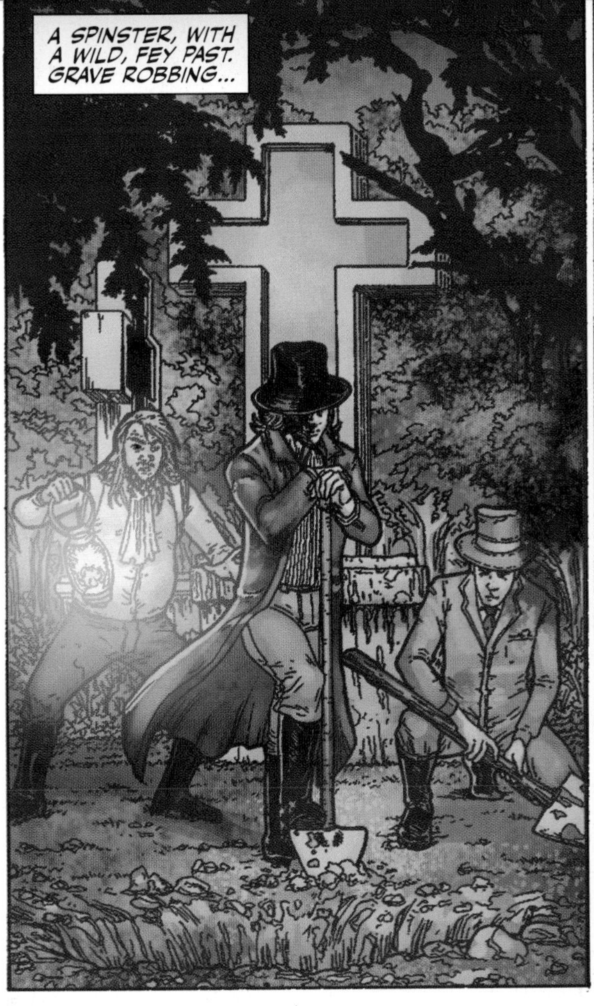
A SPINSTER, WITH A WILD, FEY PAST. GRAVE ROBBING...

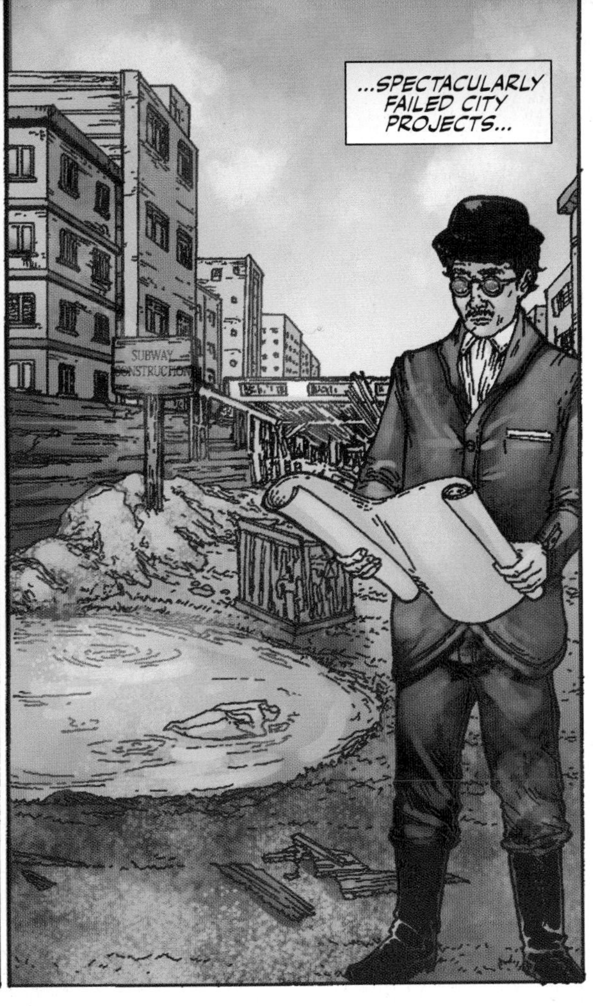
...SPECTACULARLY FAILED CITY PROJECTS...
SUBWAY CONSTRUCTION

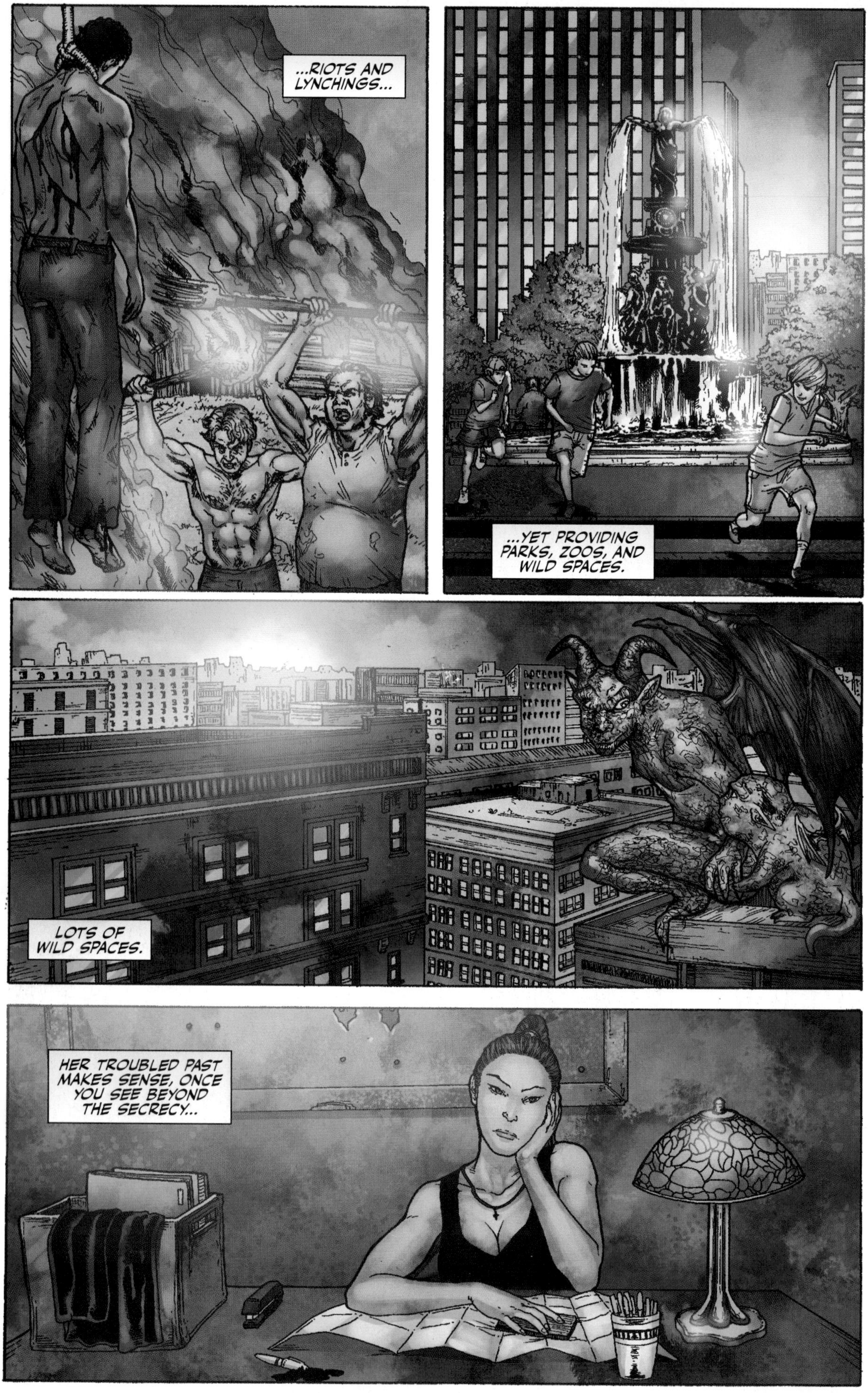
...RIOTS AND LYNCHINGS...
...YET PROVIDING PARKS, ZOOS, AND WILD SPACES.
LOTS OF WILD SPACES.
HER TROUBLED PAST MAKES SENSE, ONCE YOU SEE BEYOND THE SECRECY...

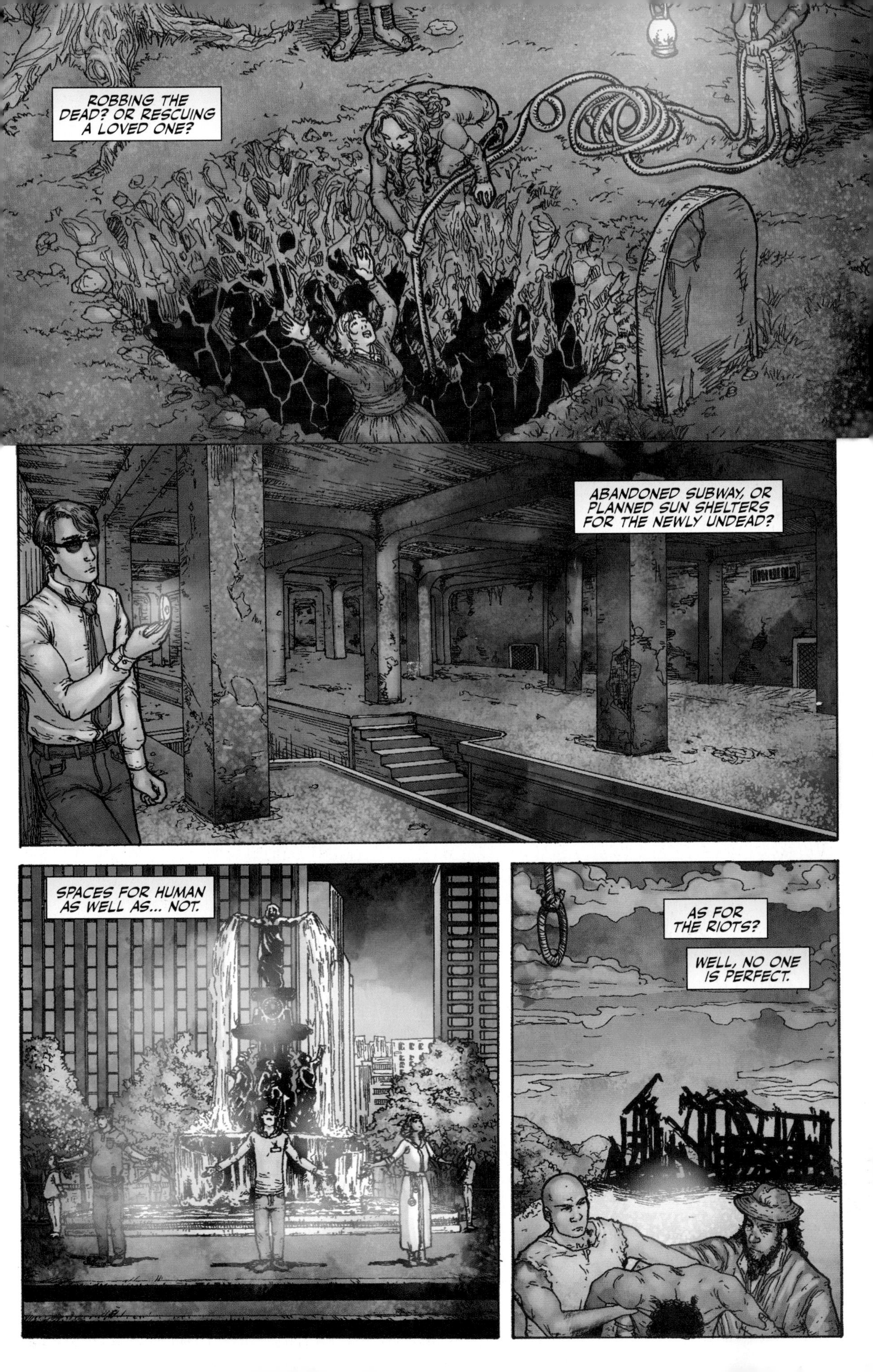

ROBBING THE DEAD? OR RESCUING A LOVED ONE?
ABANDONED SUBWAY, OR PLANNED SUN SHELTERS FOR THE NEWLY UNDEAD?
SPACES FOR HUMAN AS WELL AS... NOT.
AS FOR THE RIOTS?
WELL, NO ONE IS PERFECT.

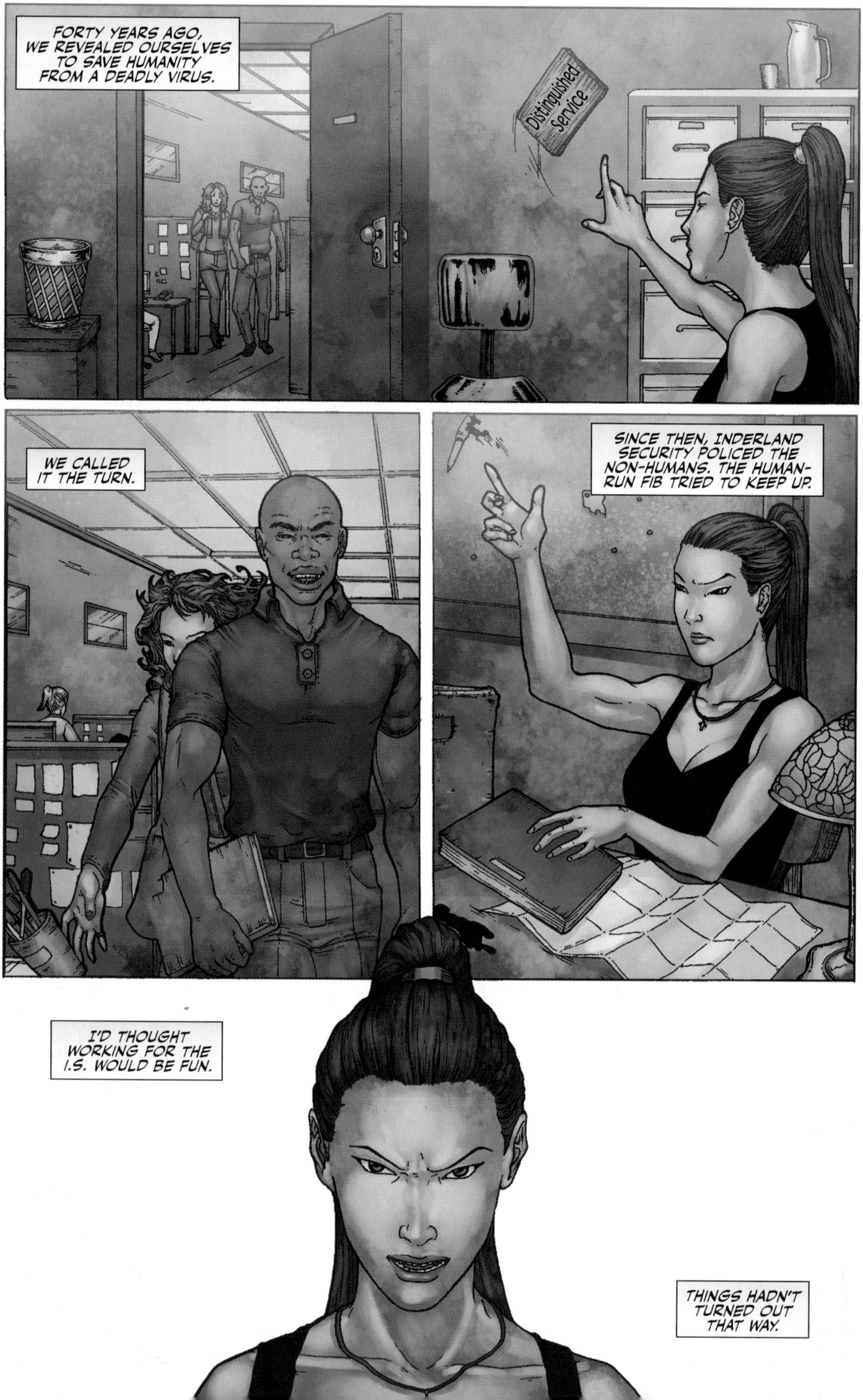
FORTY YEARS AGO, WE REVEALED OURSELVES TO SAVE HUMANITY FROM A DEADLY VIRUS.
Distinguished Service
WE CALLED IT THE TURN.
SINCE THEN, INDERLAND SECURITY POLICED THE NON-HUMANS. THE HUMAN-RUN FIB TRIED TO KEEP UP.
I'D THOUGHT WORKING FOR THE I.S. WOULD BE FUN.
THINGS HADN'T TURNED OUT THAT WAY.

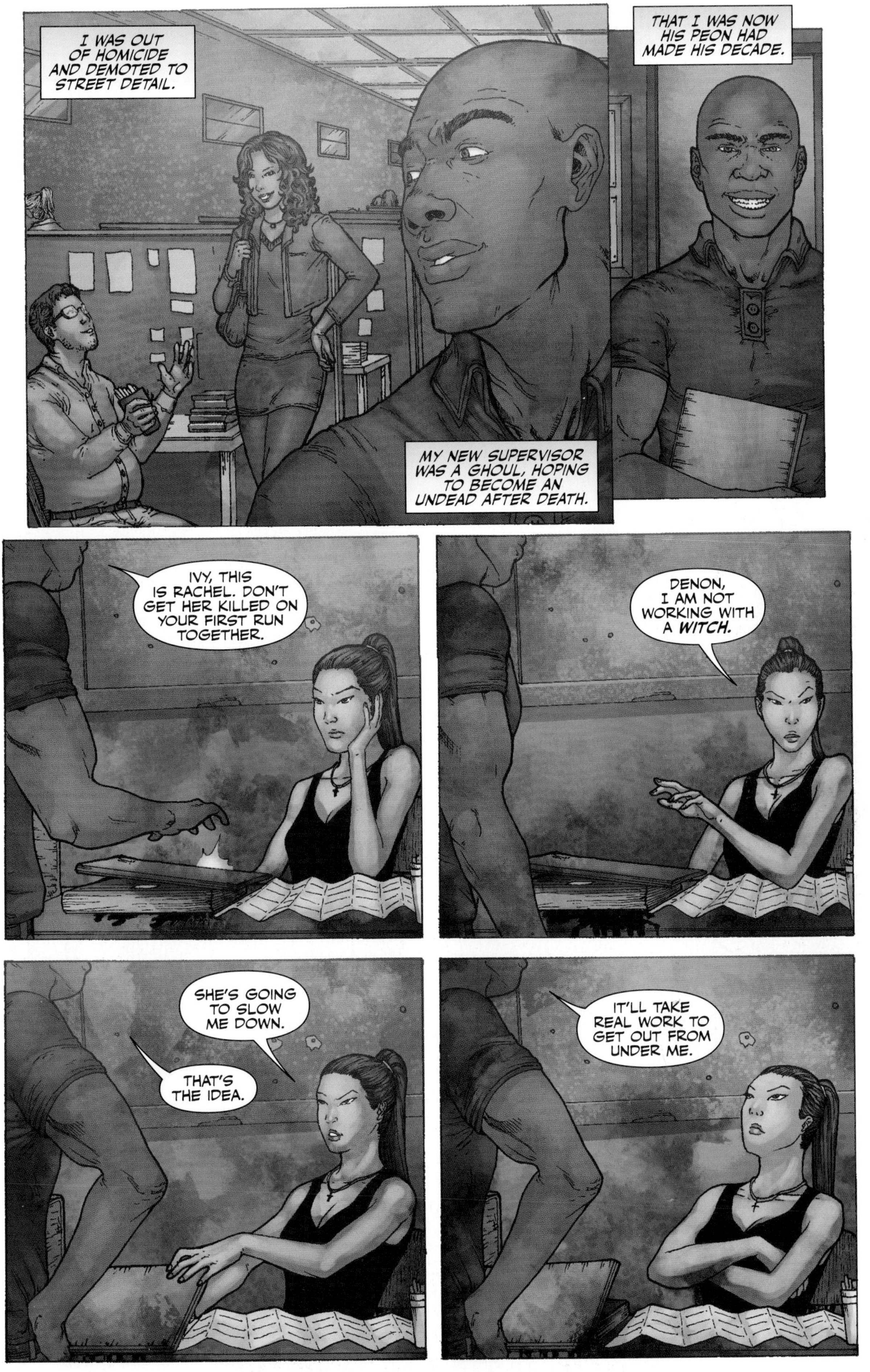
I WAS OUT OF HOMICIDE AND DEMOTED TO STREET DETAIL.
MY NEW SUPERVISOR WAS A GHOUL, HOPING TO BECOME AN UNDEAD AFTER DEATH.
THAT I WAS NOW HIS PEON HAD MADE HIS DECADE.
IVY, THIS IS RACHEL. DON'T GET HER KILLED ON YOUR FIRST RUN TOGETHER.
DENON, I AM NOT WORKING WITH A *WITCH.*
SHE'S GOING TO SLOW ME DOWN.
THAT'S THE IDEA.
IT'LL TAKE REAL WORK TO GET OUT FROM UNDER ME.

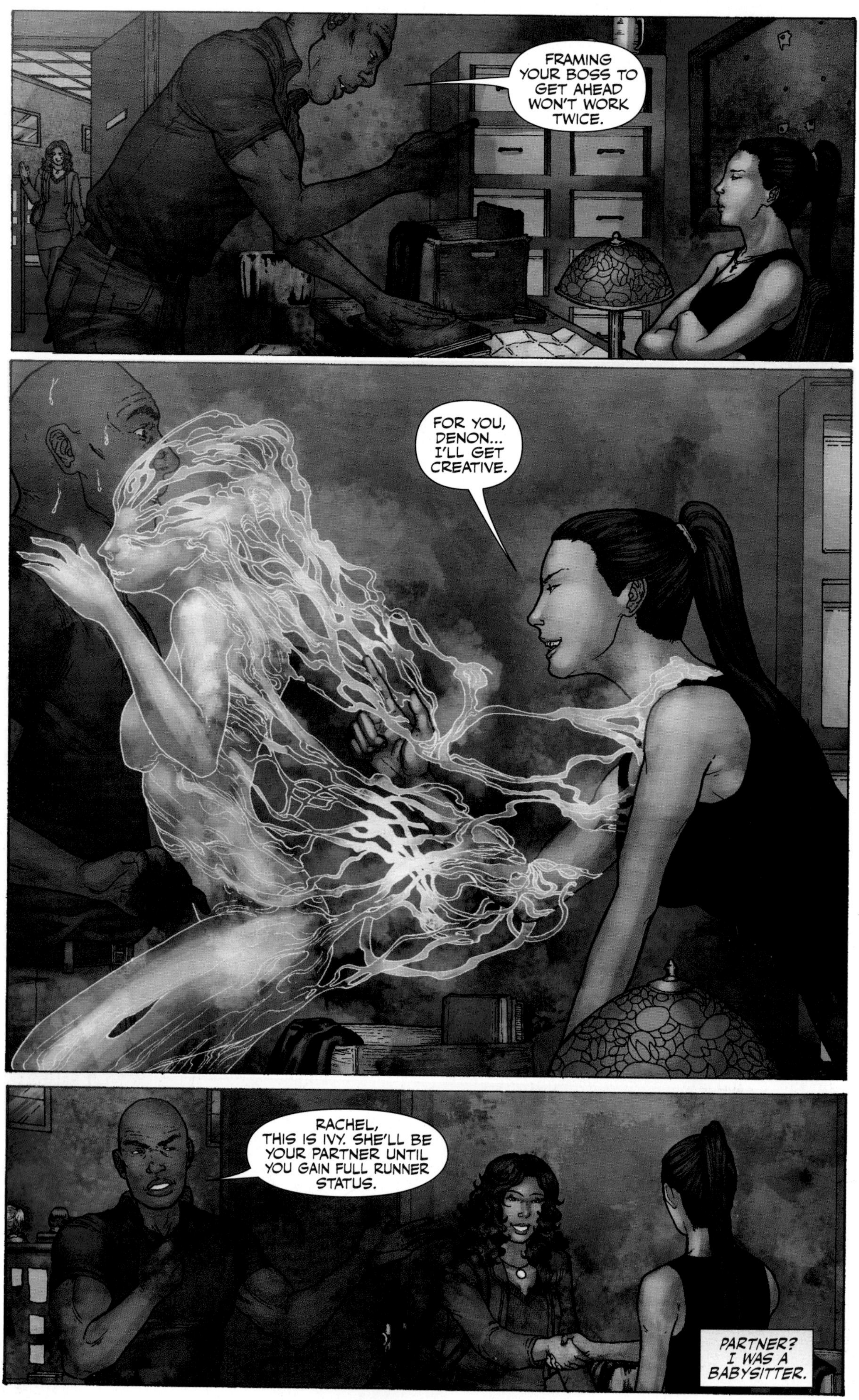
FRAMING YOUR BOSS TO GET AHEAD WON'T WORK TWICE.
FOR YOU, DENON... I'LL GET CREATIVE.
RACHEL, THIS IS IVY. SHE'LL BE YOUR PARTNER UNTIL YOU GAIN FULL RUNNER STATUS.
PARTNER? I WAS A BABYSITTER.

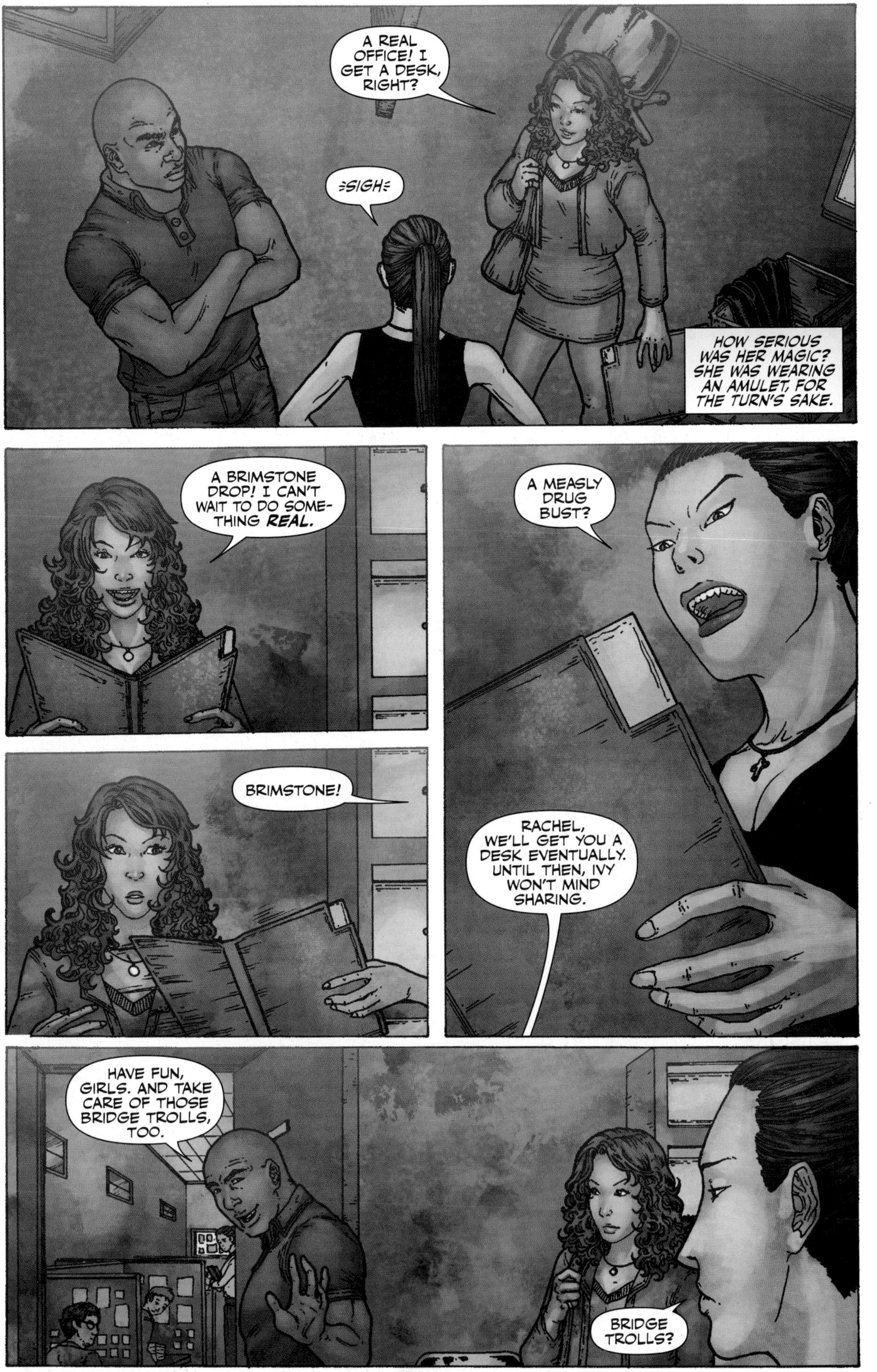
A REAL OFFICE! I GET A DESK, RIGHT?
SIGH
HOW SERIOUS WAS HER MAGIC? SHE WAS WEARING AN AMULET, FOR THE TURN'S SAKE.
A BRIMSTONE DROP! I CAN'T WAIT TO DO SOME-THING REAL.
A MEASLY DRUG BUST?
BRIMSTONE!
RACHEL, WE'LL GET YOU A DESK EVENTUALLY. UNTIL THEN, IVY WON'T MIND SHARING.
HAVE FUN, GIRLS. AND TAKE CARE OF THOSE BRIDGE TROLLS, TOO.
BRIDGE TROLLS?

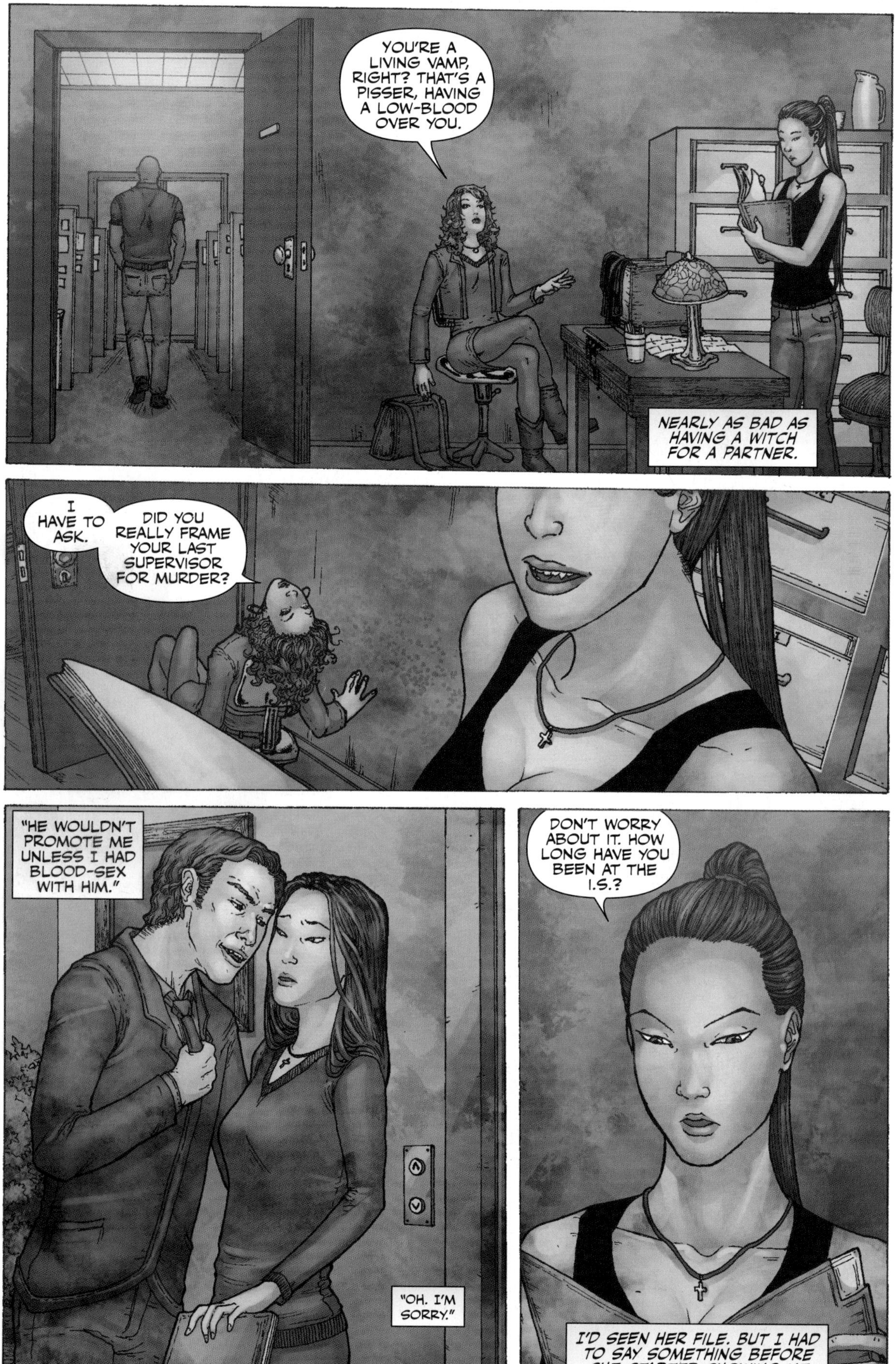

YOU'RE A LIVING VAMP, RIGHT? THAT'S A PISSER, HAVING A LOW-BLOOD OVER YOU.
NEARLY AS BAD AS HAVING A WITCH FOR A PARTNER.
I HAVE TO ASK.
DID YOU REALLY FRAME YOUR LAST SUPERVISOR FOR MURDER?
"HE WOULDN'T PROMOTE ME UNLESS I HAD BLOOD-SEX WITH HIM."
"OH. I'M SORRY."
DON'T WORRY ABOUT IT. HOW LONG HAVE YOU BEEN AT THE I.S.?
I'D SEEN HER FILE. BUT I HAD TO SAY SOMETHING BEFORE SHE STARTED SHOWING ME PICTURES OF HER CAT.

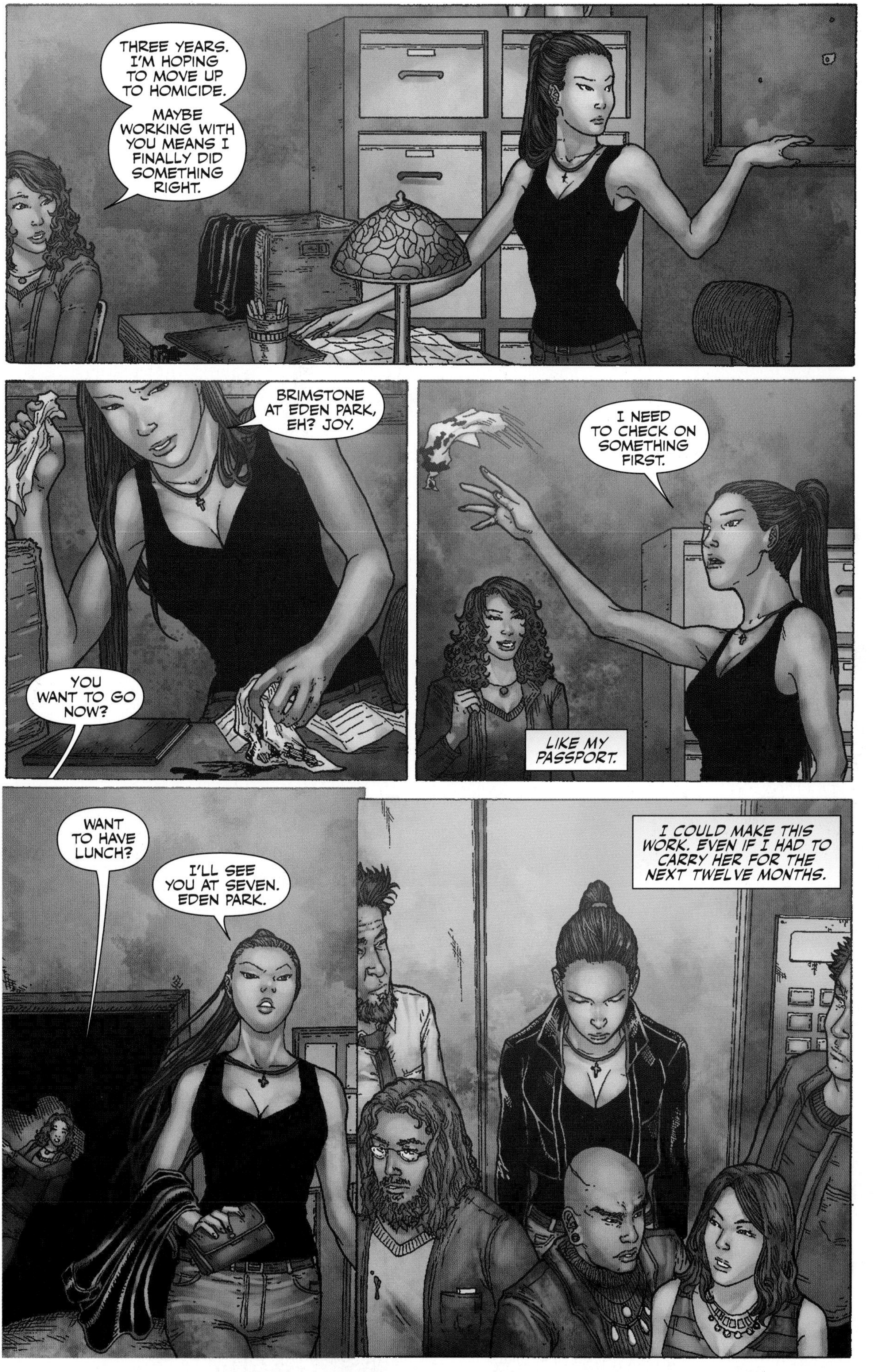
THREE YEARS. I'M HOPING TO MOVE UP TO HOMICIDE.
MAYBE WORKING WITH YOU MEANS I FINALLY DID SOMETHING RIGHT.
BRIMSTONE AT EDEN PARK, EH? JOY.
YOU WANT TO GO NOW?
I NEED TO CHECK ON SOMETHING FIRST.
LIKE MY PASSPORT.
WANT TO HAVE LUNCH?
I'LL SEE YOU AT SEVEN. EDEN PARK.
I COULD MAKE THIS WORK. EVEN IF I HAD TO CARRY HER FOR THE NEXT TWELVE MONTHS.

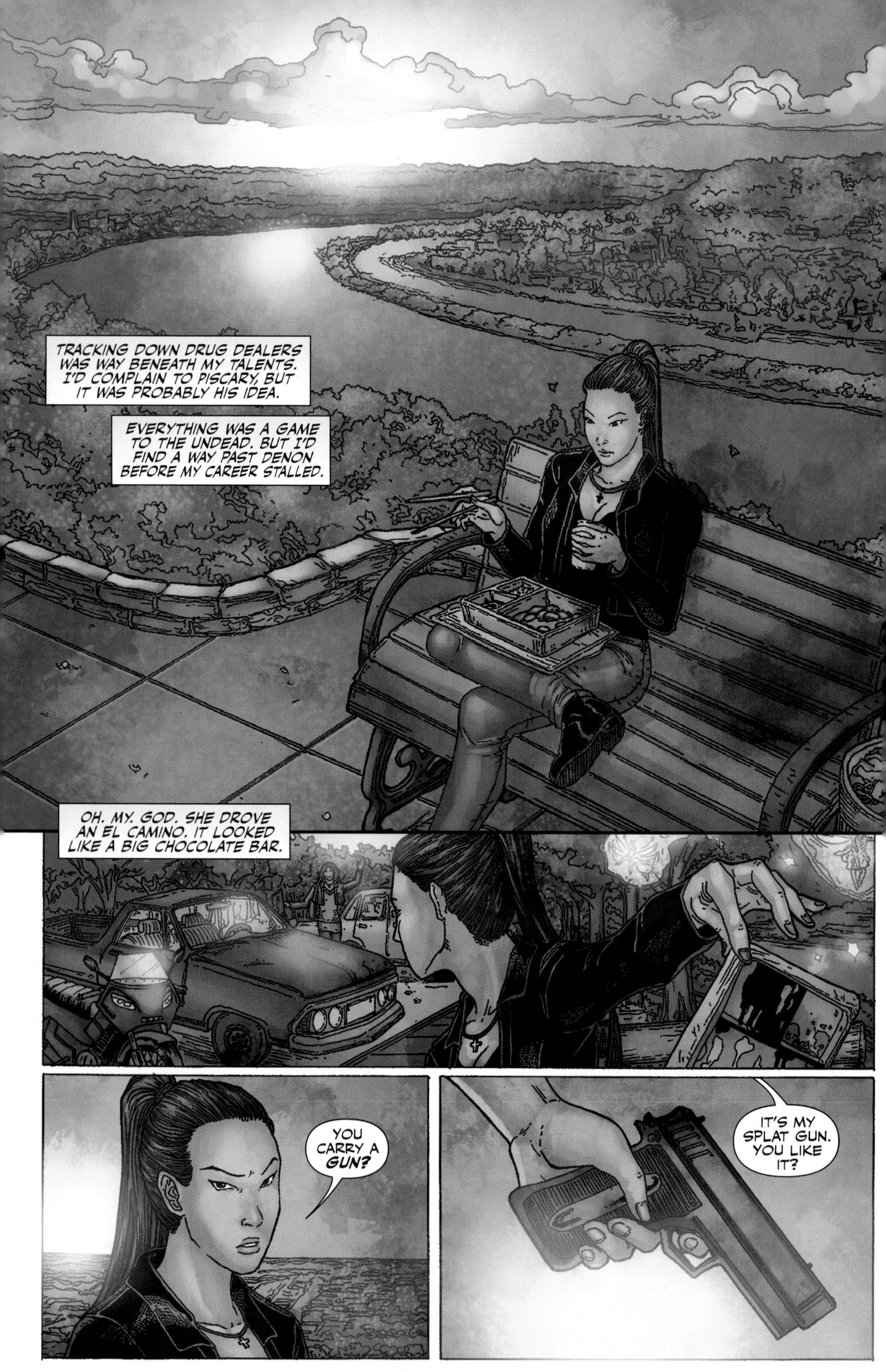
TRACKING DOWN DRUG DEALERS WAS WAY BENEATH MY TALENTS. I'D COMPLAIN TO PISCARY, BUT IT WAS PROBABLY HIS IDEA.
EVERYTHING WAS A GAME TO THE UNDEAD. BUT I'D FIND A WAY PAST DENON BEFORE MY CAREER STALLED.
OH. MY. GOD. SHE DROVE AN EL CAMINO. IT LOOKED LIKE A BIG CHOCOLATE BAR.
YOU CARRY A **GUN?**
IT'S MY SPLAT GUN. YOU LIKE IT?

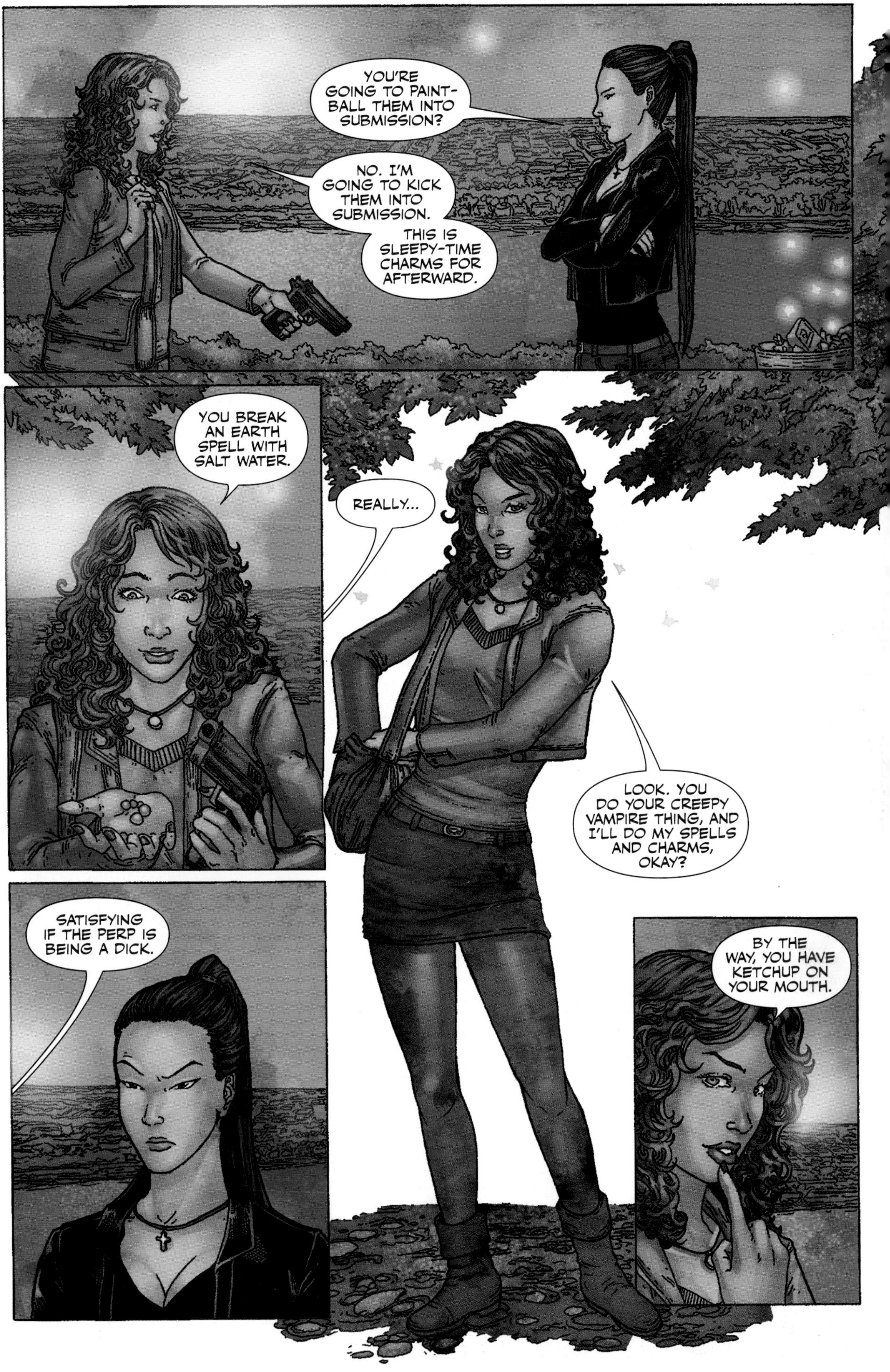
YOU'RE GOING TO PAINT-BALL THEM INTO SUBMISSION?
NO. I'M GOING TO KICK THEM INTO SUBMISSION.
THIS IS SLEEPY-TIME CHARMS FOR AFTERWARD.
YOU BREAK AN EARTH SPELL WITH SALT WATER.
REALLY...
LOOK. YOU DO YOUR CREEPY VAMPIRE THING, AND I'LL DO MY SPELLS AND CHARMS, OKAY?
SATISFYING IF THE PERP IS BEING A DICK.
BY THE WAY, YOU HAVE KETCHUP ON YOUR MOUTH.

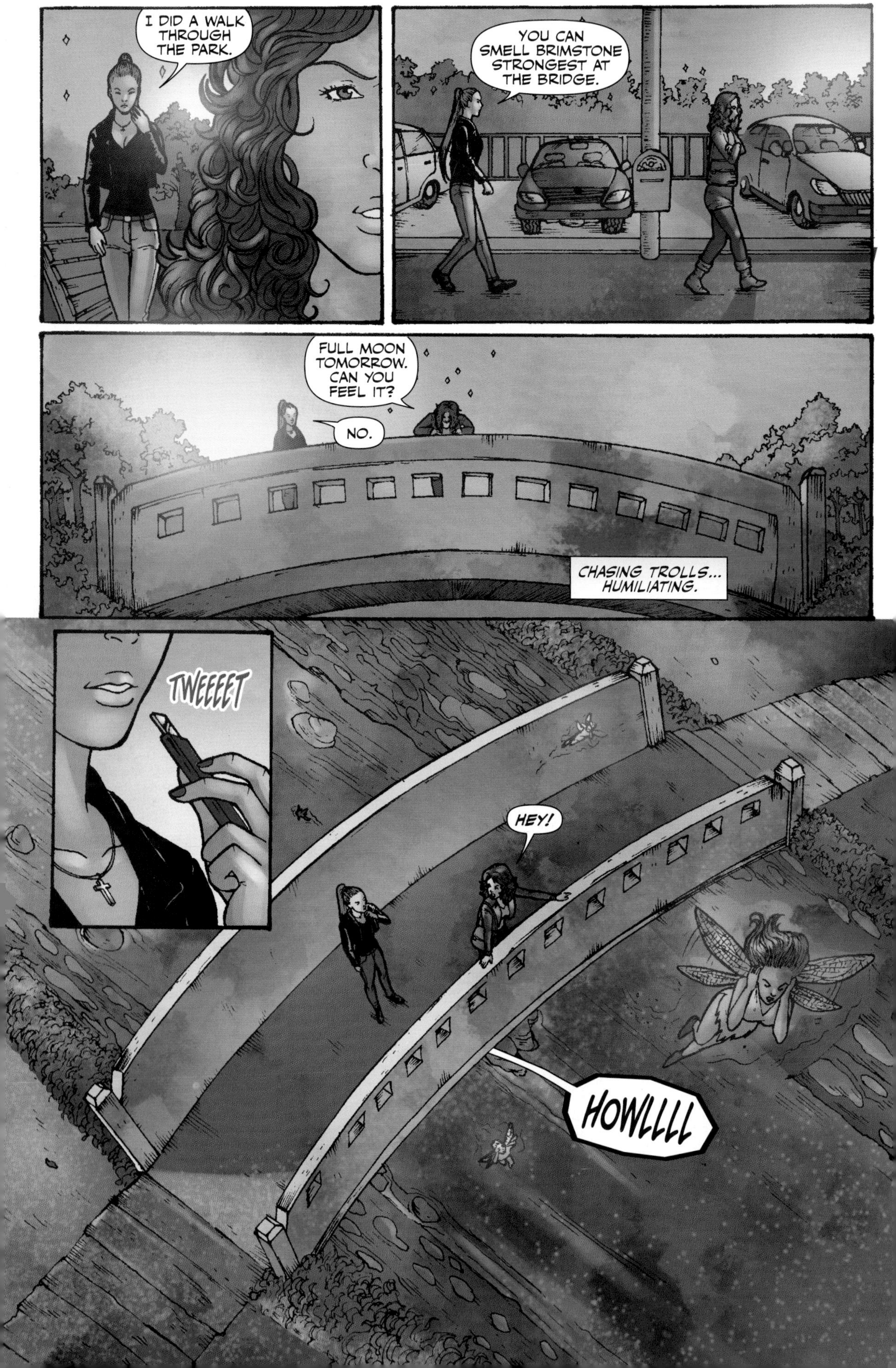
I DID A WALK THROUGH THE PARK.
YOU CAN SMELL BRIMSTONE STRONGEST AT THE BRIDGE.
FULL MOON TOMORROW. CAN YOU FEEL IT?
NO.
CHASING TROLLS... HUMILIATING.
TWEEEET
HEY!
HOWLLLL

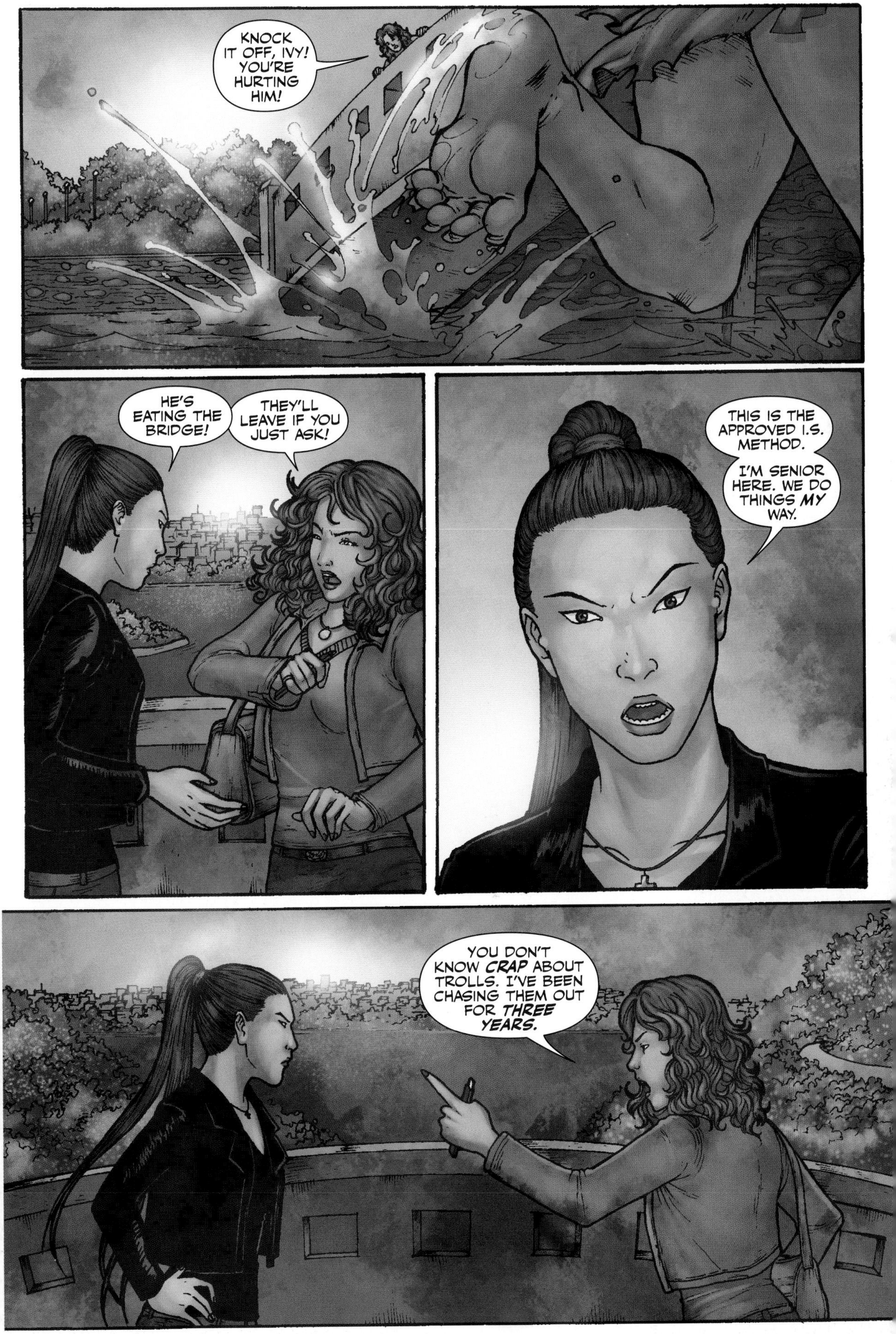
KNOCK IT OFF, IVY! YOU'RE HURTING HIM!
HE'S EATING THE BRIDGE!
THEY'LL LEAVE IF YOU JUST ASK!
THIS IS THE APPROVED I.S. METHOD.
I'M SENIOR HERE. WE DO THINGS MY WAY.
YOU DON'T KNOW CRAP ABOUT TROLLS. I'VE BEEN CHASING THEM OUT FOR THREE YEARS.

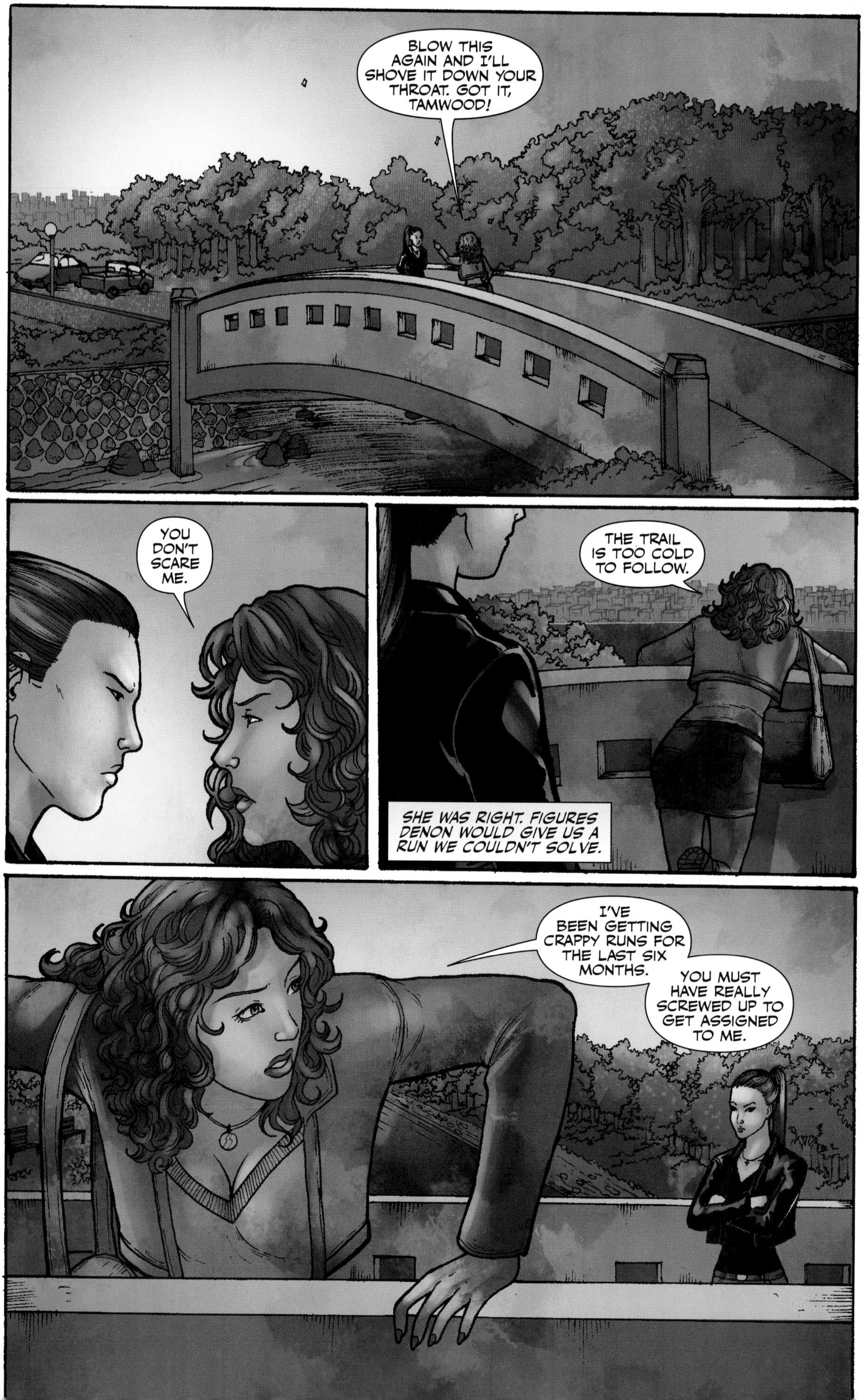

BLOW THIS AGAIN AND I'LL SHOVE IT DOWN YOUR THROAT. GOT IT, TAMWOOD!
YOU DON'T SCARE ME.
THE TRAIL IS TOO COLD TO FOLLOW.
SHE WAS RIGHT. FIGURES DENON WOULD GIVE US A RUN WE COULDN'T SOLVE.
I'VE BEEN GETTING CRAPPY RUNS FOR THE LAST SIX MONTHS.
YOU MUST HAVE REALLY SCREWED UP TO GET ASSIGNED TO ME.

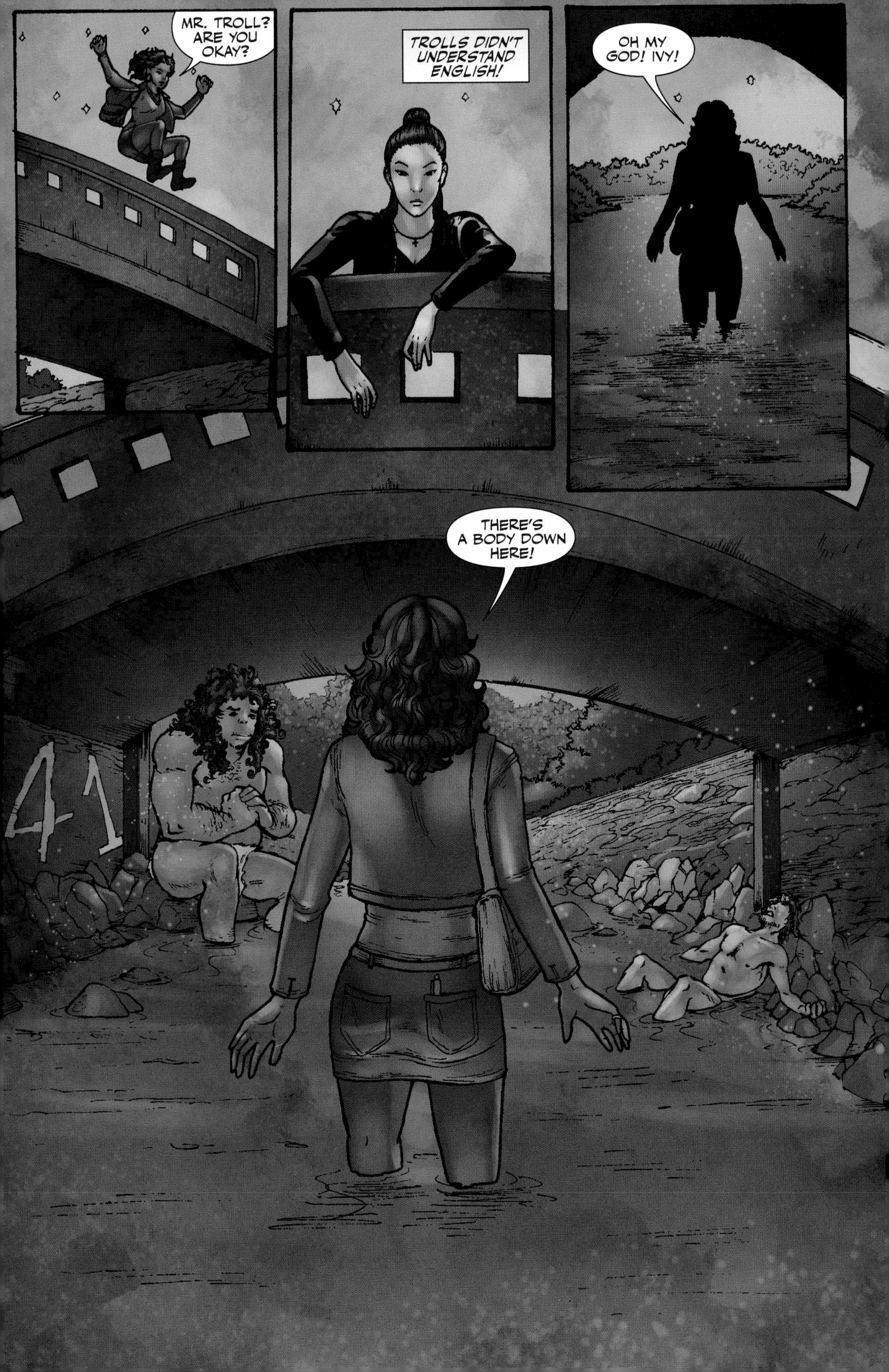
MR. TROLL? ARE YOU OKAY?
TROLLS DIDN'T UNDERSTAND ENGLISH!
OH MY GOD! IVY!
THERE'S A BODY DOWN HERE!
41

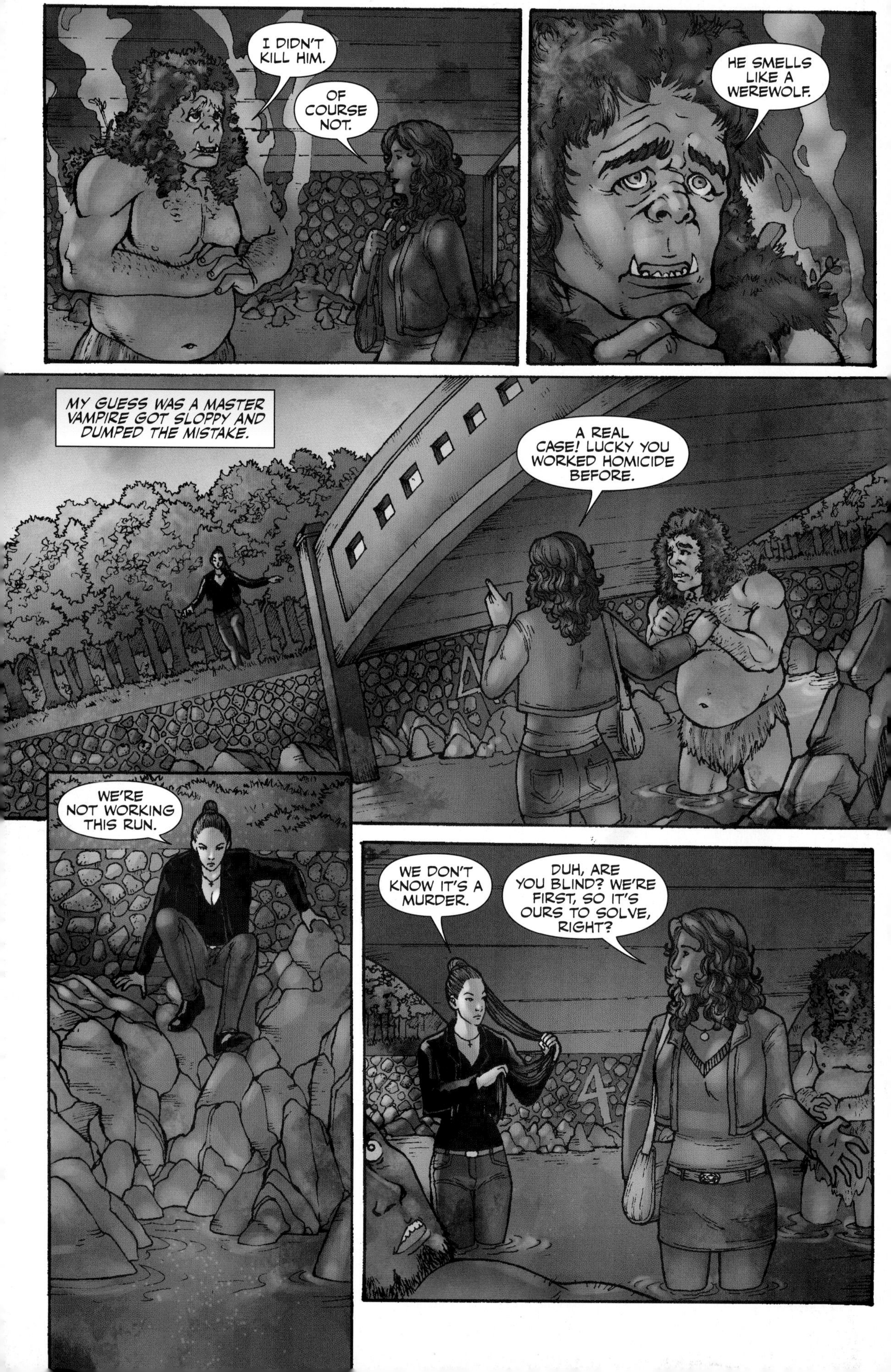
I DIDN'T KILL HIM.
OF COURSE NOT.
HE SMELLS LIKE A WEREWOLF.
MY GUESS WAS A MASTER VAMPIRE GOT SLOPPY AND DUMPED THE MISTAKE.
A REAL CASE! LUCKY YOU WORKED HOMICIDE BEFORE.
WE'RE NOT WORKING THIS RUN.
WE DON'T KNOW IT'S A MURDER.
DUH, ARE YOU BLIND? WE'RE FIRST, SO IT'S OURS TO SOLVE, RIGHT?

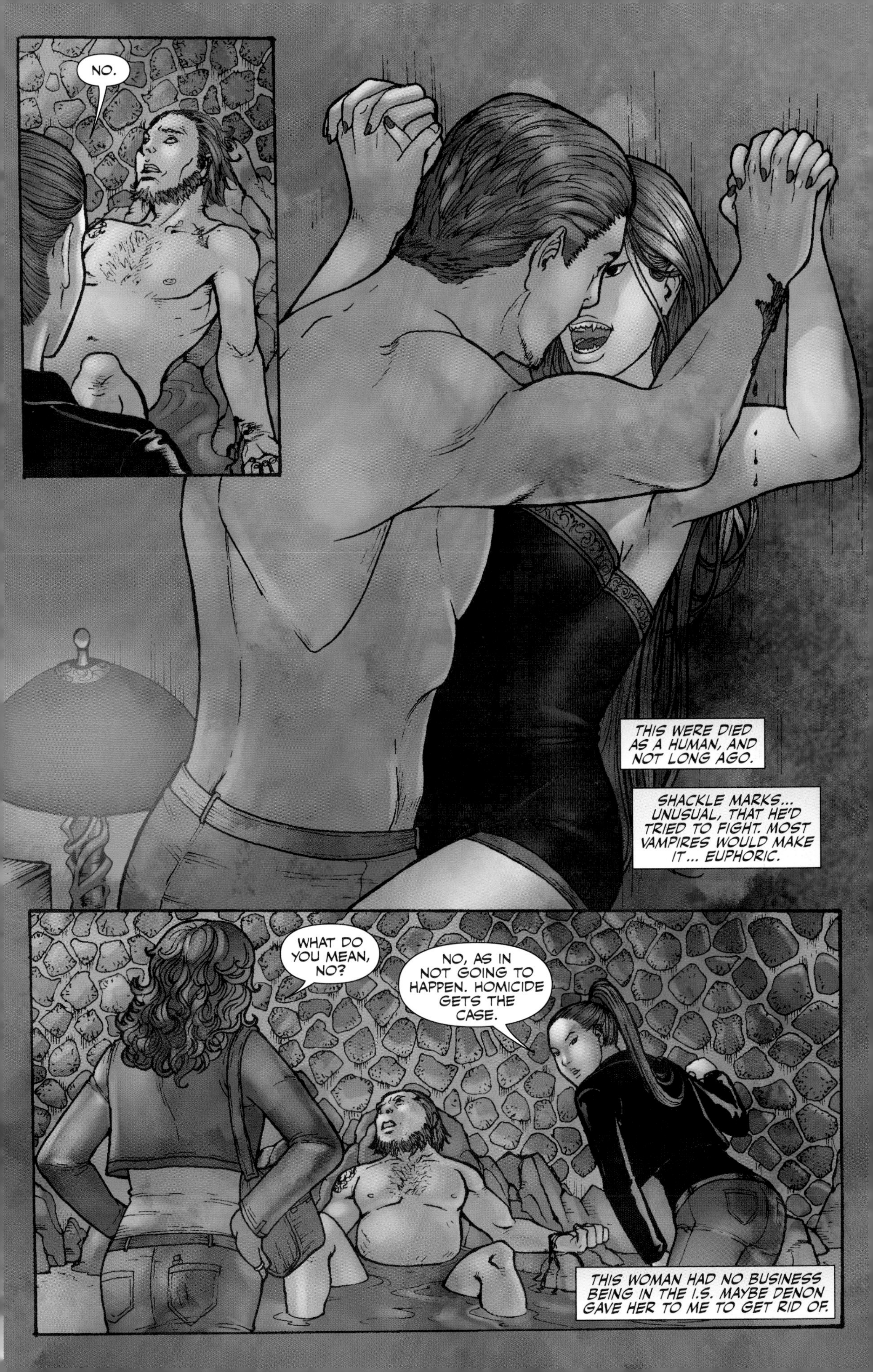
NO.
THIS WERE DIED AS A HUMAN, AND NOT LONG AGO.
SHACKLE MARKS... UNUSUAL, THAT HE'D TRIED TO FIGHT. MOST VAMPIRES WOULD MAKE IT... EUPHORIC.
WHAT DO YOU MEAN, NO?
NO, AS IN NOT GOING TO HAPPEN. HOMICIDE GETS THE CASE.
THIS WOMAN HAD NO BUSINESS BEING IN THE I.S. MAYBE DENON GAVE HER TO ME TO GET RID OF.

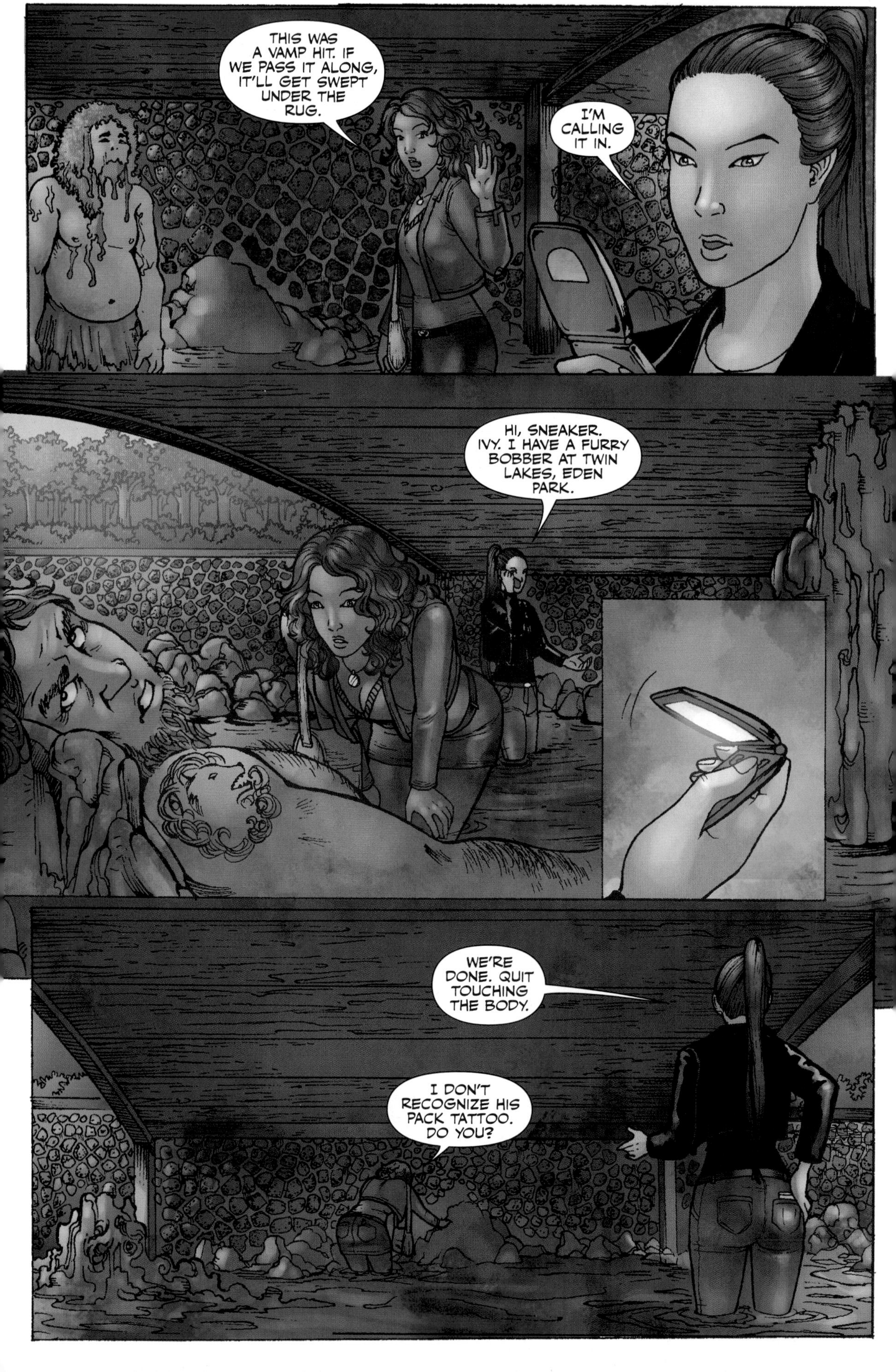
THIS WAS A VAMP HIT. IF WE PASS IT ALONG, IT'LL GET SWEPT UNDER THE RUG.
I'M CALLING IT IN.
HI, SNEAKER. IVY. I HAVE A FURRY BOBBER AT TWIN LAKES, EDEN PARK.
WE'RE DONE. QUIT TOUCHING THE BODY.
I DON'T RECOGNIZE HIS PACK TATTOO. DO YOU?

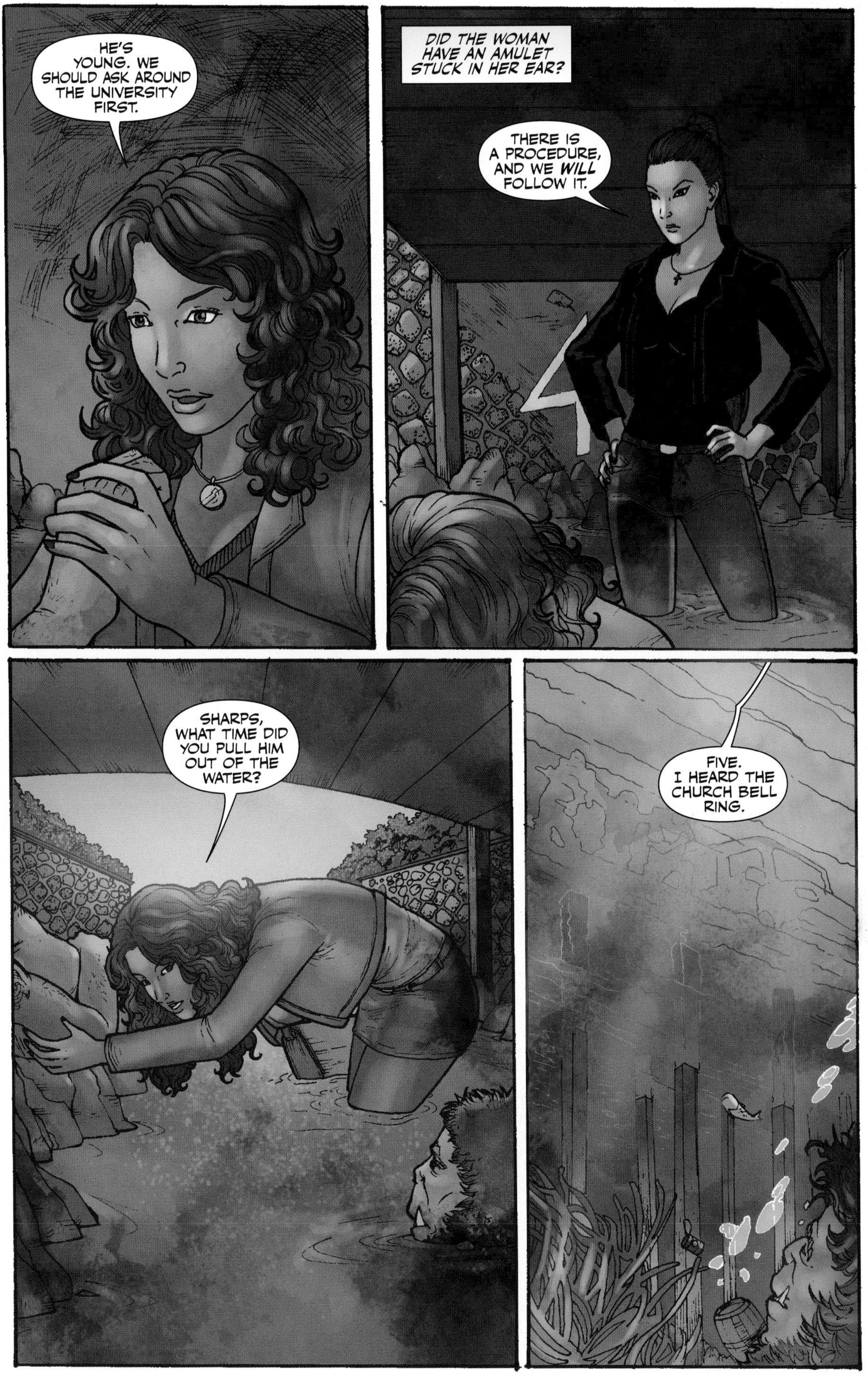
HE'S YOUNG. WE SHOULD ASK AROUND THE UNIVERSITY FIRST.
DID THE WOMAN HAVE AN AMULET STUCK IN HER EAR?
THERE IS A PROCEDURE, AND WE *WILL* FOLLOW IT.
SHARPS, WHAT TIME DID YOU PULL HIM OUT OF THE WATER?
FIVE. I HEARD THE CHURCH BELL RING.

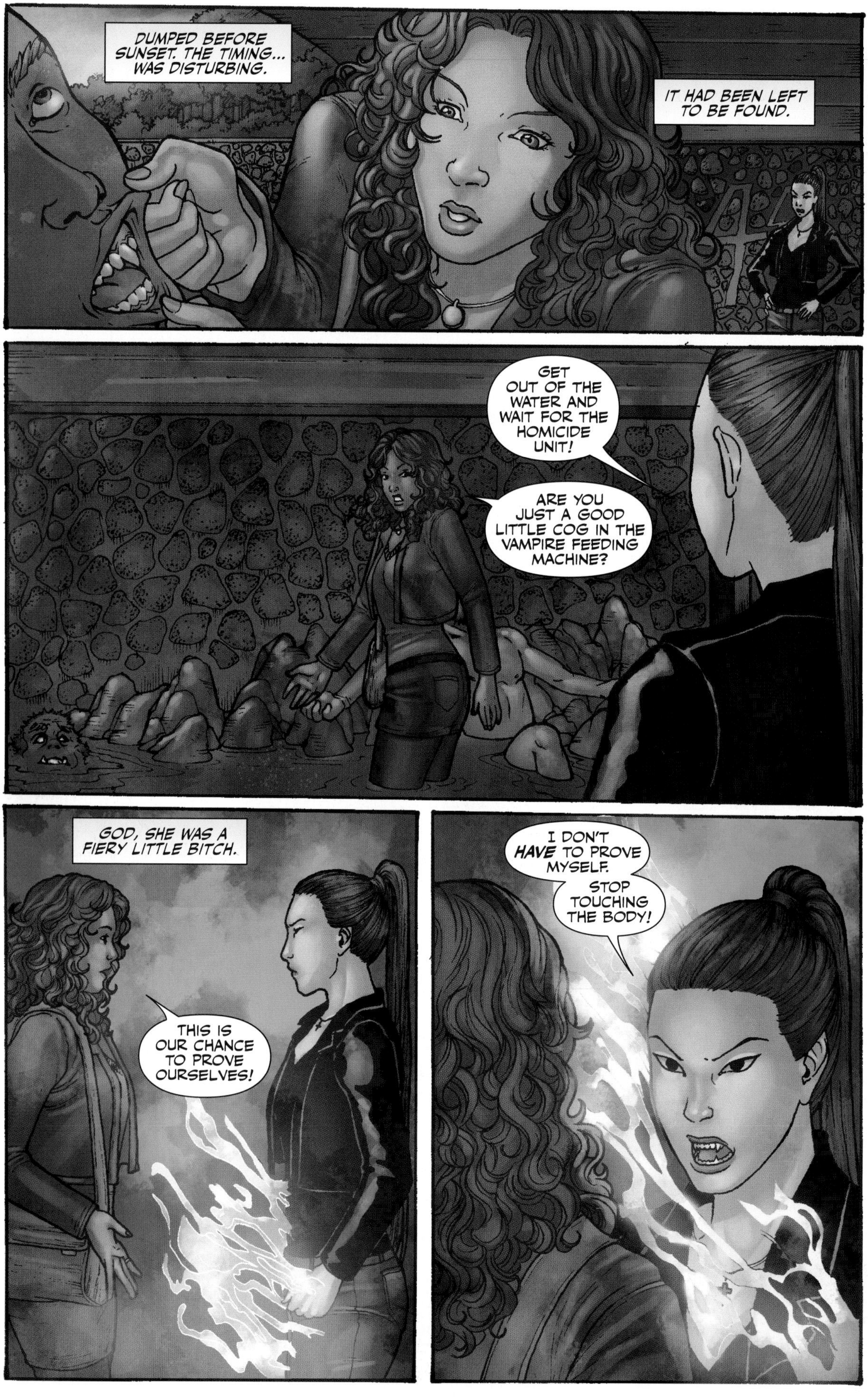
DUMPED BEFORE SUNSET. THE TIMING... WAS DISTURBING.
IT HAD BEEN LEFT TO BE FOUND.
GET OUT OF THE WATER AND WAIT FOR THE HOMICIDE UNIT!
ARE YOU JUST A GOOD LITTLE COG IN THE VAMPIRE FEEDING MACHINE?
GOD, SHE WAS A FIERY LITTLE BITCH.
THIS IS OUR CHANCE TO PROVE OURSELVES!
I DON'T HAVE TO PROVE MYSELF.
STOP TOUCHING THE BODY!

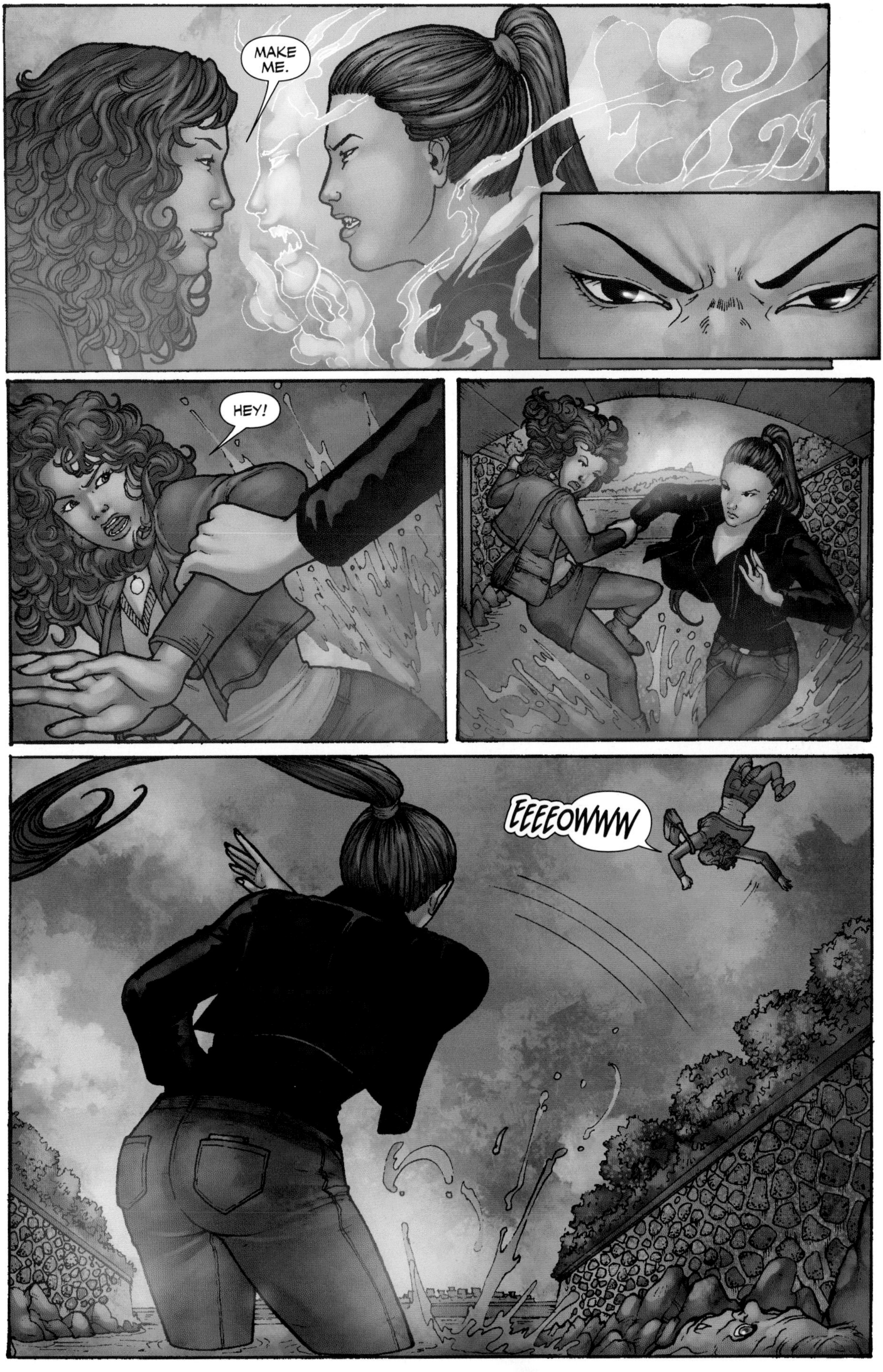
MAKE ME.
HEY!
EEEEOWWW

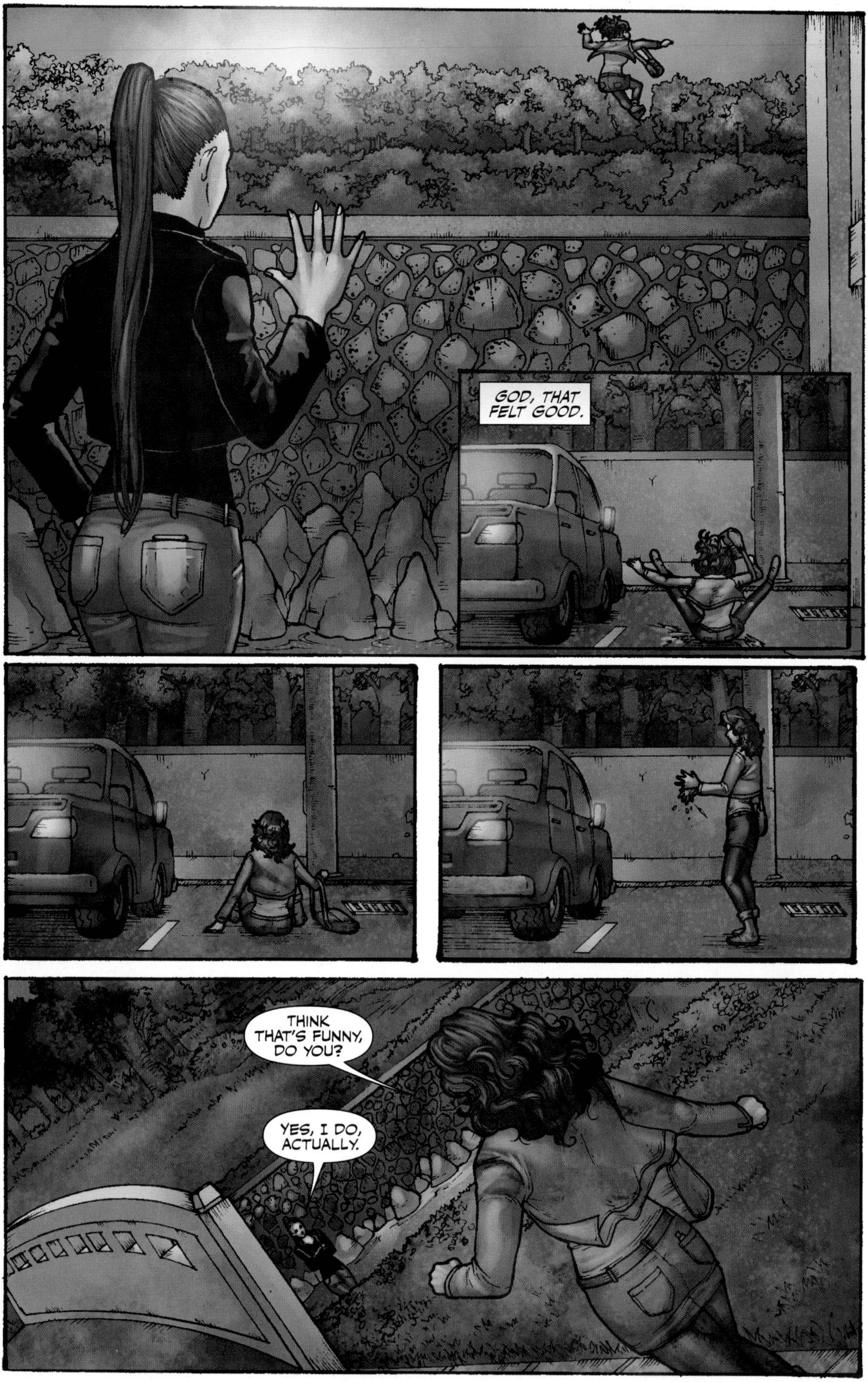
GOD, THAT FELT GOOD.
THINK THAT'S FUNNY, DO YOU?
YES, I DO, ACTUALLY.

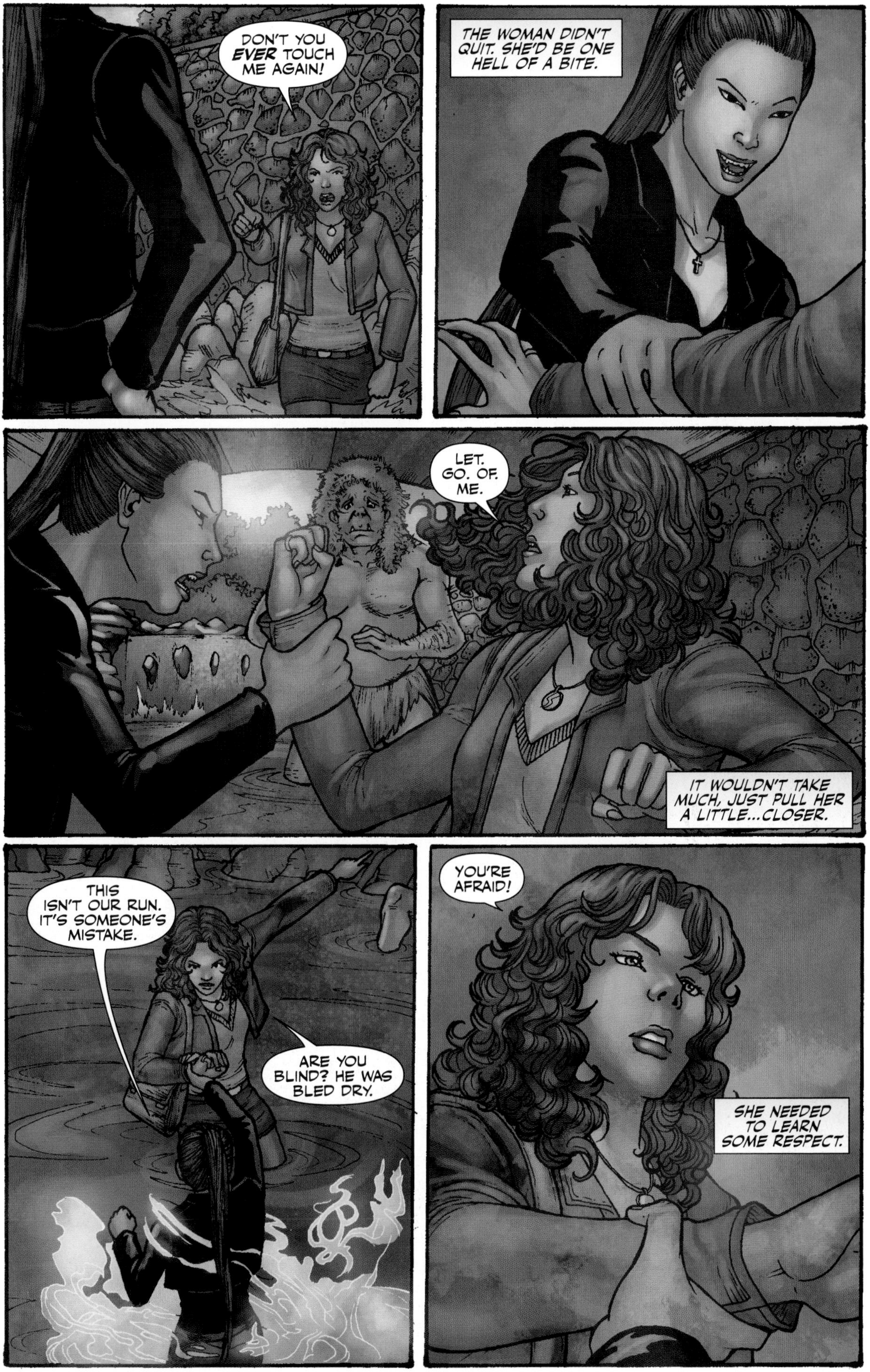
DON'T YOU EVER TOUCH ME AGAIN!
THE WOMAN DIDN'T QUIT. SHE'D BE ONE HELL OF A BITE.
LET. GO. OF. ME.
IT WOULDN'T TAKE MUCH, JUST PULL HER A LITTLE...CLOSER.
THIS ISN'T OUR RUN. IT'S SOMEONE'S MISTAKE.
ARE YOU BLIND? HE WAS BLED DRY.
YOU'RE AFRAID!
SHE NEEDED TO LEARN SOME RESPECT.

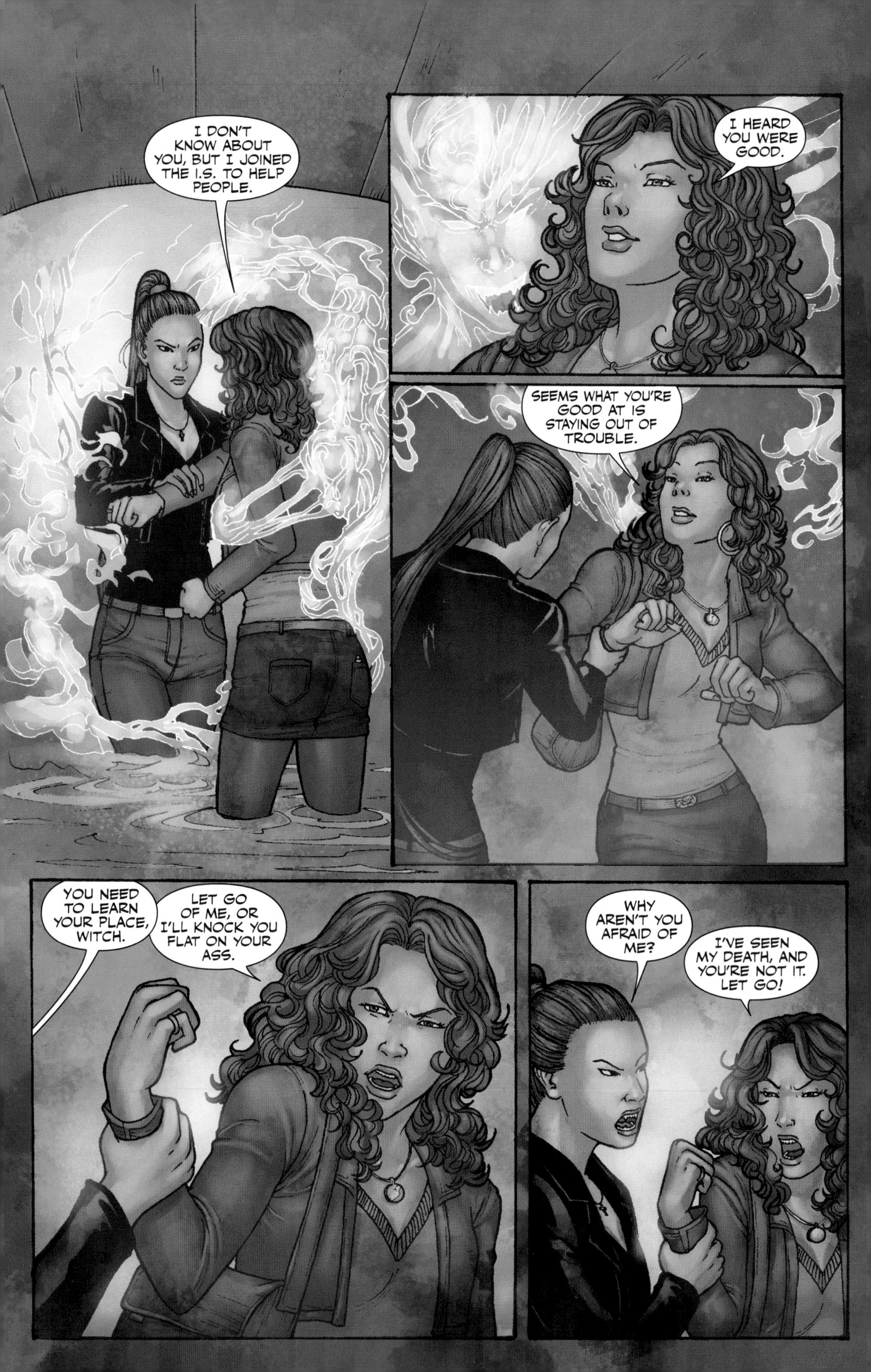
I DON'T KNOW ABOUT YOU, BUT I JOINED THE I.S. TO HELP PEOPLE.
I HEARD YOU WERE GOOD.
SEEMS WHAT YOU'RE GOOD AT IS STAYING OUT OF TROUBLE.
YOU NEED TO LEARN YOUR PLACE, WITCH.
LET GO OF ME, OR I'LL KNOCK YOU FLAT ON YOUR ASS.
WHY AREN'T YOU AFRAID OF ME?
I'VE SEEN MY DEATH, AND YOU'RE NOT IT. LET GO!

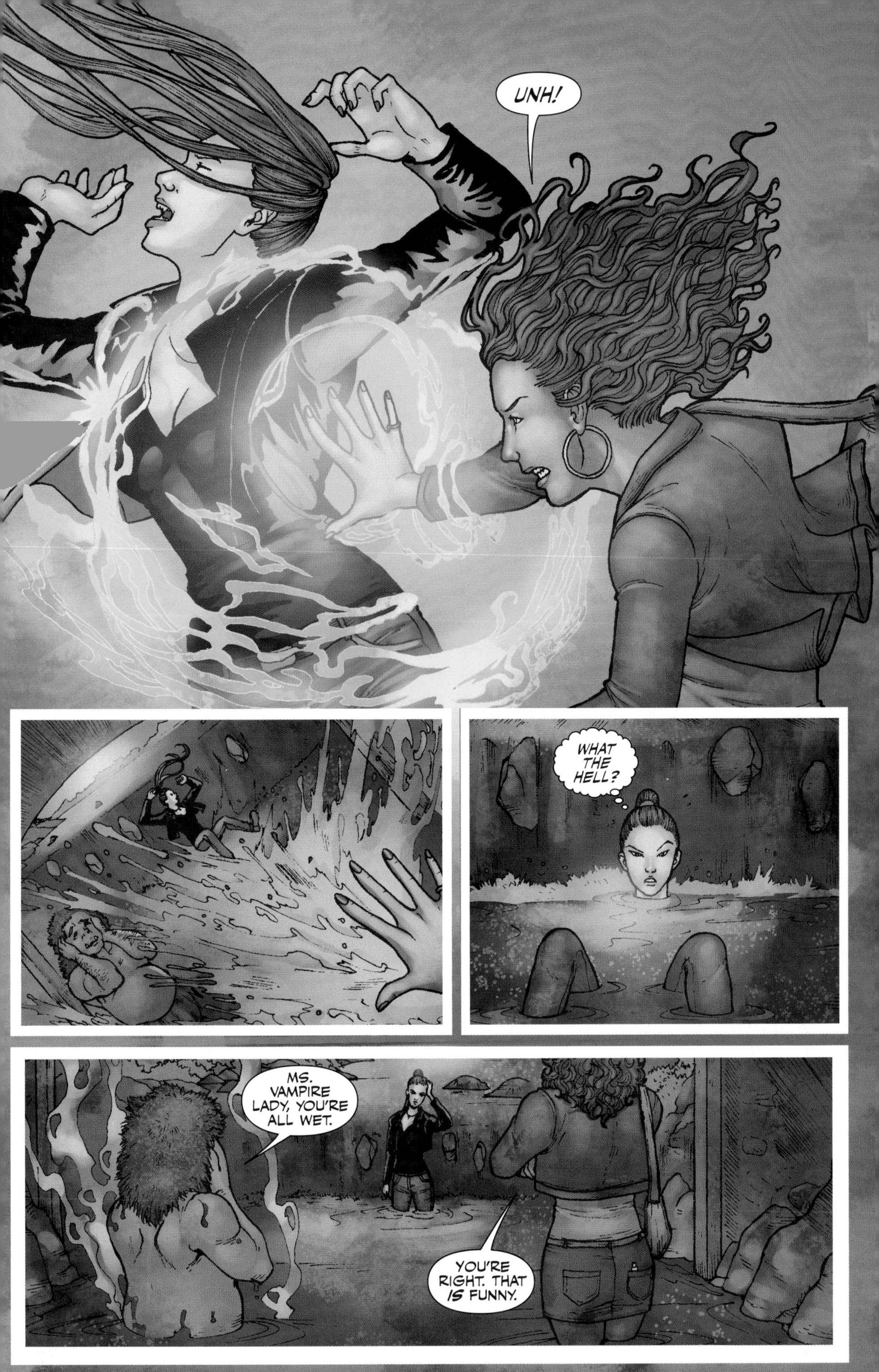
UNH!
WHAT THE HELL?
MS. VAMPIRE LADY, YOU'RE ALL WET.
YOU'RE RIGHT. THAT *IS* FUNNY.

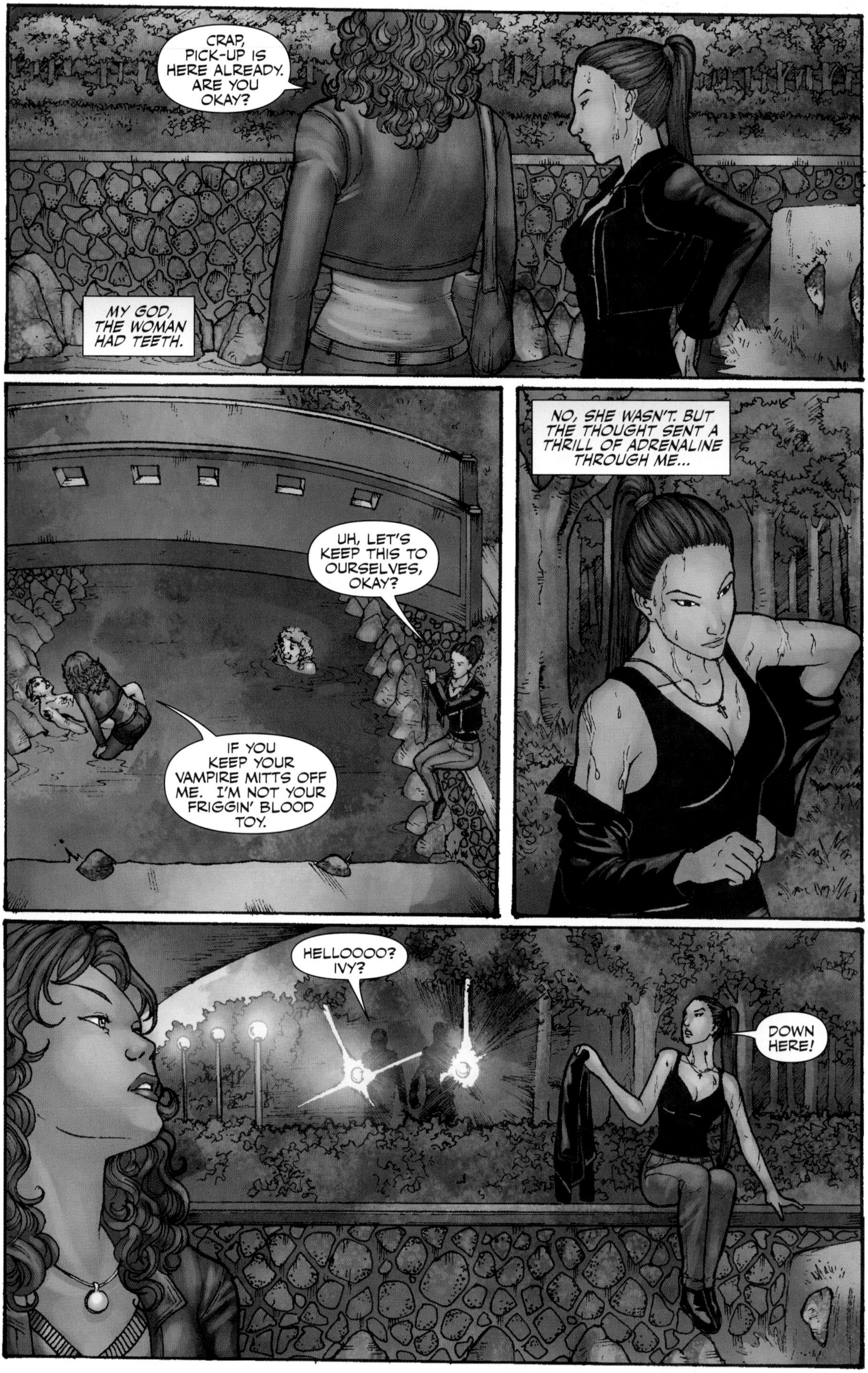
CRAP, PICK-UP IS HERE ALREADY. ARE YOU OKAY?
MY GOD, THE WOMAN HAD TEETH.
UH, LET'S KEEP THIS TO OURSELVES, OKAY?
IF YOU KEEP YOUR VAMPIRE MITTS OFF ME. I'M NOT YOUR FRIGGIN' BLOOD TOY.
NO, SHE WASN'T. BUT THE THOUGHT SENT A THRILL OF ADRENALINE THROUGH ME...
HELLOOOO? IVY?
DOWN HERE!

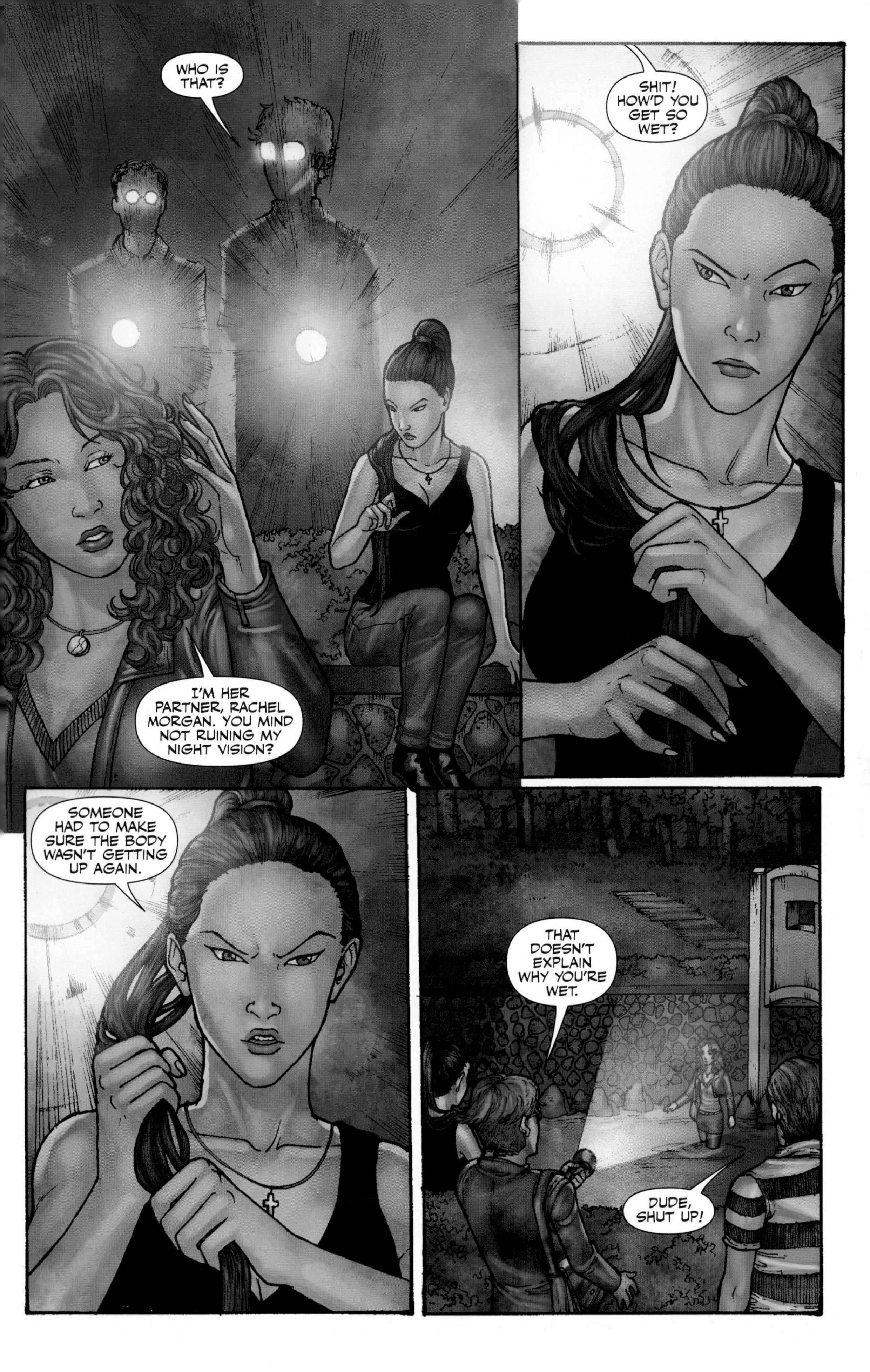
WHO IS THAT?
I'M HER PARTNER, RACHEL MORGAN. YOU MIND NOT RUINING MY NIGHT VISION?
SHIT! HOW'D YOU GET SO WET?
SOMEONE HAD TO MAKE SURE THE BODY WASN'T GETTING UP AGAIN.
THAT DOESN'T EXPLAIN WHY YOU'RE WET.
DUDE, SHUT UP!

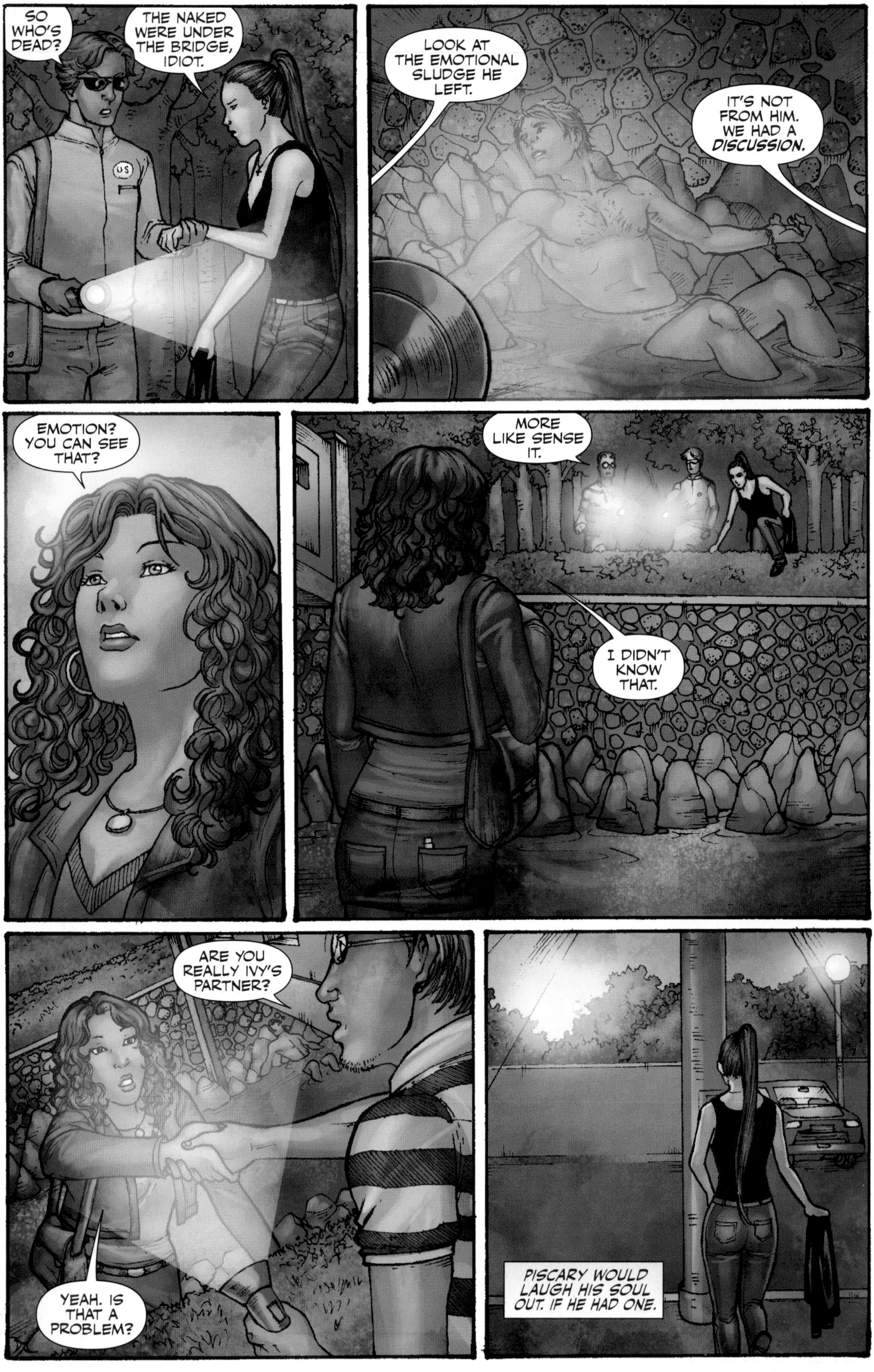
SO WHO'S DEAD?
THE NAKED WERE UNDER THE BRIDGE, IDIOT.
LOOK AT THE EMOTIONAL SLUDGE HE LEFT.
IT'S NOT FROM HIM. WE HAD A *DISCUSSION.*
EMOTION? YOU CAN SEE THAT?
MORE LIKE SENSE IT.
I DIDN'T KNOW THAT.
ARE YOU REALLY IVY'S PARTNER?
YEAH. IS THAT A PROBLEM?
PISCARY WOULD LAUGH HIS SOUL OUT. IF HE HAD ONE.

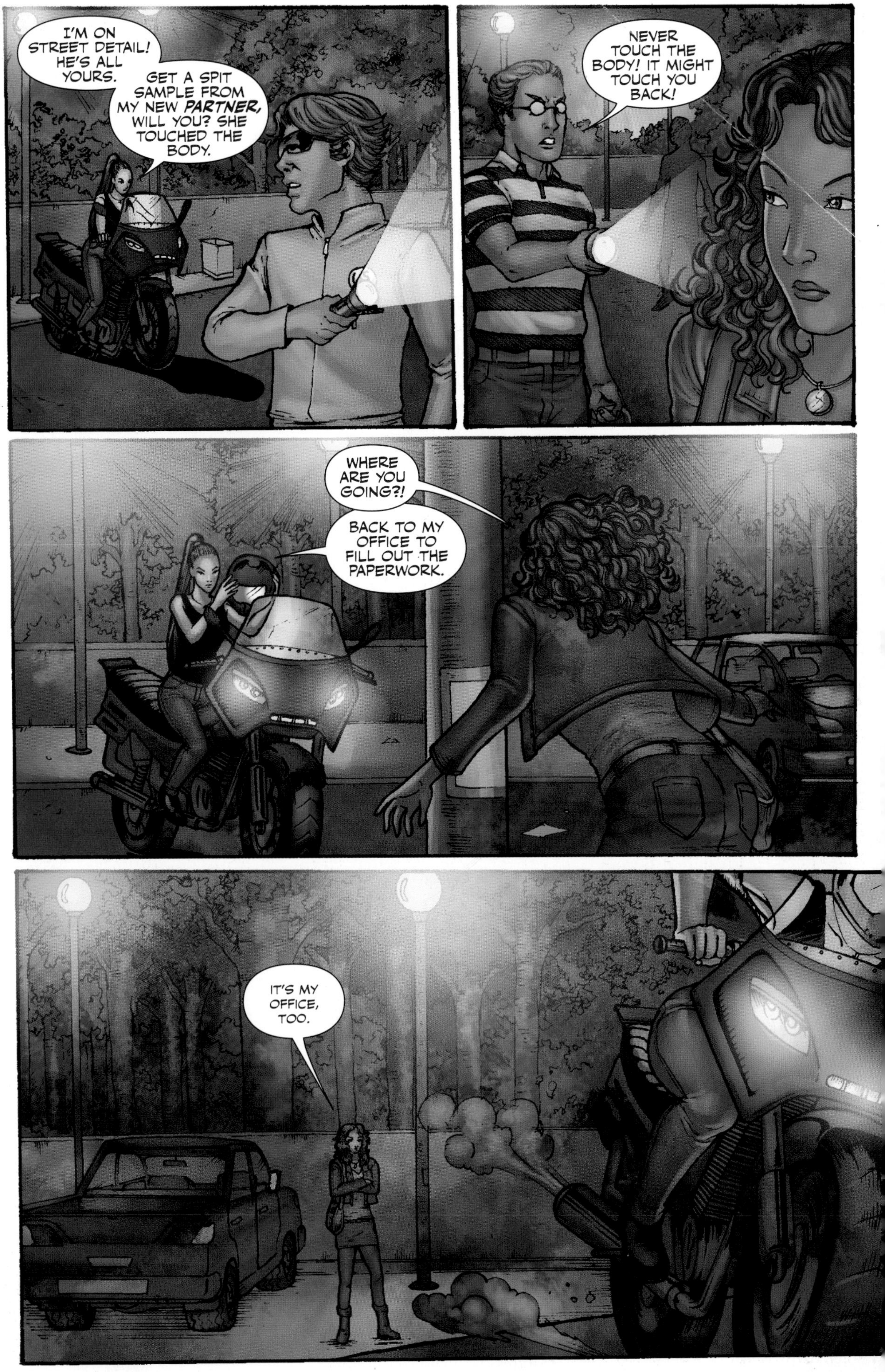
I'M ON STREET DETAIL! HE'S ALL YOURS.
GET A SPIT SAMPLE FROM MY NEW PARTNER, WILL YOU? SHE TOUCHED THE BODY.
NEVER TOUCH THE BODY! IT MIGHT TOUCH YOU BACK!
WHERE ARE YOU GOING?!
BACK TO MY OFFICE TO FILL OUT THE PAPERWORK.
IT'S MY OFFICE, TOO.

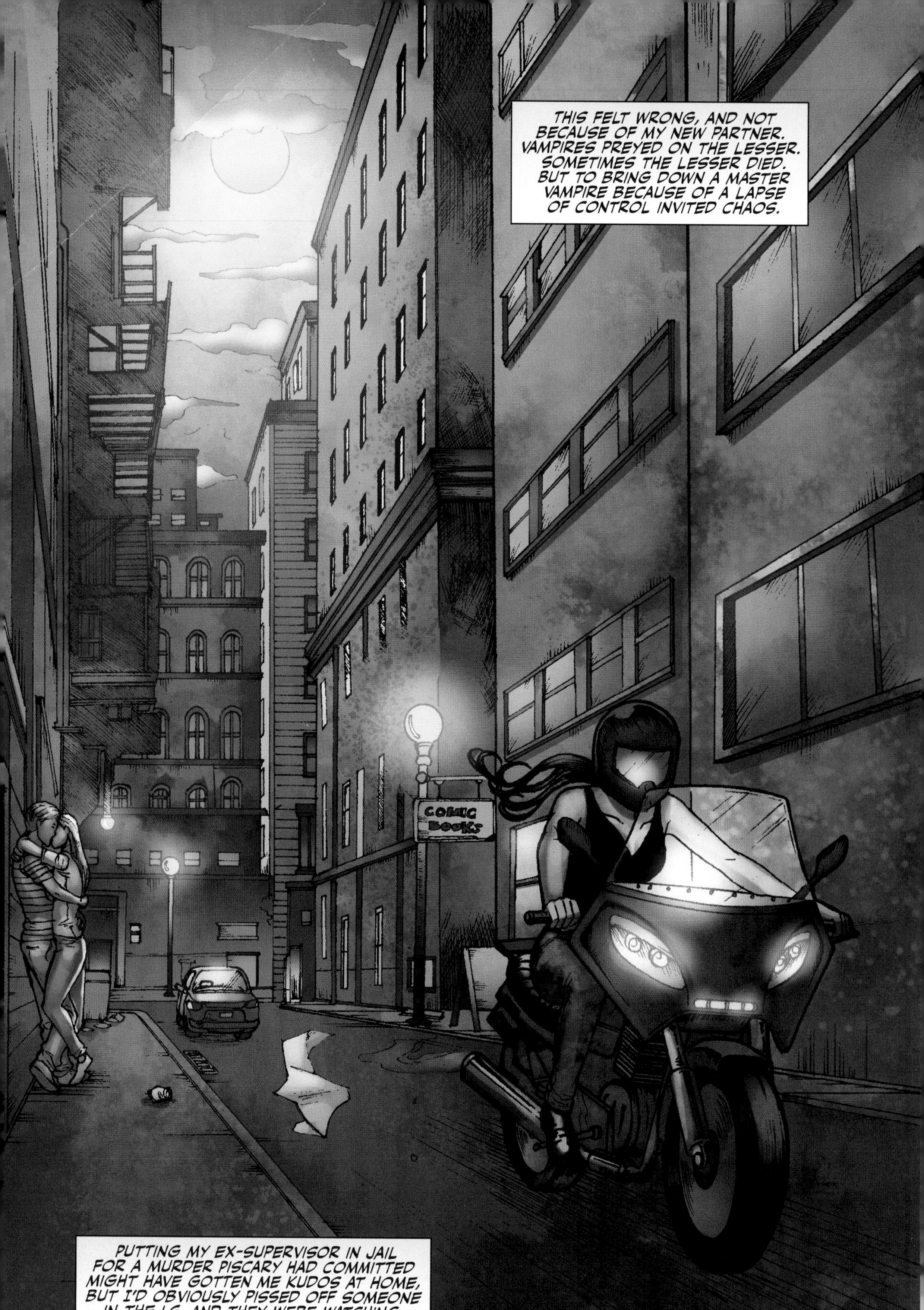
THIS FELT WRONG, AND NOT BECAUSE OF MY NEW PARTNER. VAMPIRES PREYED ON THE LESSER. SOMETIMES THE LESSER DIED. BUT TO BRING DOWN A MASTER VAMPIRE BECAUSE OF A LAPSE OF CONTROL INVITED CHAOS.
COMIC BOOKS
PUTTING MY EX-SUPERVISOR IN JAIL FOR A MURDER PISCARY HAD COMMITTED MIGHT HAVE GOTTEN ME KUDOS AT HOME, BUT I'D OBVIOUSLY PISSED OFF SOMEONE IN THE I.S. AND THEY WERE WATCHING.

CHAPTER 2

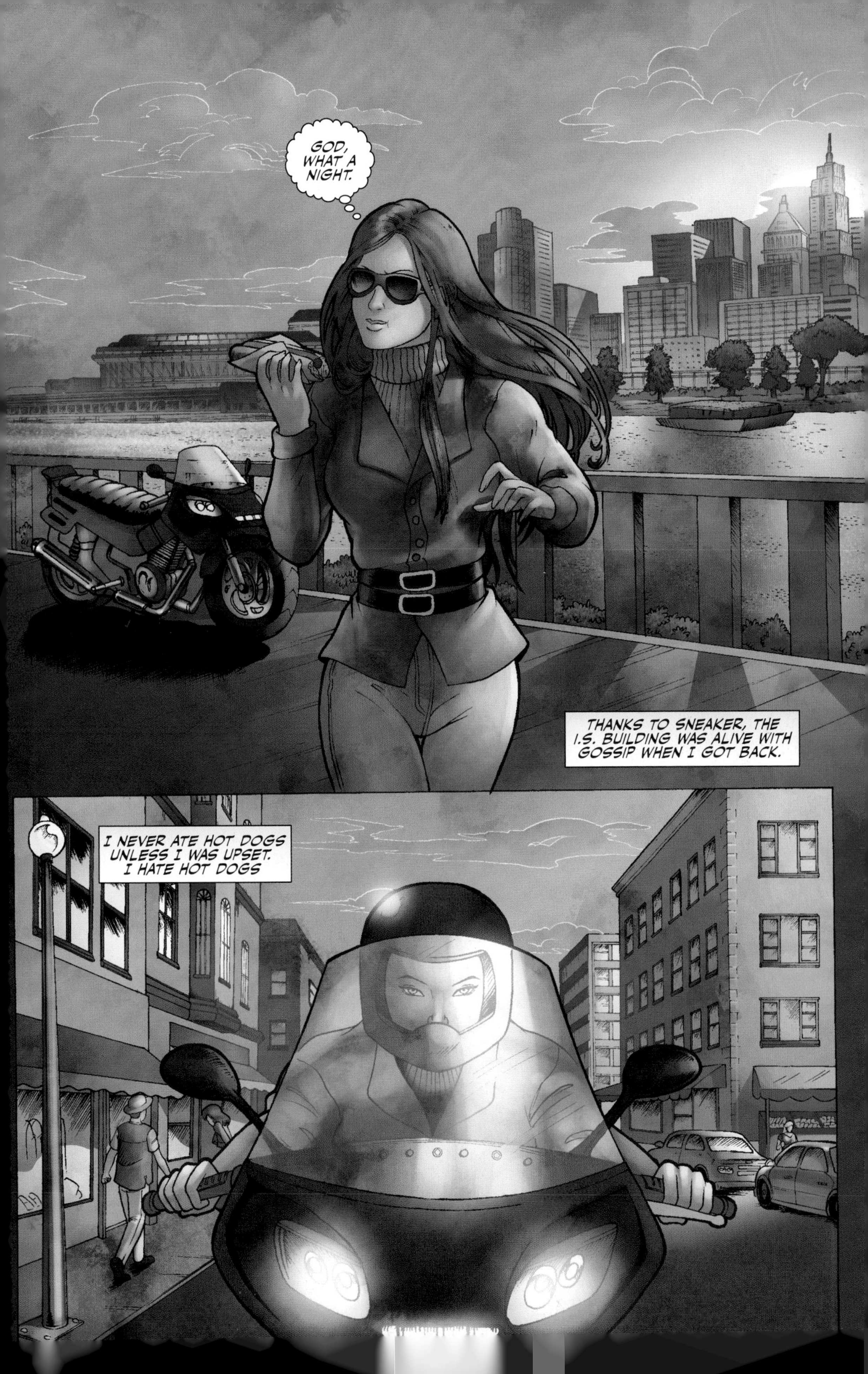
GOD, WHAT A NIGHT.
THANKS TO SNEAKER, THE I.S. BUILDING WAS ALIVE WITH GOSSIP WHEN I GOT BACK.
I NEVER ATE HOT DOGS UNLESS I WAS UPSET. I HATE HOT DOGS

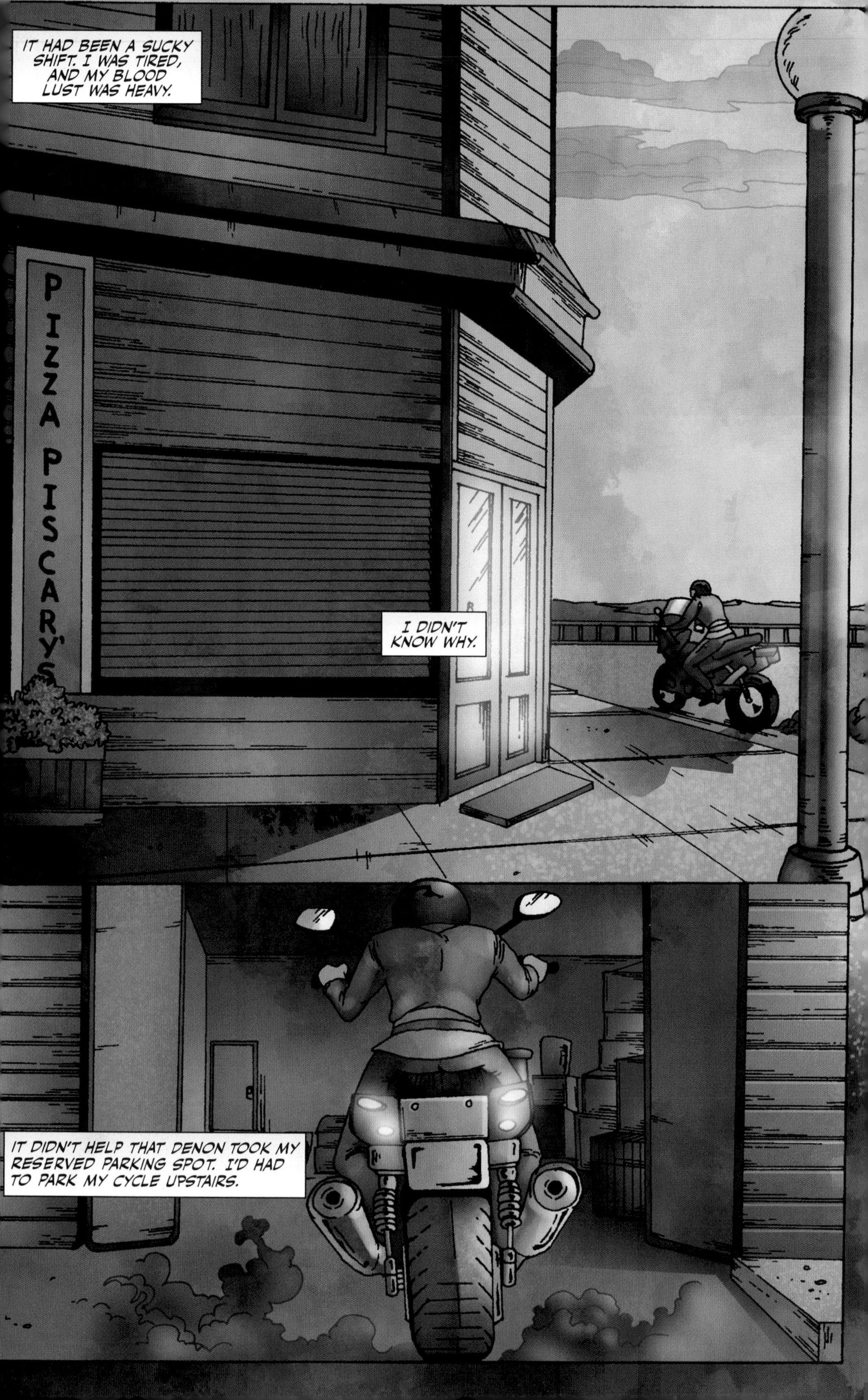
IT HAD BEEN A SUCKY SHIFT. I WAS TIRED, AND MY BLOOD LUST WAS HEAVY.
PIZZA PISCARY'S
I DIDN'T KNOW WHY.
IT DIDN'T HELP THAT DENON TOOK MY RESERVED PARKING SPOT. I'D HAD TO PARK MY CYCLE UPSTAIRS.

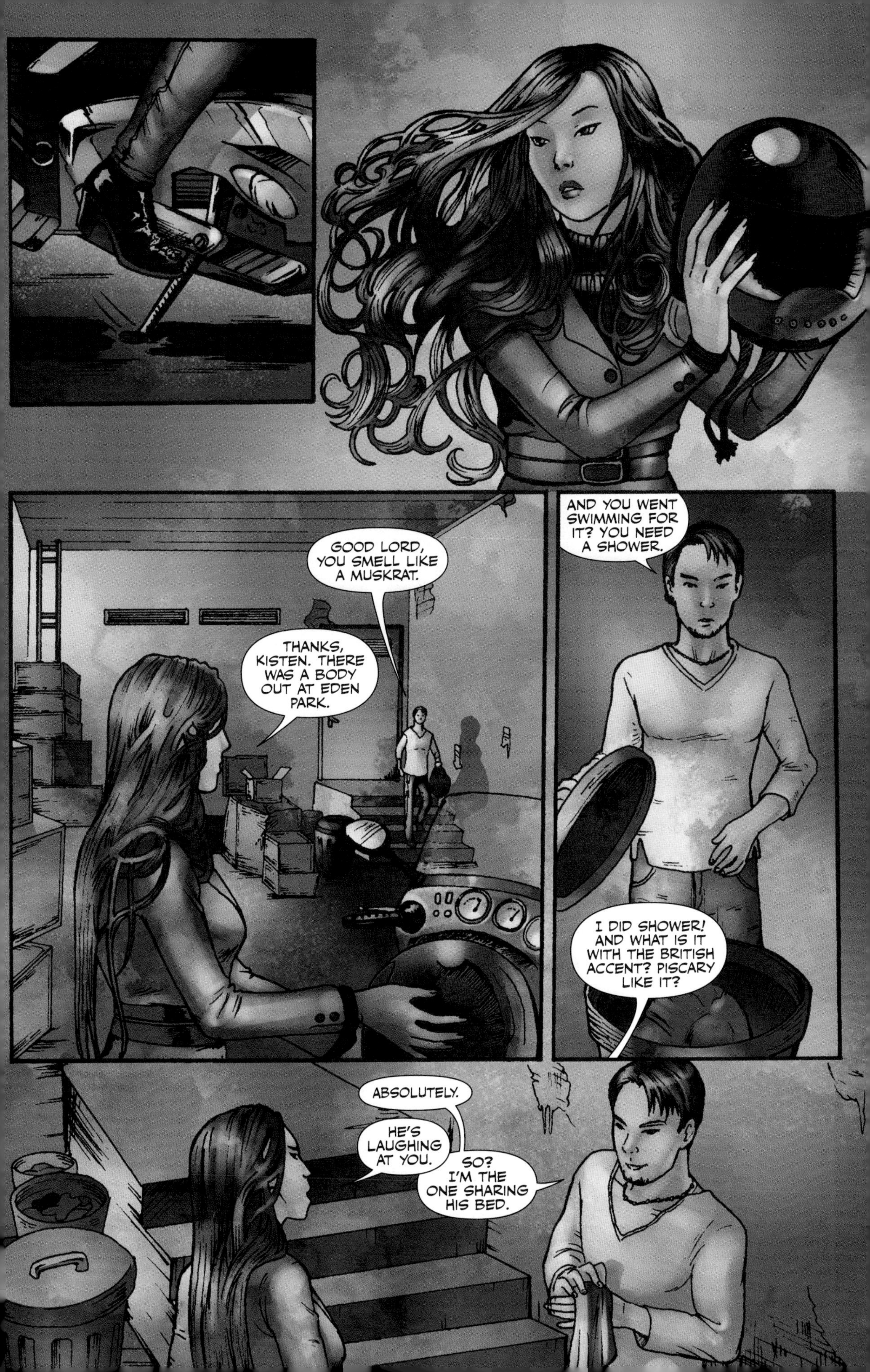
GOOD LORD, YOU SMELL LIKE A MUSKRAT.
THANKS, KISTEN. THERE WAS A BODY OUT AT EDEN PARK.
AND YOU WENT SWIMMING FOR IT? YOU NEED A SHOWER.
I DID SHOWER! AND WHAT IS IT WITH THE BRITISH ACCENT? PISCARY LIKE IT?
ABSOLUTELY.
HE'S LAUGHING AT YOU.
SO? I'M THE ONE SHARING HIS BED.

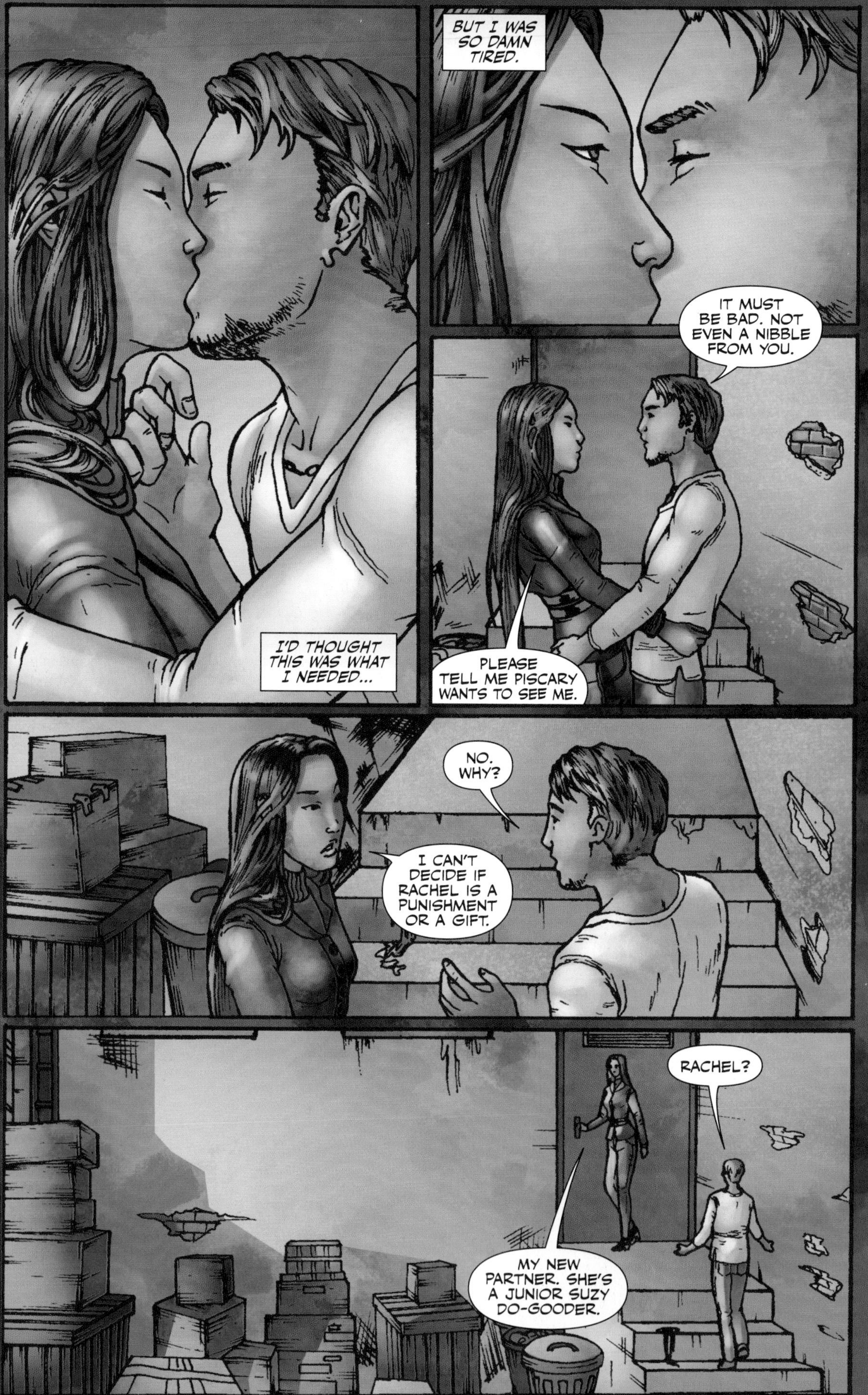
I'D THOUGHT THIS WAS WHAT I NEEDED...
BUT I WAS SO DAMN TIRED.
IT MUST BE BAD. NOT EVEN A NIBBLE FROM YOU.
PLEASE TELL ME PISCARY WANTS TO SEE ME.
NO. WHY?
I CAN'T DECIDE IF RACHEL IS A PUNISHMENT OR A GIFT.
RACHEL?
MY NEW PARTNER. SHE'S A JUNIOR SUZY DO-GOODER.

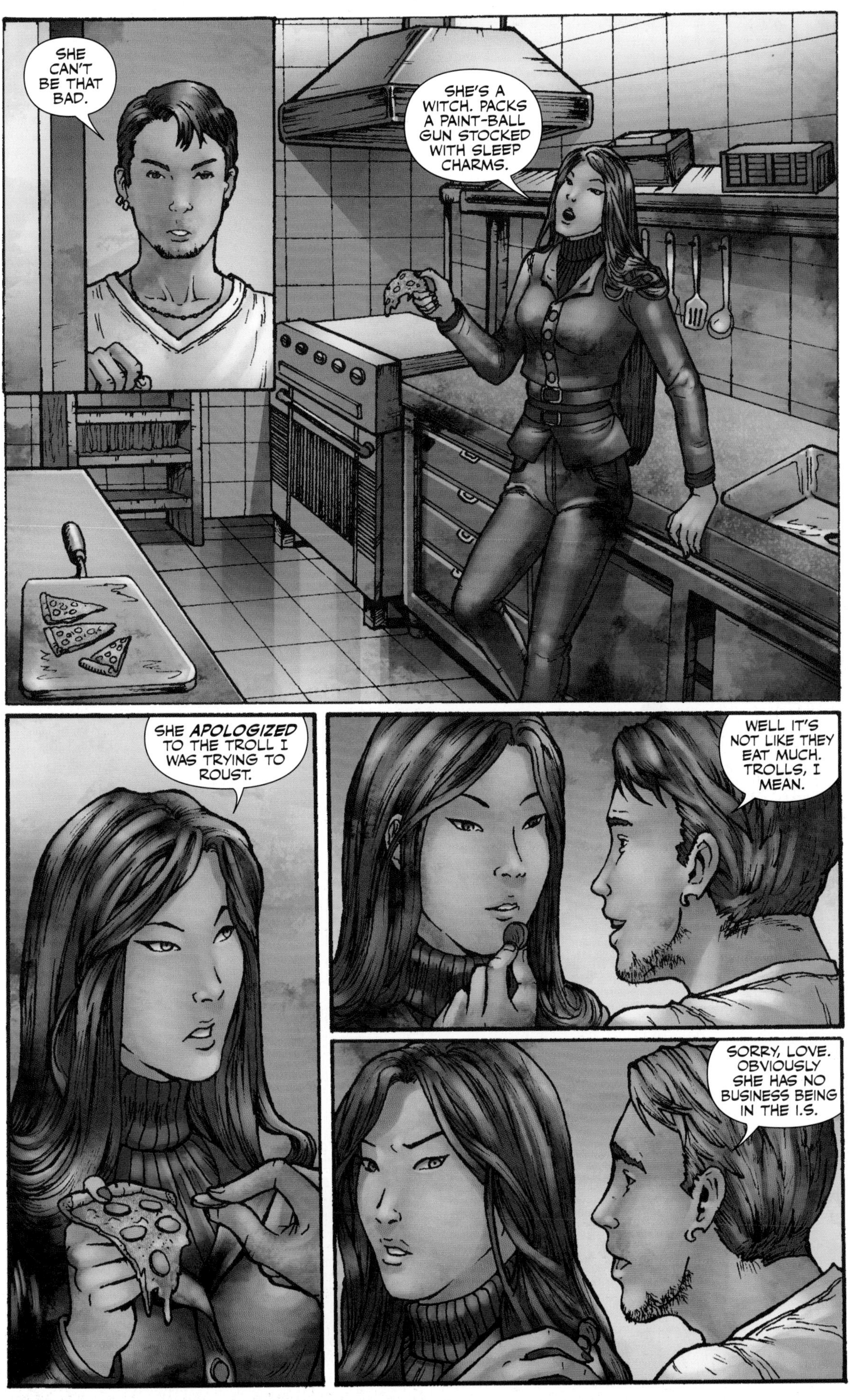
SHE CAN'T BE THAT BAD.
SHE'S A WITCH. PACKS A PAINT-BALL GUN STOCKED WITH SLEEP CHARMS.
SHE *APOLOGIZED* TO THE TROLL I WAS TRYING TO ROUST.
WELL IT'S NOT LIKE THEY EAT MUCH. TROLLS, I MEAN.
SORRY, LOVE. OBVIOUSLY SHE HAS NO BUSINESS BEING IN THE I.S.

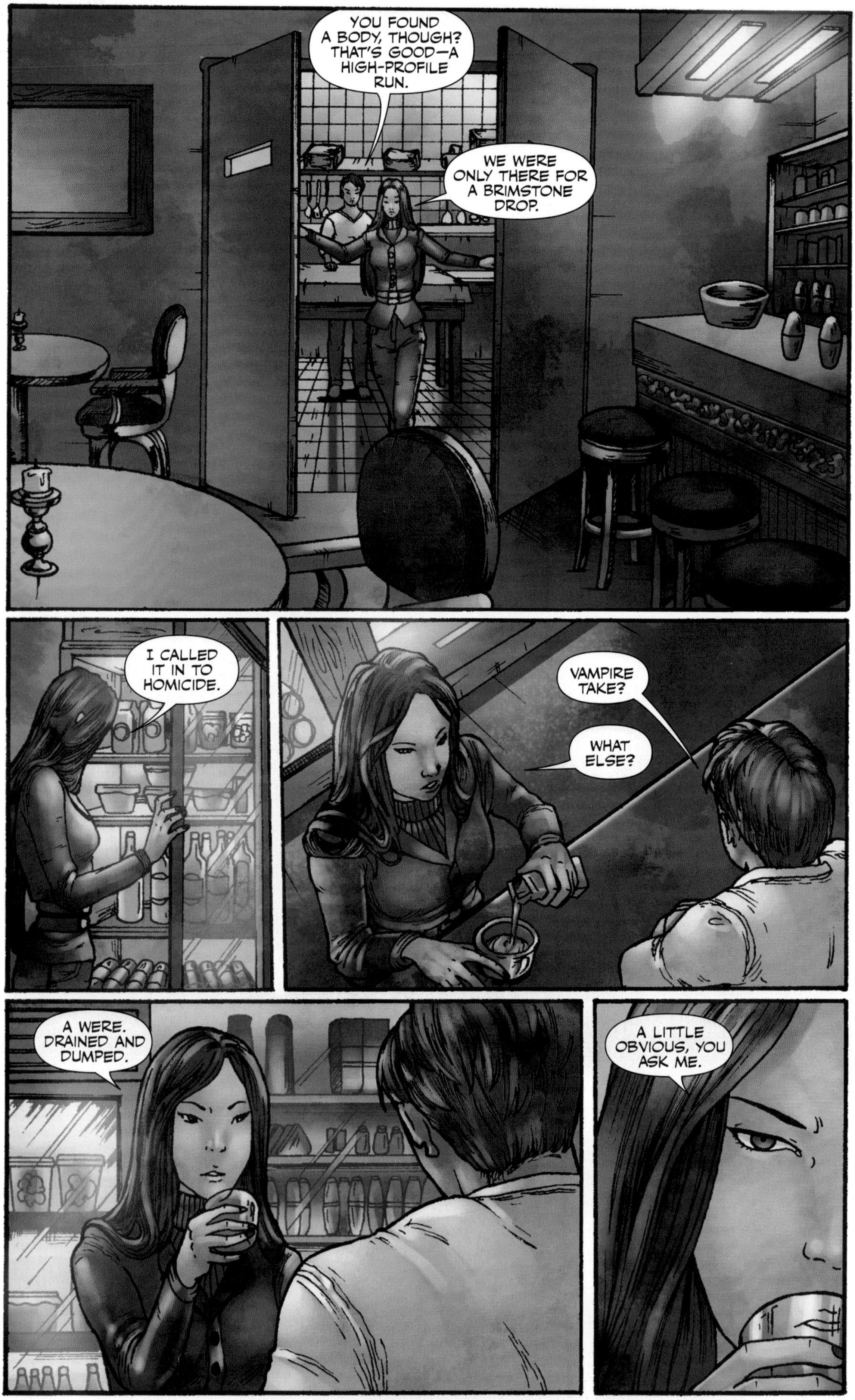
YOU FOUND A BODY, THOUGH? THAT'S GOOD—A HIGH-PROFILE RUN.
WE WERE ONLY THERE FOR A BRIMSTONE DROP.
I CALLED IT IN TO HOMICIDE.
VAMPIRE TAKE?
WHAT ELSE?
A WERE. DRAINED AND DUMPED.
A LITTLE OBVIOUS, YOU ASK ME.

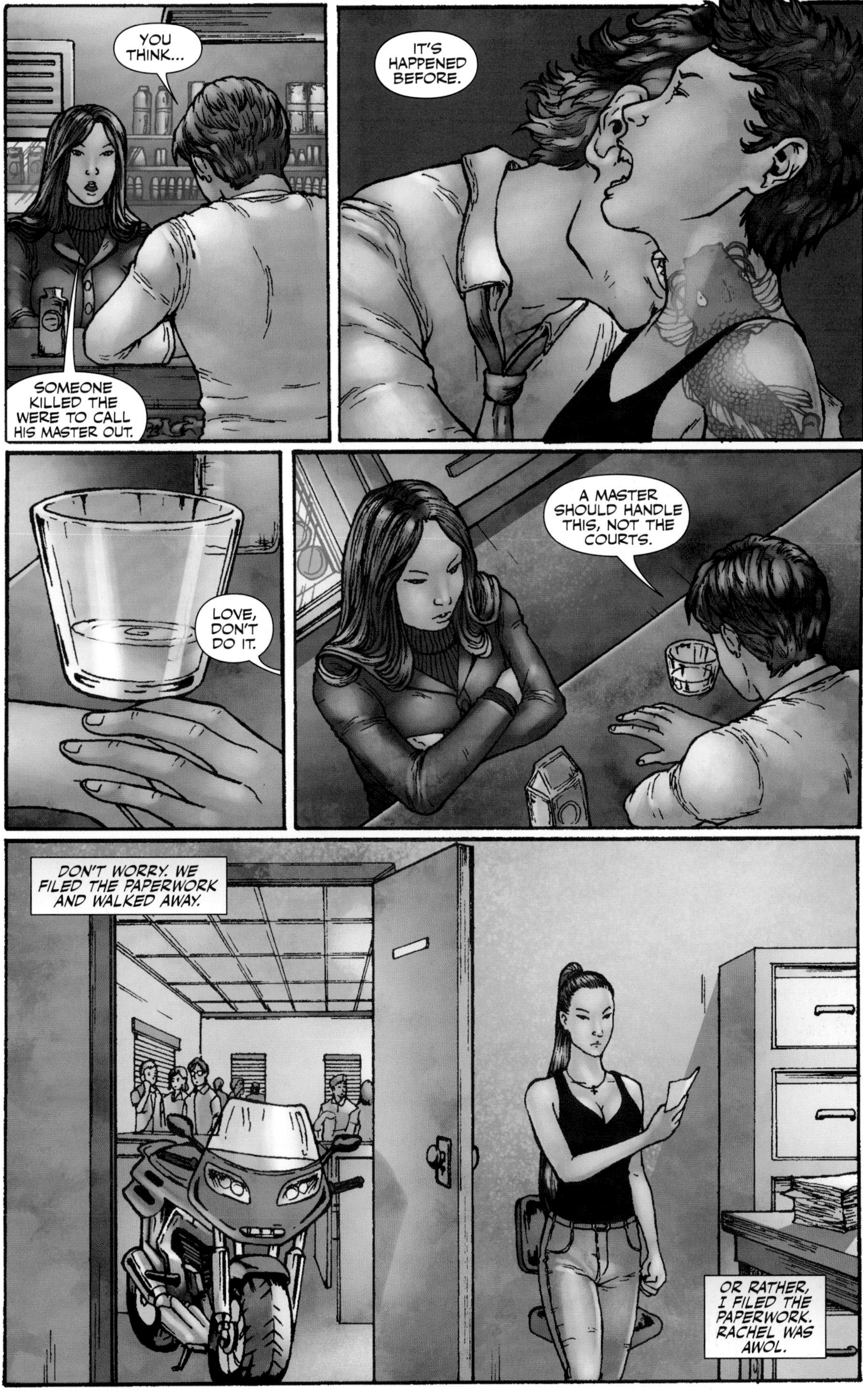
YOU THINK...
SOMEONE KILLED THE WERE TO CALL HIS MASTER OUT.
IT'S HAPPENED BEFORE.
LOVE, DON'T DO IT.
A MASTER SHOULD HANDLE THIS, NOT THE COURTS.
DON'T WORRY. WE FILED THE PAPERWORK AND WALKED AWAY.
OR RATHER, I FILED THE PAPERWORK. RACHEL WAS AWOL.

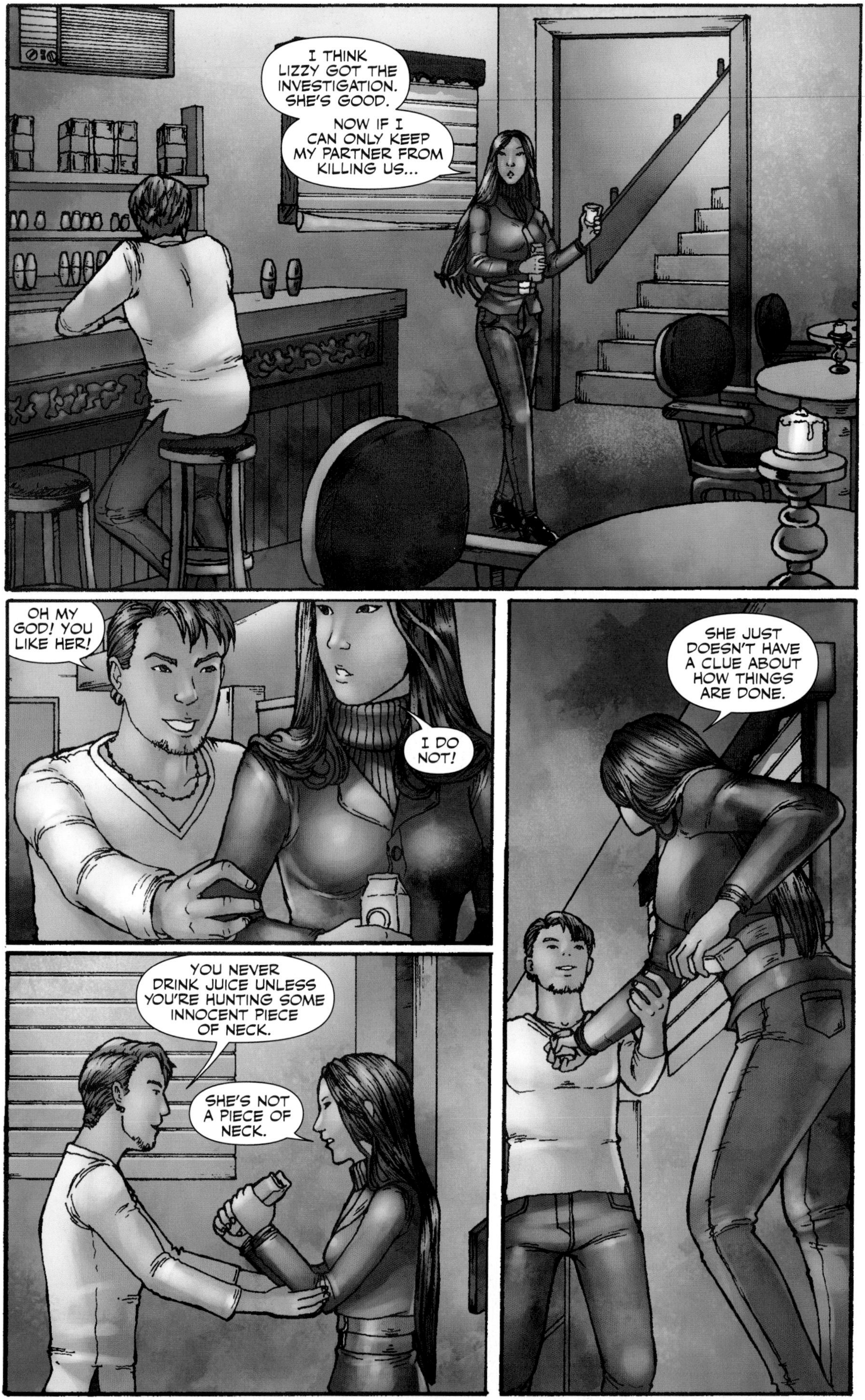
I THINK LIZZY GOT THE INVESTIGATION. SHE'S GOOD.
NOW IF I CAN ONLY KEEP MY PARTNER FROM KILLING US...
OH MY GOD! YOU LIKE HER!
I DO NOT!
YOU NEVER DRINK JUICE UNLESS YOU'RE HUNTING SOME INNOCENT PIECE OF NECK.
SHE'S NOT A PIECE OF NECK.
SHE JUST DOESN'T HAVE A CLUE ABOUT HOW THINGS ARE DONE.

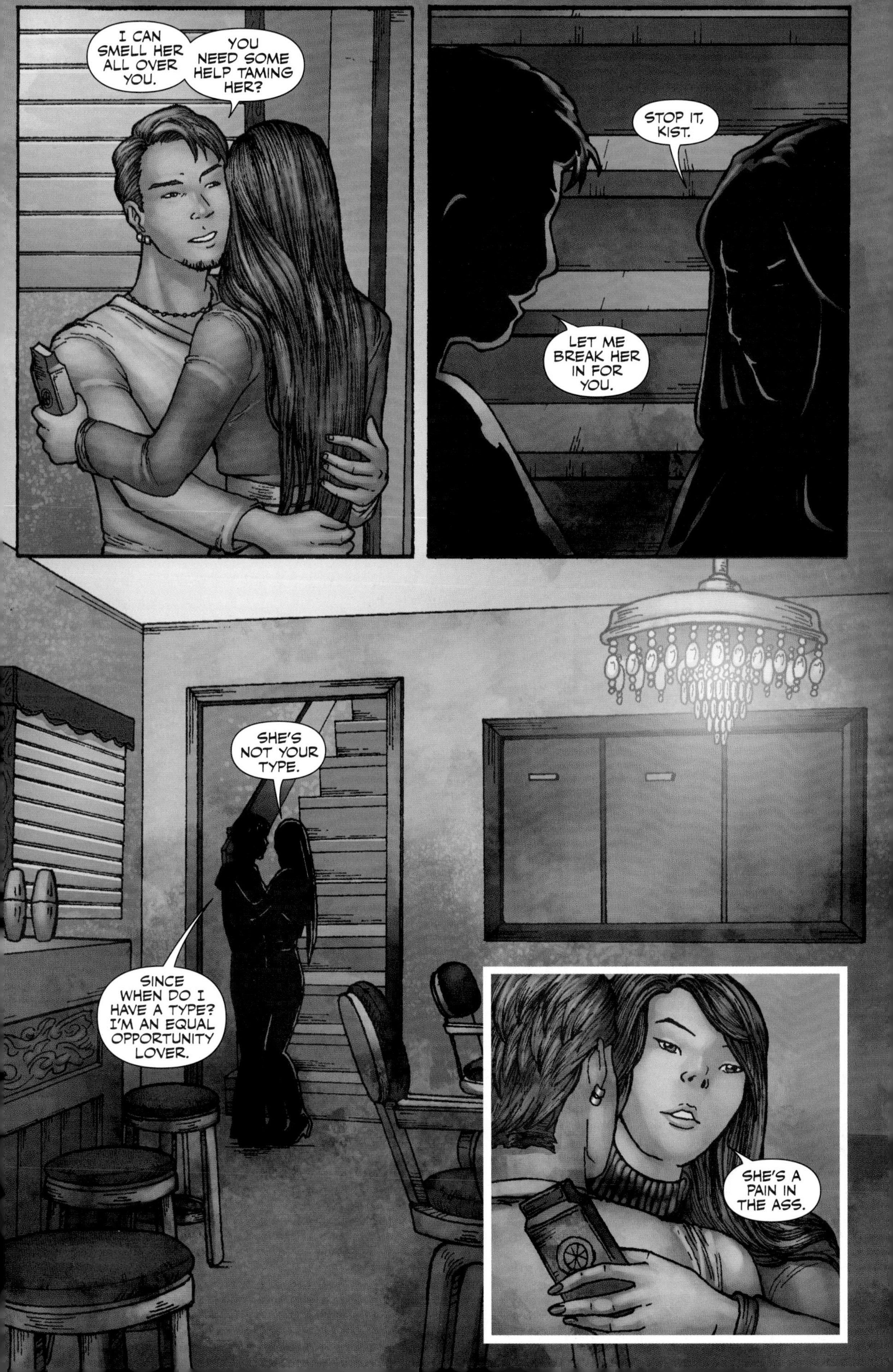
I CAN SMELL HER ALL OVER YOU.
YOU NEED SOME HELP TAMING HER?
STOP IT, KIST.
LET ME BREAK HER IN FOR YOU.
SHE'S NOT YOUR TYPE.
SINCE WHEN DO I HAVE A TYPE? I'M AN EQUAL OPPORTUNITY LOVER.
SHE'S A PAIN IN THE ASS.

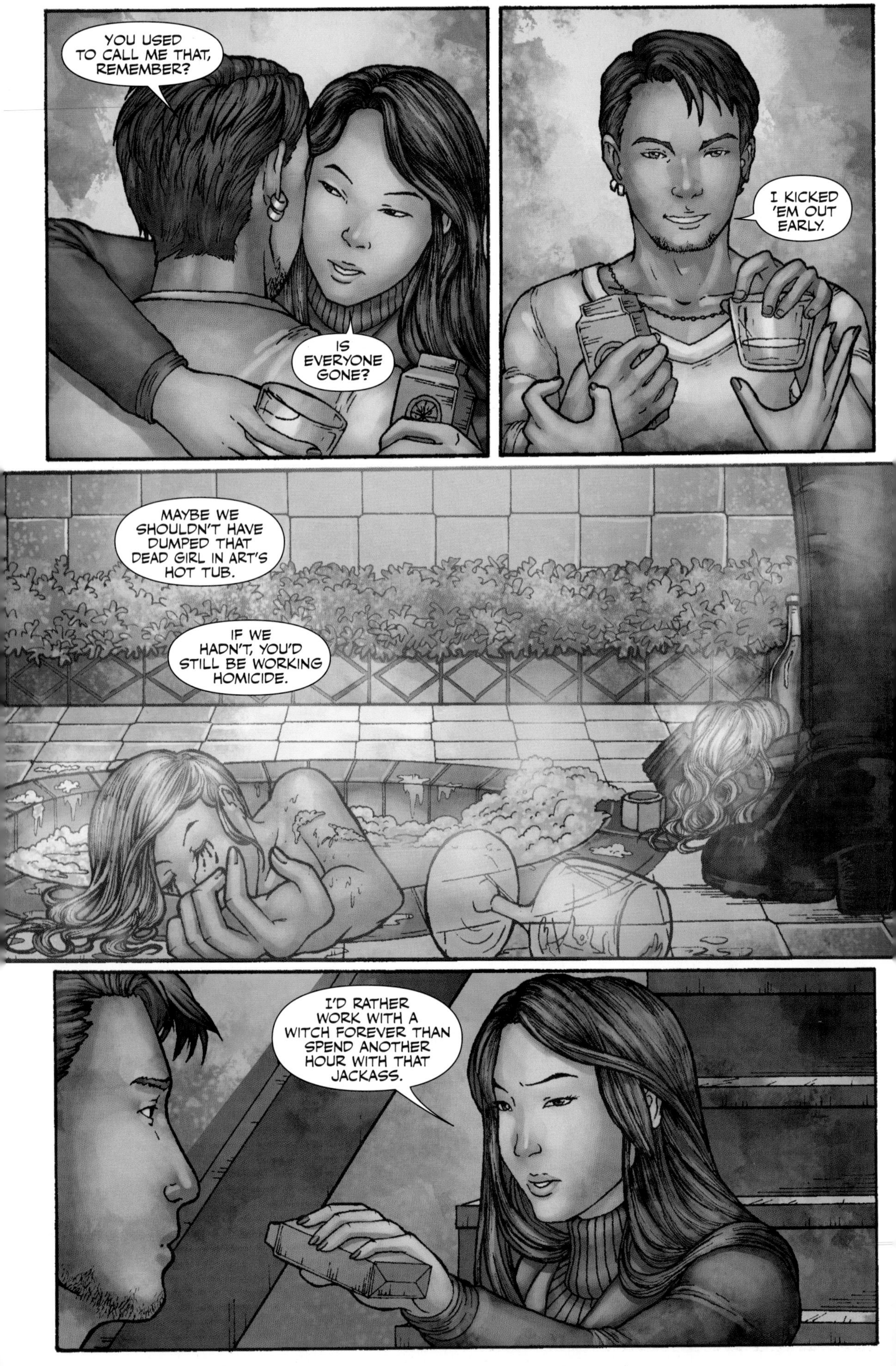
YOU USED TO CALL ME THAT, REMEMBER?
IS EVERYONE GONE?
I KICKED 'EM OUT EARLY.
MAYBE WE SHOULDN'T HAVE DUMPED THAT DEAD GIRL IN ART'S HOT TUB.
IF WE HADN'T, YOU'D STILL BE WORKING HOMICIDE.
I'D RATHER WORK WITH A WITCH FOREVER THAN SPEND ANOTHER HOUR WITH THAT JACKASS.

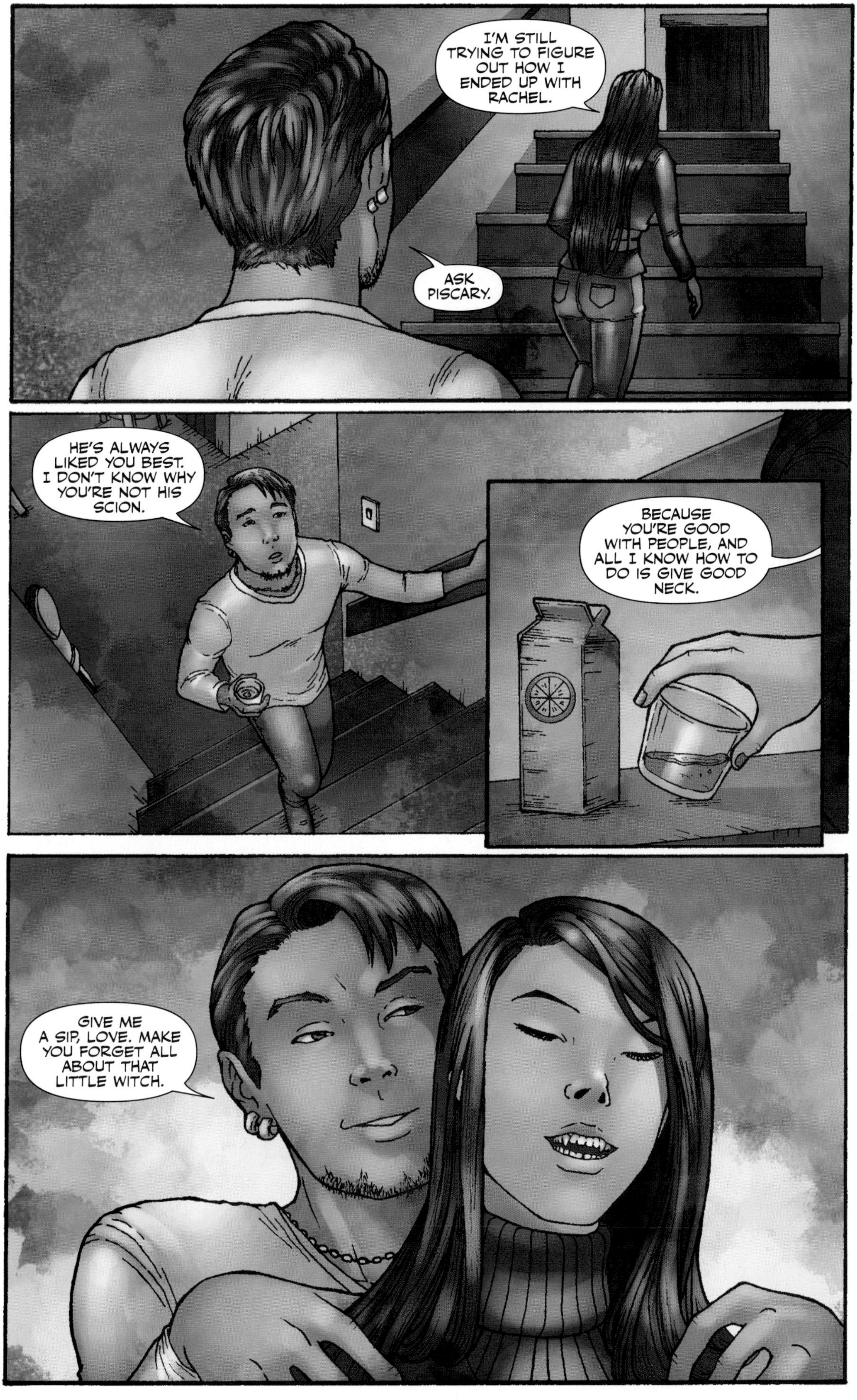
I'M STILL TRYING TO FIGURE OUT HOW I ENDED UP WITH RACHEL.
ASK PISCARY.
HE'S ALWAYS LIKED YOU BEST. I DON'T KNOW WHY YOU'RE NOT HIS SCION.
BECAUSE YOU'RE GOOD WITH PEOPLE, AND ALL I KNOW HOW TO DO IS GIVE GOOD NECK.
GIVE ME A SIP, LOVE. MAKE YOU FORGET ALL ABOUT THAT LITTLE WITCH.

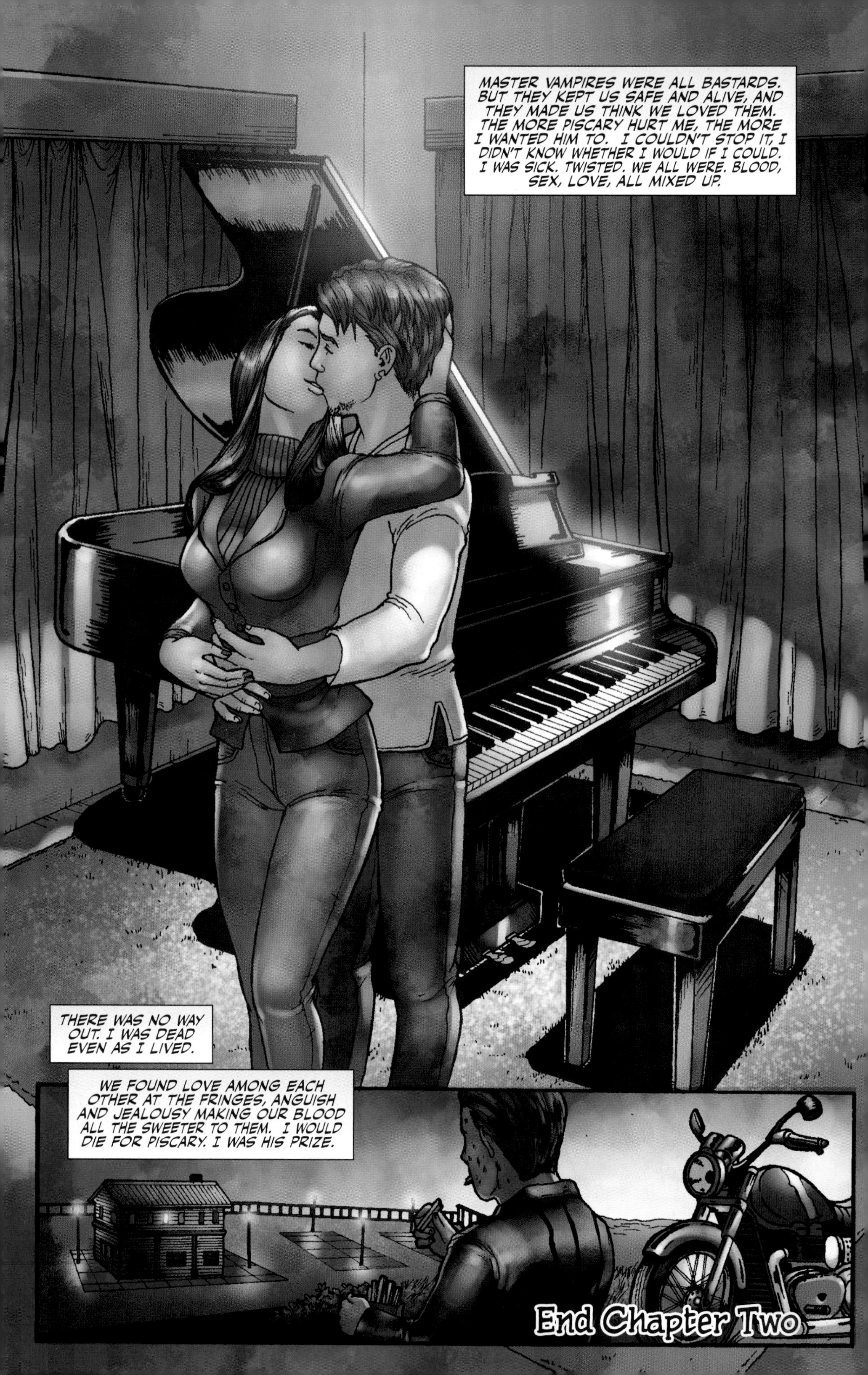
MASTER VAMPIRES WERE ALL BASTARDS. BUT THEY KEPT US SAFE AND ALIVE, AND THEY MADE US THINK WE LOVED THEM. THE MORE PISCARY HURT ME, THE MORE I WANTED HIM TO. I COULDN'T STOP IT, I DIDN'T KNOW WHETHER I WOULD IF I COULD. I WAS SICK. TWISTED. WE ALL WERE. BLOOD, SEX, LOVE, ALL MIXED UP.
THERE WAS NO WAY OUT. I WAS DEAD EVEN AS I LIVED.
WE FOUND LOVE AMONG EACH OTHER AT THE FRINGES, ANGUISH AND JEALOUSY MAKING OUR BLOOD ALL THE SWEETER TO THEM. I WOULD DIE FOR PISCARY. I WAS HIS PRIZE.
End Chapter Two

CHAPTER 3

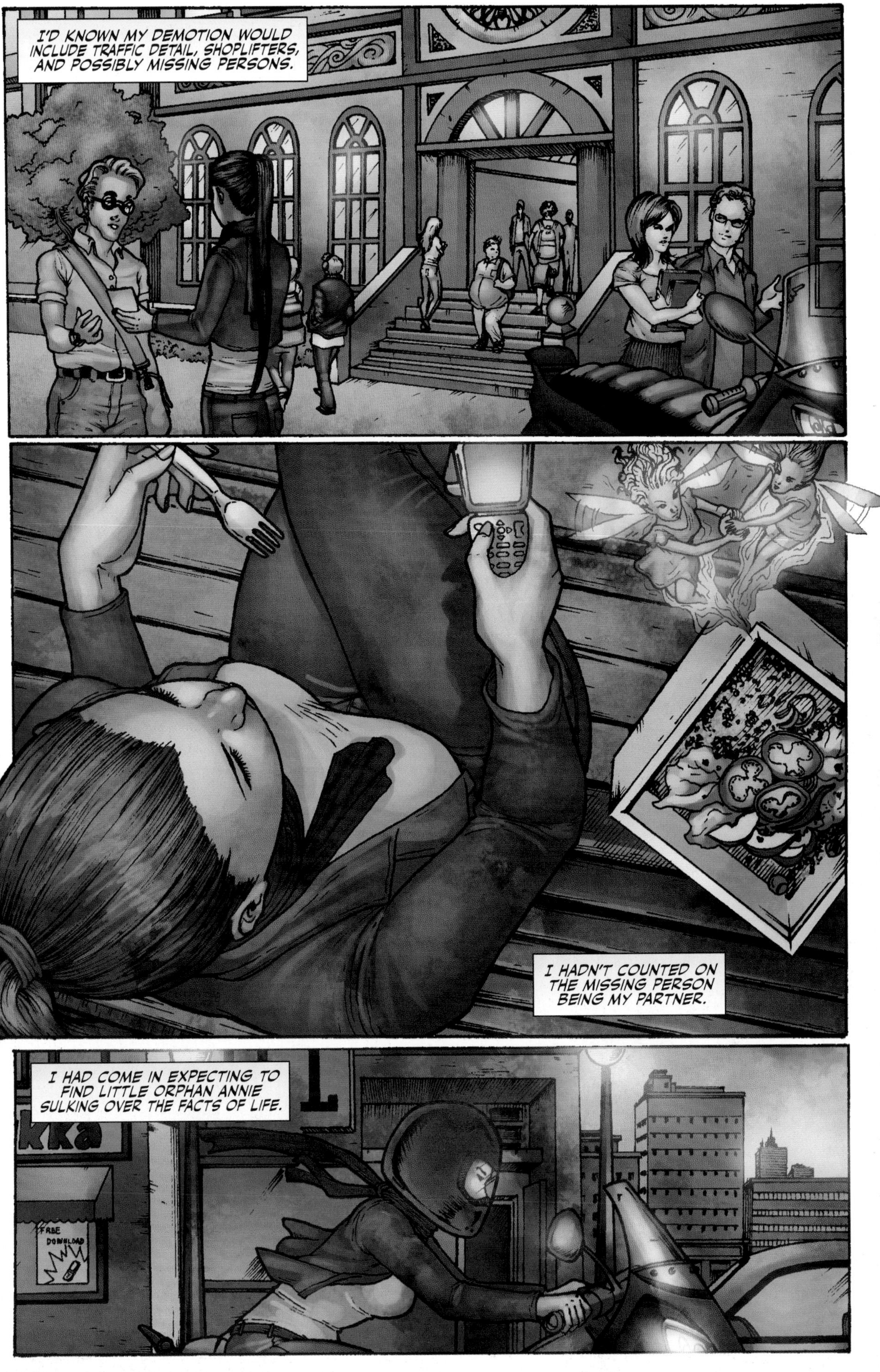
I'D KNOWN MY DEMOTION WOULD INCLUDE TRAFFIC DETAIL, SHOPLIFTERS, AND POSSIBLY MISSING PERSONS.
I HADN'T COUNTED ON THE MISSING PERSON BEING MY PARTNER.
I HAD COME IN EXPECTING TO FIND LITTLE ORPHAN ANNIE SULKING OVER THE FACTS OF LIFE.
FREE DOWNLOAD

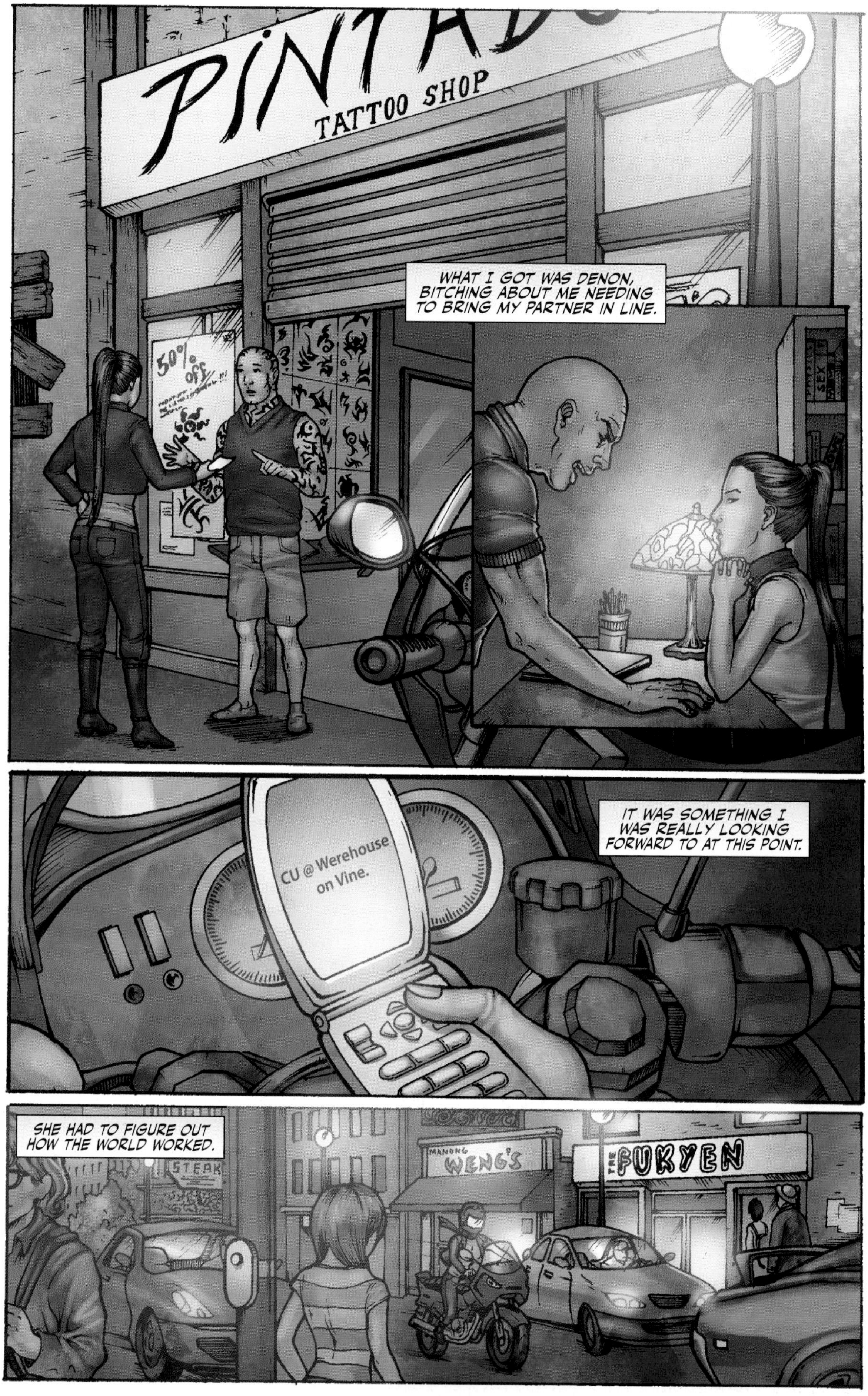

PINTADO
TATTOO SHOP
50% off
WHAT I GOT WAS DENON, BITCHING ABOUT ME NEEDING TO BRING MY PARTNER IN LINE.
SEX
IT WAS SOMETHING I WAS REALLY LOOKING FORWARD TO AT THIS POINT.
CU @ Werehouse on Vine.
SHE HAD TO FIGURE OUT HOW THE WORLD WORKED.
STEAK
MANONG WENG'S
THE FUKYEN

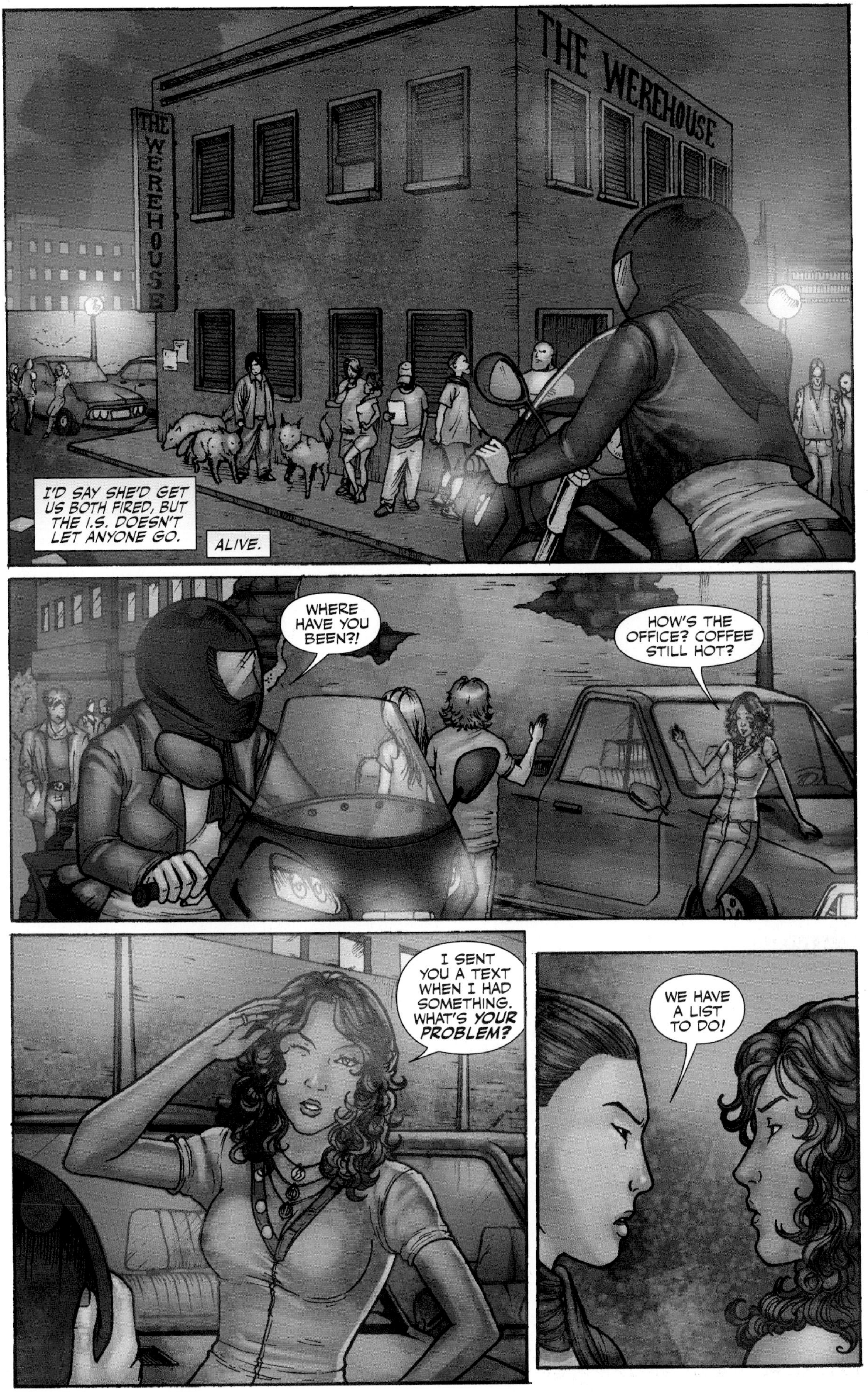
THE WEREHOUSE
THE WEREHOUSE
I'D SAY SHE'D GET US BOTH FIRED, BUT THE I.S. DOESN'T LET ANYONE GO.
ALIVE.
WHERE HAVE YOU BEEN?!
HOW'S THE OFFICE? COFFEE STILL HOT?
I SENT YOU A TEXT WHEN I HAD SOMETHING. WHAT'S *YOUR PROBLEM?*
WE HAVE A LIST TO DO!

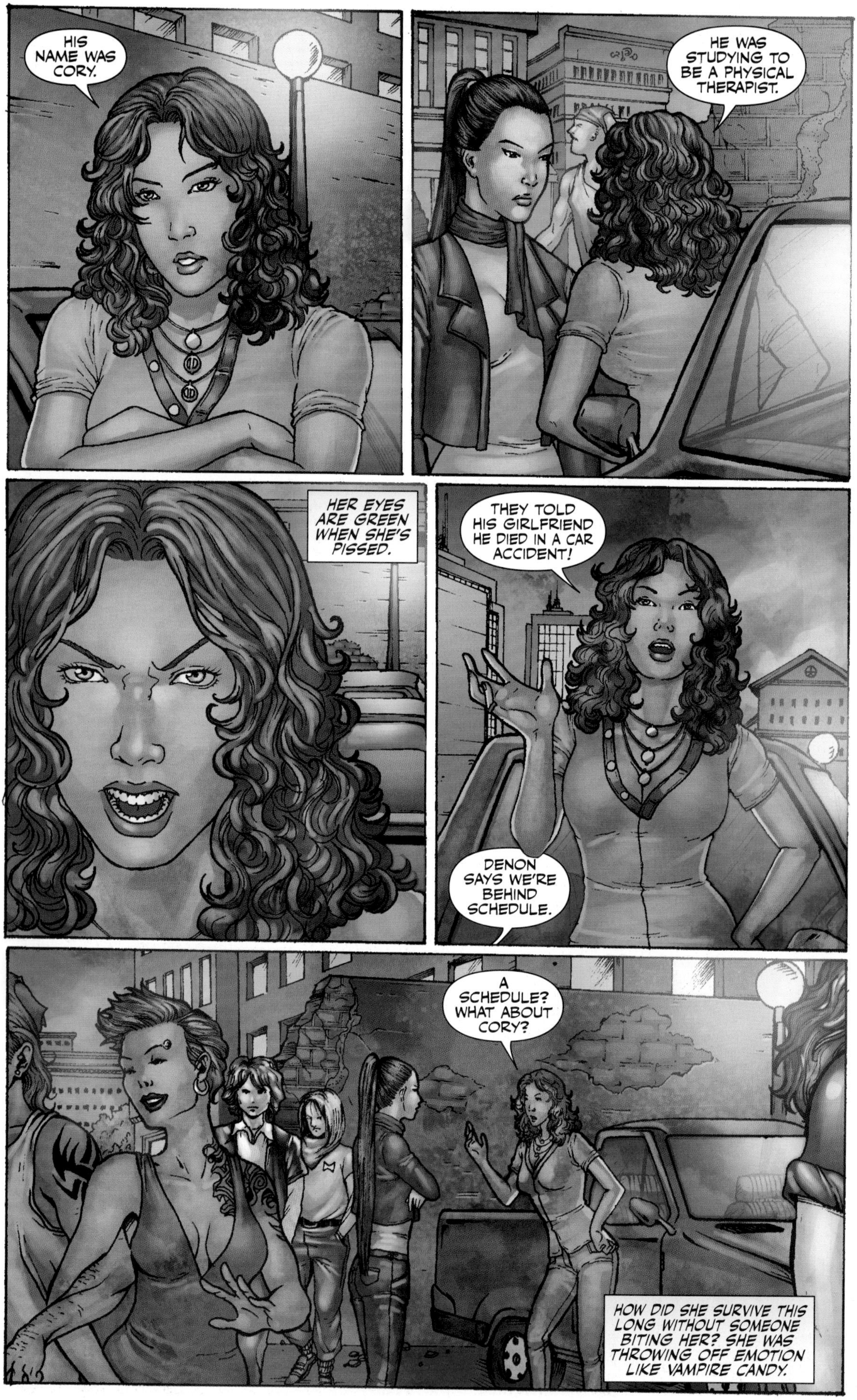
HIS NAME WAS CORY.
HE WAS STUDYING TO BE A PHYSICAL THERAPIST.
HER EYES ARE GREEN WHEN SHE'S PISSED.
THEY TOLD HIS GIRLFRIEND HE DIED IN A CAR ACCIDENT!
DENON SAYS WE'RE BEHIND SCHEDULE.
A SCHEDULE? WHAT ABOUT CORY?
HOW DID SHE SURVIVE THIS LONG WITHOUT SOMEONE BITING HER? SHE WAS THROWING OFF EMOTION LIKE VAMPIRE CANDY.

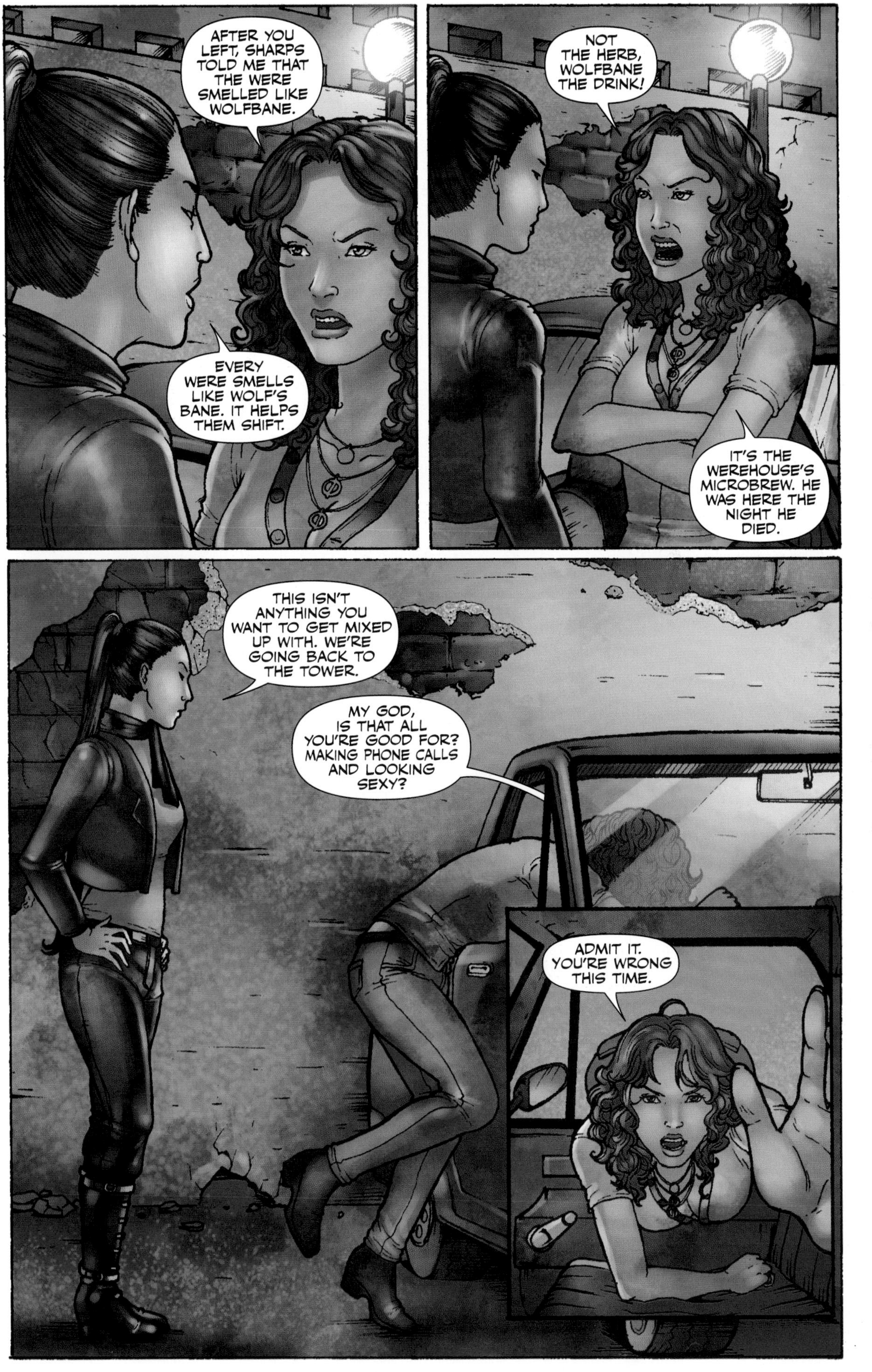
AFTER YOU LEFT, SHARPS TOLD ME THAT THE WERE SMELLED LIKE WOLFBANE.
EVERY WERE SMELLS LIKE WOLF'S BANE. IT HELPS THEM SHIFT.
NOT THE HERB, WOLFBANE THE DRINK!
IT'S THE WEREHOUSE'S MICROBREW. HE WAS HERE THE NIGHT HE DIED.
THIS ISN'T ANYTHING YOU WANT TO GET MIXED UP WITH. WE'RE GOING BACK TO THE TOWER.
MY GOD, IS THAT ALL YOU'RE GOOD FOR? MAKING PHONE CALLS AND LOOKING SEXY?
ADMIT IT. YOU'RE WRONG THIS TIME.

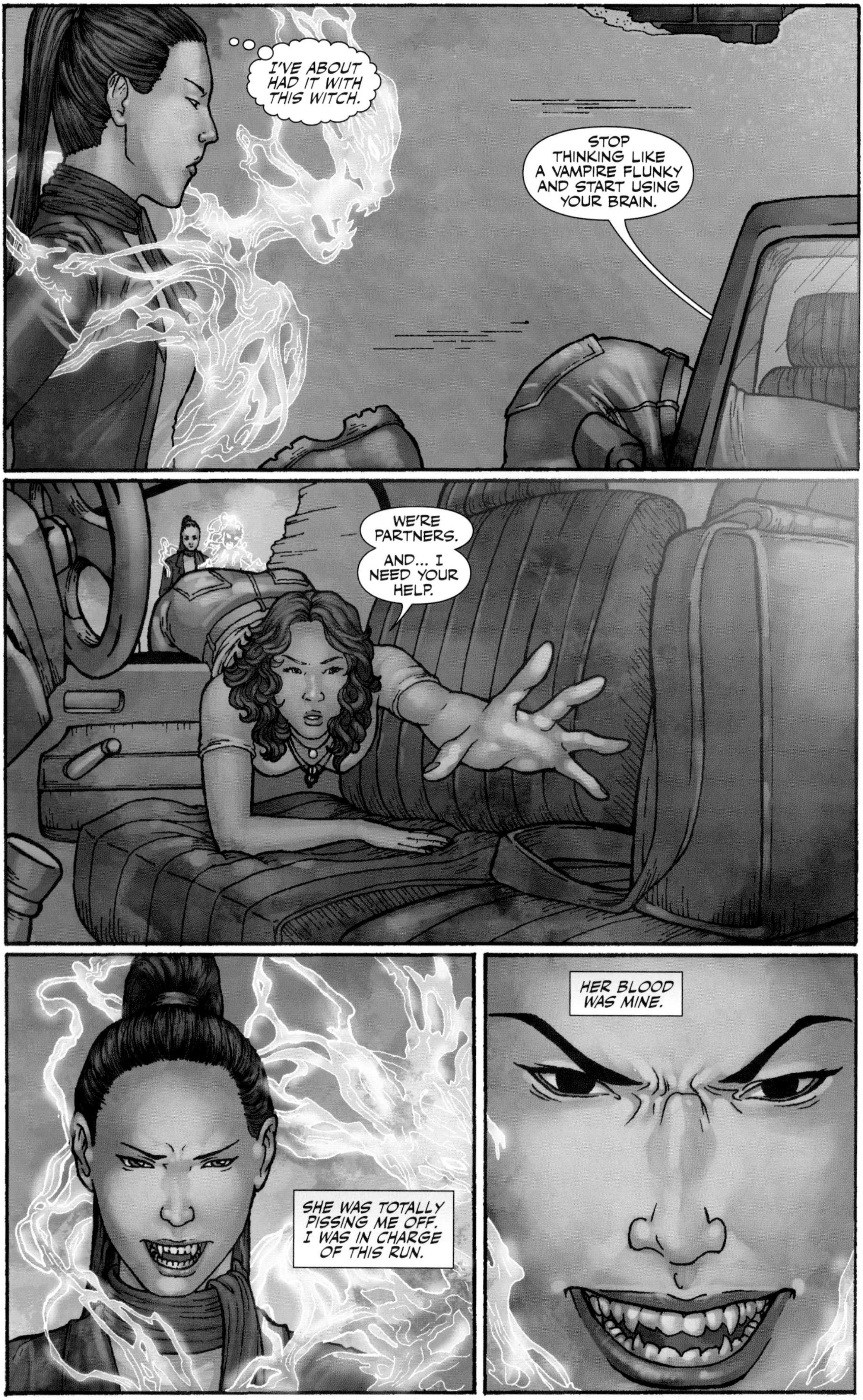
I'VE ABOUT HAD IT WITH THIS WITCH.
STOP THINKING LIKE A VAMPIRE FLUNKY AND START USING YOUR BRAIN.
WE'RE PARTNERS.
AND... I NEED YOUR HELP.
SHE WAS TOTALLY PISSING ME OFF. I WAS IN CHARGE OF THIS RUN.
HER BLOOD WAS MINE.

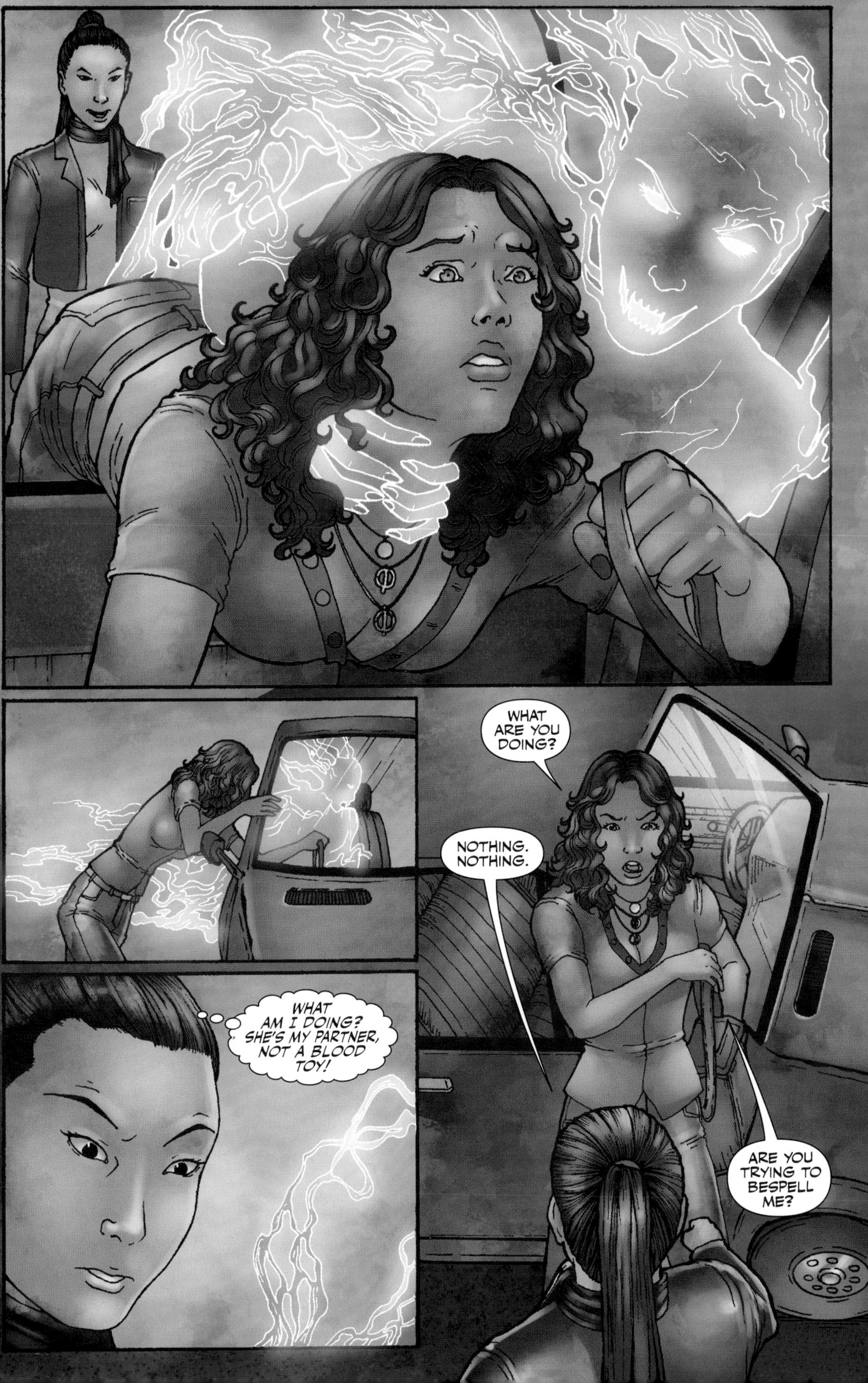
WHAT ARE YOU DOING?
NOTHING. NOTHING.
WHAT AM I DOING? SHE'S MY PARTNER, NOT A BLOOD TOY!
ARE YOU TRYING TO BESPELL ME?

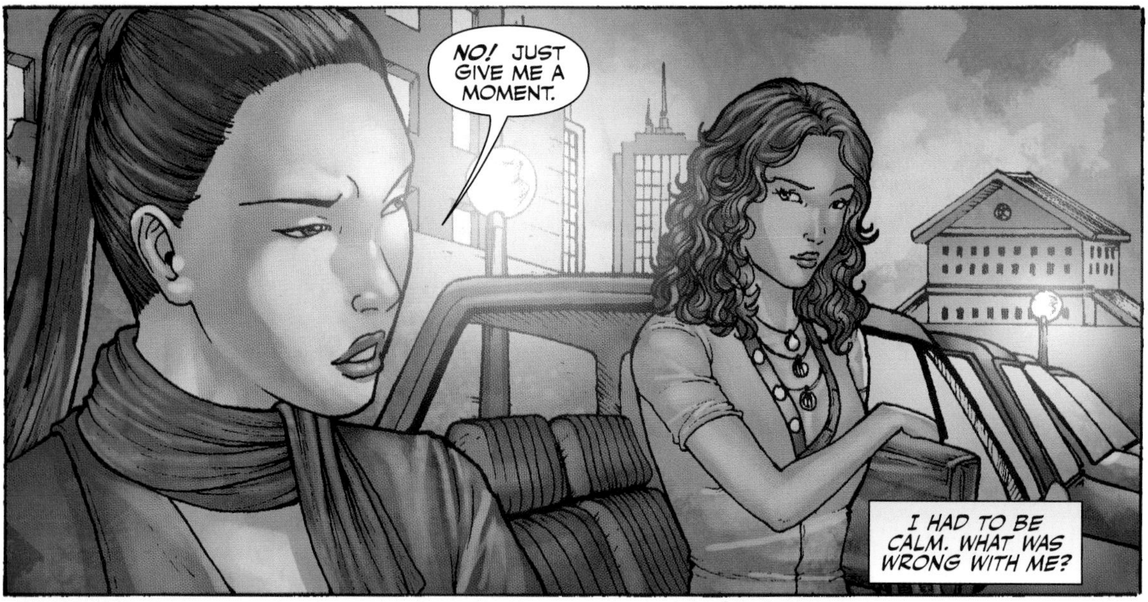
NO! JUST GIVE ME A MOMENT.
I HAD TO BE CALM. WHAT WAS WRONG WITH ME?

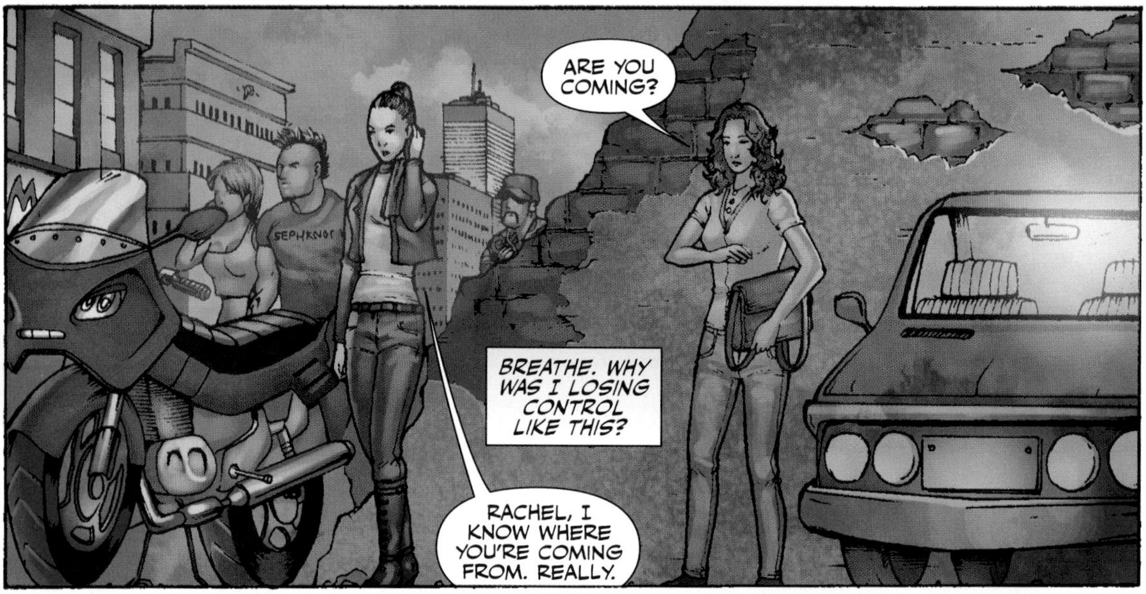
ARE YOU COMING?
SEPHKNOT
BREATHE. WHY WAS I LOSING CONTROL LIKE THIS?
RACHEL, I KNOW WHERE YOU'RE COMING FROM. REALLY.

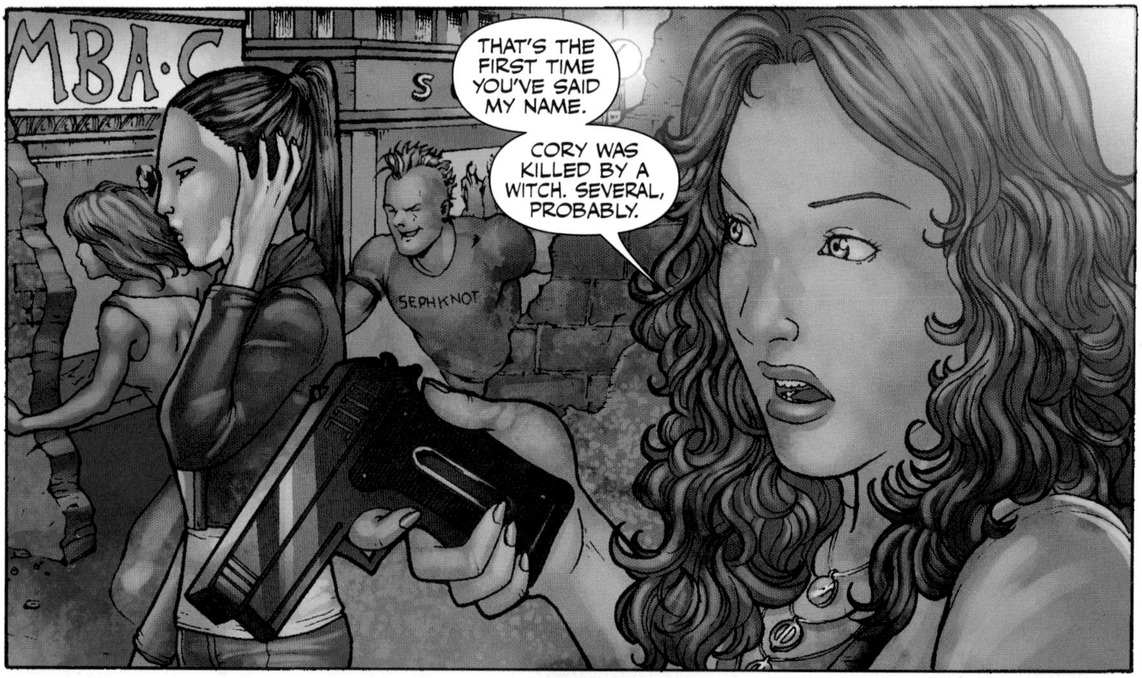
THAT'S THE FIRST TIME YOU'VE SAID MY NAME.
CORY WAS KILLED BY A WITCH. SEVERAL, PROBABLY.
SEPHKNOT

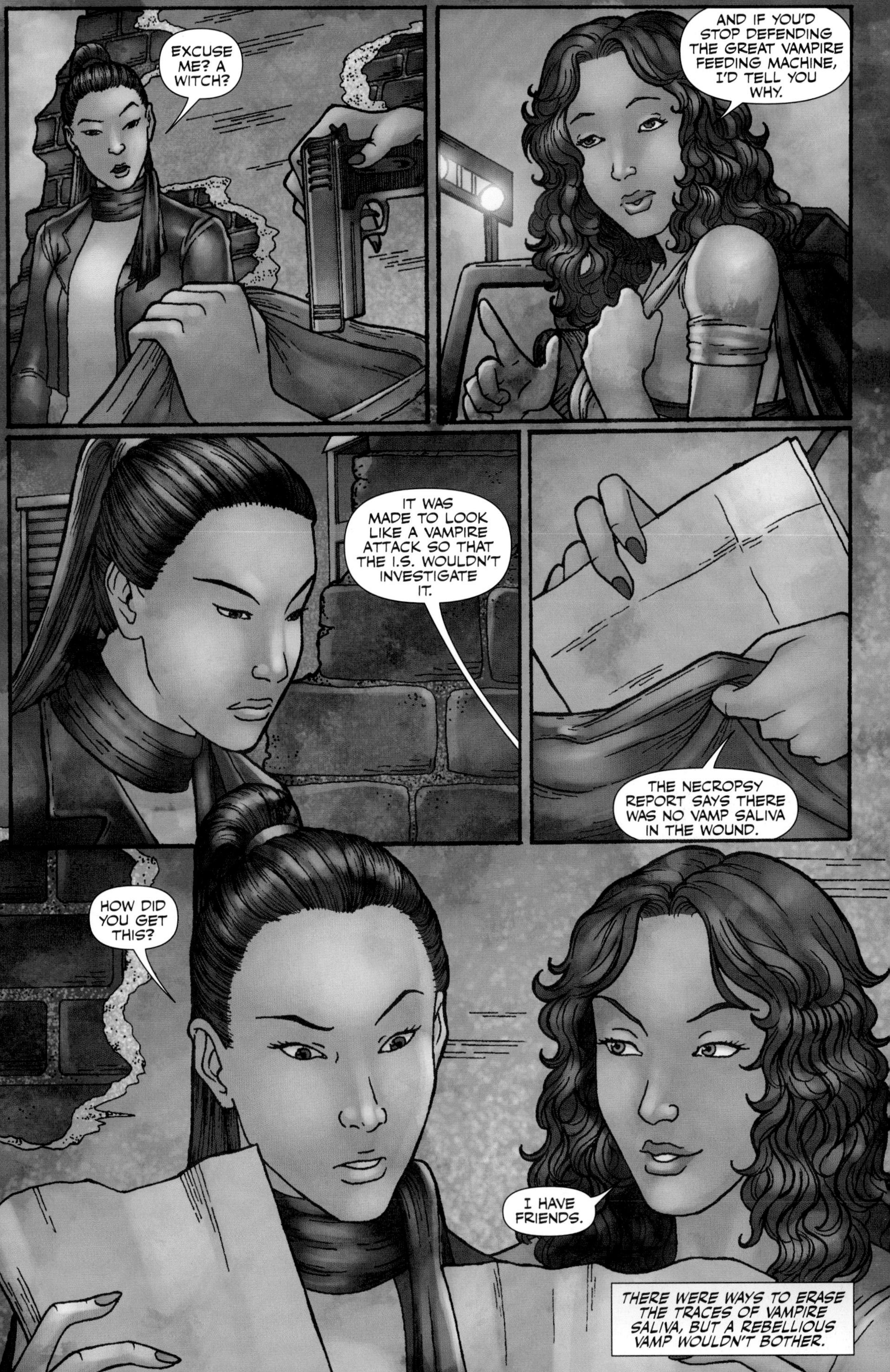
EXCUSE ME? A WITCH?
AND IF YOU'D STOP DEFENDING THE GREAT VAMPIRE FEEDING MACHINE, I'D TELL YOU WHY.
IT WAS MADE TO LOOK LIKE A VAMPIRE ATTACK SO THAT THE I.S. WOULDN'T INVESTIGATE IT.
THE NECROPSY REPORT SAYS THERE WAS NO VAMP SALIVA IN THE WOUND.
HOW DID YOU GET THIS?
I HAVE FRIENDS.
THERE WERE WAYS TO ERASE THE TRACES OF VAMPIRE SALIVA, BUT A REBELLIOUS VAMP WOULDN'T BOTHER.

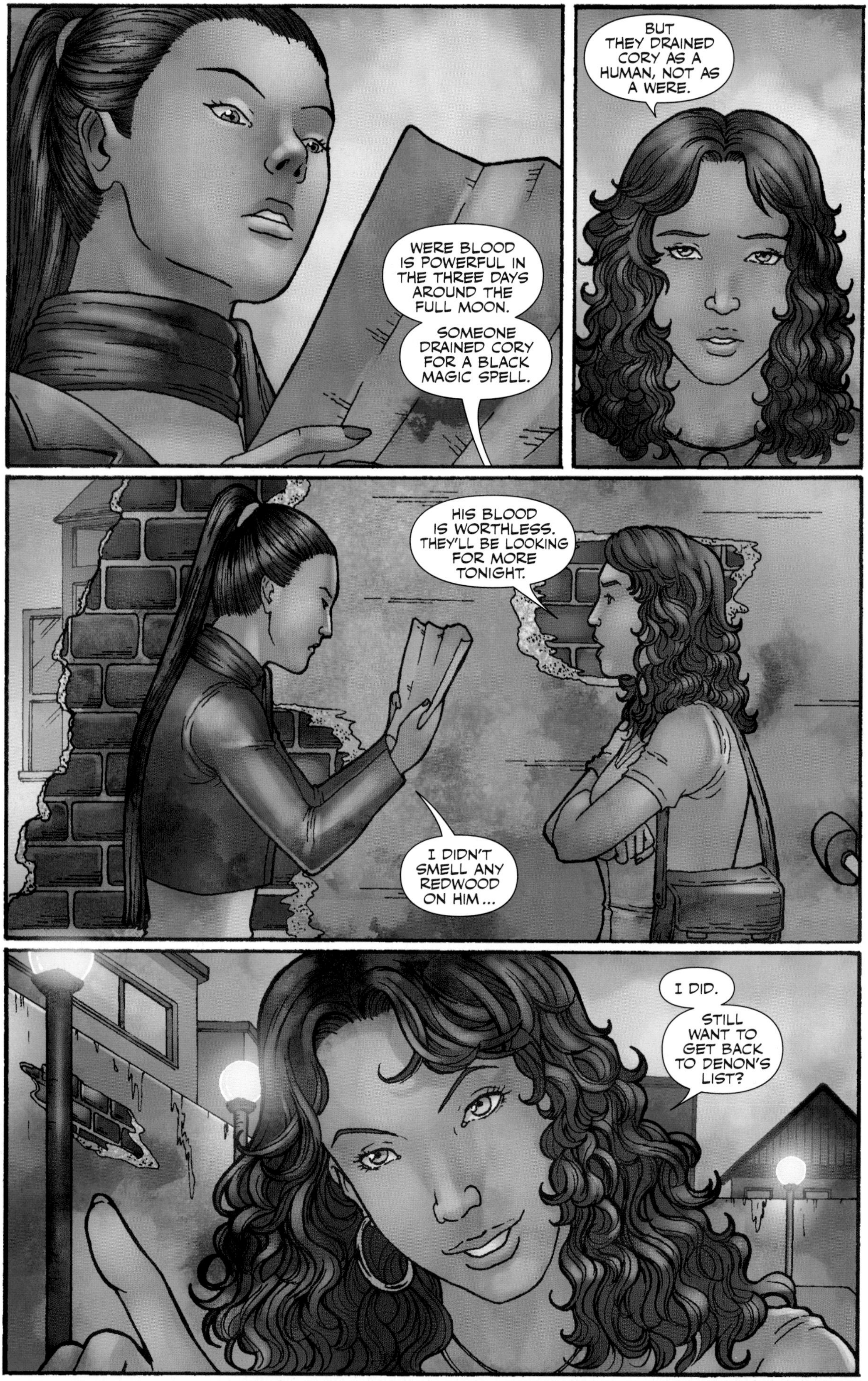
BUT THEY DRAINED CORY AS A HUMAN, NOT AS A WERE.
WERE BLOOD IS POWERFUL IN THE THREE DAYS AROUND THE FULL MOON.
SOMEONE DRAINED CORY FOR A BLACK MAGIC SPELL.
HIS BLOOD IS WORTHLESS. THEY'LL BE LOOKING FOR MORE TONIGHT.
I DIDN'T SMELL ANY REDWOOD ON HIM...
I DID.
STILL WANT TO GET BACK TO DENON'S LIST?

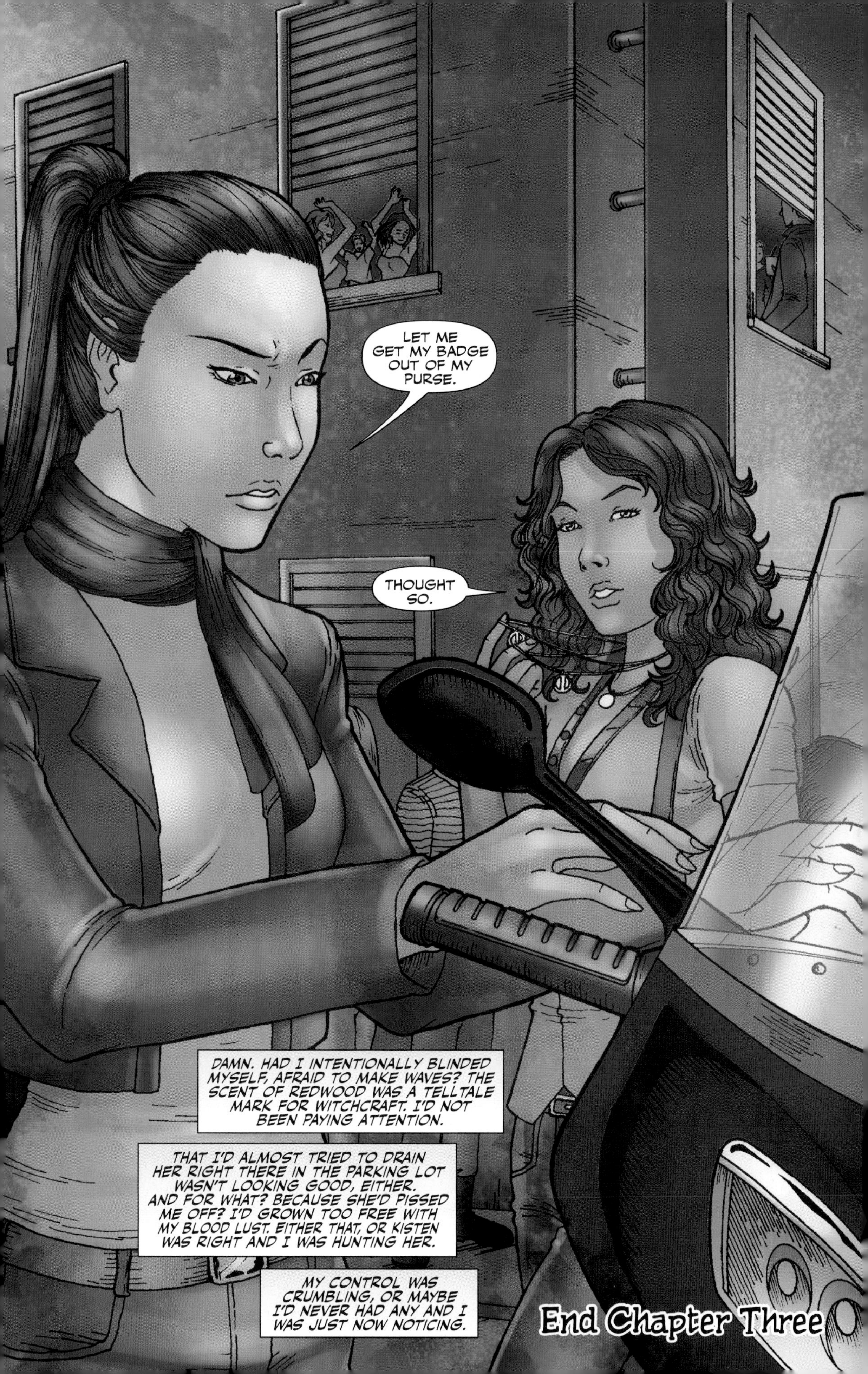
LET ME GET MY BADGE OUT OF MY PURSE.
THOUGHT SO.
DAMN. HAD I INTENTIONALLY BLINDED MYSELF, AFRAID TO MAKE WAVES? THE SCENT OF REDWOOD WAS A TELLTALE MARK FOR WITCHCRAFT. I'D NOT BEEN PAYING ATTENTION.
THAT I'D ALMOST TRIED TO DRAIN HER RIGHT THERE IN THE PARKING LOT WASN'T LOOKING GOOD, EITHER. AND FOR WHAT? BECAUSE SHE'D PISSED ME OFF? I'D GROWN TOO FREE WITH MY BLOOD LUST. EITHER THAT, OR KISTEN WAS RIGHT AND I WAS HUNTING HER.
MY CONTROL WAS CRUMBLING, OR MAYBE I'D NEVER HAD ANY AND I WAS JUST NOW NOTICING.
End Chapter Three

CHAPTER 4

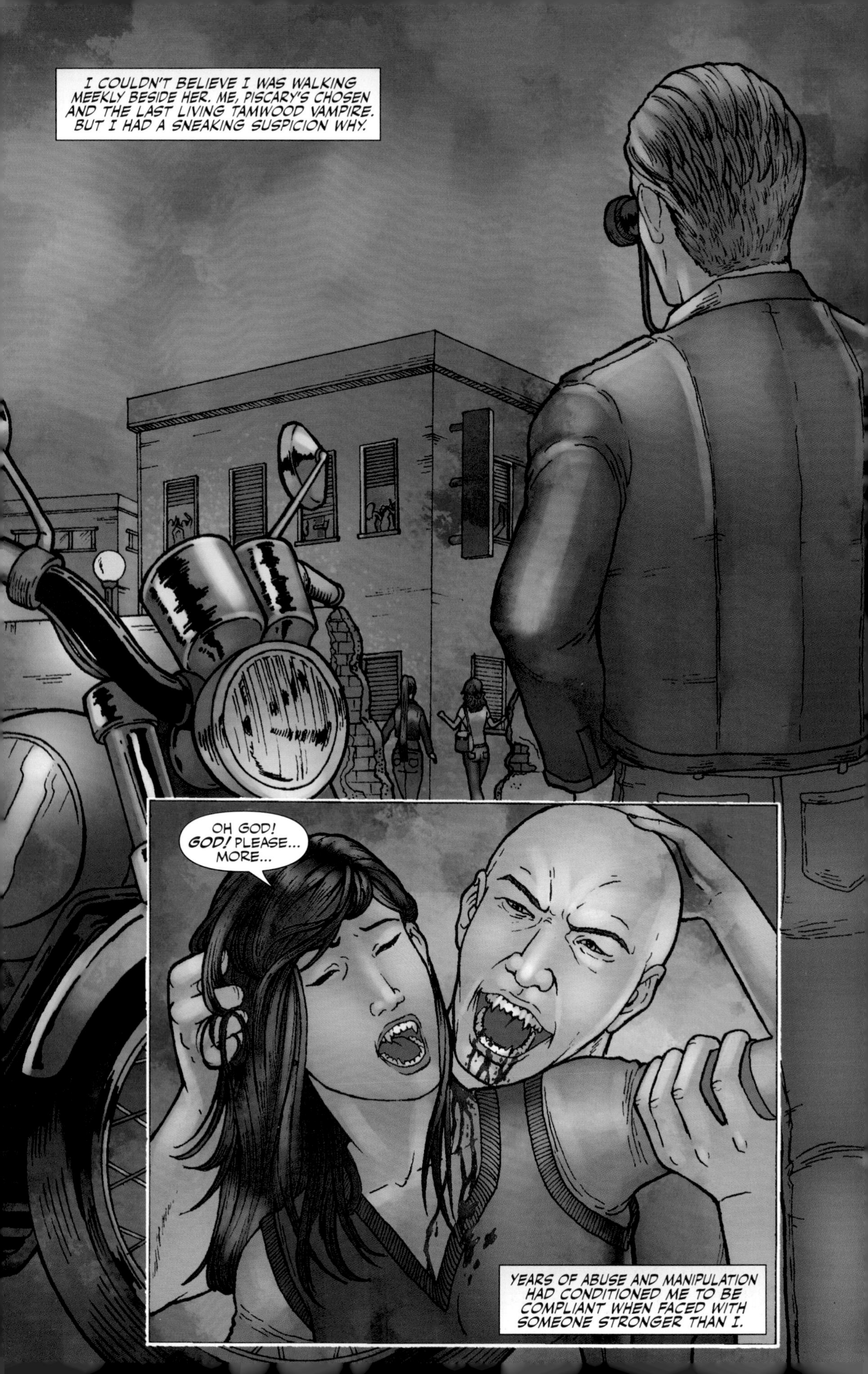
I COULDN'T BELIEVE I WAS WALKING MEEKLY BESIDE HER. ME, PISCARY'S CHOSEN AND THE LAST LIVING TAMWOOD VAMPIRE. BUT I HAD A SNEAKING SUSPICION WHY.
OH GOD! GOD! PLEASE... MORE...
YEARS OF ABUSE AND MANIPULATION HAD CONDITIONED ME TO BE COMPLIANT WHEN FACED WITH SOMEONE STRONGER THAN I.

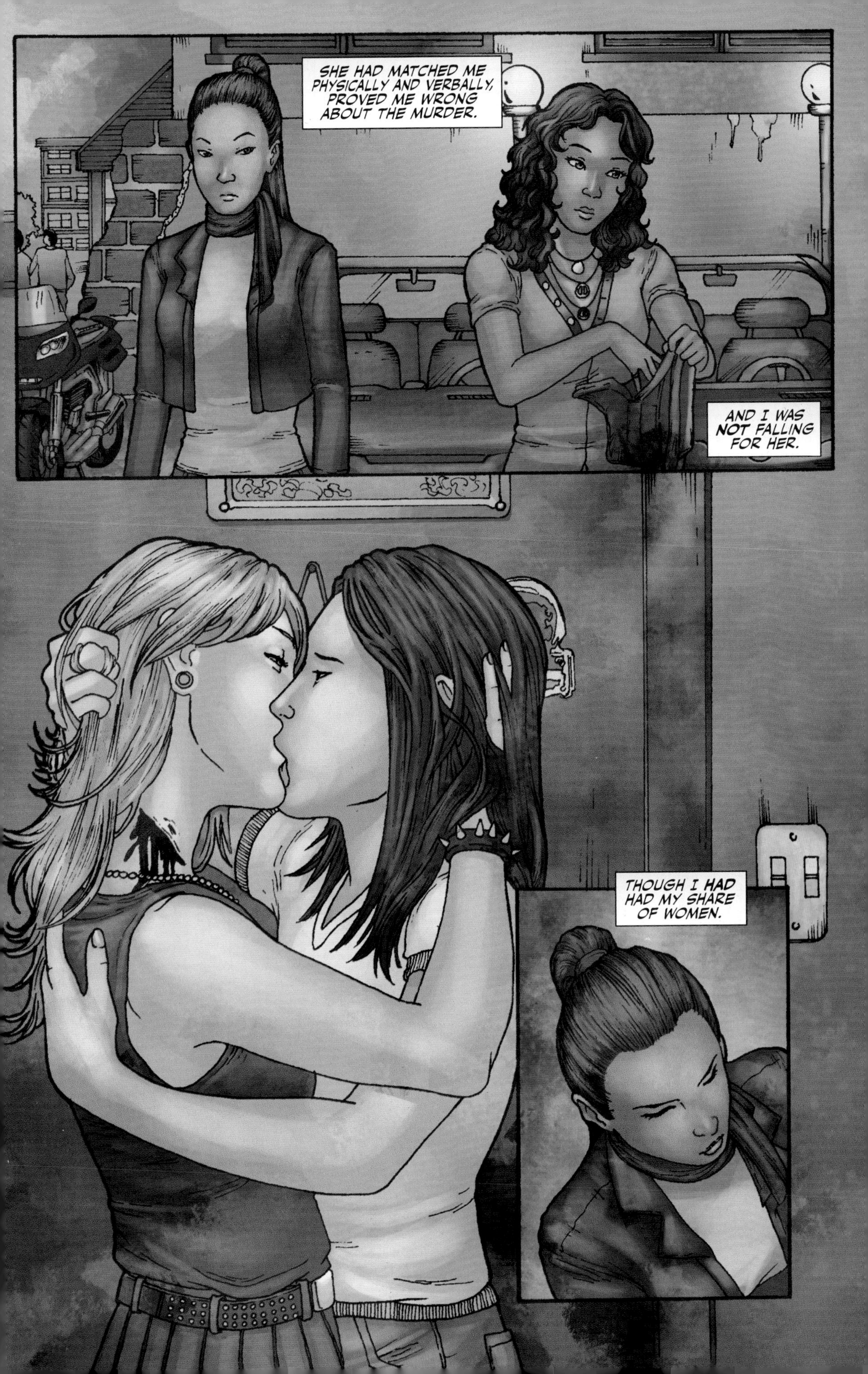
SHE HAD MATCHED ME PHYSICALLY AND VERBALLY, PROVED ME WRONG ABOUT THE MURDER.
AND I WAS NOT FALLING FOR HER.
THOUGH I HAD HAD MY SHARE OF WOMEN.

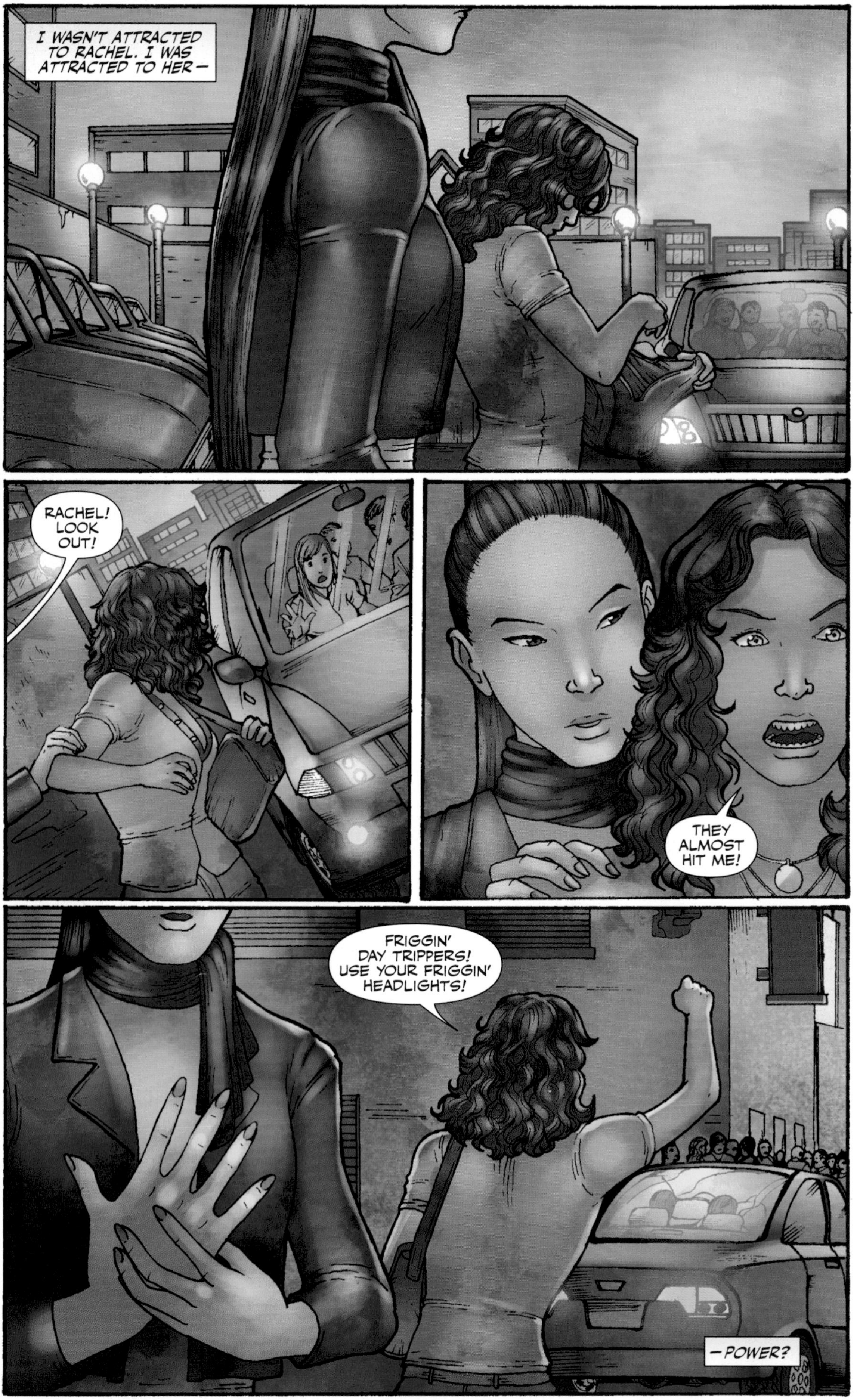
I WASN'T ATTRACTED TO RACHEL. I WAS ATTRACTED TO HER—
RACHEL! LOOK OUT!
THEY ALMOST HIT ME!
FRIGGIN' DAY TRIPPERS! USE YOUR FRIGGIN' HEADLIGHTS!
—POWER?

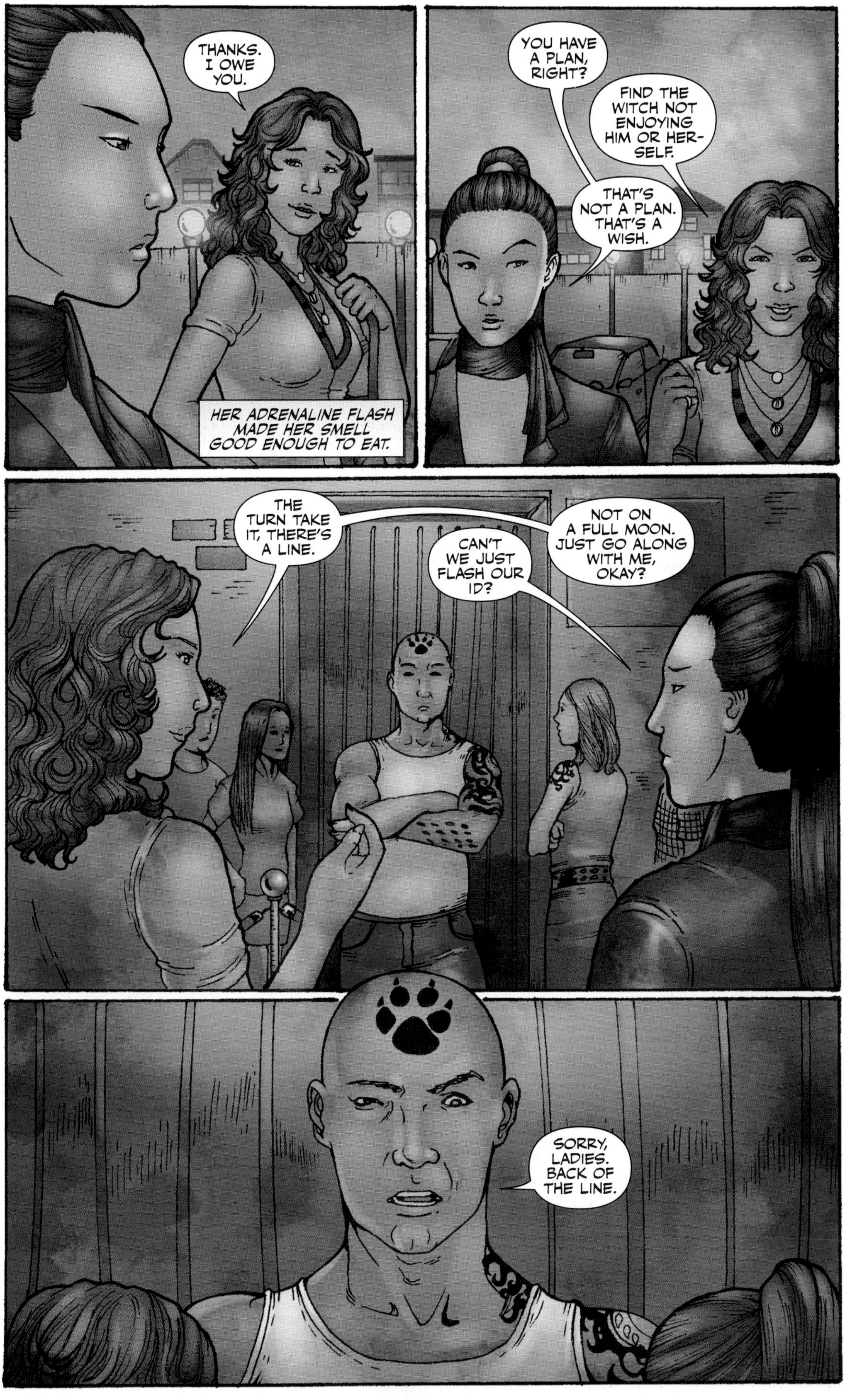
THANKS. I OWE YOU.
HER ADRENALINE FLASH MADE HER SMELL GOOD ENOUGH TO EAT.
YOU HAVE A PLAN, RIGHT?
FIND THE WITCH NOT ENJOYING HIM OR HER-SELF.
THAT'S NOT A PLAN. THAT'S A WISH.
THE TURN TAKE IT, THERE'S A LINE.
CAN'T WE JUST FLASH OUR ID?
NOT ON A FULL MOON. JUST GO ALONG WITH ME, OKAY?
SORRY, LADIES. BACK OF THE LINE.

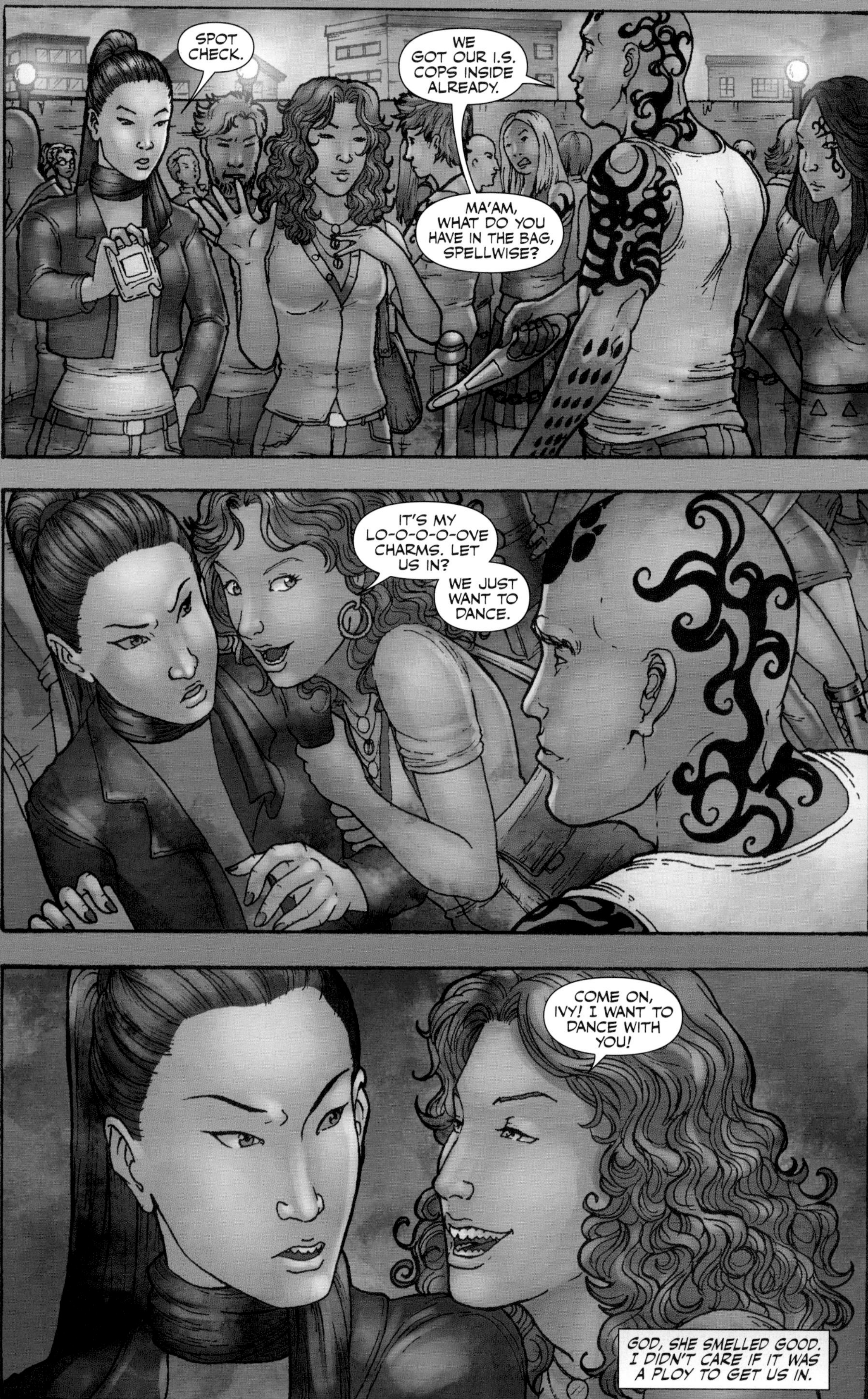
SPOT CHECK.
WE GOT OUR I.S. COPS INSIDE ALREADY.
MA'AM, WHAT DO YOU HAVE IN THE BAG, SPELLWISE?
IT'S MY LO-O-O-O-OVE CHARMS. LET US IN?
WE JUST WANT TO DANCE.
COME ON, IVY! I WANT TO DANCE WITH YOU!
GOD, SHE SMELLED GOOD. I DIDN'T CARE IF IT WAS A PLOY TO GET US IN.

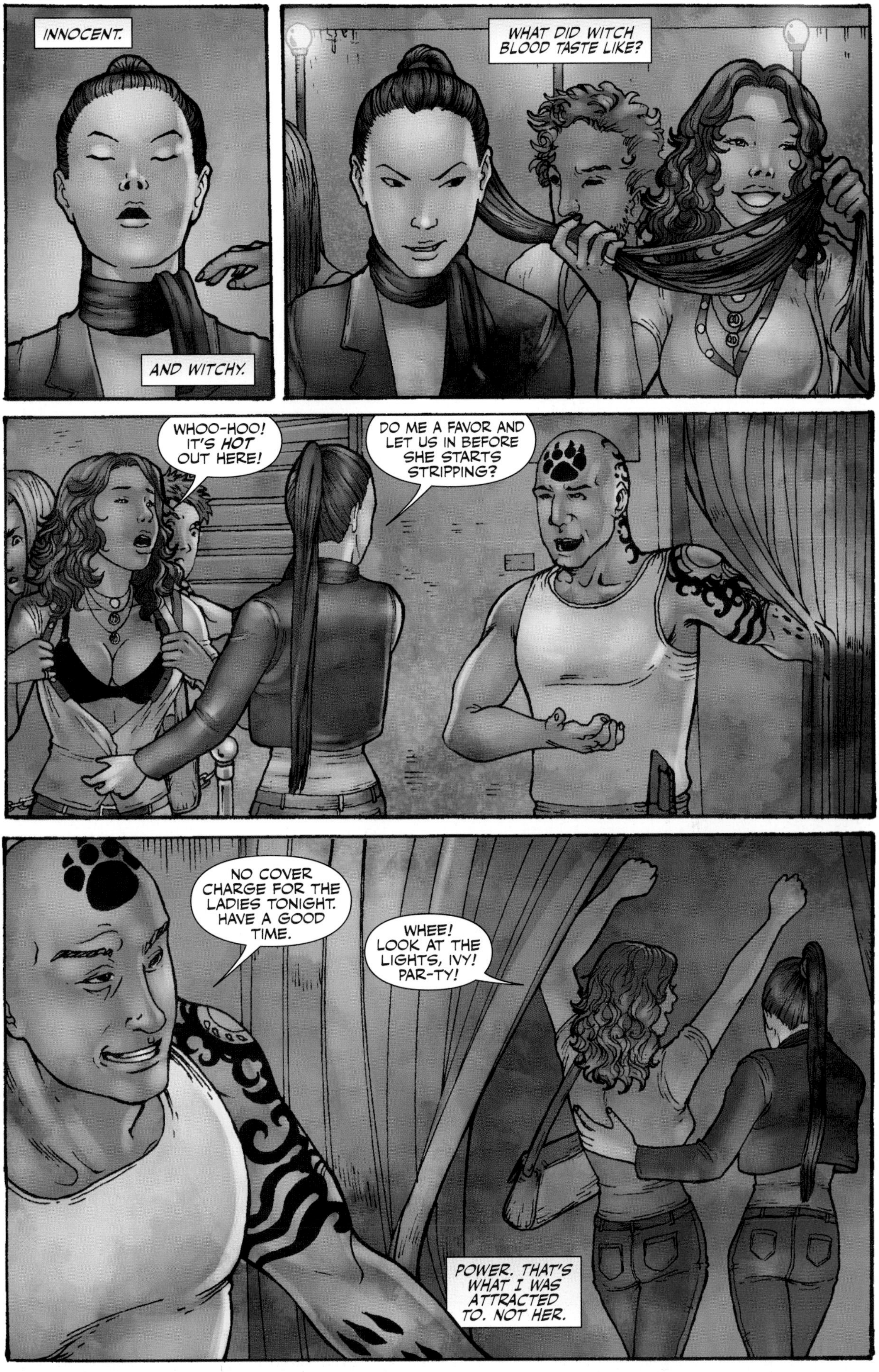

INNOCENT.
AND WITCHY.
WHAT DID WITCH BLOOD TASTE LIKE?
WHOO-HOO! IT'S *HOT* OUT HERE!
DO ME A FAVOR AND LET US IN BEFORE SHE STARTS STRIPPING?
NO COVER CHARGE FOR THE LADIES TONIGHT. HAVE A GOOD TIME.
WHEE! LOOK AT THE LIGHTS, IVY! PAR-TY!
POWER. THAT'S WHAT I WAS ATTRACTED TO. NOT HER.

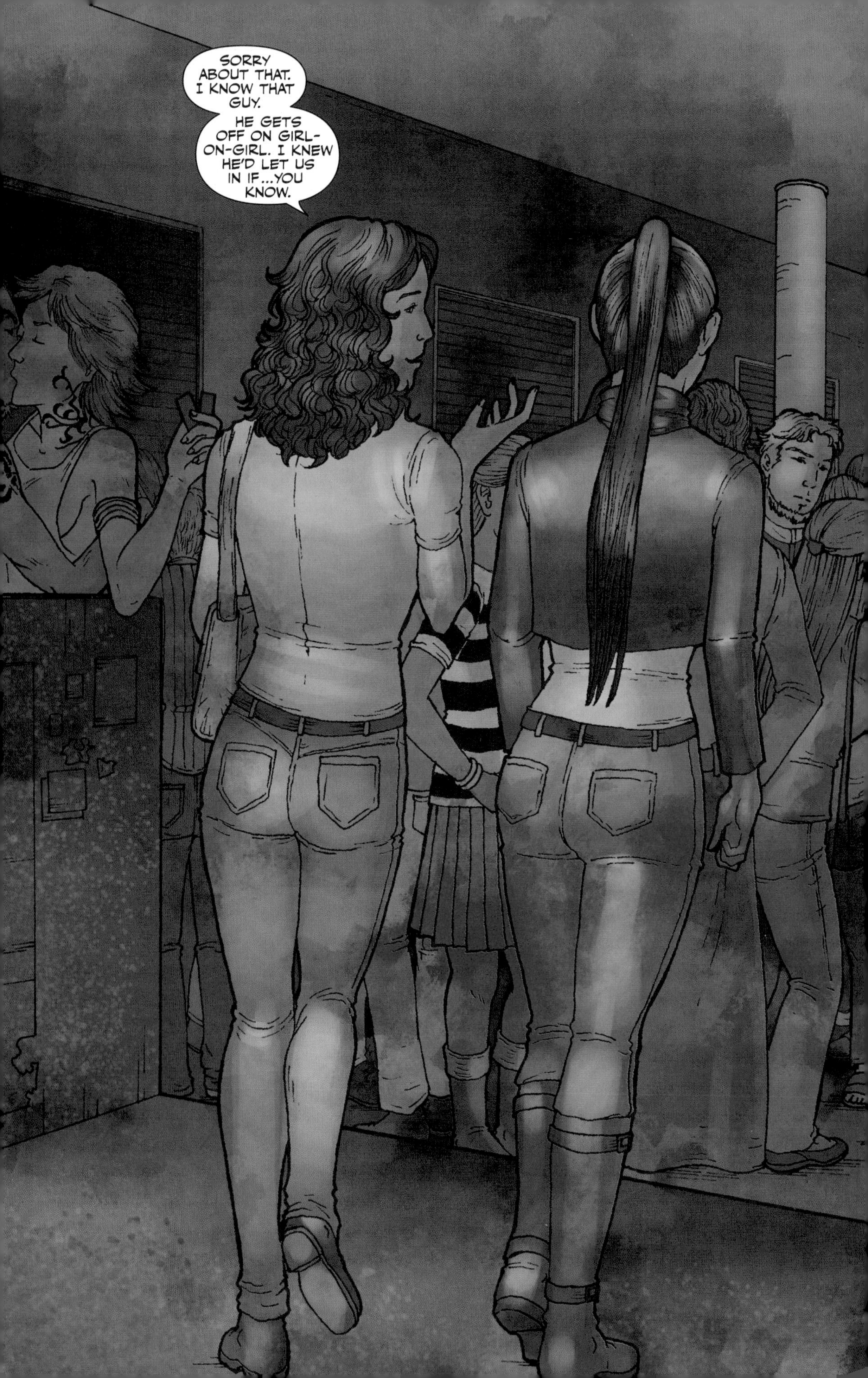
SORRY ABOUT THAT. I KNOW THAT GUY.
HE GETS OFF ON GIRL-ON-GIRL. I KNEW HE'D LET US IN IF...YOU KNOW.

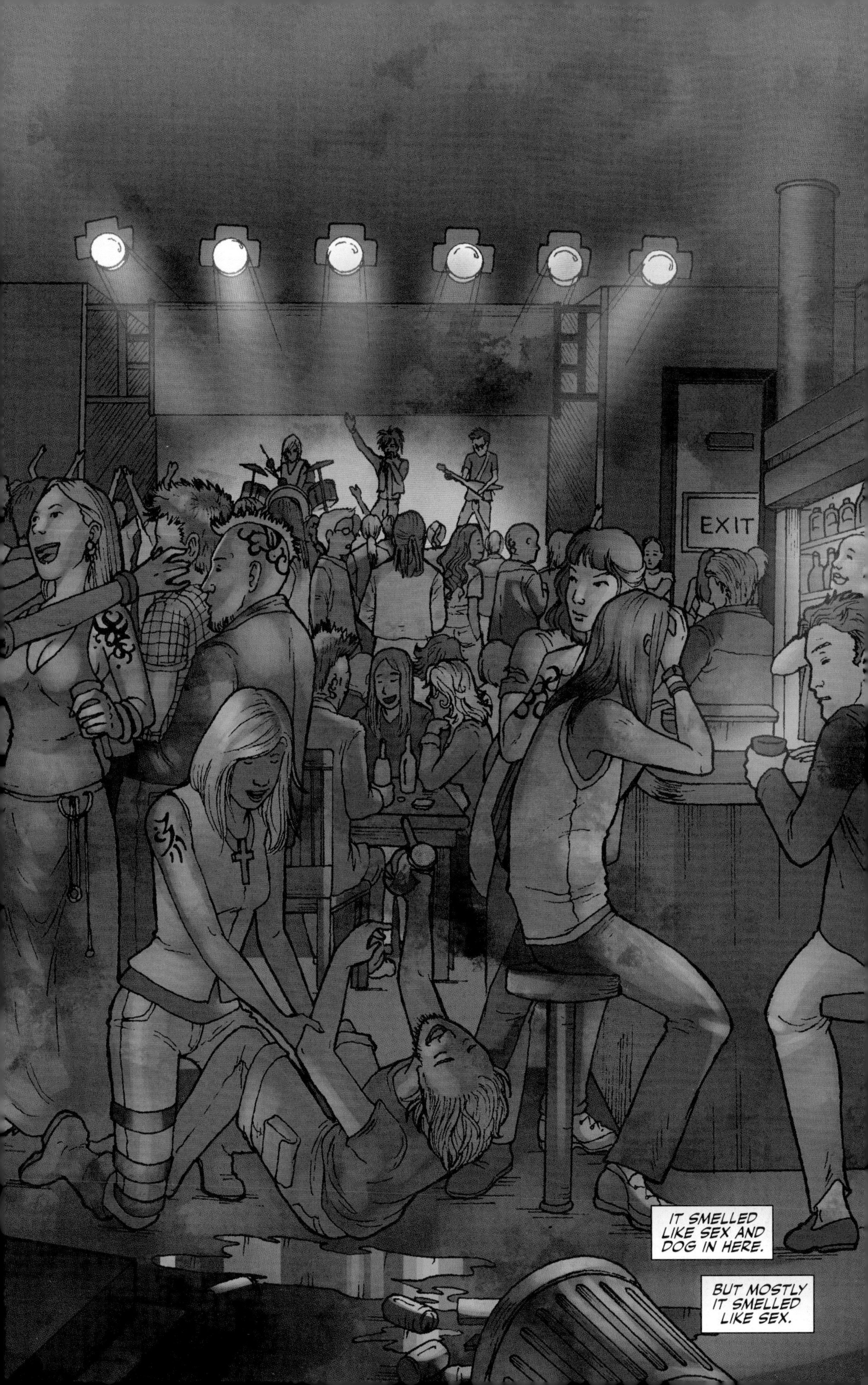
EXIT
IT SMELLED LIKE SEX AND DOG IN HERE.
BUT MOSTLY IT SMELLED LIKE SEX.

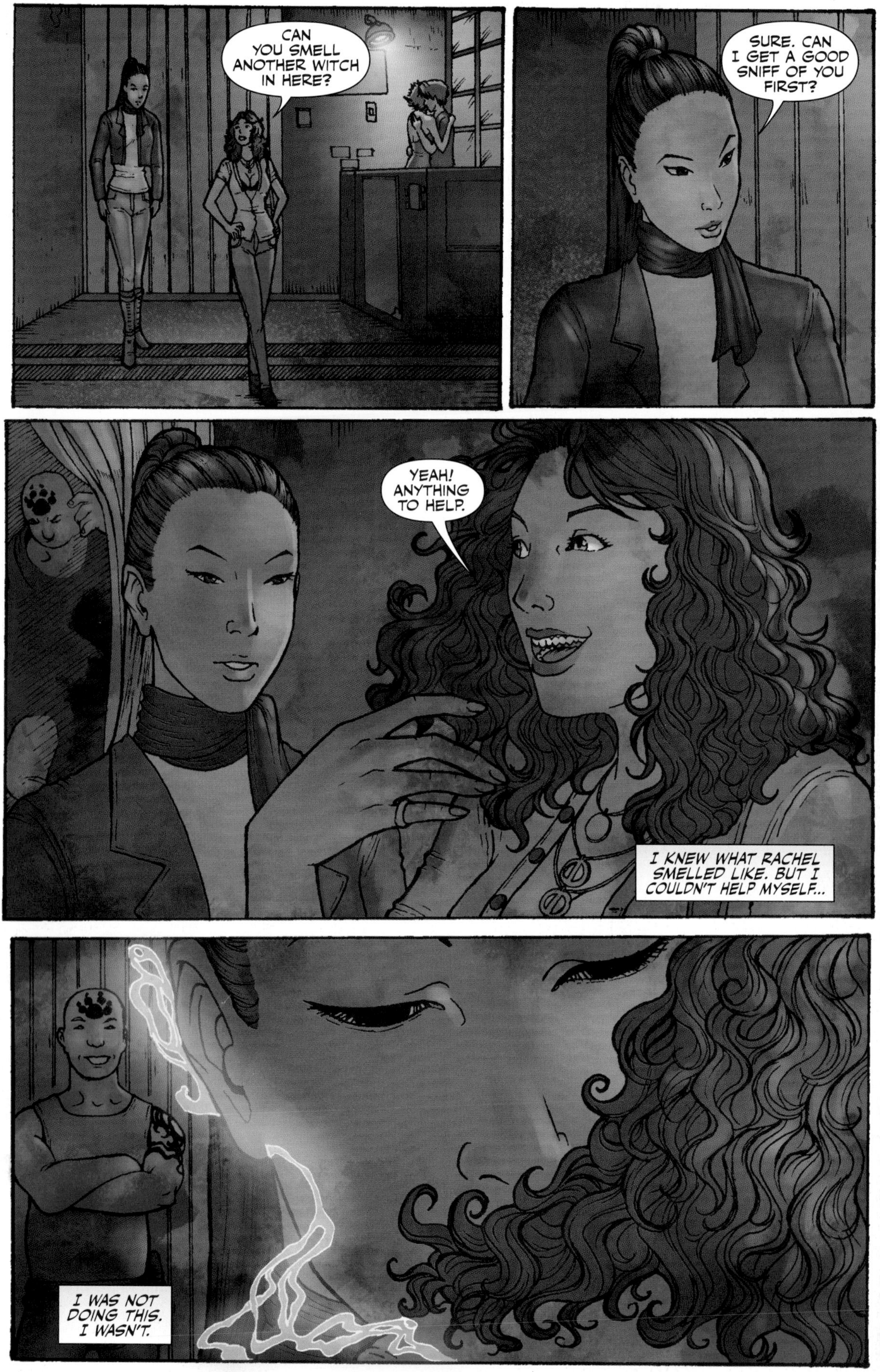
CAN YOU SMELL ANOTHER WITCH IN HERE?
SURE. CAN I GET A GOOD SNIFF OF YOU FIRST?
YEAH! ANYTHING TO HELP.
I KNEW WHAT RACHEL SMELLED LIKE. BUT I COULDN'T HELP MYSELF...
I WAS NOT DOING THIS. I WASN'T.

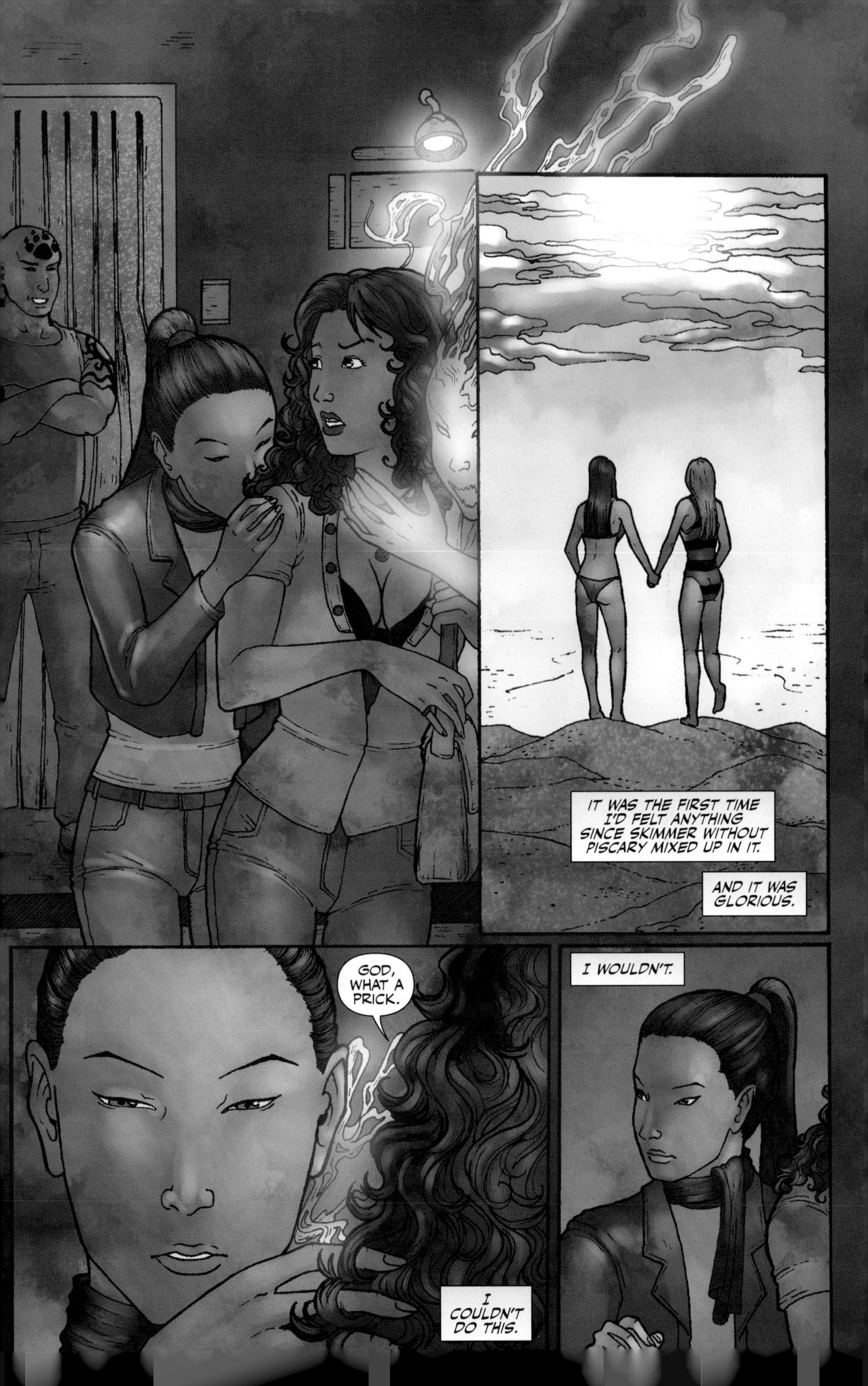
IT WAS THE FIRST TIME I'D FELT ANYTHING SINCE SKIMMER WITHOUT PISCARY MIXED UP IN IT.
AND IT WAS GLORIOUS.
GOD, WHAT A PRICK.
I COULDN'T DO THIS.
I WOULDN'T.

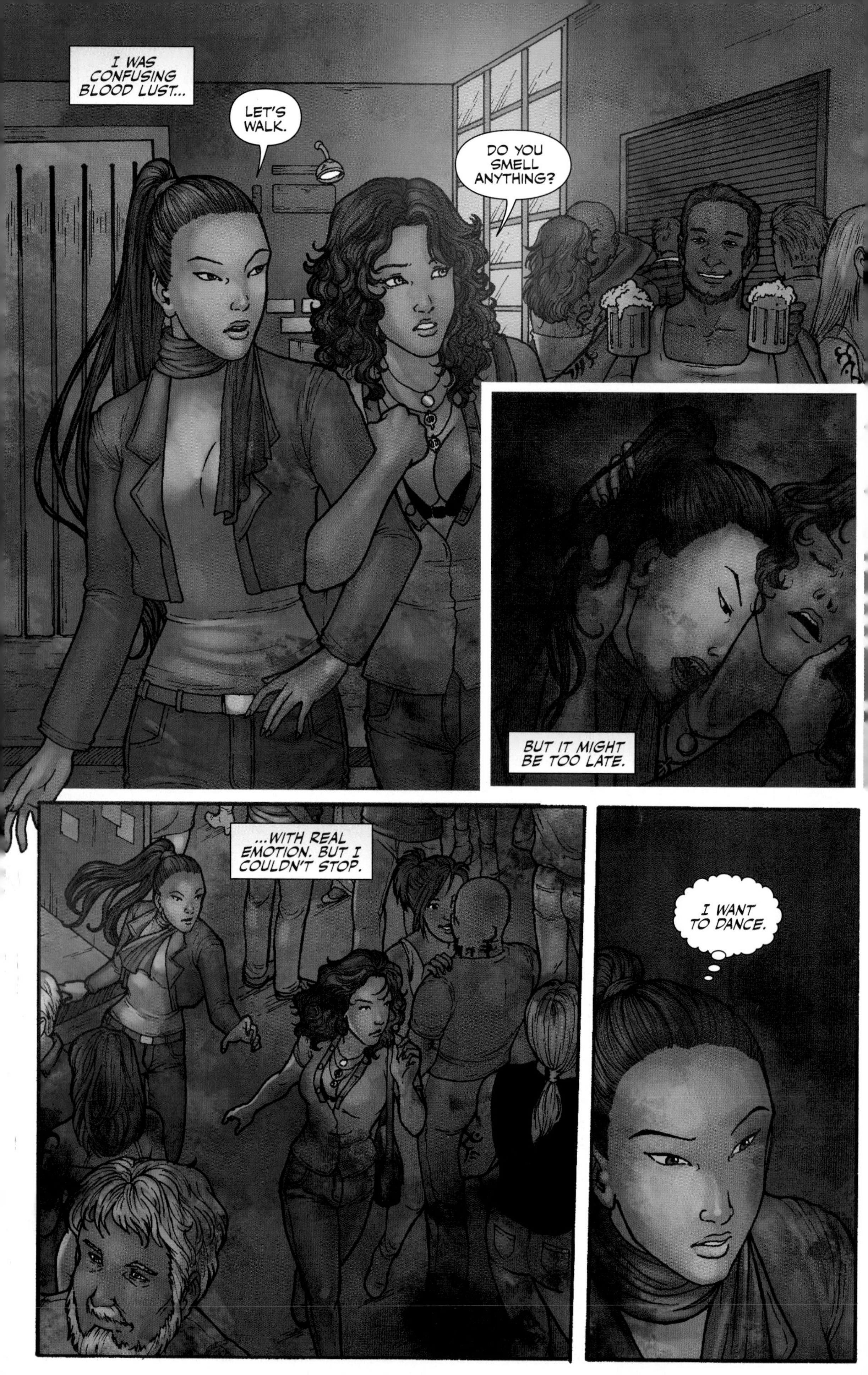
I WAS CONFUSING BLOOD LUST...
LET'S WALK.
DO YOU SMELL ANYTHING?
BUT IT MIGHT BE TOO LATE.
...WITH REAL EMOTION. BUT I COULDN'T STOP.
I WANT TO DANCE.

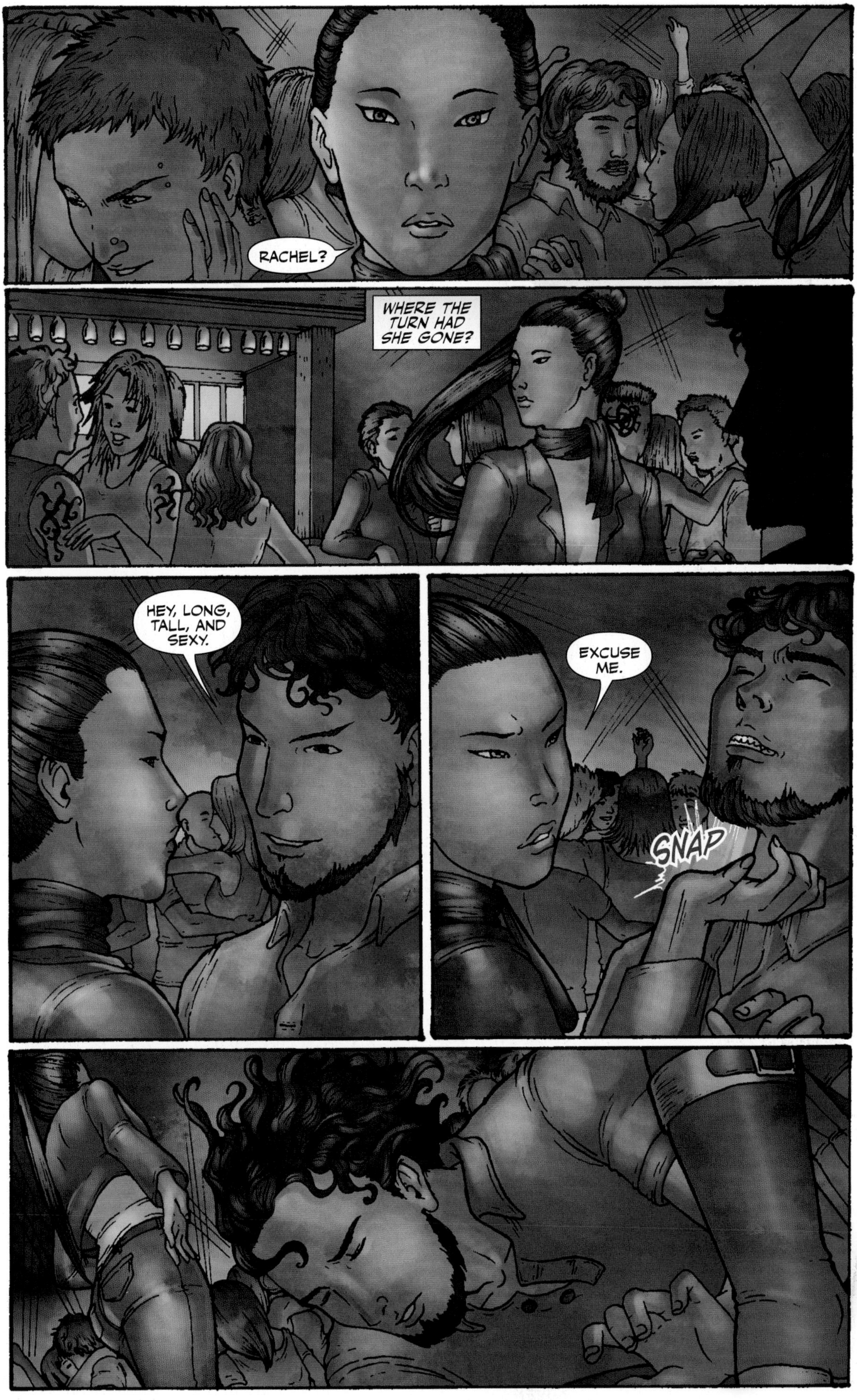
RACHEL?
WHERE THE TURN HAD SHE GONE?
HEY, LONG, TALL, AND SEXY.
EXCUSE ME.
SNAP

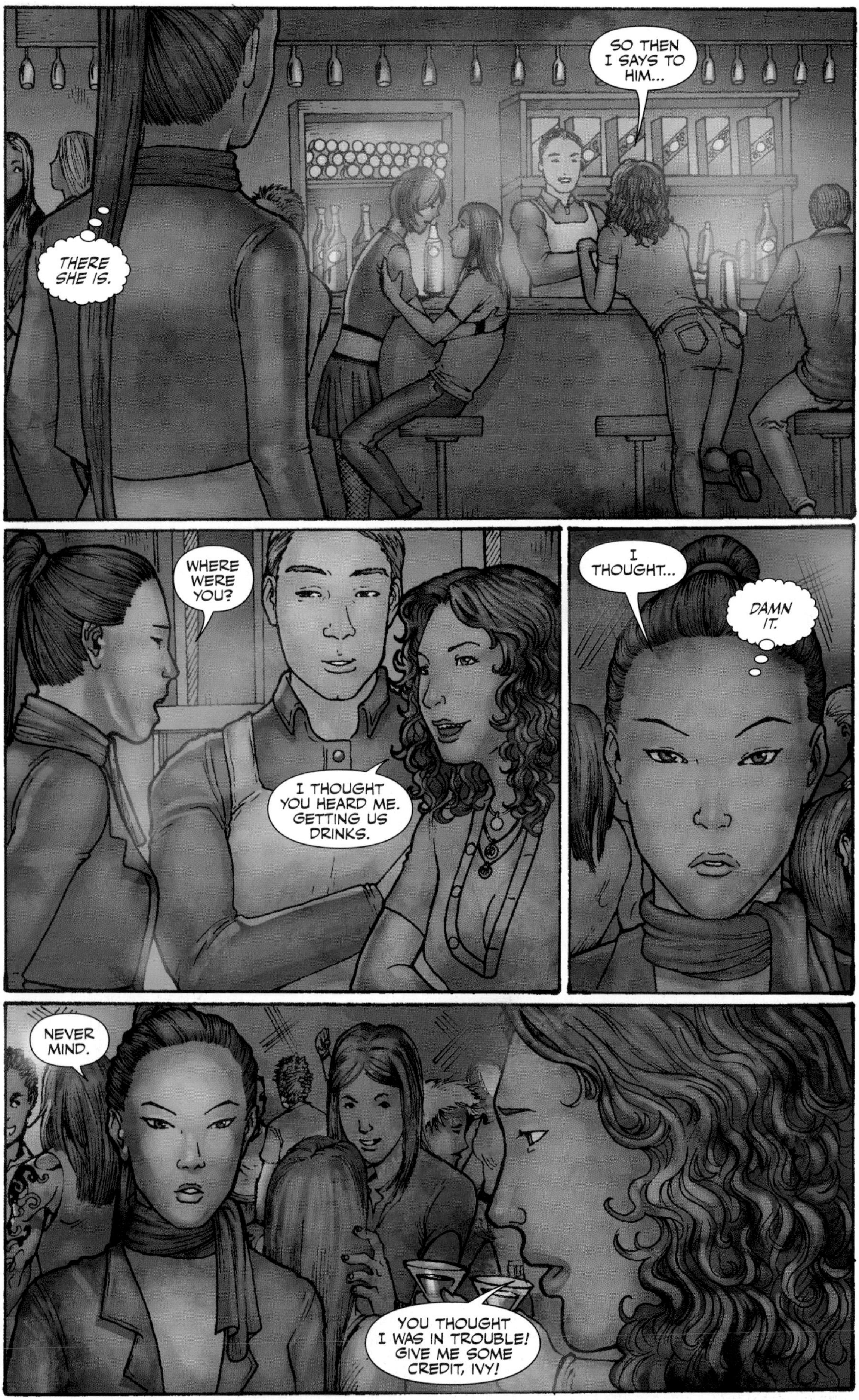
SO THEN I SAYS TO HIM...
THERE SHE IS.
WHERE WERE YOU?
I THOUGHT YOU HEARD ME. GETTING US DRINKS.
I THOUGHT...
DAMN IT.
NEVER MIND.
YOU THOUGHT I WAS IN TROUBLE! GIVE ME SOME CREDIT, IVY!

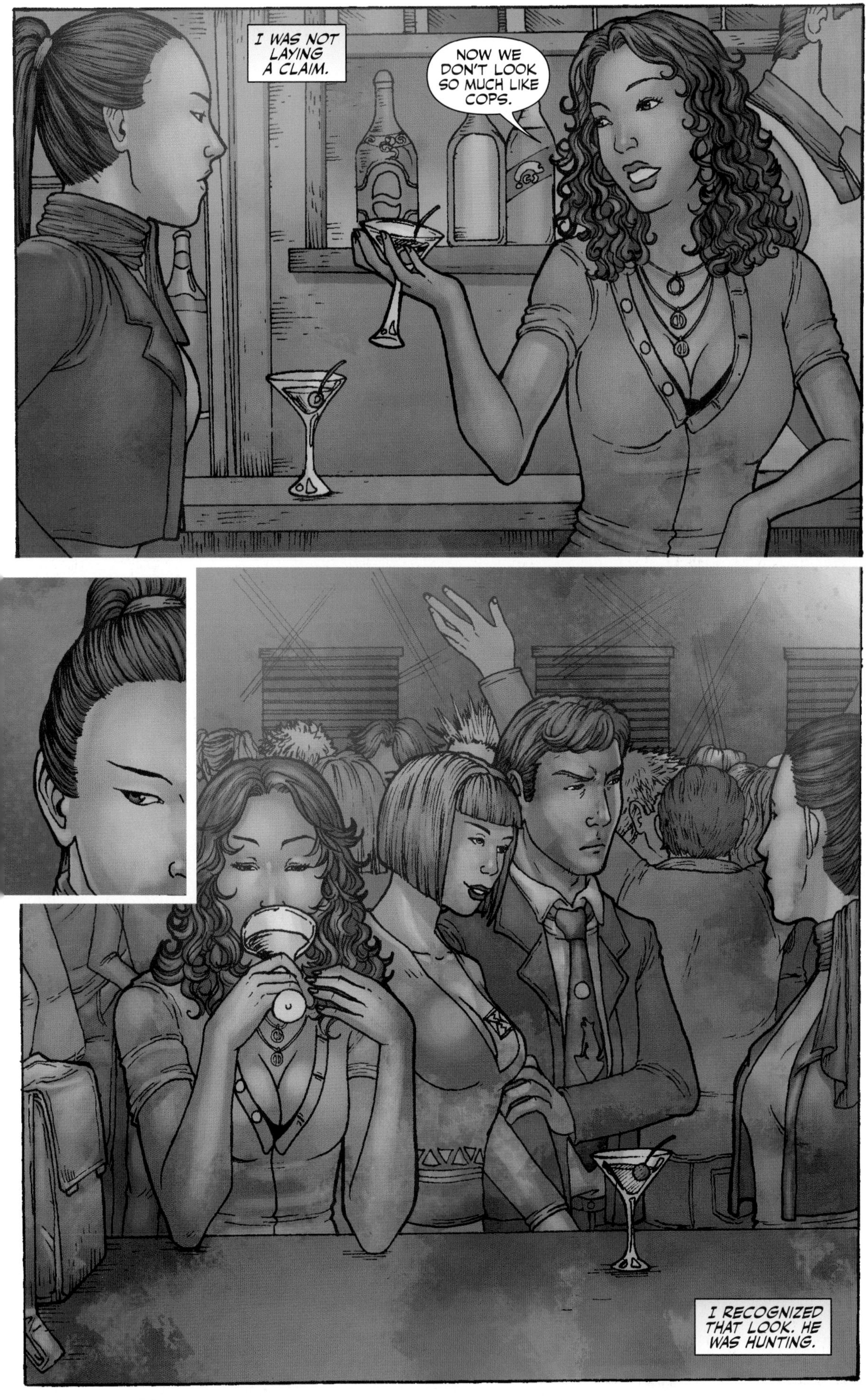
I WAS NOT LAYING A CLAIM.
NOW WE DON'T LOOK SO MUCH LIKE COPS.
I RECOGNIZED THAT LOOK. HE WAS HUNTING.

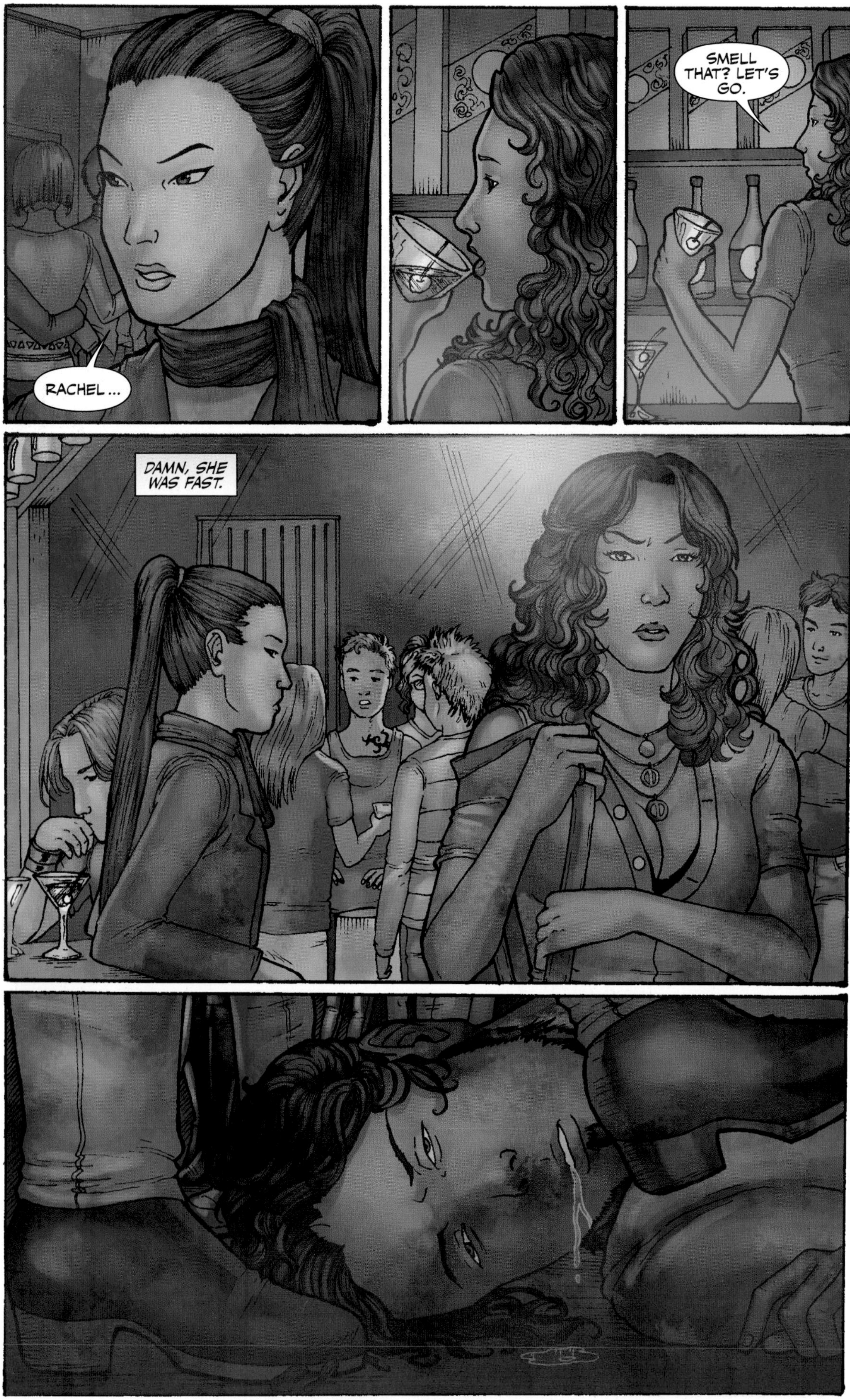
RACHEL...
SMELL THAT? LET'S GO.
DAMN, SHE WAS FAST.

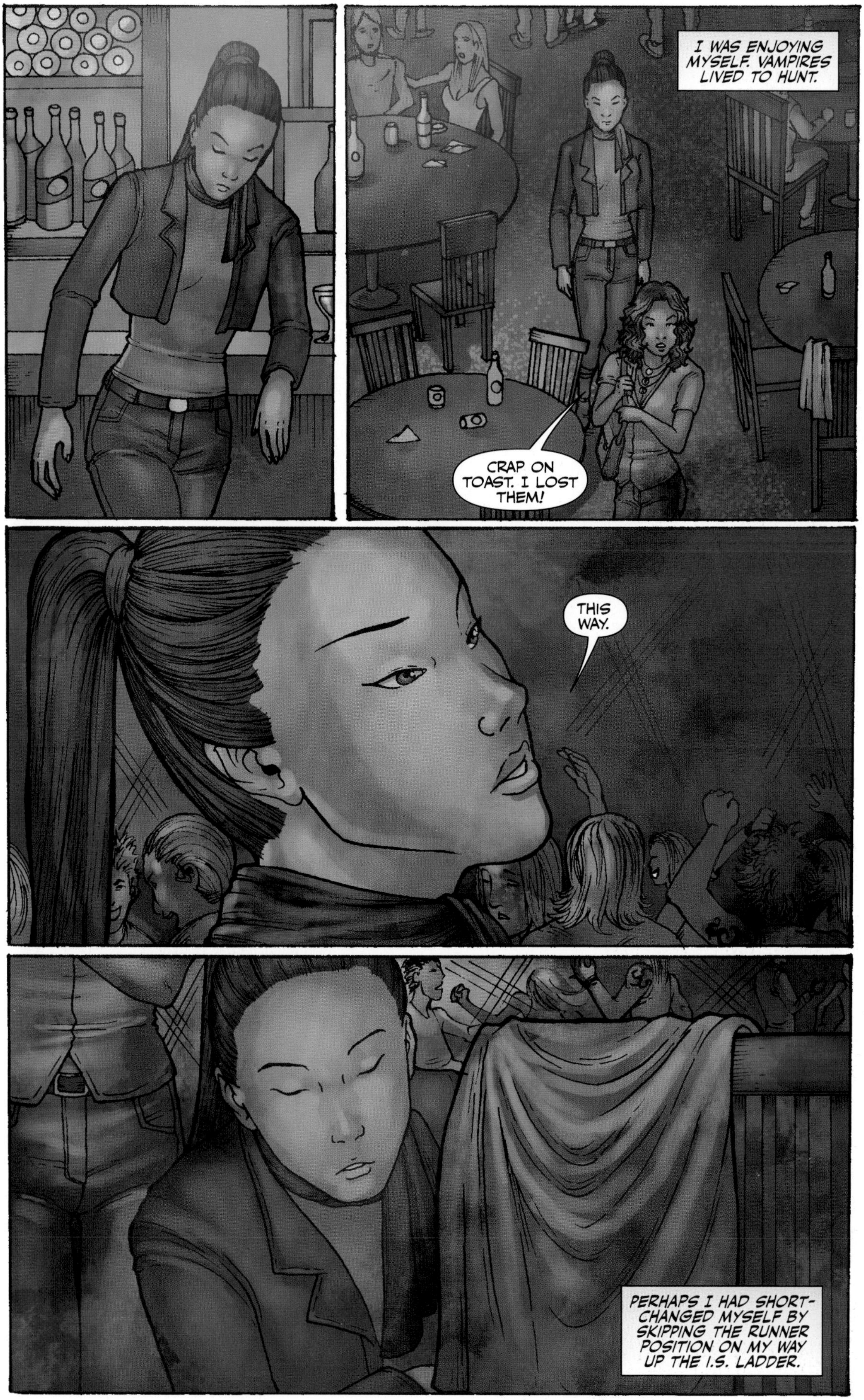
I WAS ENJOYING MYSELF. VAMPIRES LIVED TO HUNT.
CRAP ON TOAST. I LOST THEM!
THIS WAY.
PERHAPS I HAD SHORT-CHANGED MYSELF BY SKIPPING THE RUNNER POSITION ON MY WAY UP THE I.S. LADDER.

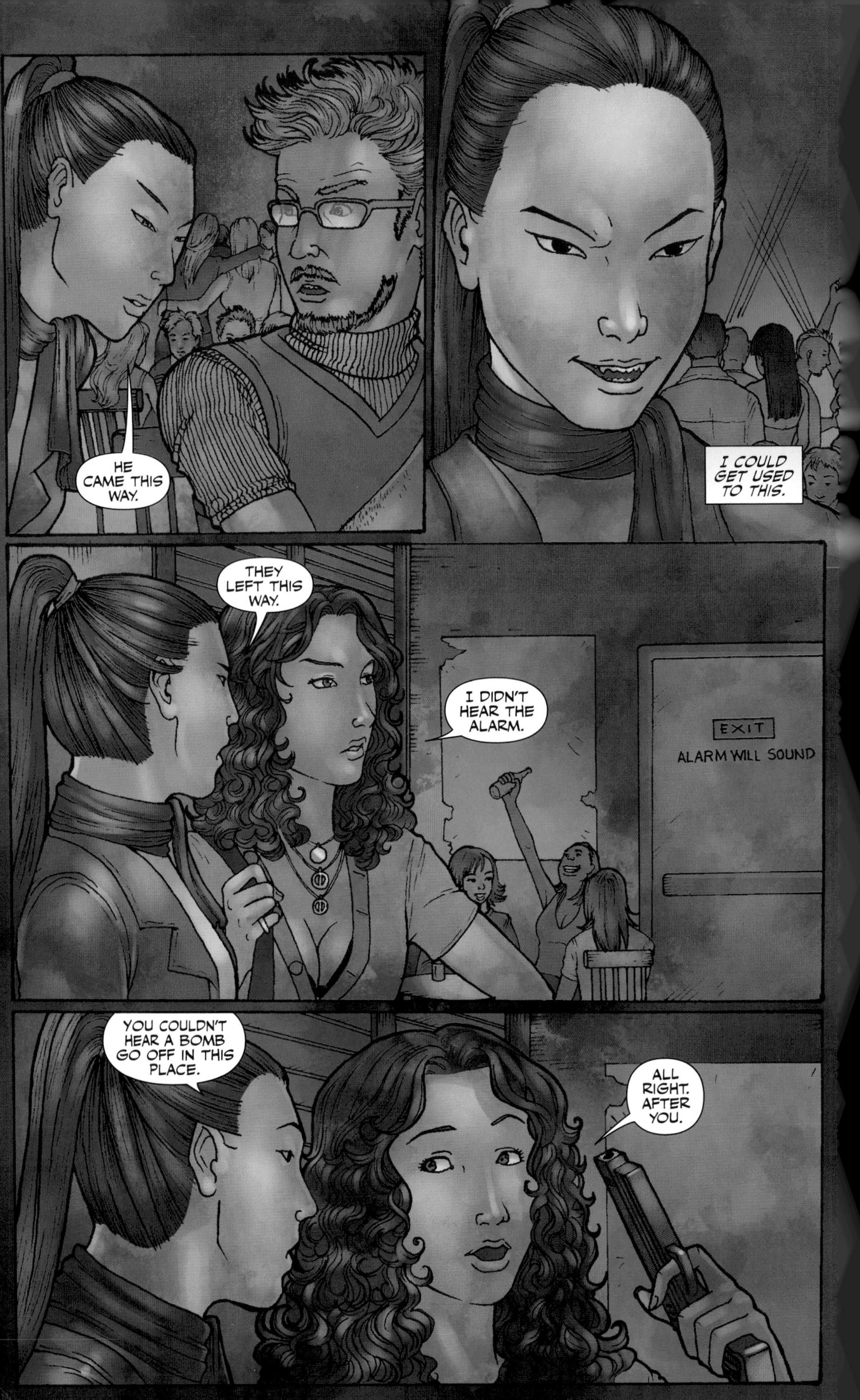
HE CAME THIS WAY.
I COULD GET USED TO THIS.
THEY LEFT THIS WAY.
I DIDN'T HEAR THE ALARM.
EXIT
ALARM WILL SOUND
YOU COULDN'T HEAR A BOMB GO OFF IN THIS PLACE.
ALL RIGHT. AFTER YOU.

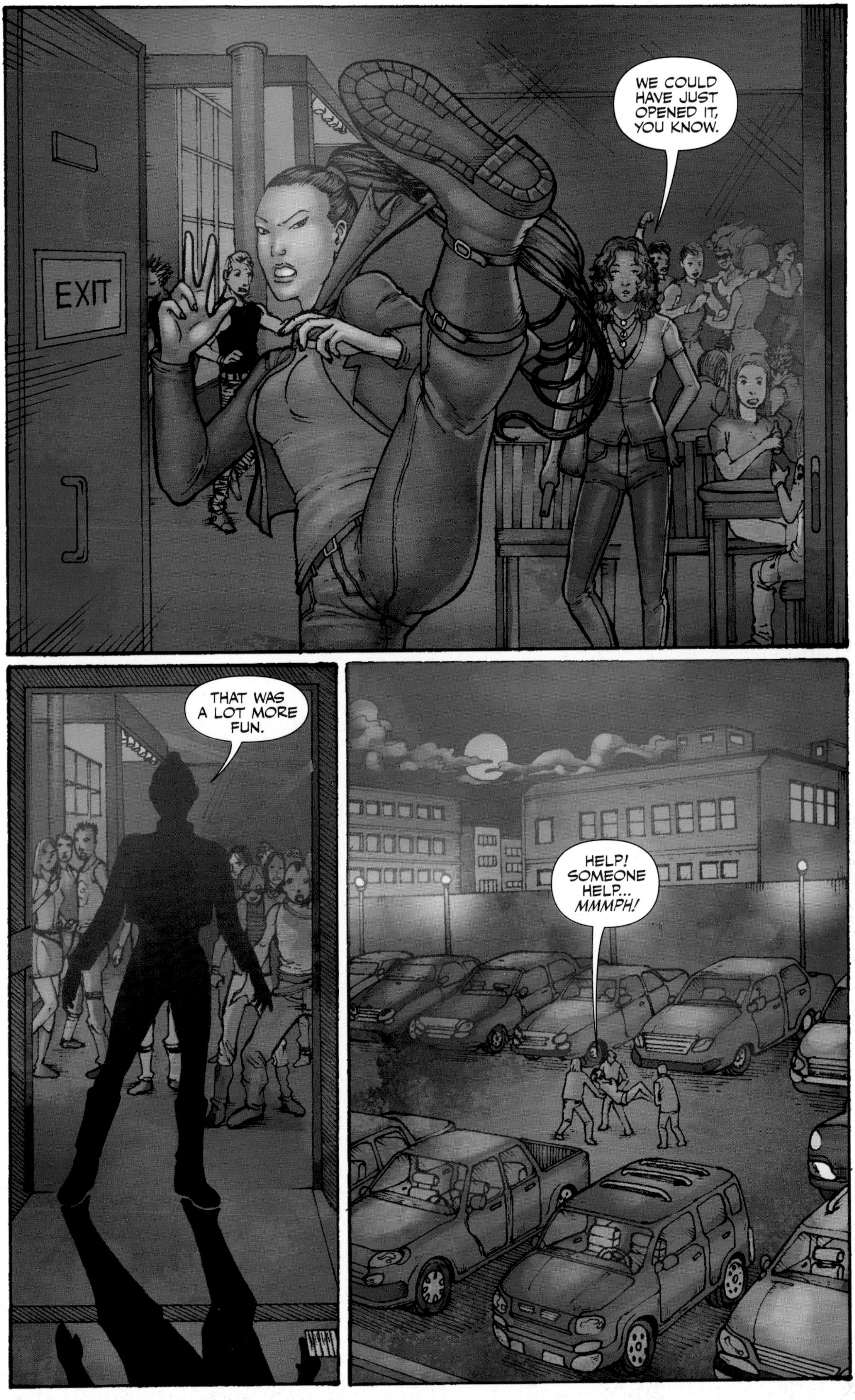
EXIT
WE COULD HAVE JUST OPENED IT, YOU KNOW.
THAT WAS A LOT MORE FUN.
HELP! SOMEONE HELP... MMMPH!

IT'S A WITCH COVEN! BE CAREFUL!

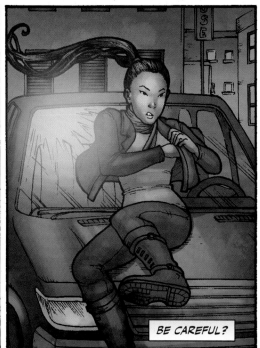

BE CAREFUL?

I.S.! GET OUT OF THE VEHICLE!

HELP ME! PLEASE!

YOU KNOW WHY THE I.S. ONLY SENDS WITCHES AFTER WITCHES?

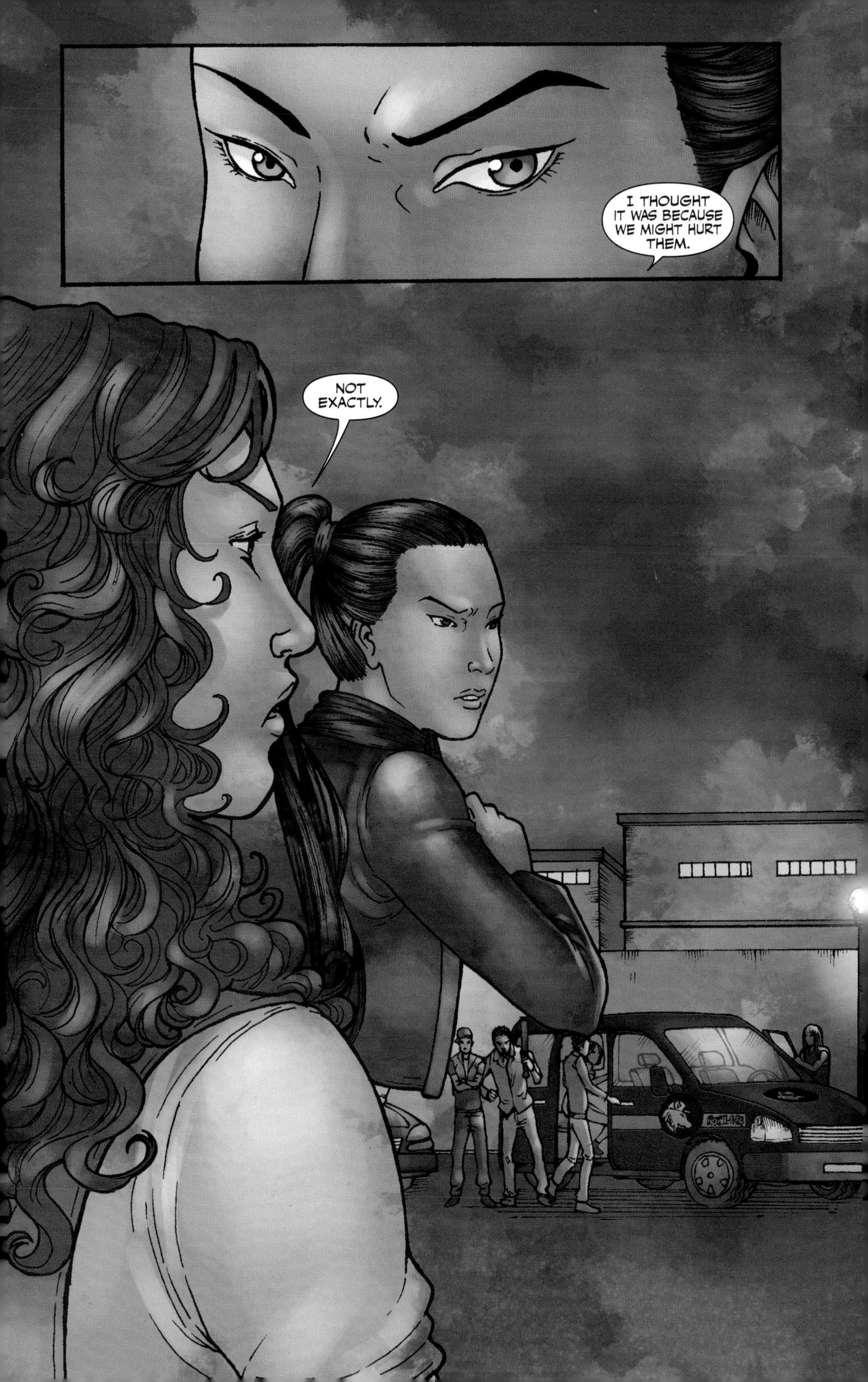
I THOUGHT IT WAS BECAUSE WE MIGHT HURT THEM.
NOT EXACTLY.

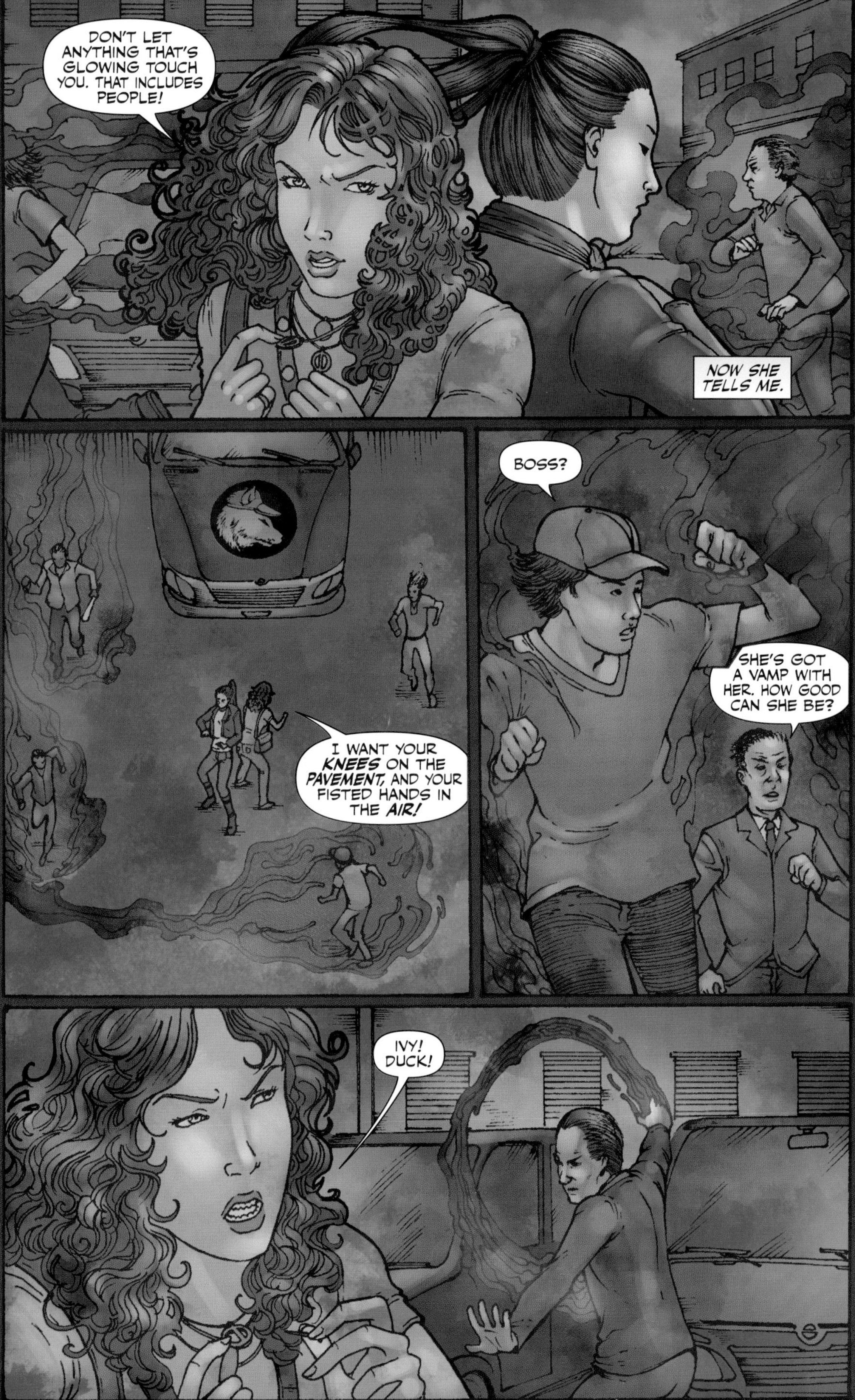
DON'T LET ANYTHING THAT'S GLOWING TOUCH YOU. THAT INCLUDES PEOPLE!
NOW SHE TELLS ME.
I WANT YOUR KNEES ON THE PAVEMENT, AND YOUR FISTED HANDS IN THE AIR!
BOSS?
SHE'S GOT A VAMP WITH HER. HOW GOOD CAN SHE BE?
IVY! DUCK!

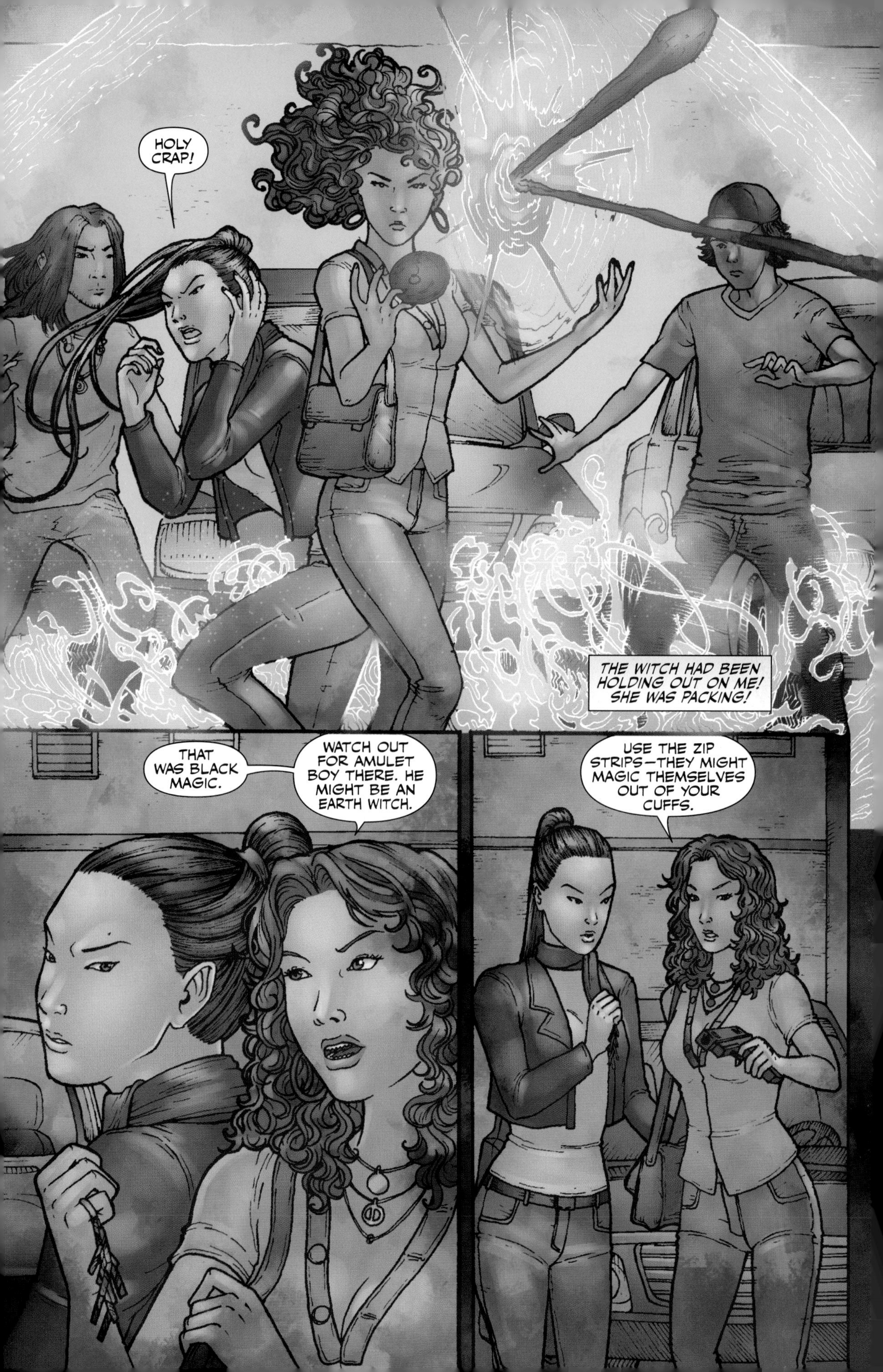
HOLY CRAP!
THE WITCH HAD BEEN HOLDING OUT ON ME! SHE WAS PACKING!
THAT WAS BLACK MAGIC.
WATCH OUT FOR AMULET BOY THERE. HE MIGHT BE AN EARTH WITCH.
USE THE ZIP STRIPS—THEY MIGHT MAGIC THEMSELVES OUT OF YOUR CUFFS.

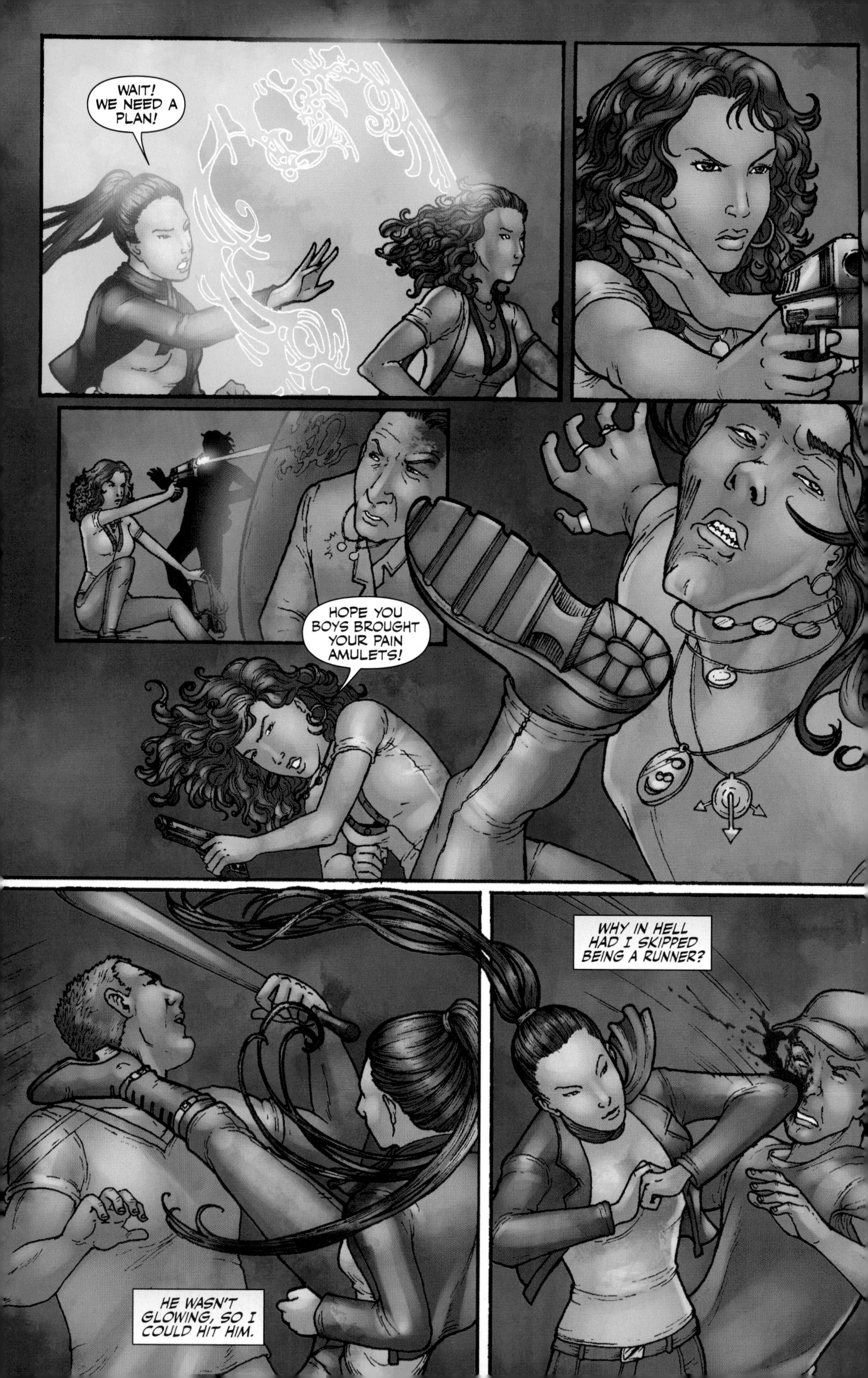
WAIT! WE NEED A PLAN!
HOPE YOU BOYS BROUGHT YOUR PAIN AMULETS!
HE WASN'T GLOWING, SO I COULD HIT HIM.
WHY IN HELL HAD I SKIPPED BEING A RUNNER?

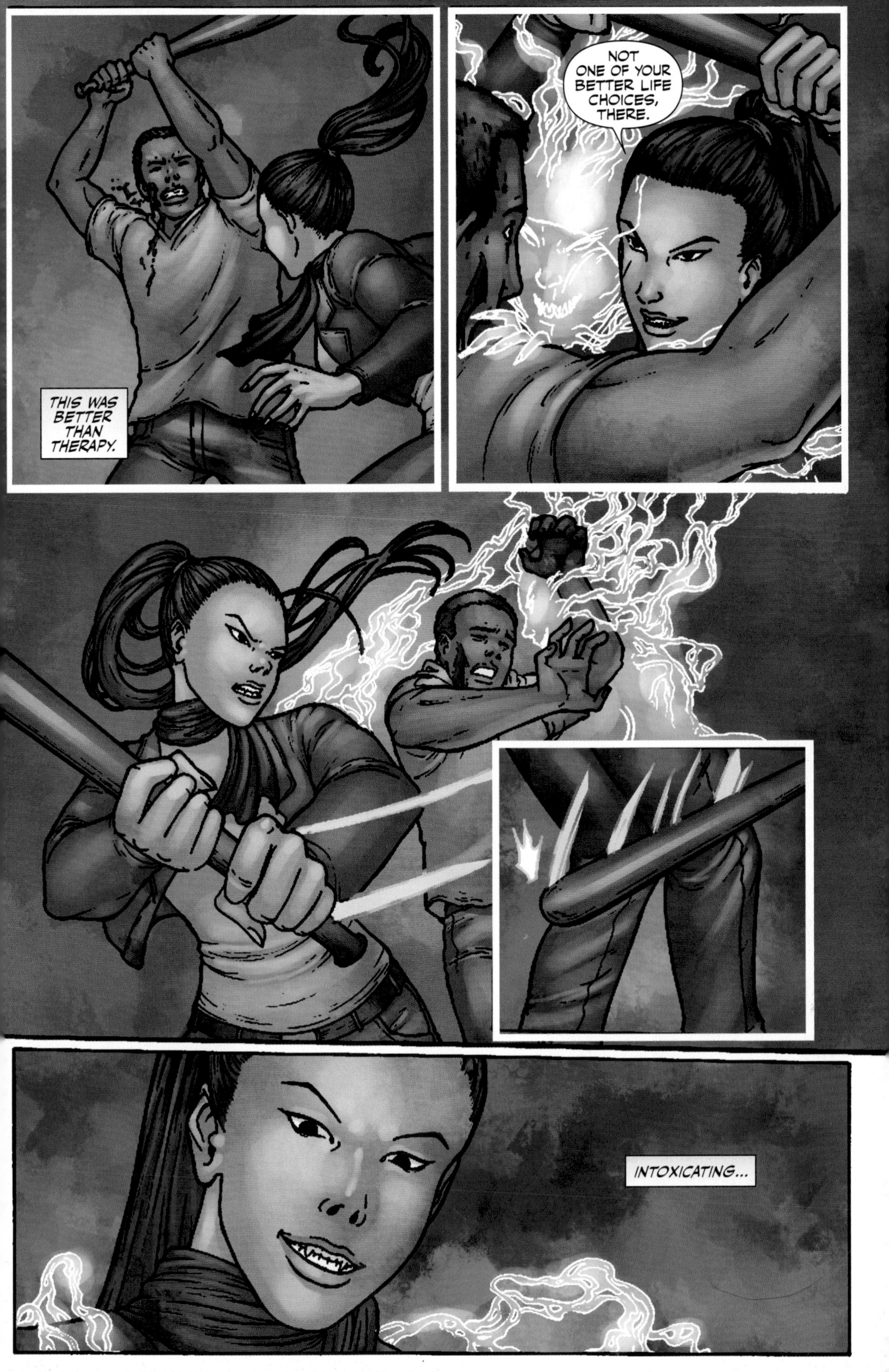
THIS WAS BETTER THAN THERAPY.
NOT ONE OF YOUR BETTER LIFE CHOICES, THERE.
INTOXICATING...

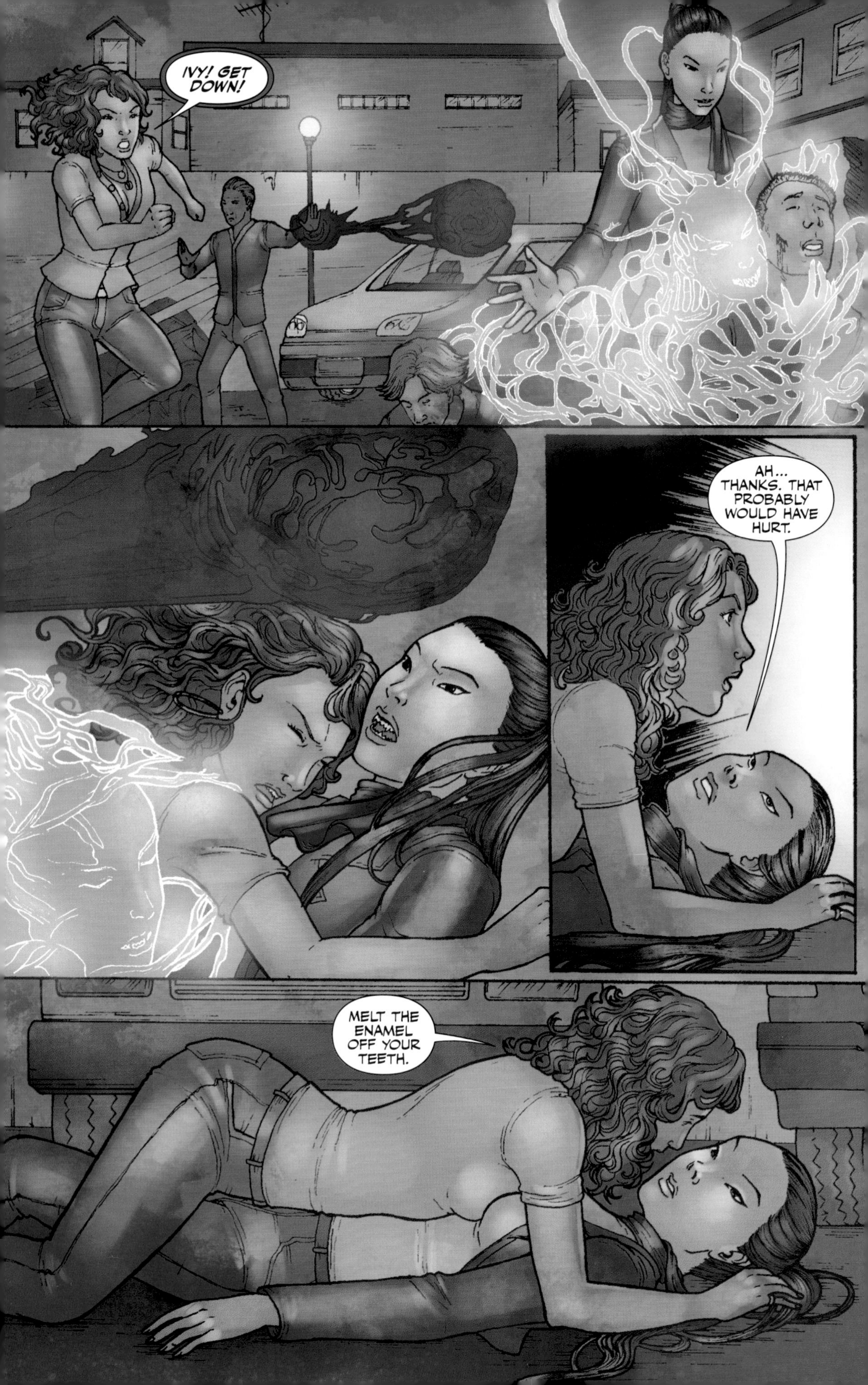
IVY! GET DOWN!
AH... THANKS. THAT PROBABLY WOULD HAVE HURT.
MELT THE ENAMEL OFF YOUR TEETH.

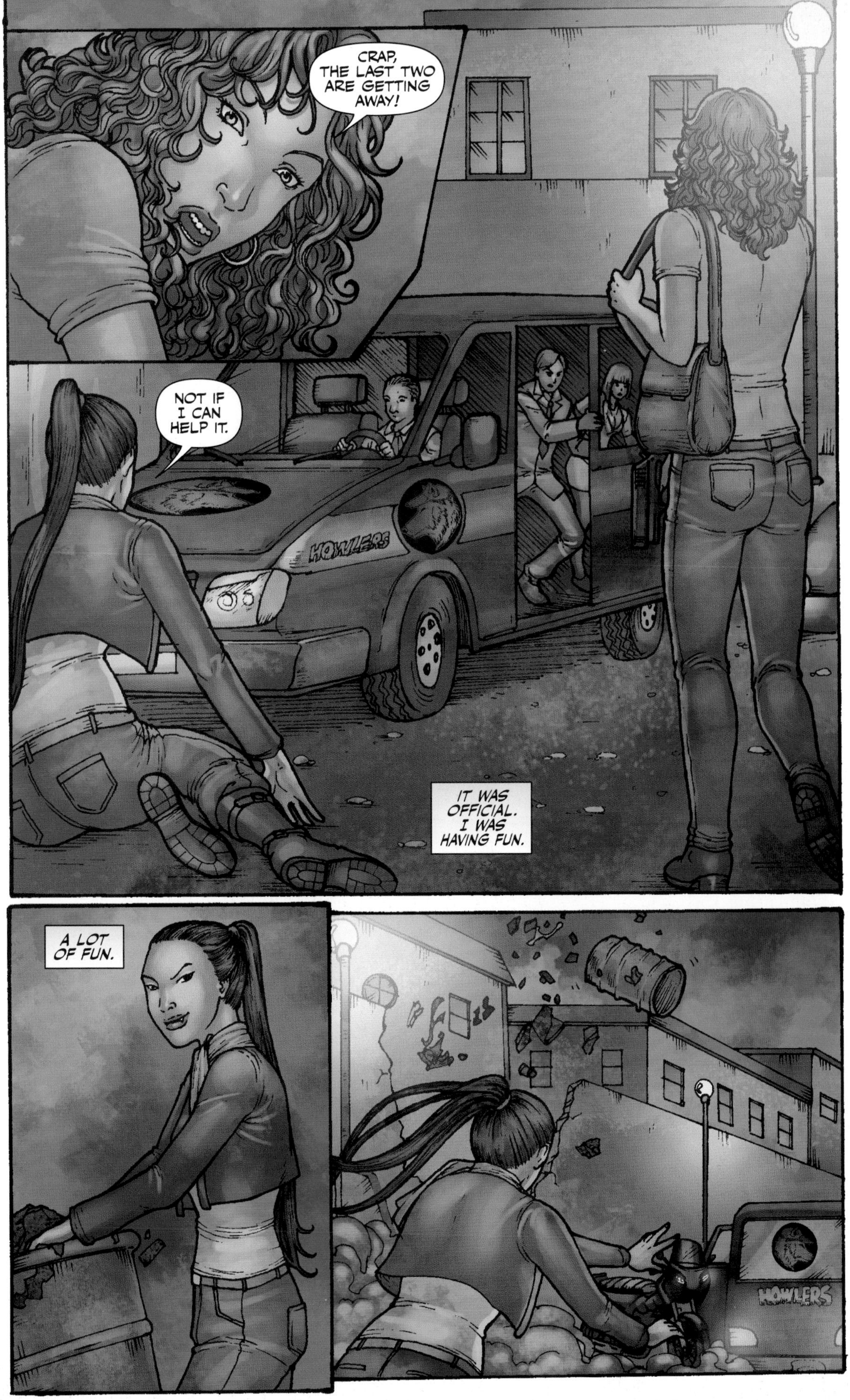
CRAP, THE LAST TWO ARE GETTING AWAY!
NOT IF I CAN HELP IT.
HOWLERS
IT WAS OFFICIAL. I WAS HAVING FUN.
A LOT OF FUN.
HOWLERS

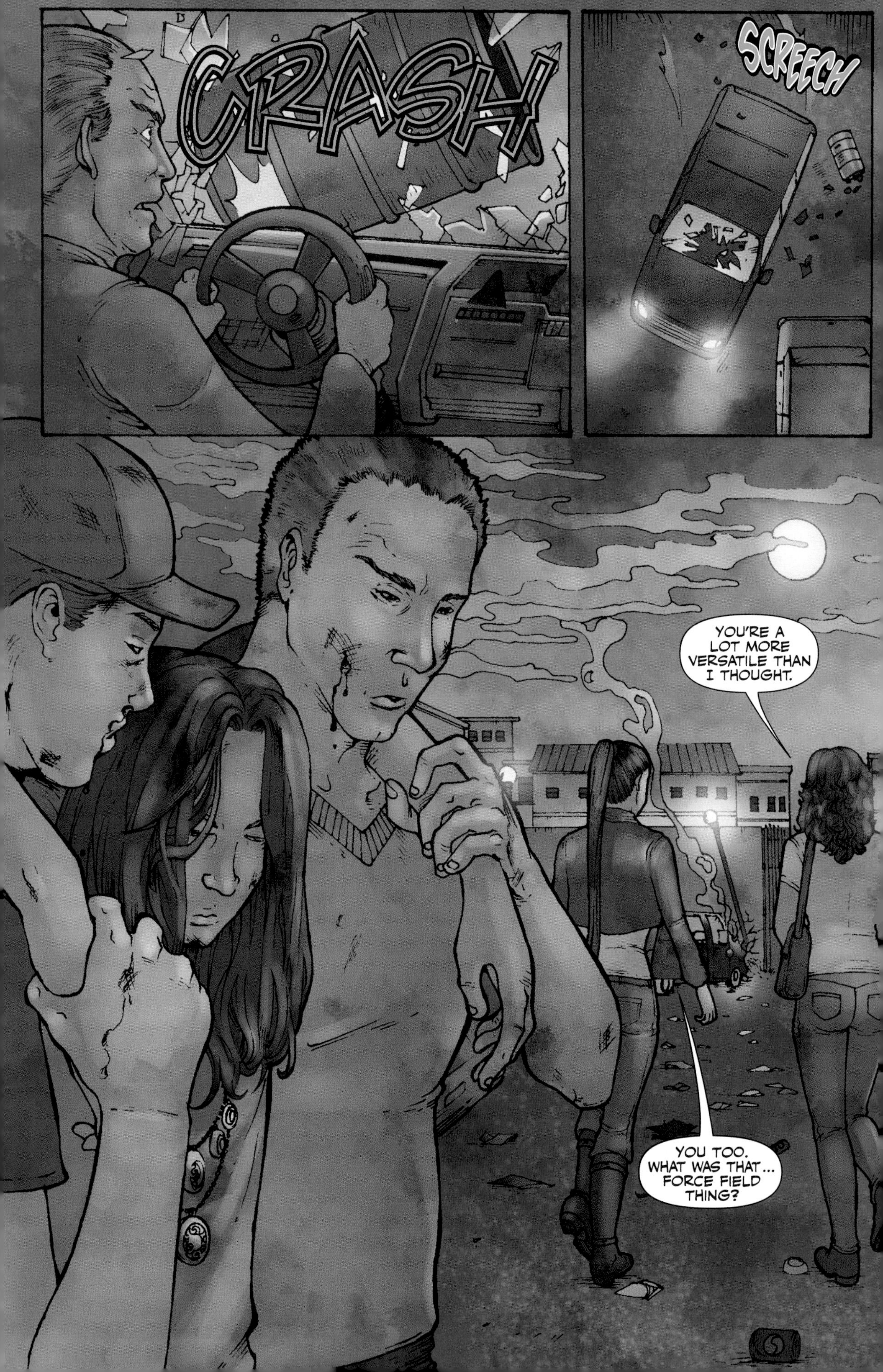
CRASH
SCREECH
YOU'RE A LOT MORE VERSATILE THAN I THOUGHT.
YOU TOO. WHAT WAS THAT... FORCE FIELD THING?

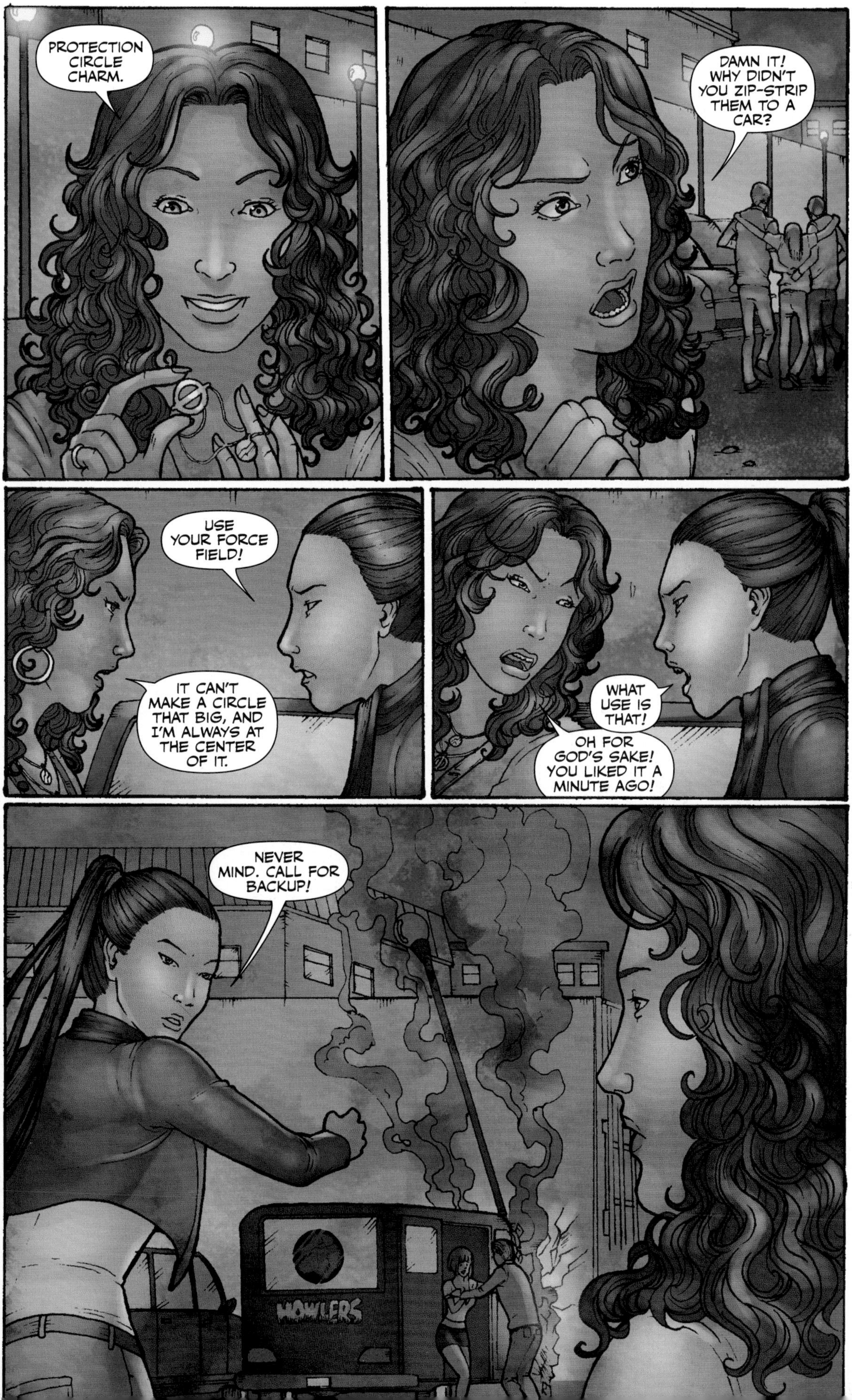
PROTECTION CIRCLE CHARM.
DAMN IT! WHY DIDN'T YOU ZIP-STRIP THEM TO A CAR?
USE YOUR FORCE FIELD!
IT CAN'T MAKE A CIRCLE THAT BIG, AND I'M ALWAYS AT THE CENTER OF IT.
WHAT USE IS THAT!
OH FOR GOD'S SAKE! YOU LIKED IT A MINUTE AGO!
NEVER MIND. CALL FOR BACKUP!
HOWLERS

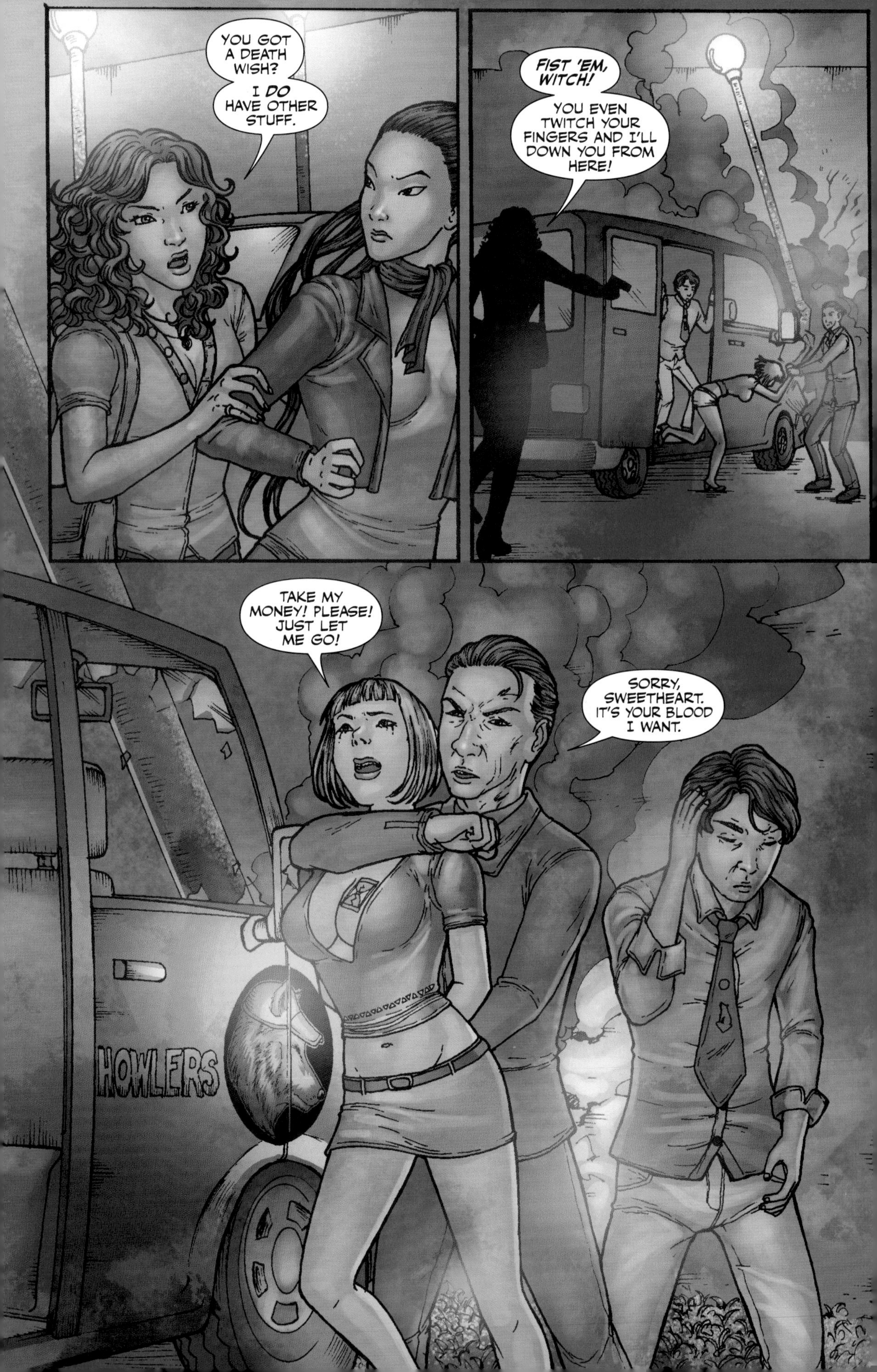

YOU GOT A DEATH WISH?
I *DO* HAVE OTHER STUFF.
FIST 'EM, WITCH!
YOU EVEN TWITCH YOUR FINGERS AND I'LL DOWN YOU FROM HERE!
TAKE MY MONEY! PLEASE! JUST LET ME GO!
SORRY, SWEETHEART. IT'S YOUR BLOOD I WANT.
HOWLERS

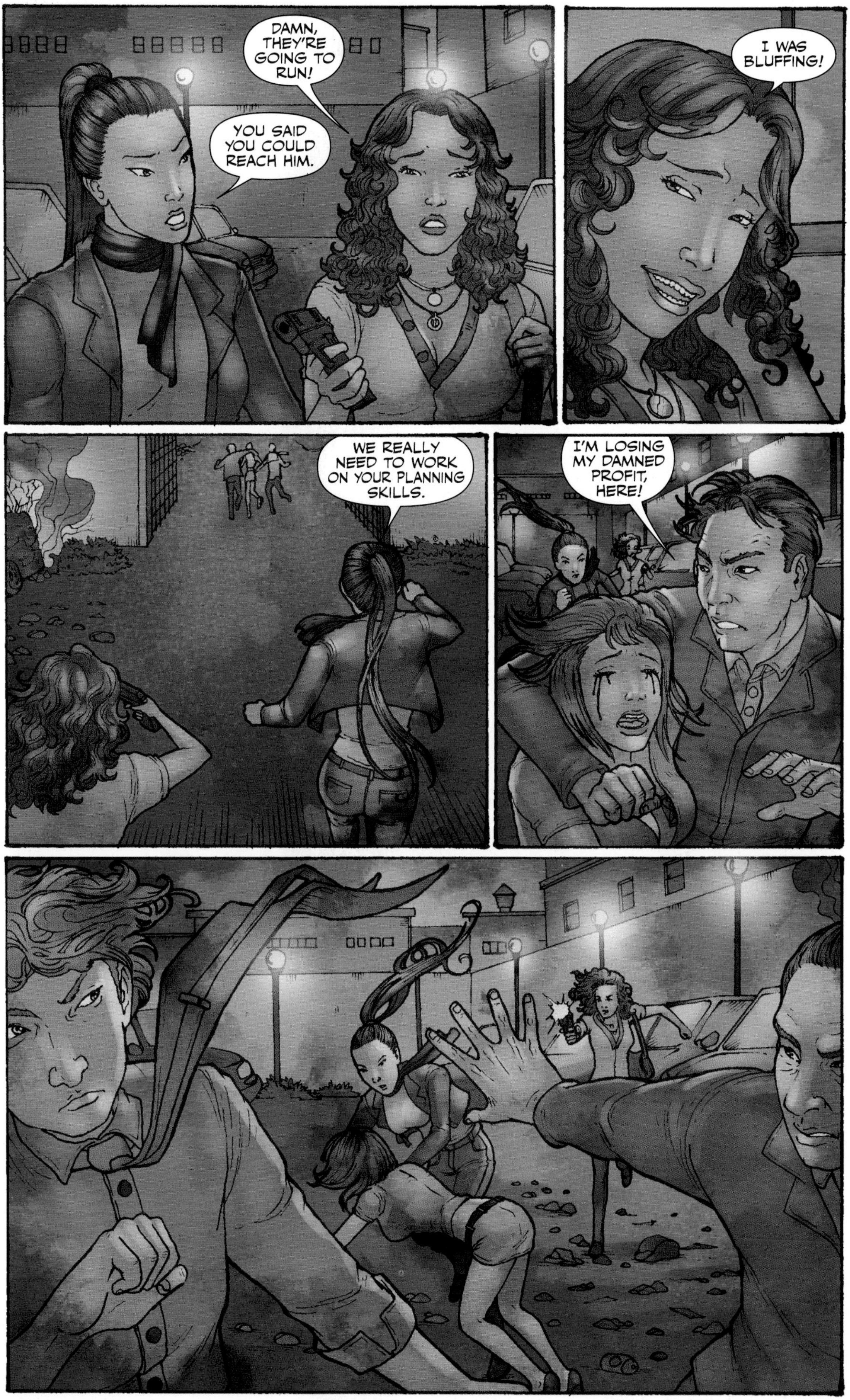
DAMN, THEY'RE GOING TO RUN!
YOU SAID YOU COULD REACH HIM.
I WAS BLUFFING!
WE REALLY NEED TO WORK ON YOUR PLANNING SKILLS.
I'M LOSING MY DAMNED PROFIT, HERE!

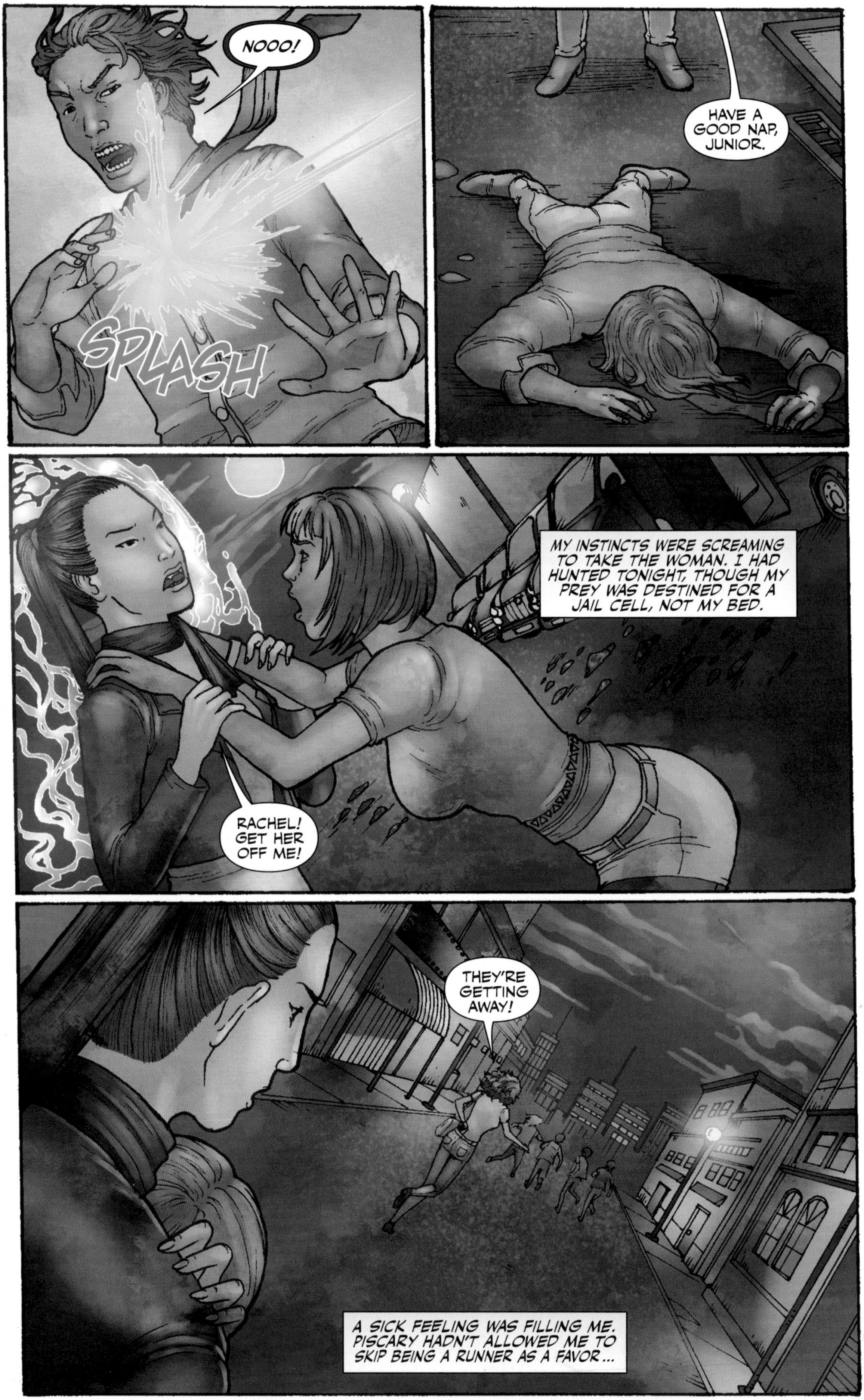
NOOO!
SPLASH
HAVE A GOOD NAP, JUNIOR.
MY INSTINCTS WERE SCREAMING TO TAKE THE WOMAN. I HAD HUNTED TONIGHT, THOUGH MY PREY WAS DESTINED FOR A JAIL CELL, NOT MY BED.
RACHEL! GET HER OFF ME!
THEY'RE GETTING AWAY!
A SICK FEELING WAS FILLING ME. PISCARY HADN'T ALLOWED ME TO SKIP BEING A RUNNER AS A FAVOR...

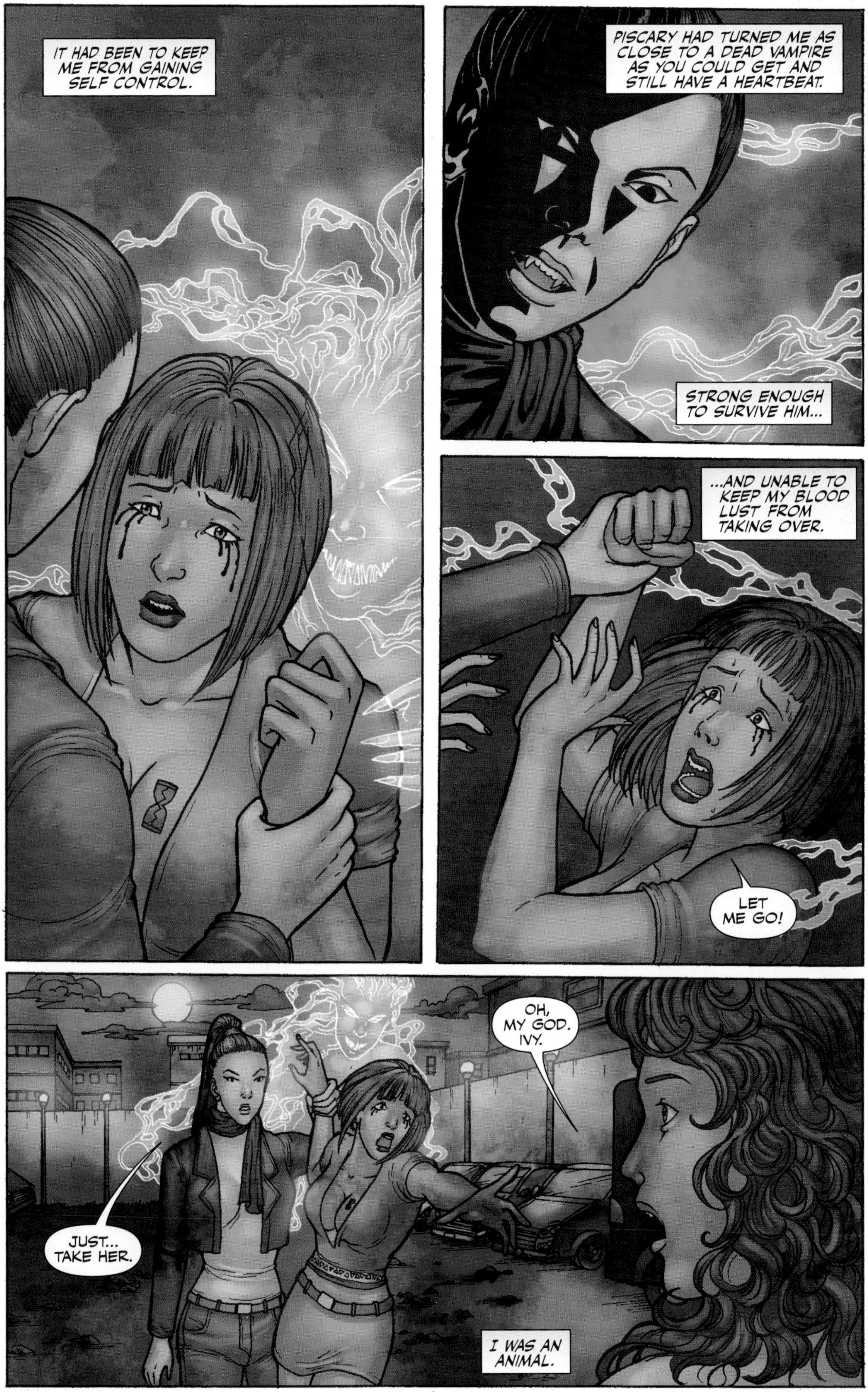
IT HAD BEEN TO KEEP ME FROM GAINING SELF CONTROL.
PISCARY HAD TURNED ME AS CLOSE TO A DEAD VAMPIRE AS YOU COULD GET AND STILL HAVE A HEARTBEAT.
STRONG ENOUGH TO SURVIVE HIM...
...AND UNABLE TO KEEP MY BLOOD LUST FROM TAKING OVER.
LET ME GO!
JUST... TAKE HER.
OH, MY GOD. IVY.
I WAS AN ANIMAL.

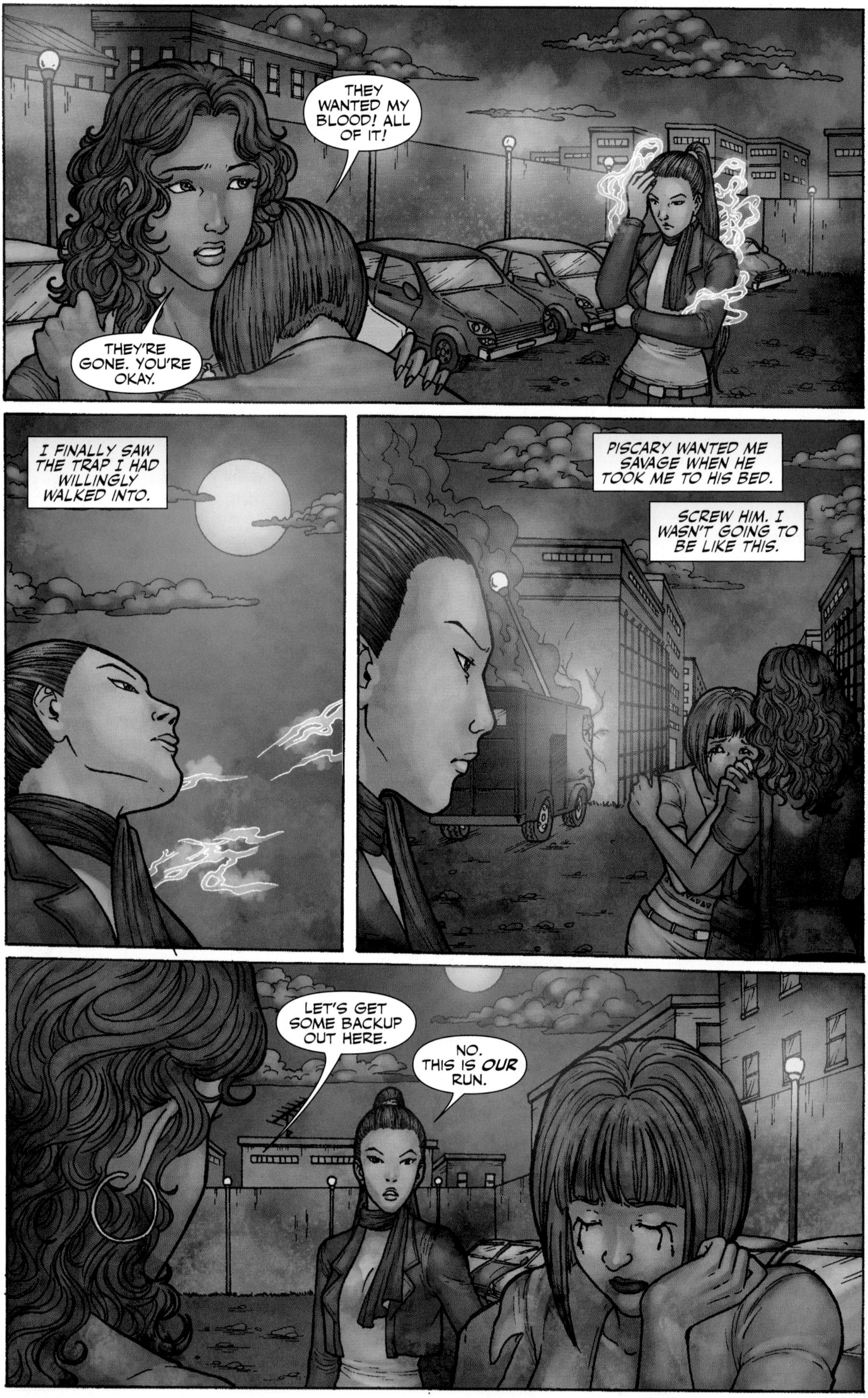
THEY WANTED MY BLOOD! ALL OF IT!
THEY'RE GONE. YOU'RE OKAY.
I FINALLY SAW THE TRAP I HAD WILLINGLY WALKED INTO.
PISCARY WANTED ME SAVAGE WHEN HE TOOK ME TO HIS BED.
SCREW HIM. I WASN'T GOING TO BE LIKE THIS.
LET'S GET SOME BACKUP OUT HERE.
NO. THIS IS OUR RUN.

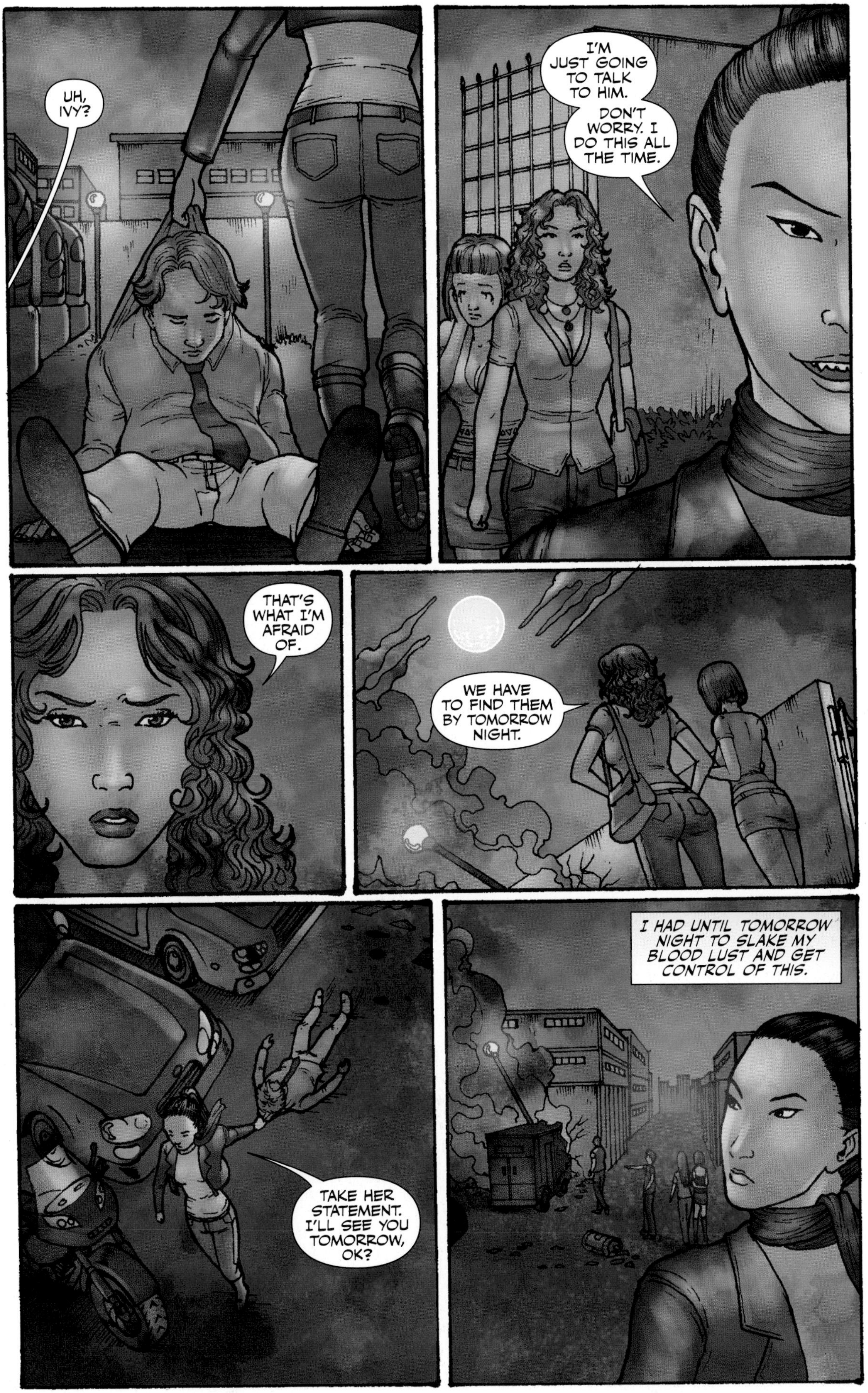
UH, IVY?
I'M JUST GOING TO TALK TO HIM.
DON'T WORRY. I DO THIS ALL THE TIME.
THAT'S WHAT I'M AFRAID OF.
WE HAVE TO FIND THEM BY TOMORROW NIGHT.
TAKE HER STATEMENT. I'LL SEE YOU TOMORROW, OK?
I HAD UNTIL TOMORROW NIGHT TO SLAKE MY BLOOD LUST AND GET CONTROL OF THIS.

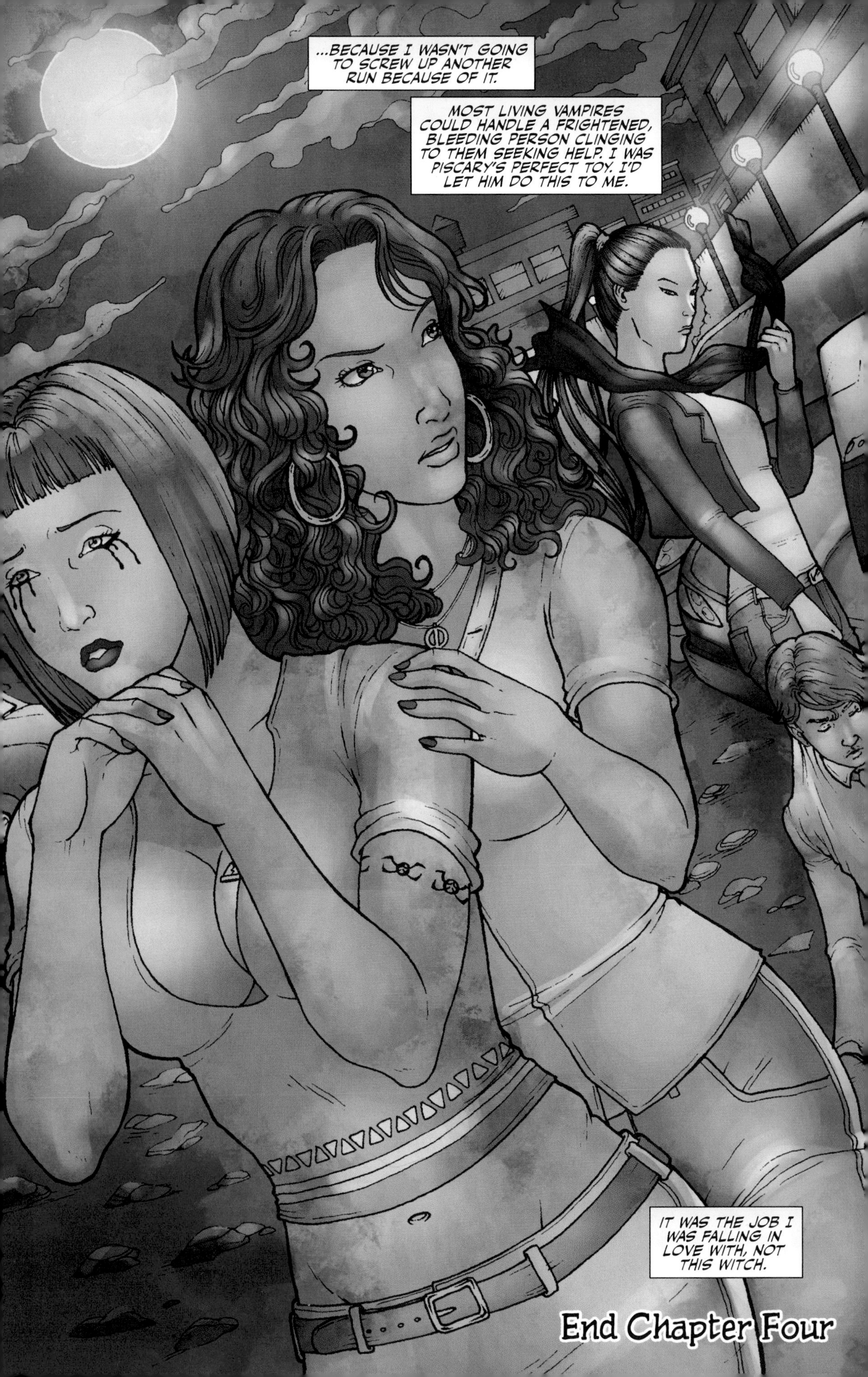
...BECAUSE I WASN'T GOING TO SCREW UP ANOTHER RUN BECAUSE OF IT.
MOST LIVING VAMPIRES COULD HANDLE A FRIGHTENED, BLEEDING PERSON CLINGING TO THEM SEEKING HELP. I WAS PISCARY'S PERFECT TOY. I'D LET HIM DO THIS TO ME.
IT WAS THE JOB I WAS FALLING IN LOVE WITH, NOT THIS WITCH.
End Chapter Four

CHAPTER 5

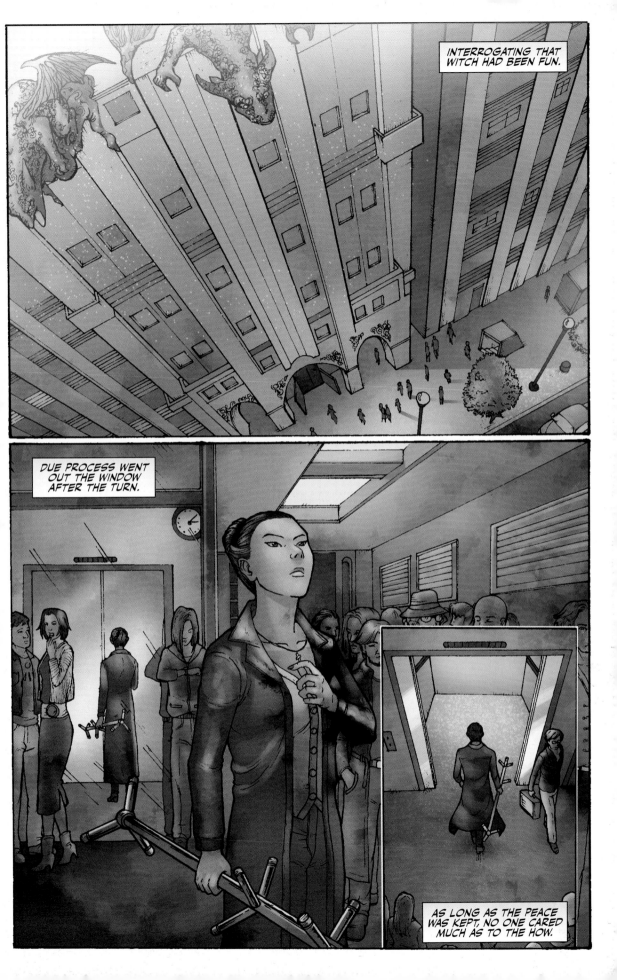

INTERROGATING THAT WITCH HAD BEEN FUN.

DUE PROCESS WENT OUT THE WINDOW AFTER THE TURN.

AS LONG AS THE PEACE WAS KEPT, NO ONE CARED MUCH AS TO THE HOW.

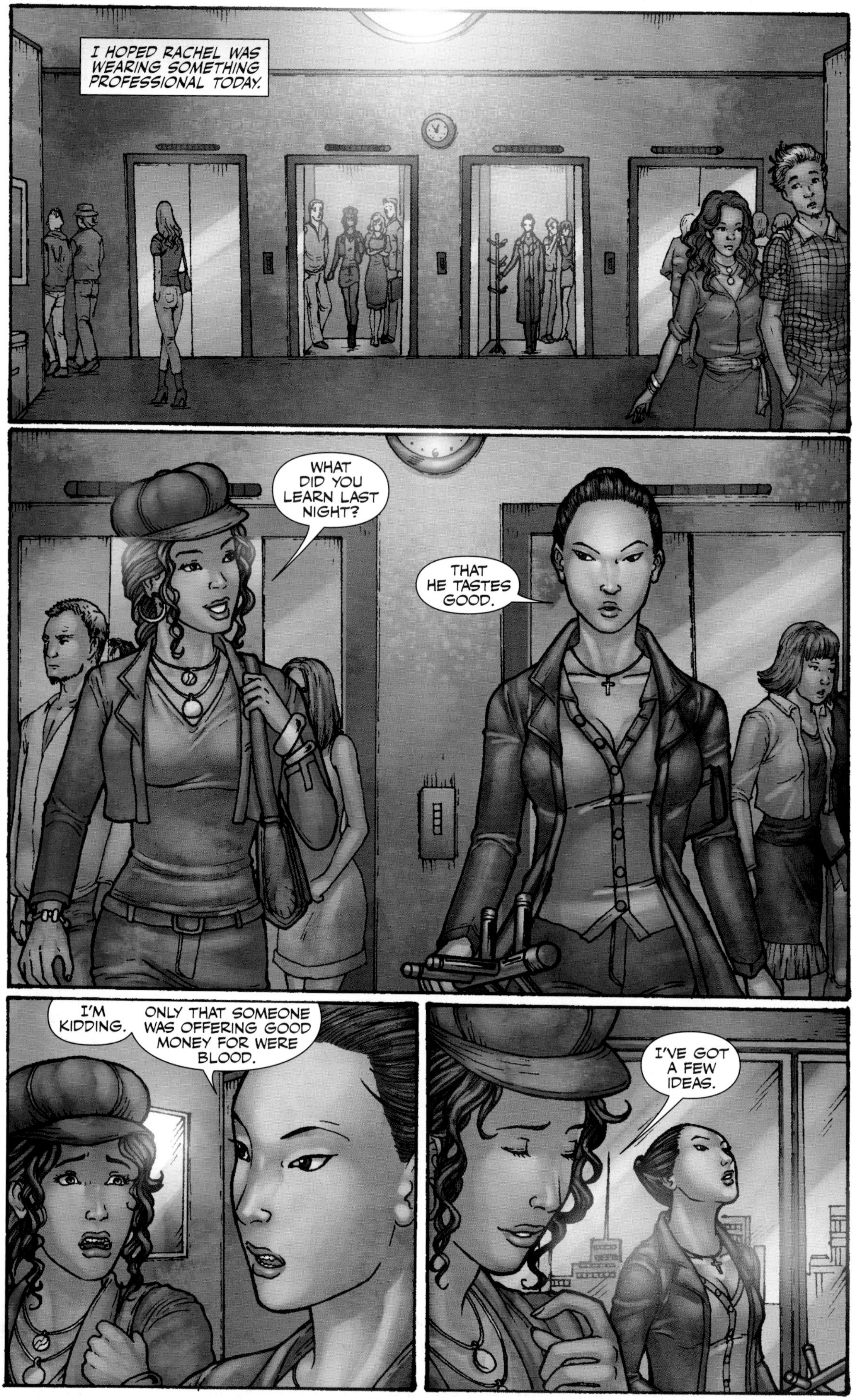
I HOPED RACHEL WAS WEARING SOMETHING PROFESSIONAL TODAY.
WHAT DID YOU LEARN LAST NIGHT?
THAT HE TASTES GOOD.
I'M KIDDING.
ONLY THAT SOMEONE WAS OFFERING GOOD MONEY FOR WERE BLOOD.
I'VE GOT A FEW IDEAS.

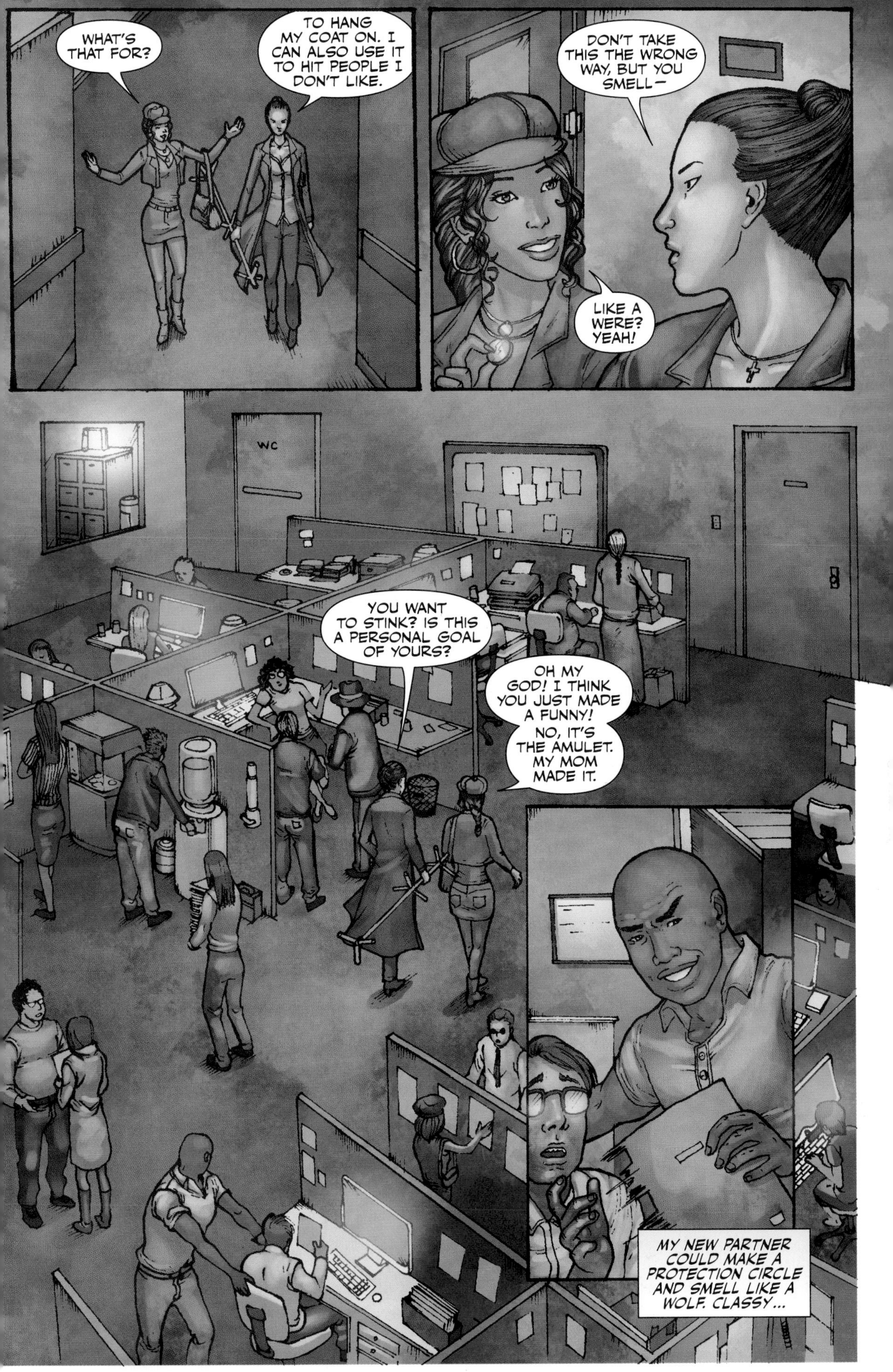
WHAT'S THAT FOR?
TO HANG MY COAT ON. I CAN ALSO USE IT TO HIT PEOPLE I DON'T LIKE.
DON'T TAKE THIS THE WRONG WAY, BUT YOU SMELL—
LIKE A WERE? YEAH!
WC
YOU WANT TO STINK? IS THIS A PERSONAL GOAL OF YOURS?
OH MY GOD! I THINK YOU JUST MADE A FUNNY!
NO, IT'S THE AMULET. MY MOM MADE IT.
MY NEW PARTNER COULD MAKE A PROTECTION CIRCLE AND SMELL LIKE A WOLF. CLASSY...

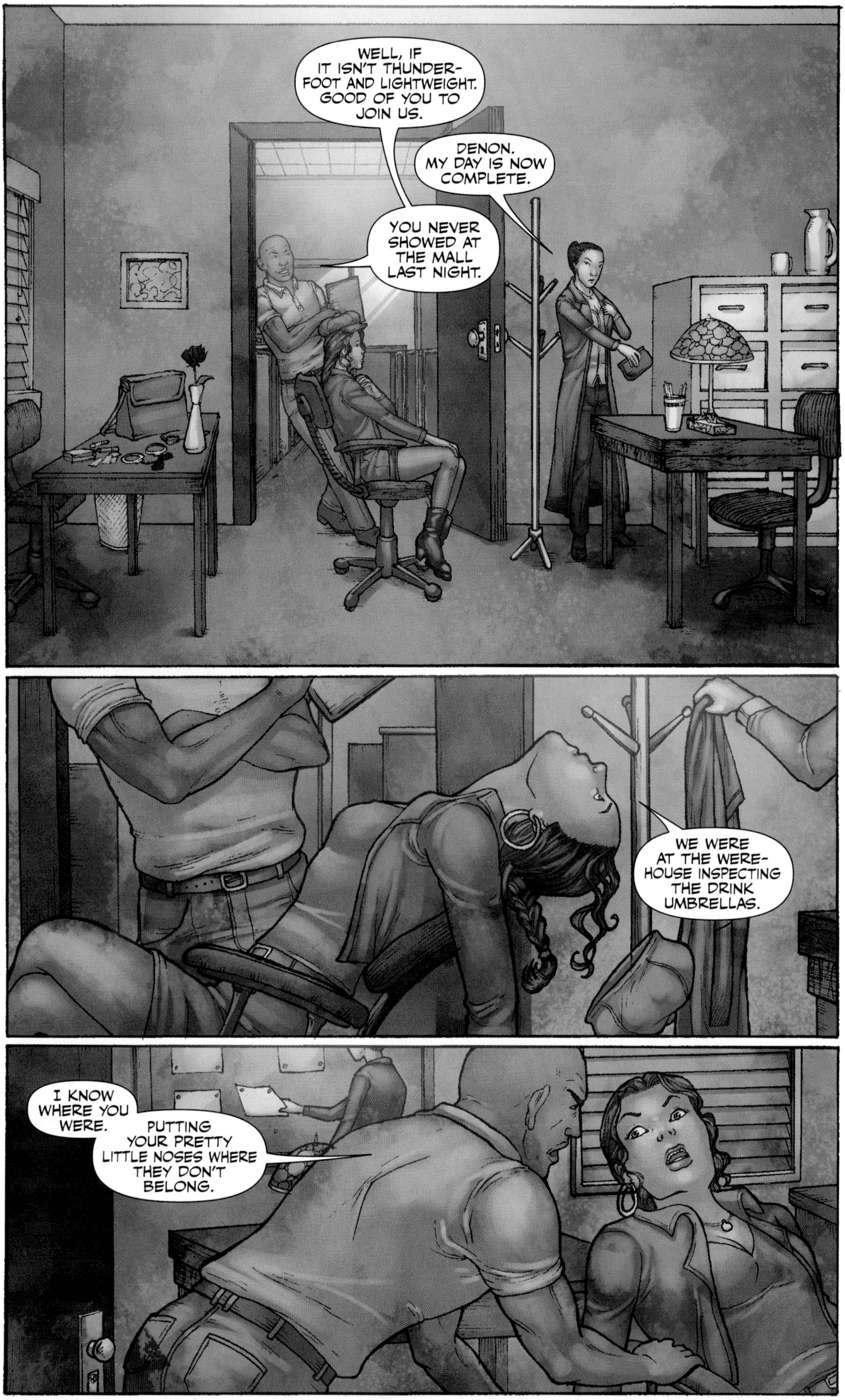
WELL, IF IT ISN'T THUNDER-FOOT AND LIGHTWEIGHT. GOOD OF YOU TO JOIN US.
DENON. MY DAY IS NOW COMPLETE.
YOU NEVER SHOWED AT THE MALL LAST NIGHT.
WE WERE AT THE WERE-HOUSE INSPECTING THE DRINK UMBRELLAS.
I KNOW WHERE YOU WERE.
PUTTING YOUR PRETTY LITTLE NOSES WHERE THEY DON'T BELONG.

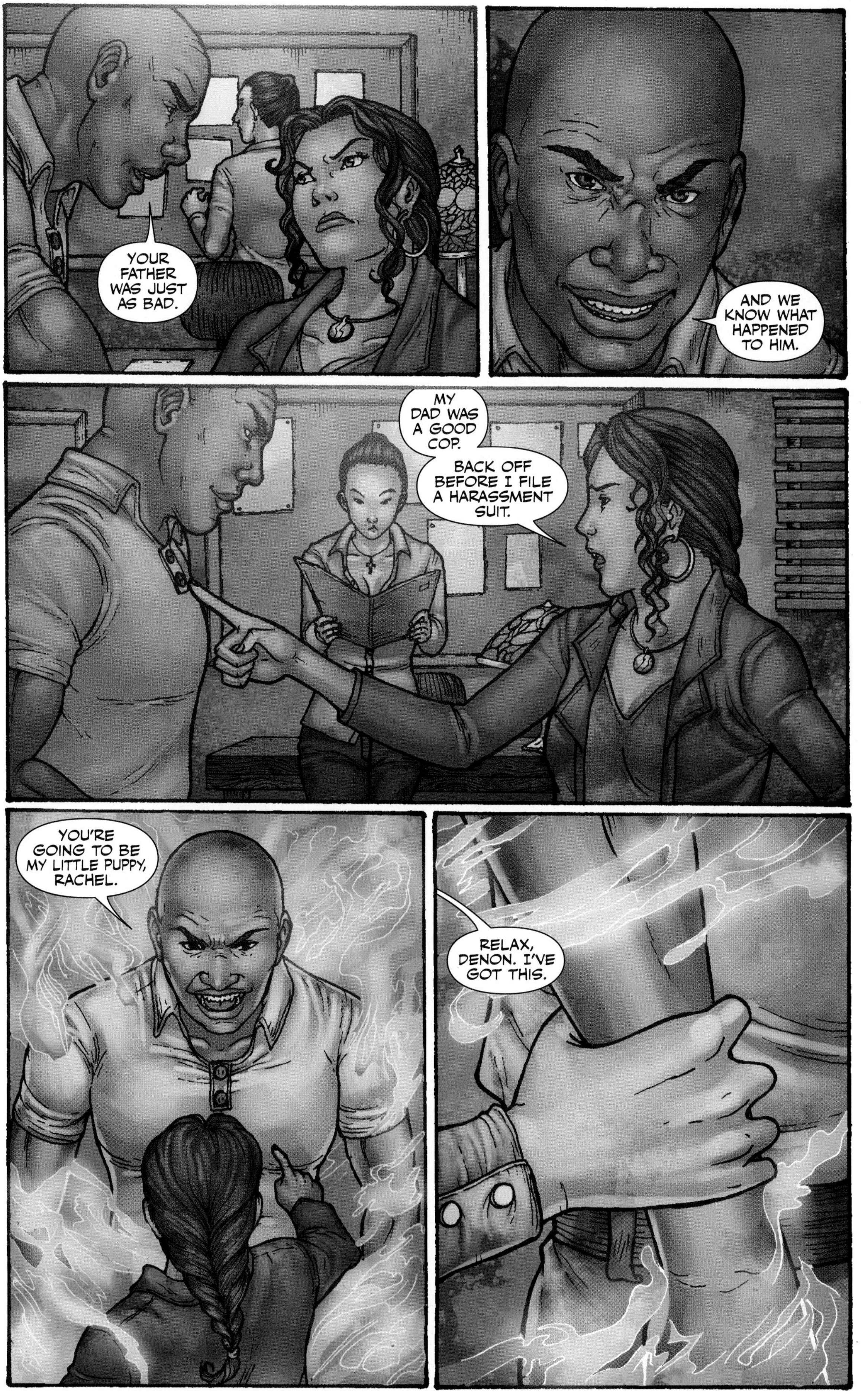
YOUR FATHER WAS JUST AS BAD.
AND WE KNOW WHAT HAPPENED TO HIM.
MY DAD WAS A GOOD COP.
BACK OFF BEFORE I FILE A HARASSMENT SUIT.
YOU'RE GOING TO BE MY LITTLE PUPPY, RACHEL.
RELAX, DENON. I'VE GOT THIS.

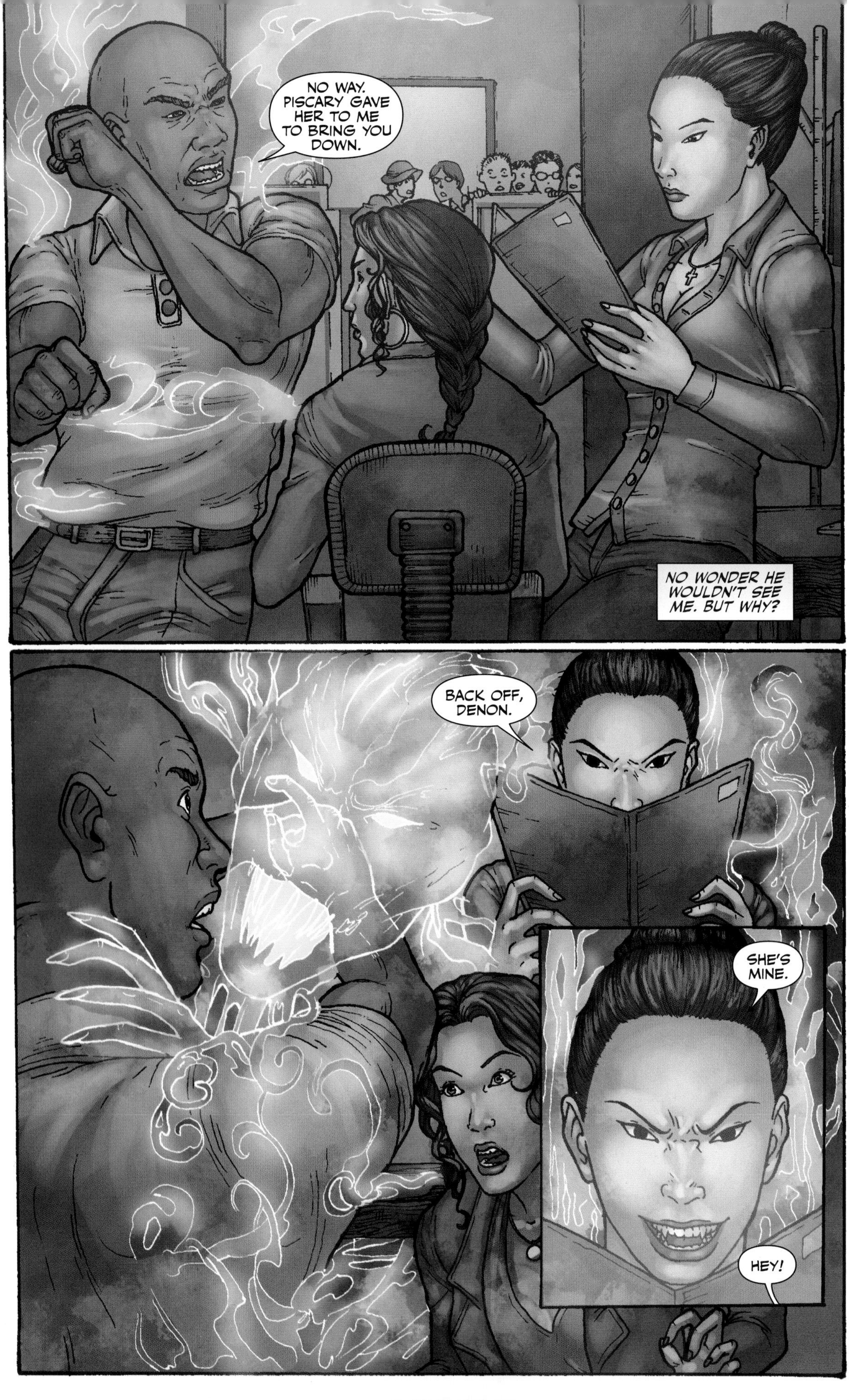
NO WAY. PISCARY GAVE HER TO ME TO BRING YOU DOWN.
NO WONDER HE WOULDN'T SEE ME. BUT WHY?
BACK OFF, DENON.
SHE'S MINE.
HEY!

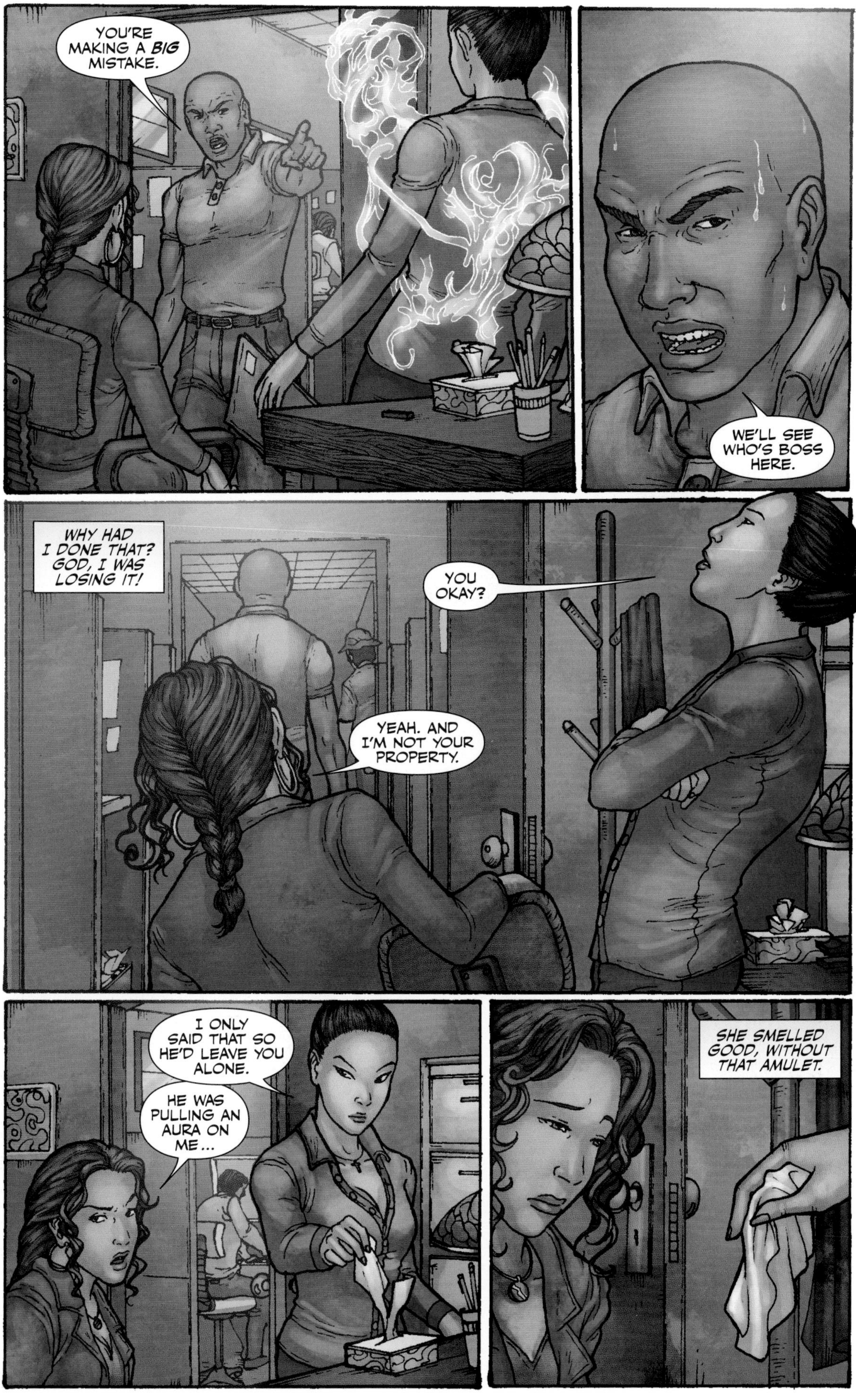
YOU'RE MAKING A BIG MISTAKE.
WE'LL SEE WHO'S BOSS HERE.
WHY HAD I DONE THAT? GOD, I WAS LOSING IT!
YOU OKAY?
YEAH. AND I'M NOT YOUR PROPERTY.
I ONLY SAID THAT SO HE'D LEAVE YOU ALONE.
HE WAS PULLING AN AURA ON ME...
SHE SMELLED GOOD, WITHOUT THAT AMULET.

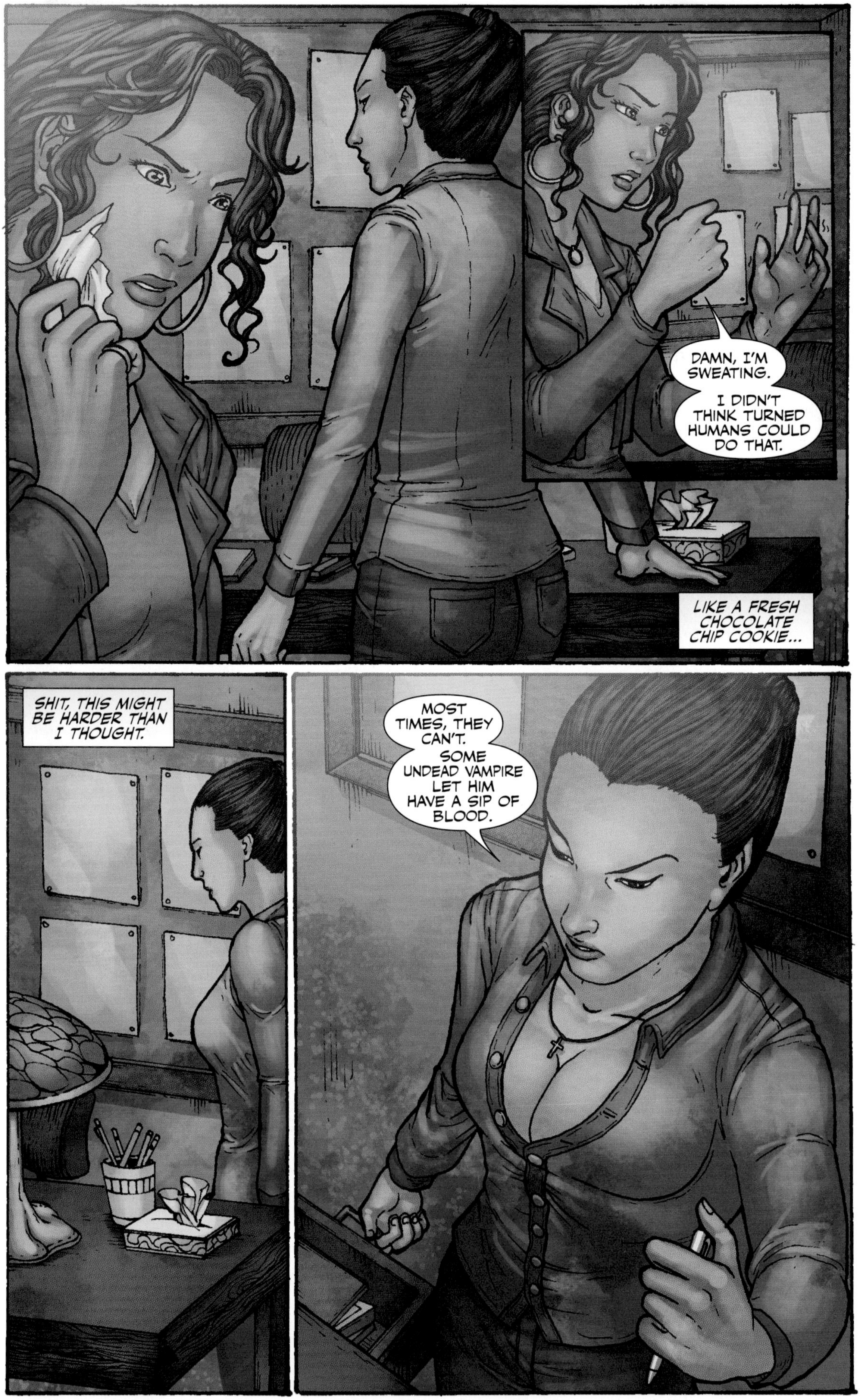
DAMN, I'M SWEATING.
I DIDN'T THINK TURNED HUMANS COULD DO THAT.
LIKE A FRESH CHOCOLATE CHIP COOKIE...
SHIT, THIS MIGHT BE HARDER THAN I THOUGHT.
MOST TIMES, THEY CAN'T.
SOME UNDEAD VAMPIRE LET HIM HAVE A SIP OF BLOOD.

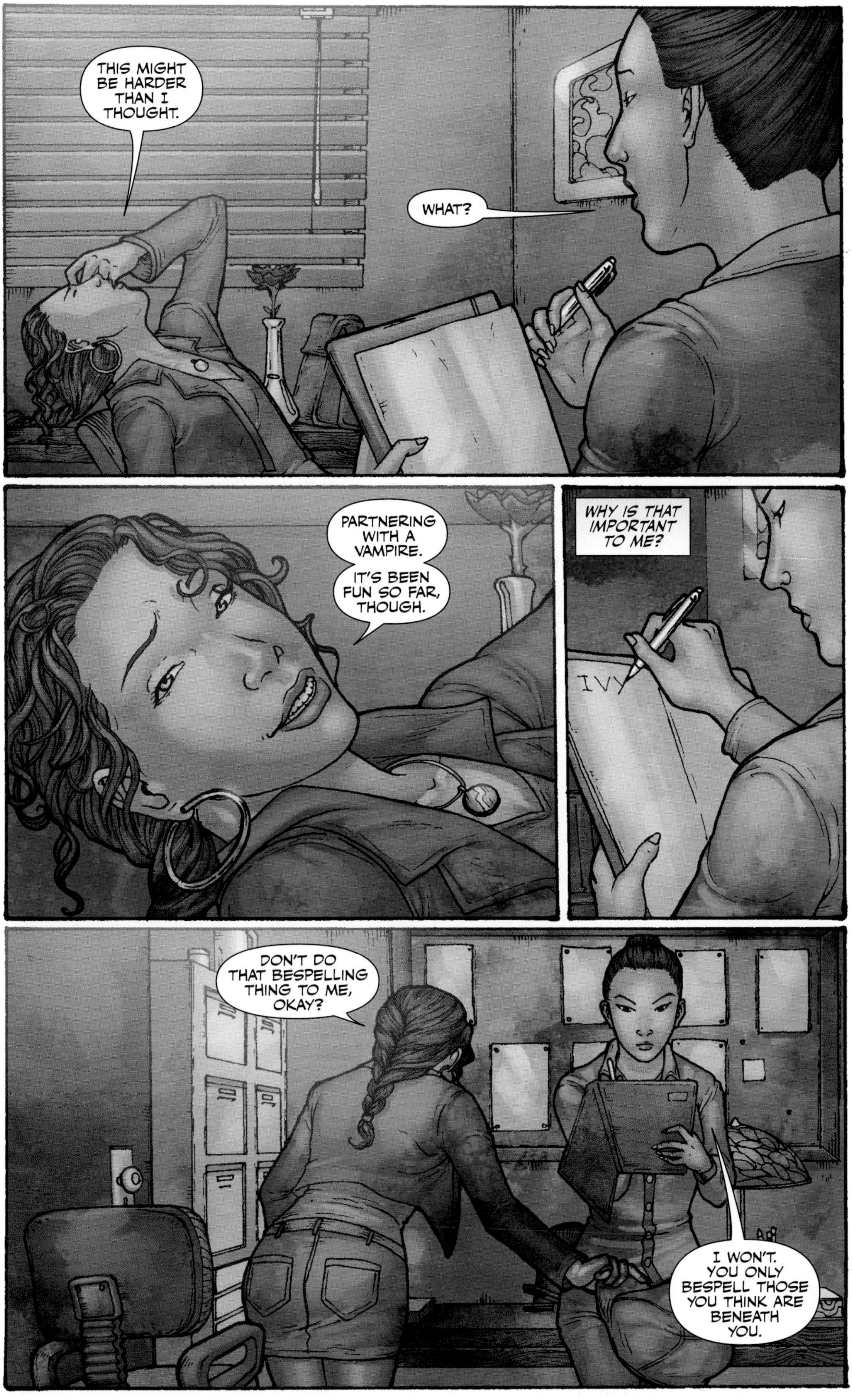

THIS MIGHT BE HARDER THAN I THOUGHT.
WHAT?
PARTNERING WITH A VAMPIRE.
IT'S BEEN FUN SO FAR, THOUGH.
WHY IS THAT IMPORTANT TO ME?
IVY
DON'T DO THAT BESPELLING THING TO ME, OKAY?
I WON'T. YOU ONLY BESPELL THOSE YOU THINK ARE BENEATH YOU.

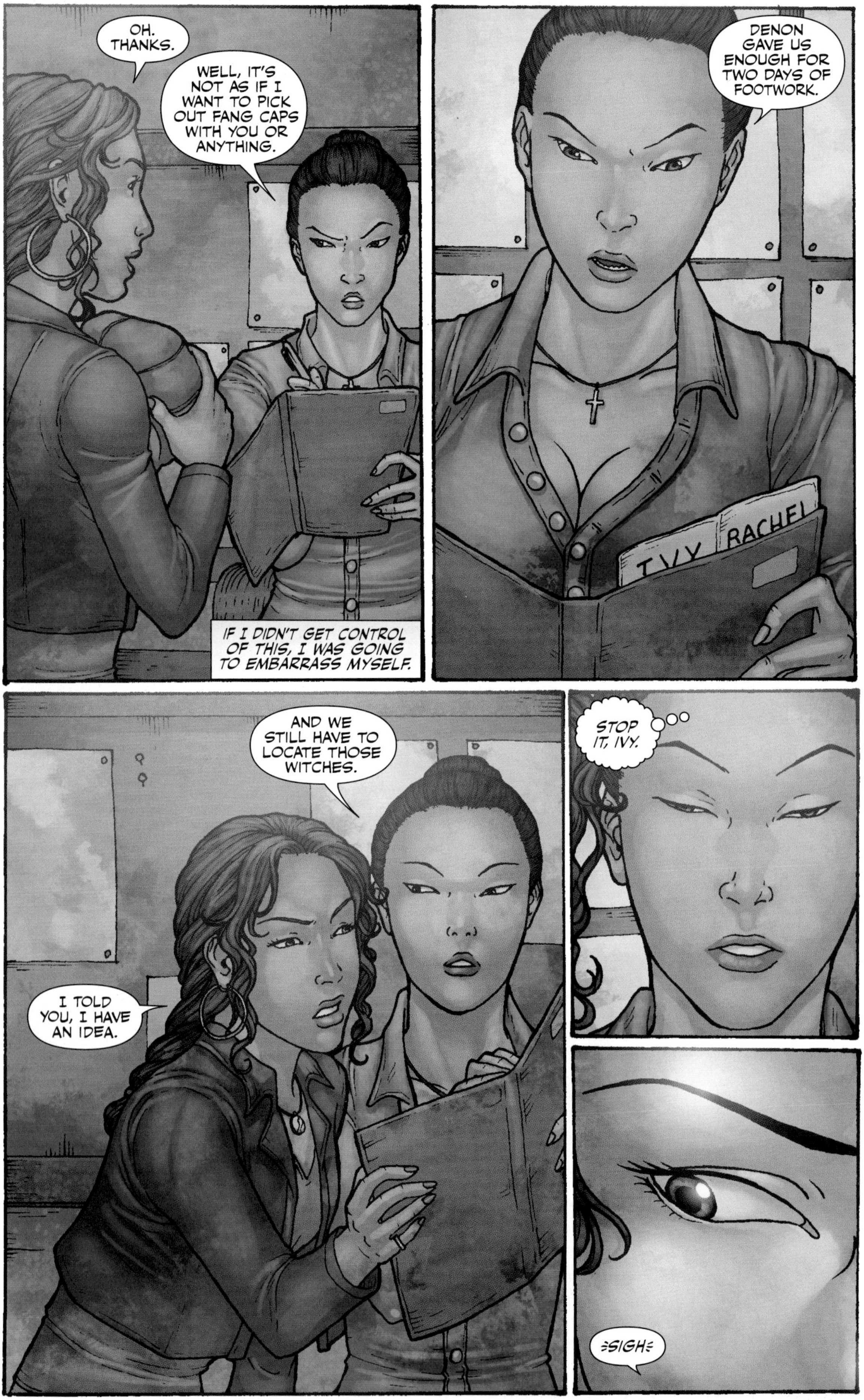
OH. THANKS.
WELL, IT'S NOT AS IF I WANT TO PICK OUT FANG CAPS WITH YOU OR ANYTHING.
IF I DIDN'T GET CONTROL OF THIS, I WAS GOING TO EMBARRASS MYSELF.
DENON GAVE US ENOUGH FOR TWO DAYS OF FOOTWORK.
IVY
RACHEL
AND WE STILL HAVE TO LOCATE THOSE WITCHES.
I TOLD YOU, I HAVE AN IDEA.
STOP IT, IVY.
SIGH

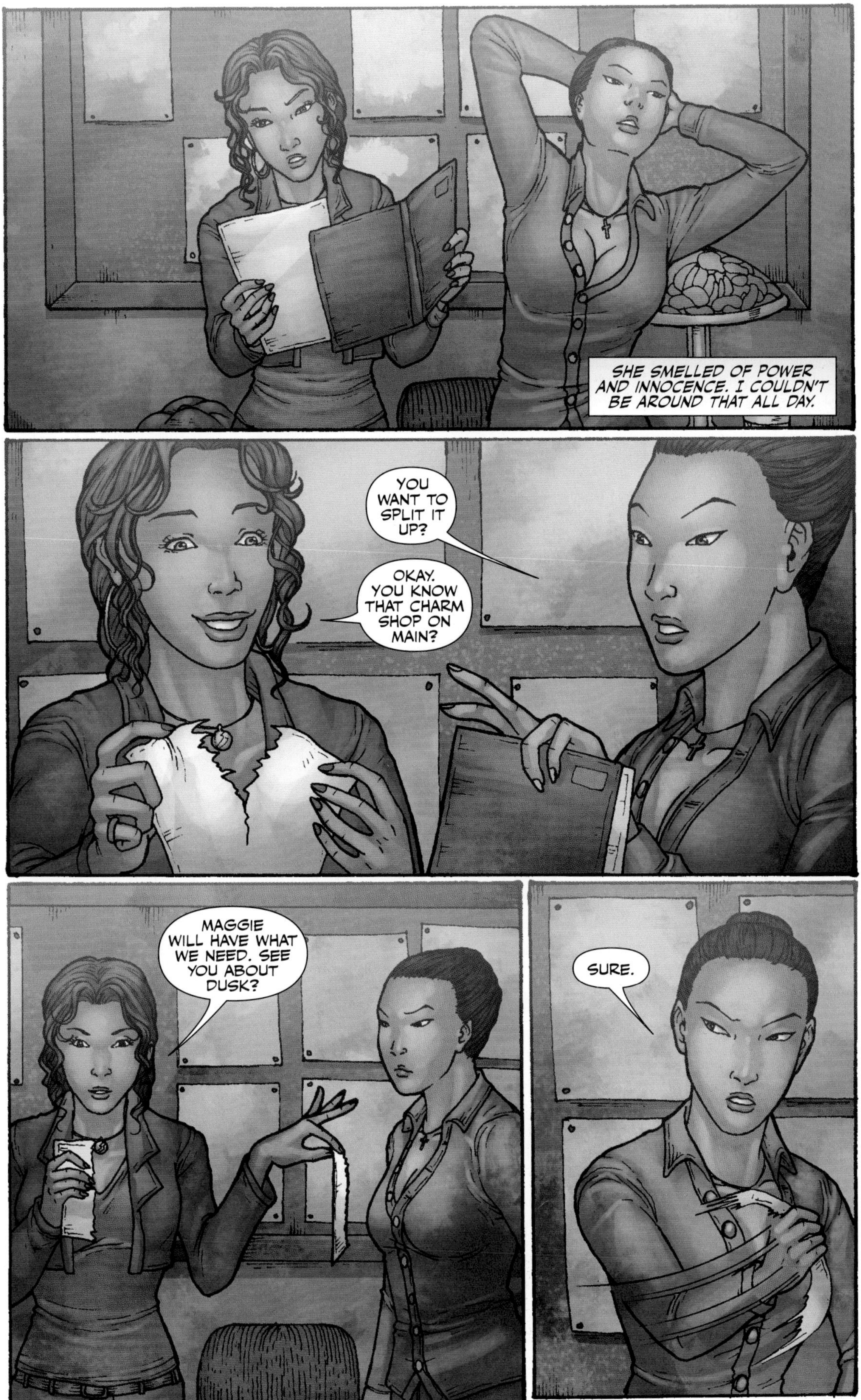
SHE SMELLED OF POWER AND INNOCENCE. I COULDN'T BE AROUND THAT ALL DAY.
YOU WANT TO SPLIT IT UP?
OKAY. YOU KNOW THAT CHARM SHOP ON MAIN?
MAGGIE WILL HAVE WHAT WE NEED. SEE YOU ABOUT DUSK?
SURE.

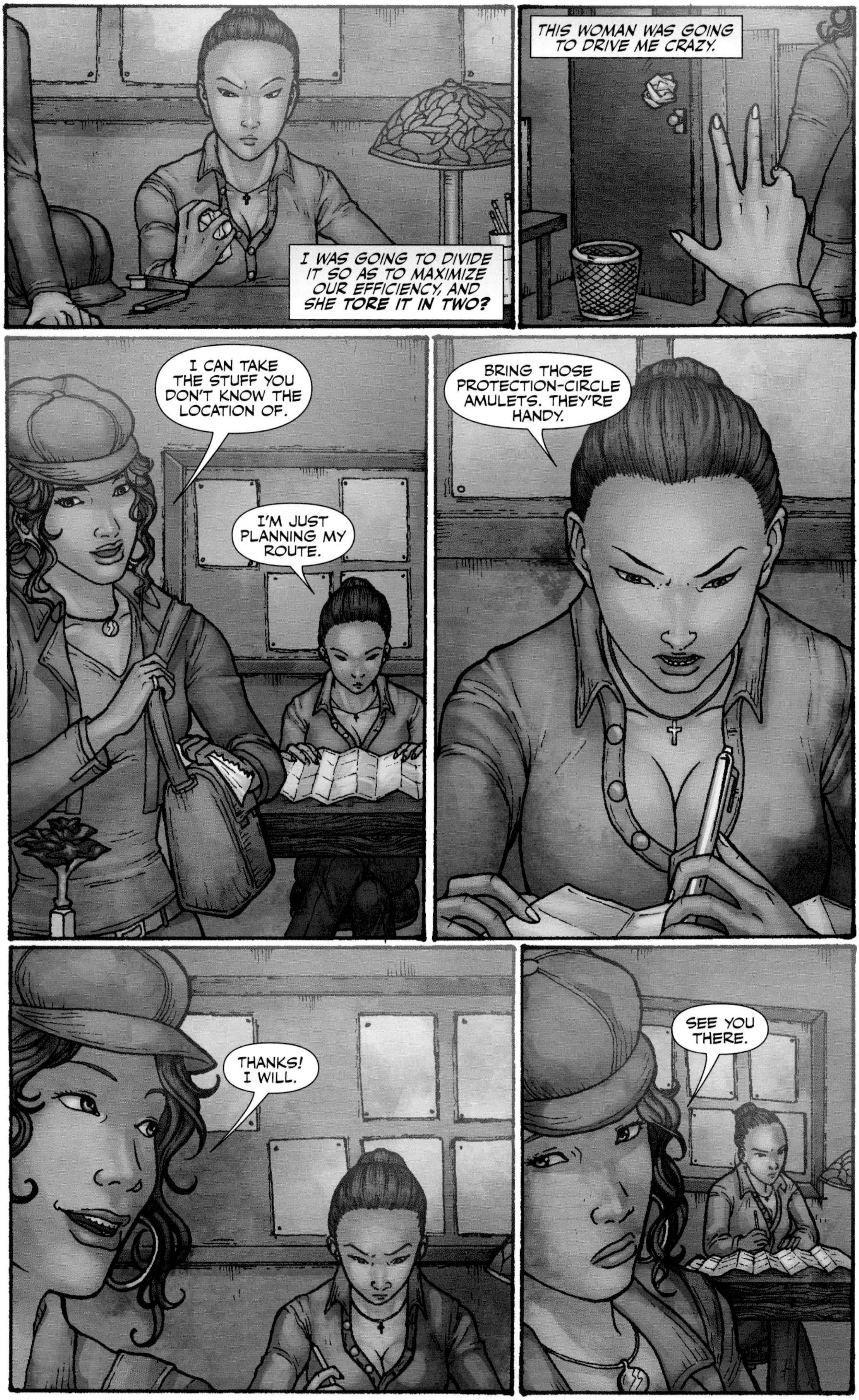
I WAS GOING TO DIVIDE IT SO AS TO MAXIMIZE OUR EFFICIENCY, AND SHE TORE IT IN TWO?
THIS WOMAN WAS GOING TO DRIVE ME CRAZY.
I CAN TAKE THE STUFF YOU DON'T KNOW THE LOCATION OF.
I'M JUST PLANNING MY ROUTE.
BRING THOSE PROTECTION-CIRCLE AMULETS. THEY'RE HANDY.
THANKS! I WILL.
SEE YOU THERE.

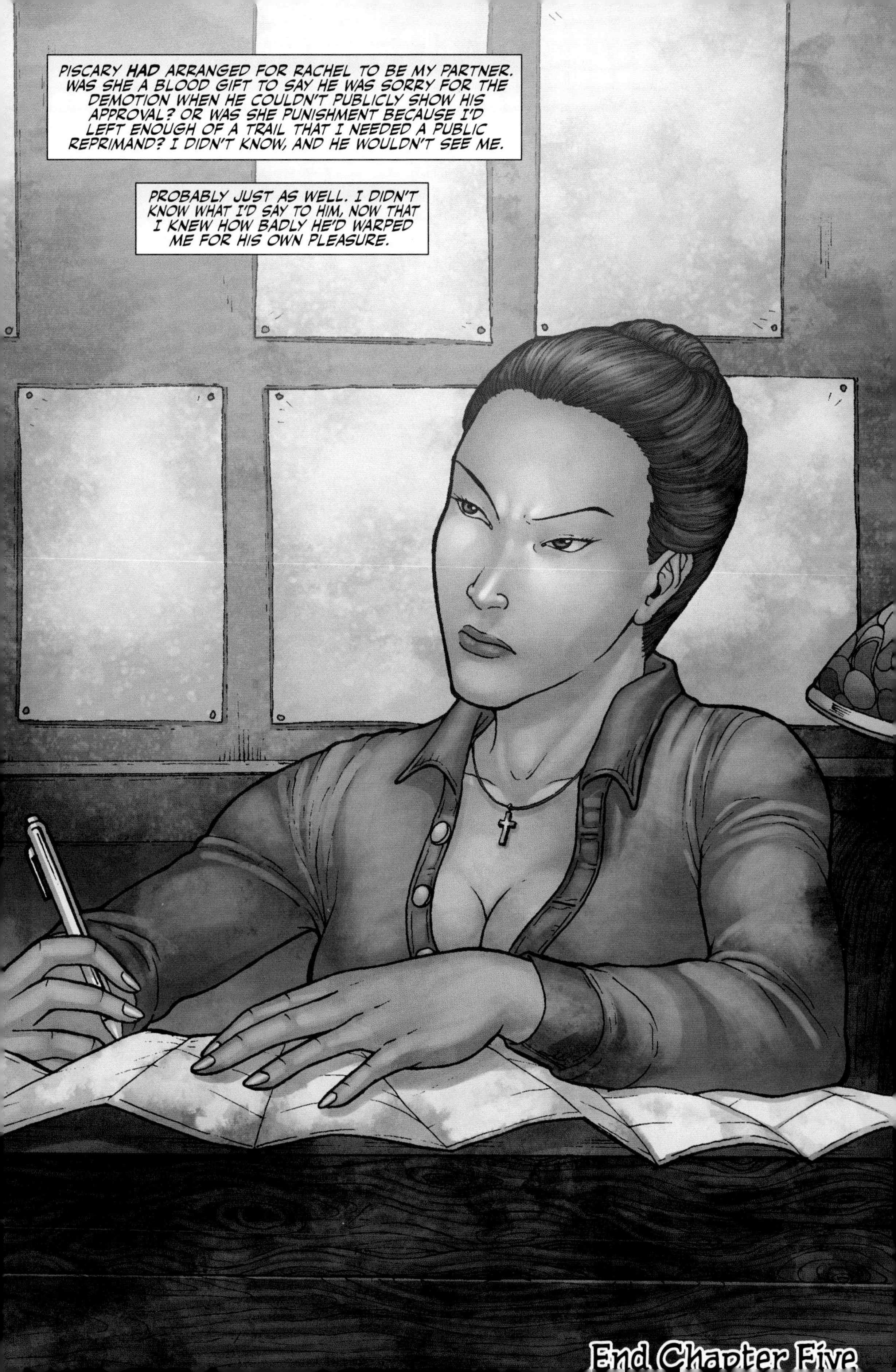
PISCARY **HAD** ARRANGED FOR RACHEL TO BE MY PARTNER. WAS SHE A BLOOD GIFT TO SAY HE WAS SORRY FOR THE DEMOTION WHEN HE COULDN'T PUBLICLY SHOW HIS APPROVAL? OR WAS SHE PUNISHMENT BECAUSE I'D LEFT ENOUGH OF A TRAIL THAT I NEEDED A PUBLIC REPRIMAND? I DIDN'T KNOW, AND HE WOULDN'T SEE ME.
PROBABLY JUST AS WELL. I DIDN'T KNOW WHAT I'D SAY TO HIM, NOW THAT I KNEW HOW BADLY HE'D WARPED ME FOR HIS OWN PLEASURE.
End Chapter Five

CHAPTER 6

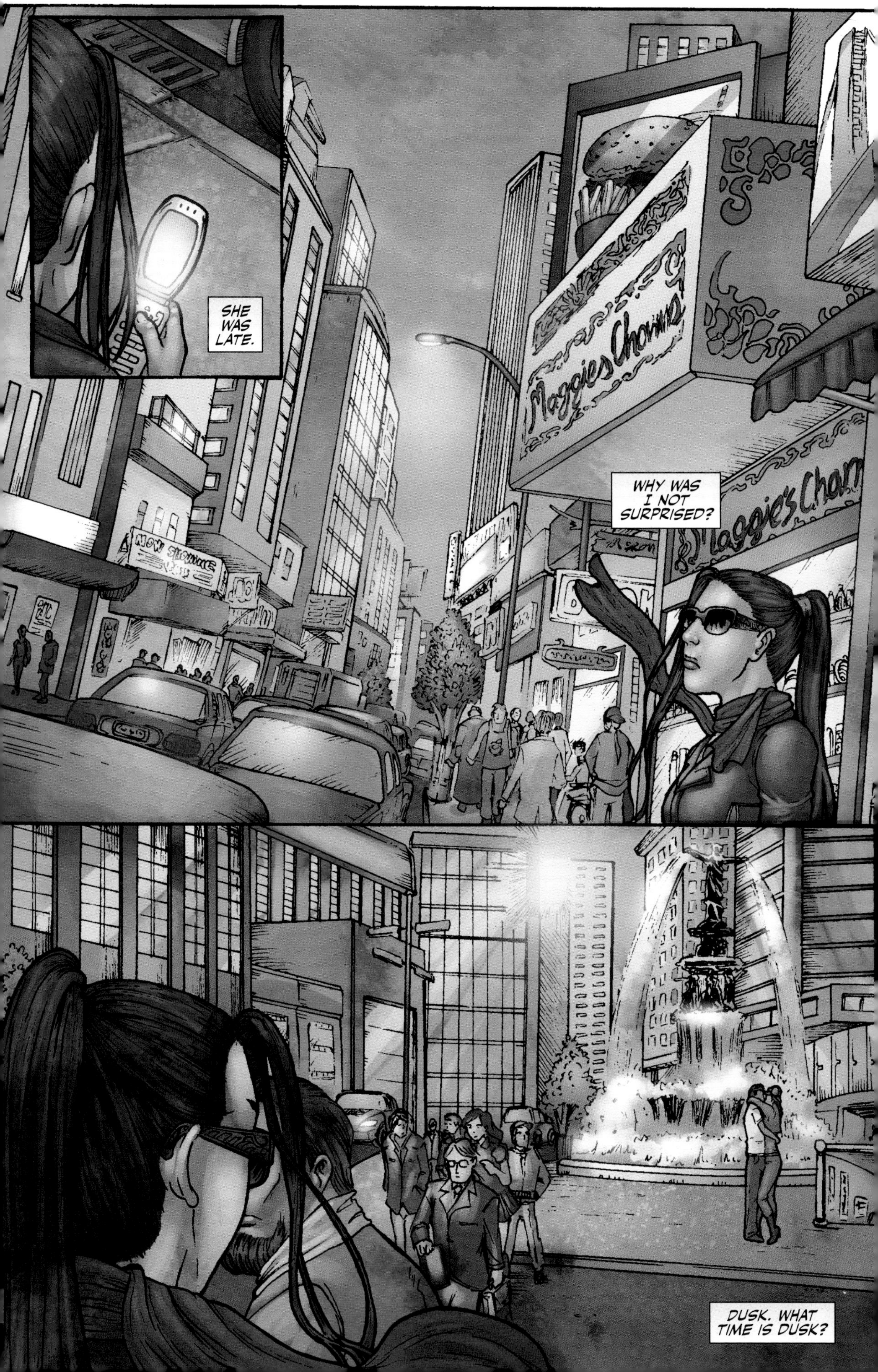
SHE WAS LATE.
WHY WAS I NOT SURPRISED?
DUSK. WHAT TIME IS DUSK?

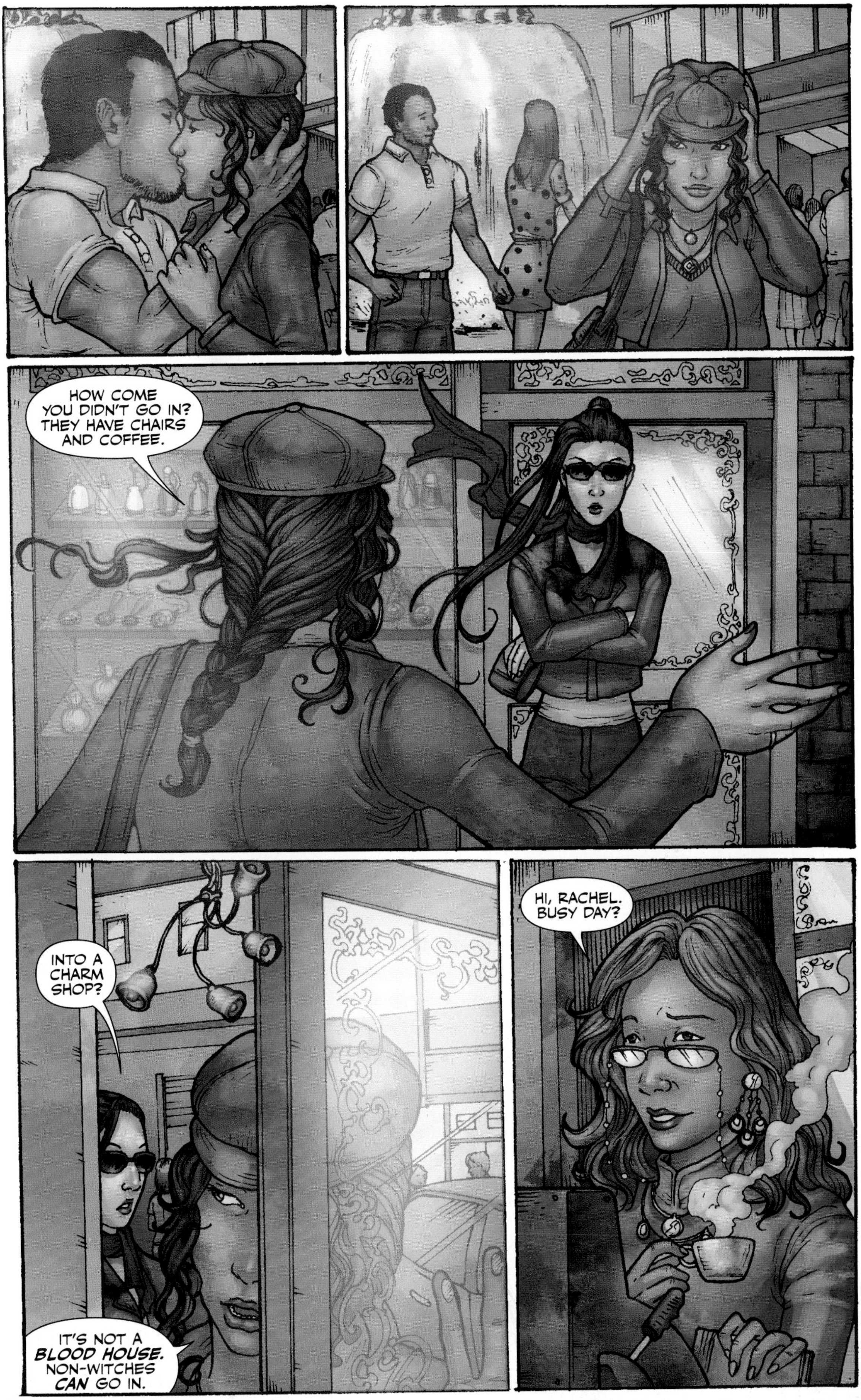
HOW COME YOU DIDN'T GO IN? THEY HAVE CHAIRS AND COFFEE.
INTO A CHARM SHOP?
IT'S NOT A BLOOD HOUSE. NON-WITCHES CAN GO IN.
HI, RACHEL. BUSY DAY?

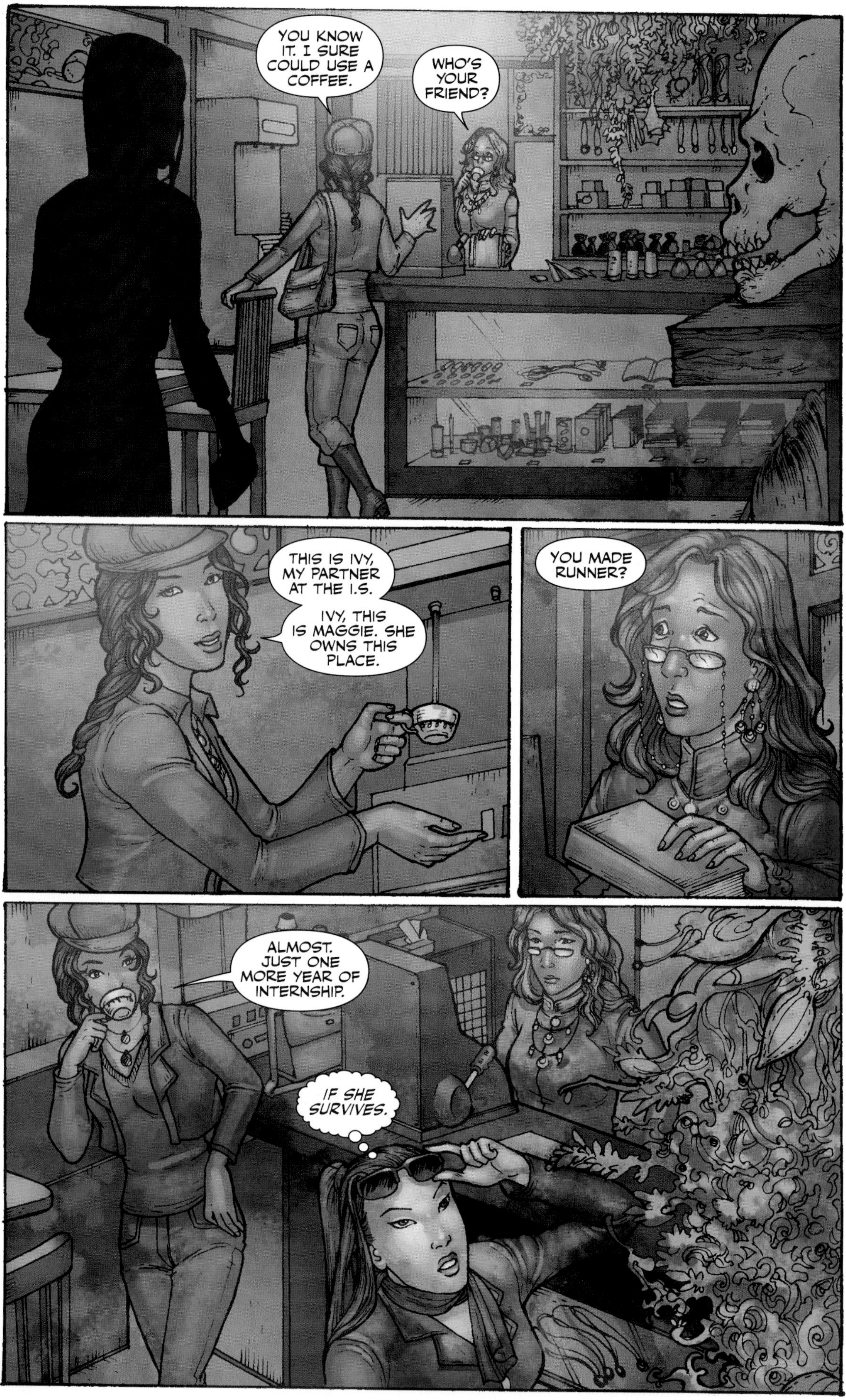
YOU KNOW IT. I SURE COULD USE A COFFEE.
WHO'S YOUR FRIEND?
THIS IS IVY, MY PARTNER AT THE I.S.
IVY, THIS IS MAGGIE. SHE OWNS THIS PLACE.
YOU MADE RUNNER?
ALMOST. JUST ONE MORE YEAR OF INTERNSHIP.
IF SHE SURVIVES.

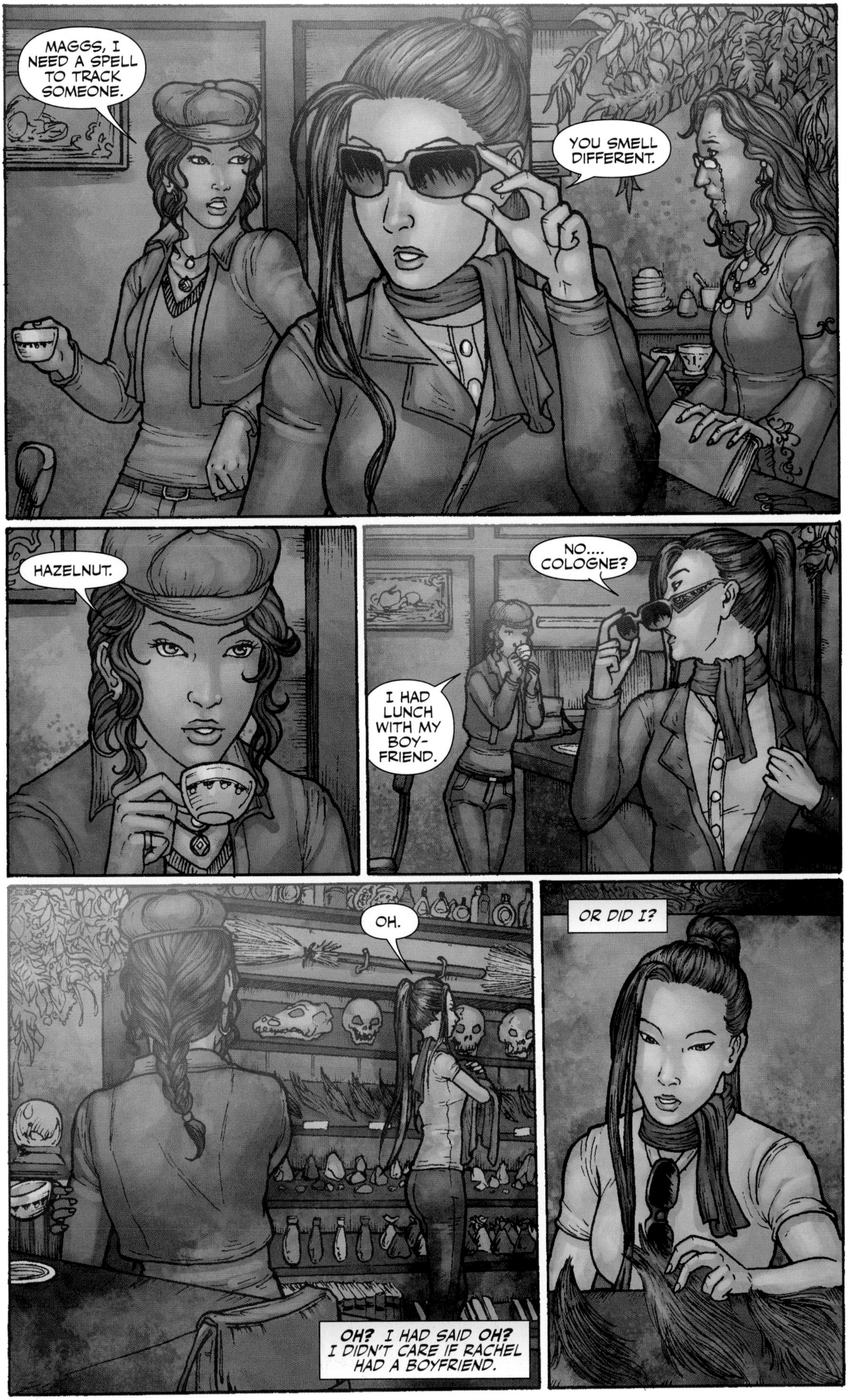
MAGGS, I NEED A SPELL TO TRACK SOMEONE.
YOU SMELL DIFFERENT.
HAZELNUT.
NO.... COLOGNE?
I HAD LUNCH WITH MY BOY-FRIEND.
OH.
OH? I HAD SAID OH? I DIDN'T CARE IF RACHEL HAD A BOYFRIEND.
OR DID I?

TRACKING CHARM. EXPENSIVE. WHO WE LOOKING FOR?

WHAT DO YOU HAVE THAT'S CHEAP?

NO SUCH THING AS A CHEAP FINDING CHARM.

ANYTHING THAT LOCATES LARGE AMOUNTS OF BLOOD?

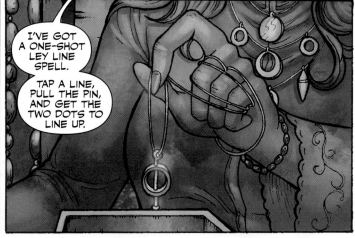

I'VE GOT A ONE-SHOT LEY LINE SPELL.

TAP A LINE, PULL THE PIN, AND GET THE TWO DOTS TO LINE UP.

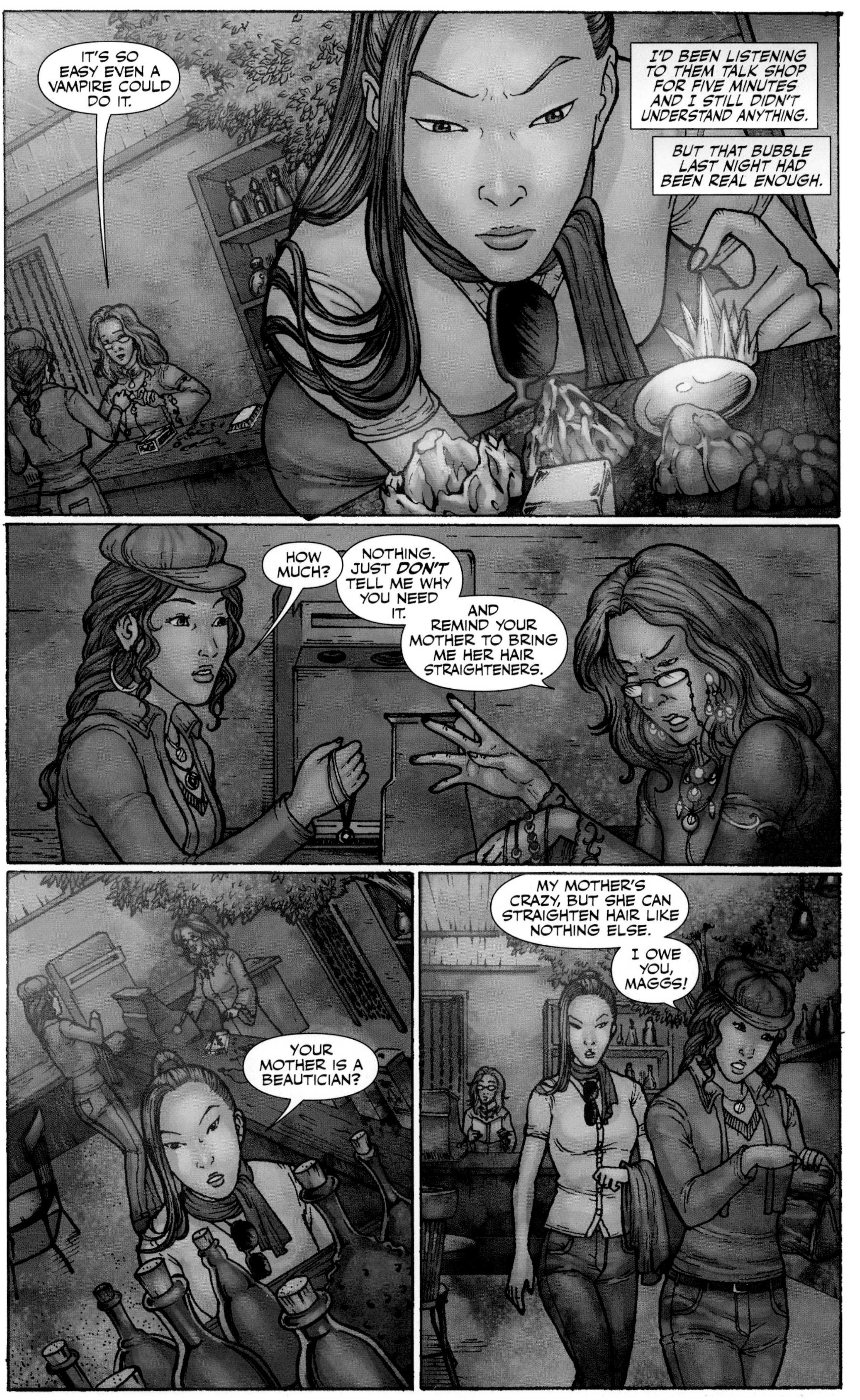
IT'S SO EASY EVEN A VAMPIRE COULD DO IT.
I'D BEEN LISTENING TO THEM TALK SHOP FOR FIVE MINUTES AND I STILL DIDN'T UNDERSTAND ANYTHING.
BUT THAT BUBBLE LAST NIGHT HAD BEEN REAL ENOUGH.
HOW MUCH?
NOTHING. JUST DON'T TELL ME WHY YOU NEED IT.
AND REMIND YOUR MOTHER TO BRING ME HER HAIR STRAIGHTENERS.
YOUR MOTHER IS A BEAUTICIAN?
MY MOTHER'S CRAZY, BUT SHE CAN STRAIGHTEN HAIR LIKE NOTHING ELSE.
I OWE YOU, MAGGS!

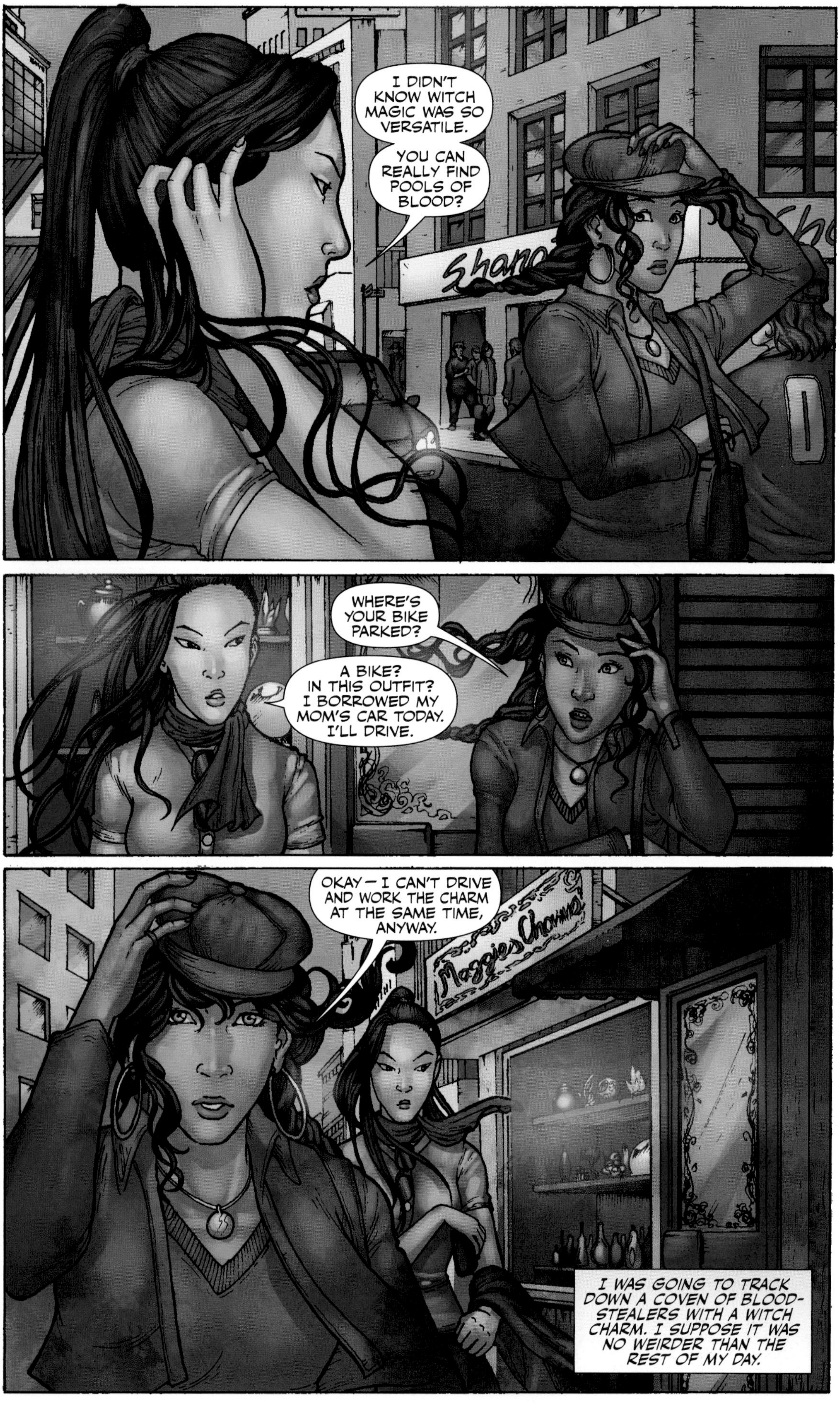
I DIDN'T KNOW WITCH MAGIC WAS SO VERSATILE.
YOU CAN REALLY FIND POOLS OF BLOOD?
WHERE'S YOUR BIKE PARKED?
A BIKE? IN THIS OUTFIT? I BORROWED MY MOM'S CAR TODAY. I'LL DRIVE.
OKAY — I CAN'T DRIVE AND WORK THE CHARM AT THE SAME TIME, ANYWAY.
Maggie's Charms
I WAS GOING TO TRACK DOWN A COVEN OF BLOOD-STEALERS WITH A WITCH CHARM. I SUPPOSE IT WAS NO WEIRDER THAN THE REST OF MY DAY.

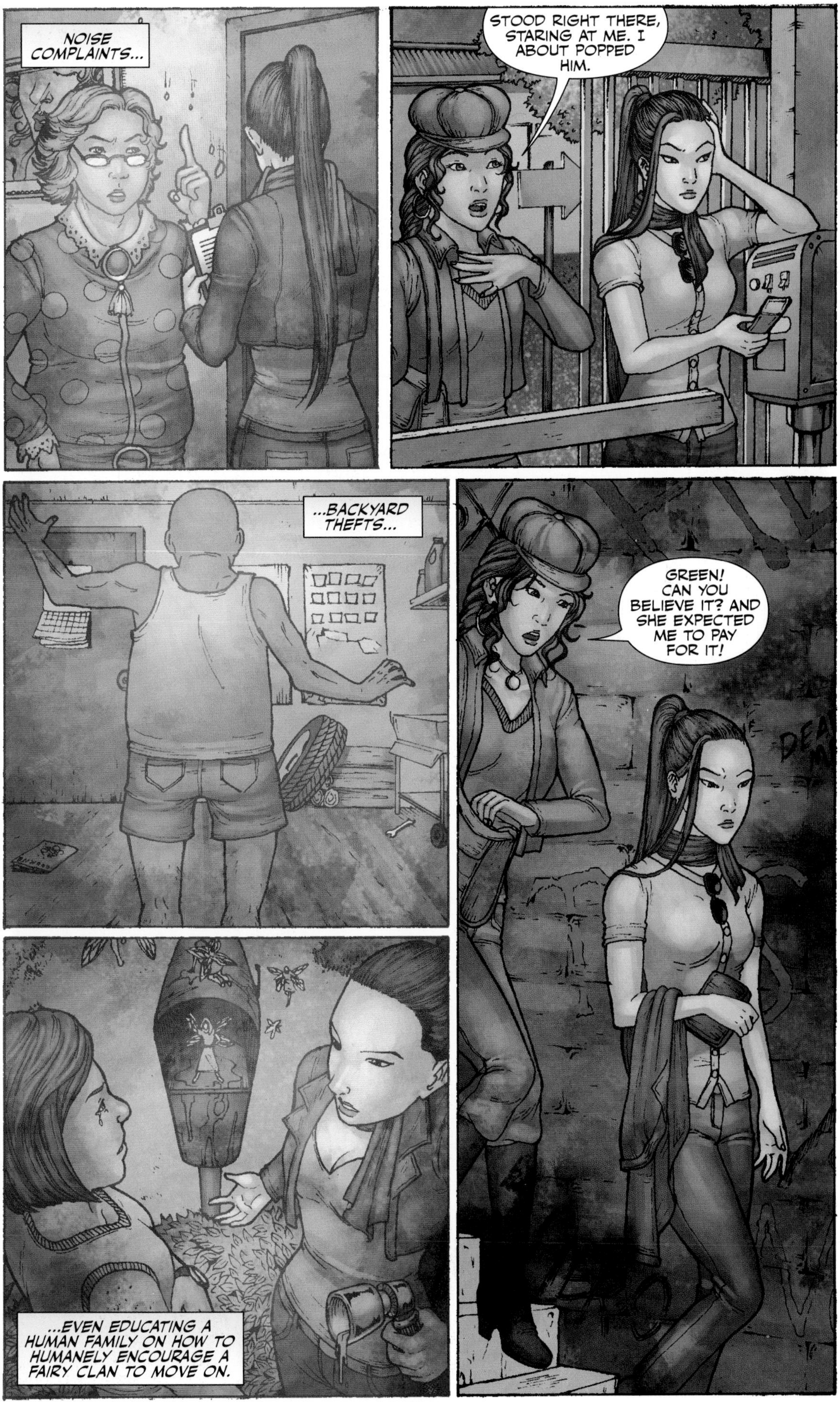
NOISE COMPLAINTS...
STOOD RIGHT THERE, STARING AT ME. I ABOUT POPPED HIM.
...BACKYARD THEFTS...
GREEN! CAN YOU BELIEVE IT? AND SHE EXPECTED ME TO PAY FOR IT!
...EVEN EDUCATING A HUMAN FAMILY ON HOW TO HUMANELY ENCOURAGE A FAIRY CLAN TO MOVE ON.

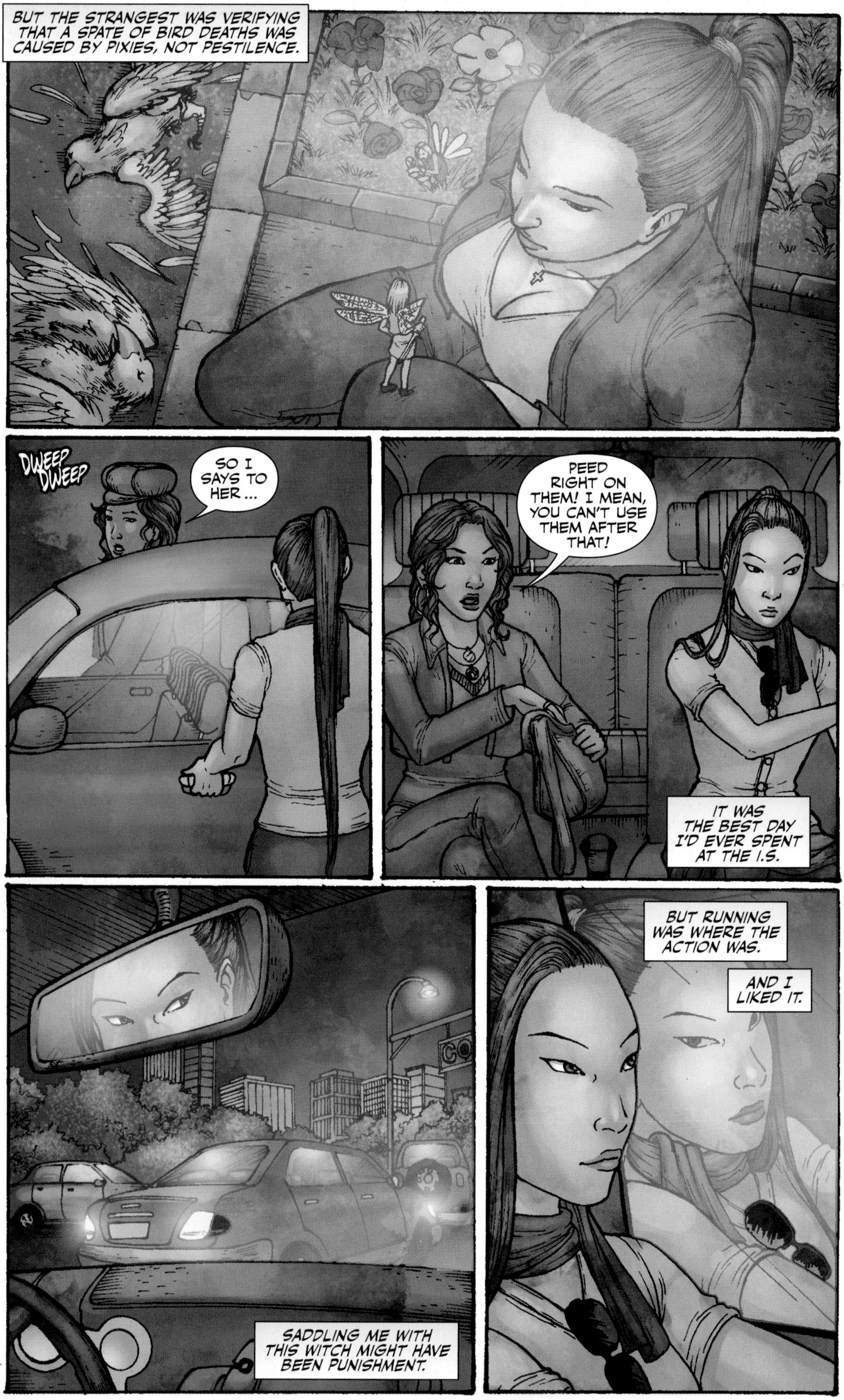
BUT THE STRANGEST WAS VERIFYING THAT A SPATE OF BIRD DEATHS WAS CAUSED BY PIXIES, NOT PESTILENCE.
DWEEP DWEEP
SO I SAYS TO HER...
PEED RIGHT ON THEM! I MEAN, YOU CAN'T USE THEM AFTER THAT!
IT WAS THE BEST DAY I'D EVER SPENT AT THE I.S.
SADDLING ME WITH THIS WITCH MIGHT HAVE BEEN PUNISHMENT.
BUT RUNNING WAS WHERE THE ACTION WAS.
AND I LIKED IT.

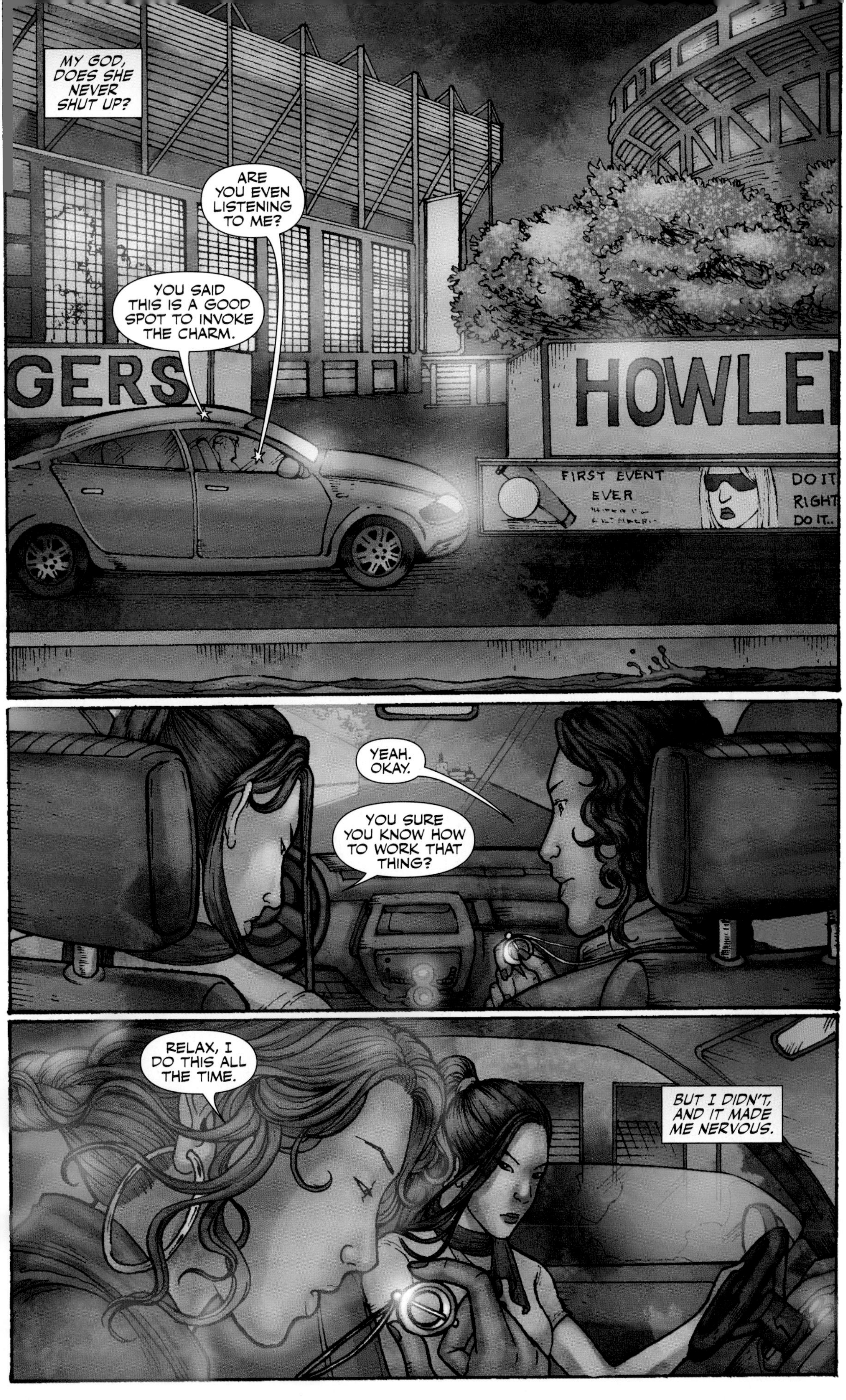
MY GOD, DOES SHE NEVER SHUT UP?
ARE YOU EVEN LISTENING TO ME?
YOU SAID THIS IS A GOOD SPOT TO INVOKE THE CHARM.
GERS
HOWLE
FIRST EVENT EVER
DO IT RIGHT DO IT..
YEAH. OKAY.
YOU SURE YOU KNOW HOW TO WORK THAT THING?
RELAX, I DO THIS ALL THE TIME.
BUT I DIDN'T, AND IT MADE ME NERVOUS.

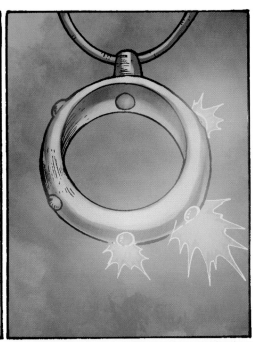

SHE LOOKED FREAKY WHEN SHE DID HER MAGIC. POWERFUL...

IT'S NOT THE WITCH, IVY. KNOCK IT OFF.

I'M GOING TO GUESS THE INDUSTRIAL PARK. WE GOT THEM!

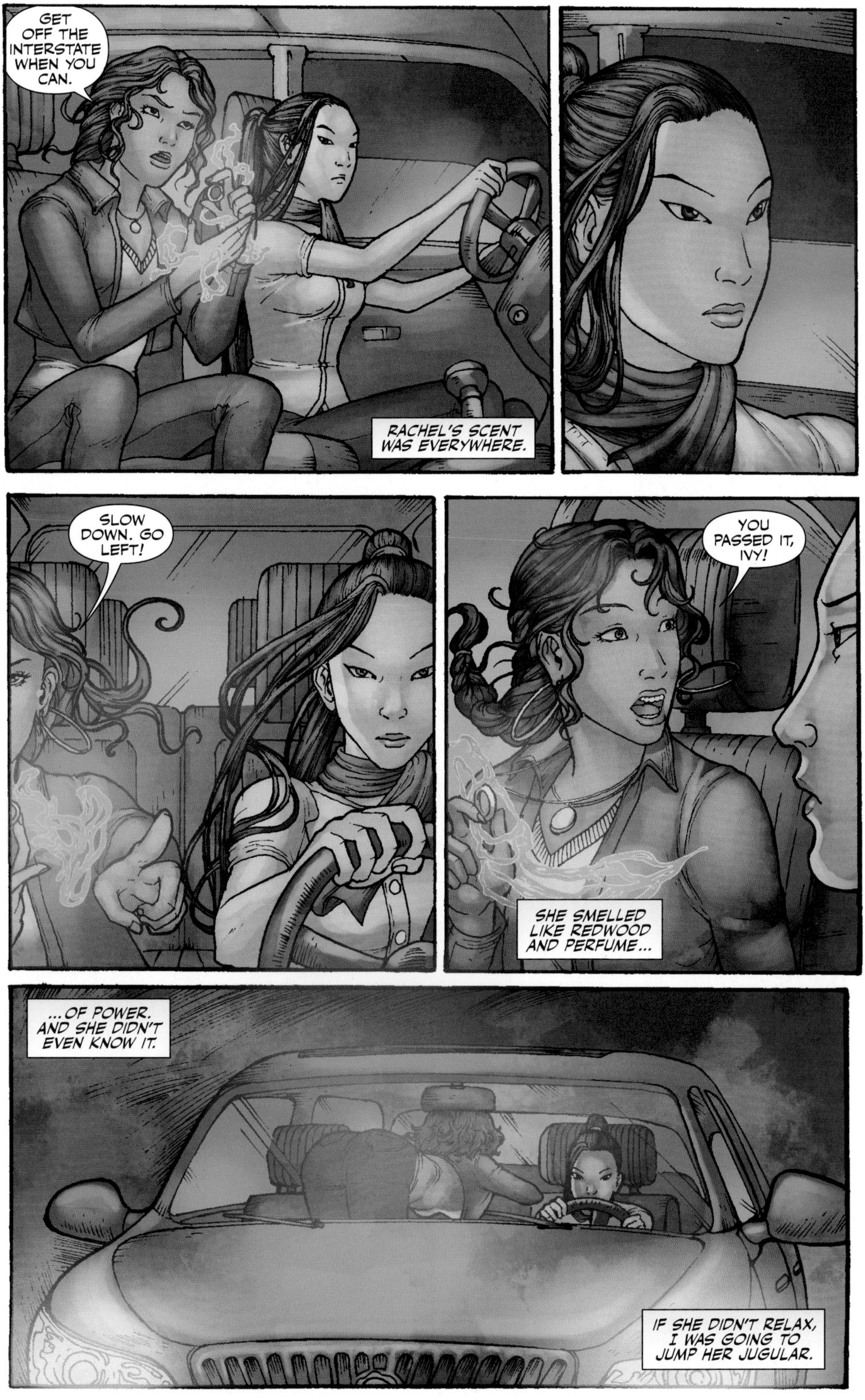
GET OFF THE INTERSTATE WHEN YOU CAN.
RACHEL'S SCENT WAS EVERYWHERE.
SLOW DOWN. GO LEFT!
YOU PASSED IT, IVY!
SHE SMELLED LIKE REDWOOD AND PERFUME...
...OF POWER. AND SHE DIDN'T EVEN KNOW IT.
IF SHE DIDN'T RELAX, I WAS GOING TO JUMP HER JUGULAR.

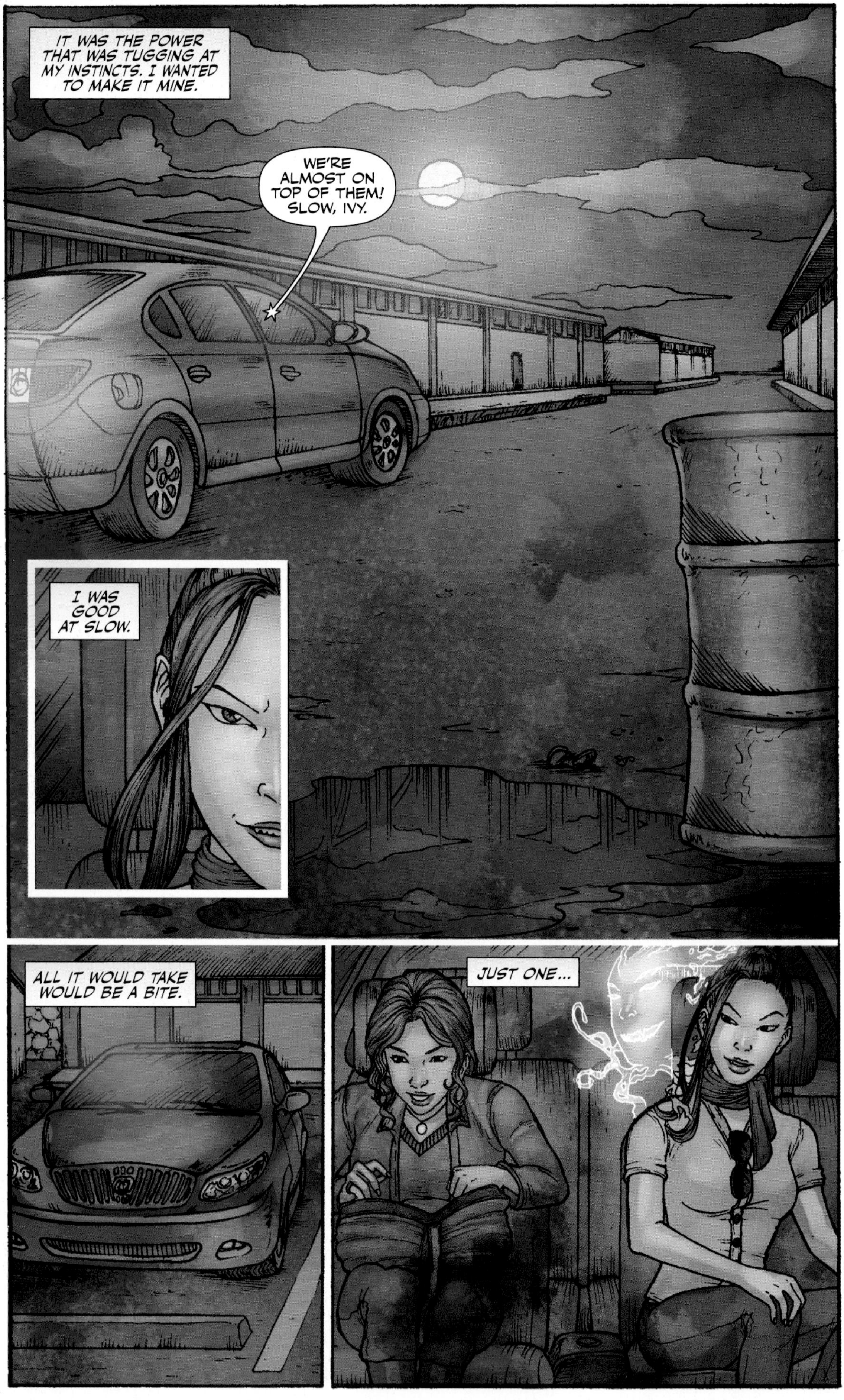
IT WAS THE POWER THAT WAS TUGGING AT MY INSTINCTS. I WANTED TO MAKE IT MINE.
WE'RE ALMOST ON TOP OF THEM! SLOW, IVY.
I WAS GOOD AT SLOW.
ALL IT WOULD TAKE WOULD BE A BITE.
JUST ONE...

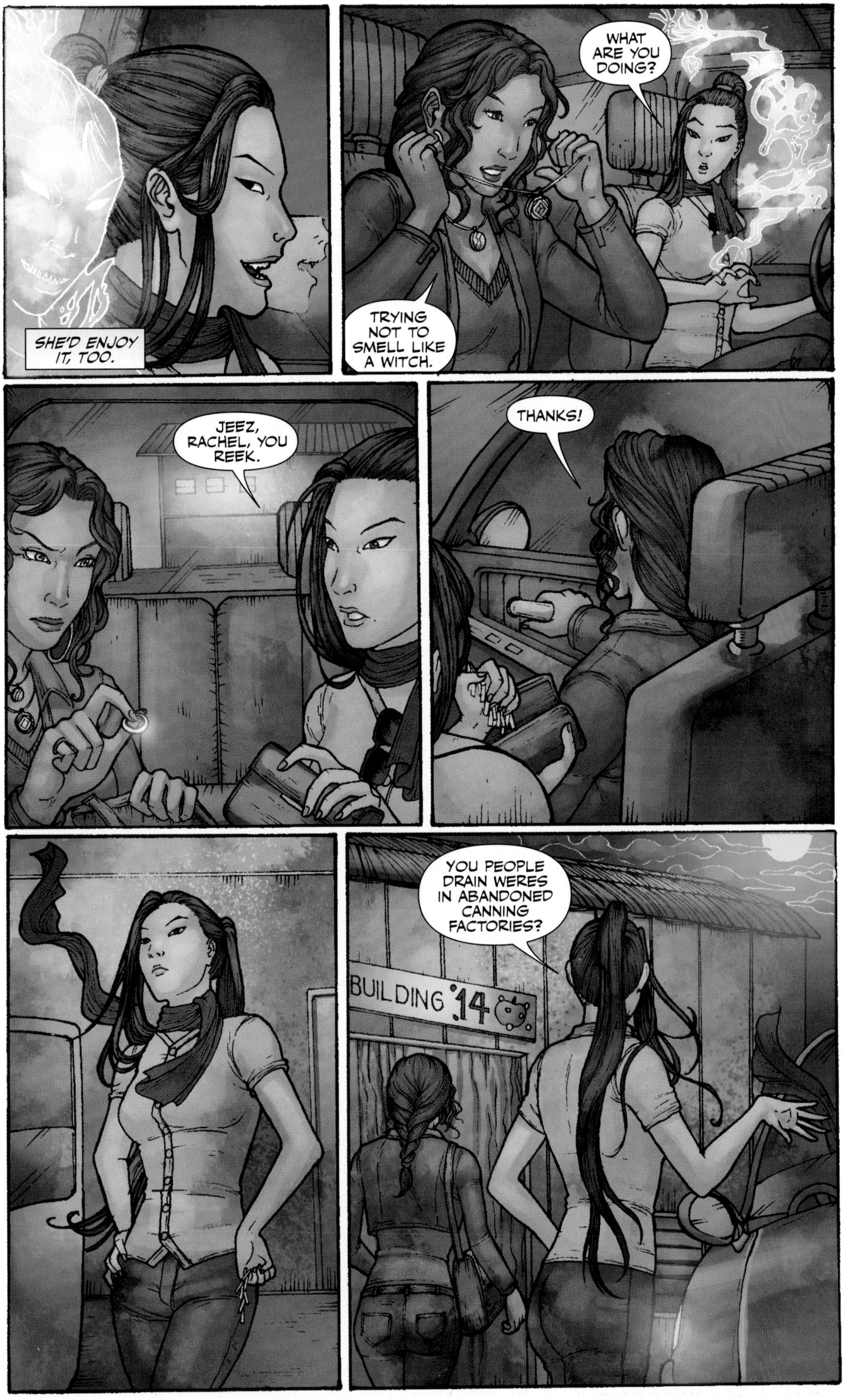
SHE'D ENJOY IT, TOO.
WHAT ARE YOU DOING?
TRYING NOT TO SMELL LIKE A WITCH.
JEEZ, RACHEL, YOU REEK.
THANKS!
YOU PEOPLE DRAIN WERES IN ABANDONED CANNING FACTORIES?
BUILDING 14

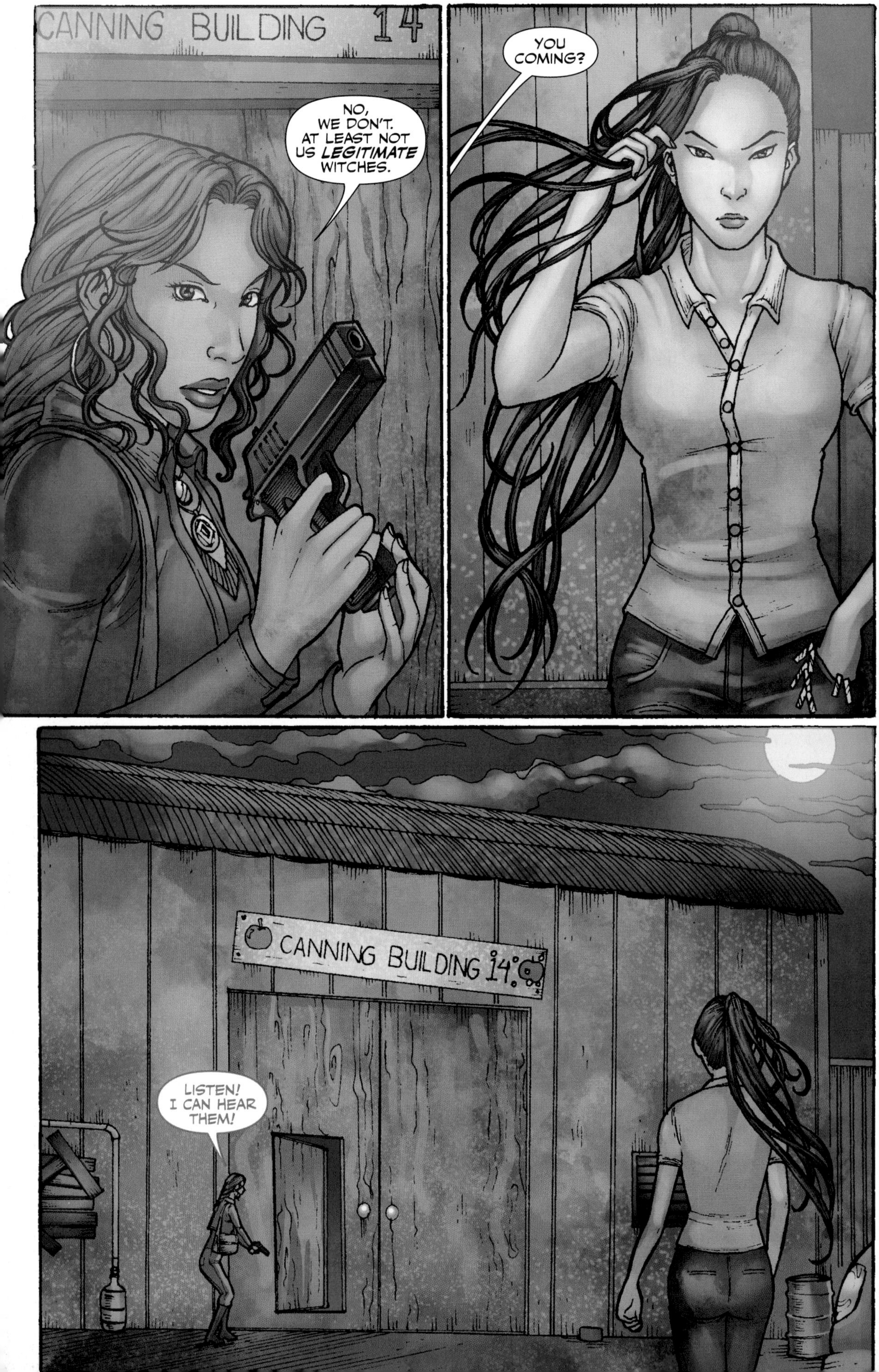
CANNING BUILDING 14
NO, WE DON'T. AT LEAST NOT US LEGITIMATE WITCHES.
YOU COMING?
CANNING BUILDING 14
LISTEN! I CAN HEAR THEM!

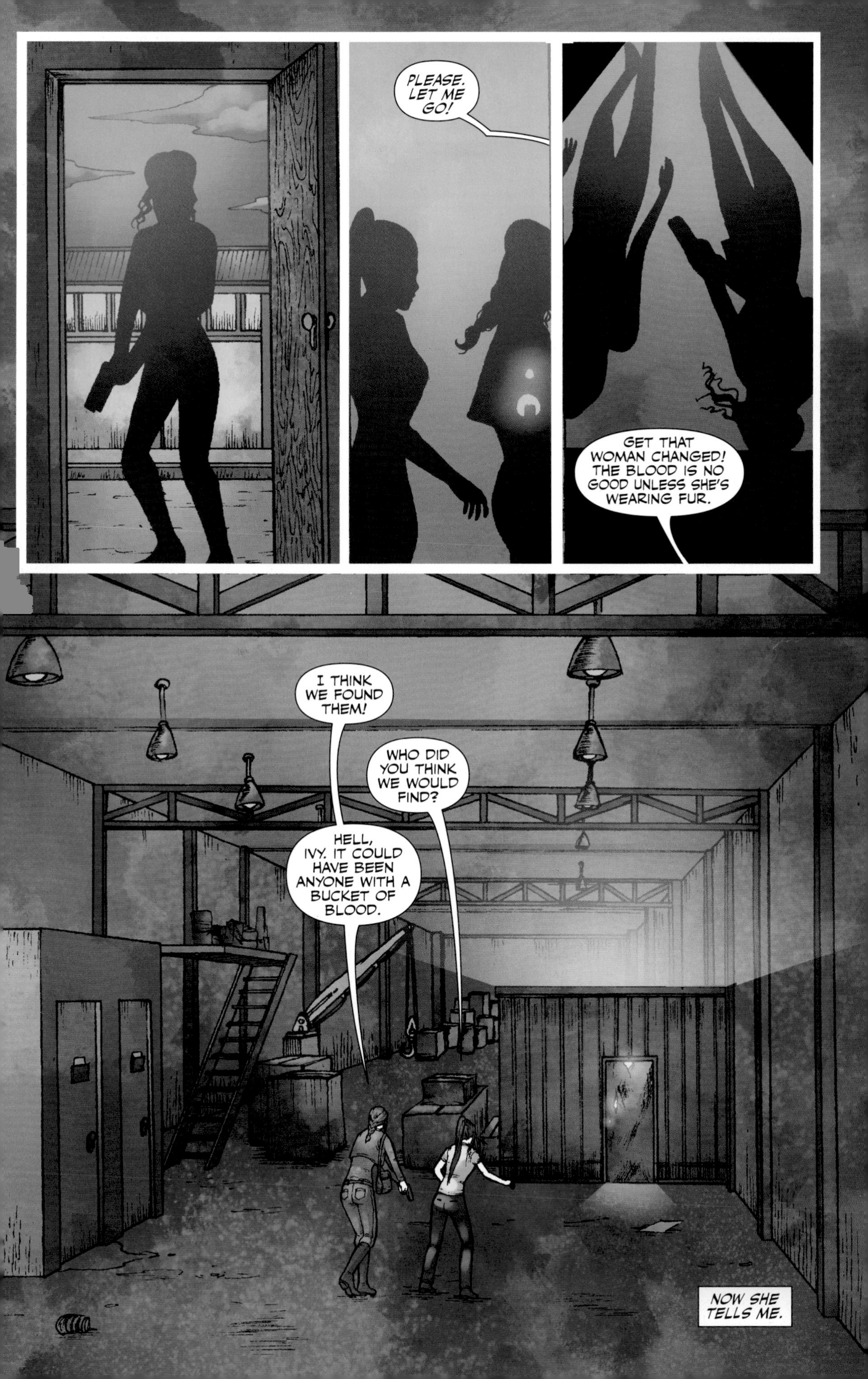

PLEASE. LET ME GO!
GET THAT WOMAN CHANGED! THE BLOOD IS NO GOOD UNLESS SHE'S WEARING FUR.
I THINK WE FOUND THEM!
WHO DID YOU THINK WE WOULD FIND?
HELL, IVY. IT COULD HAVE BEEN ANYONE WITH A BUCKET OF BLOOD.
NOW SHE TELLS ME.

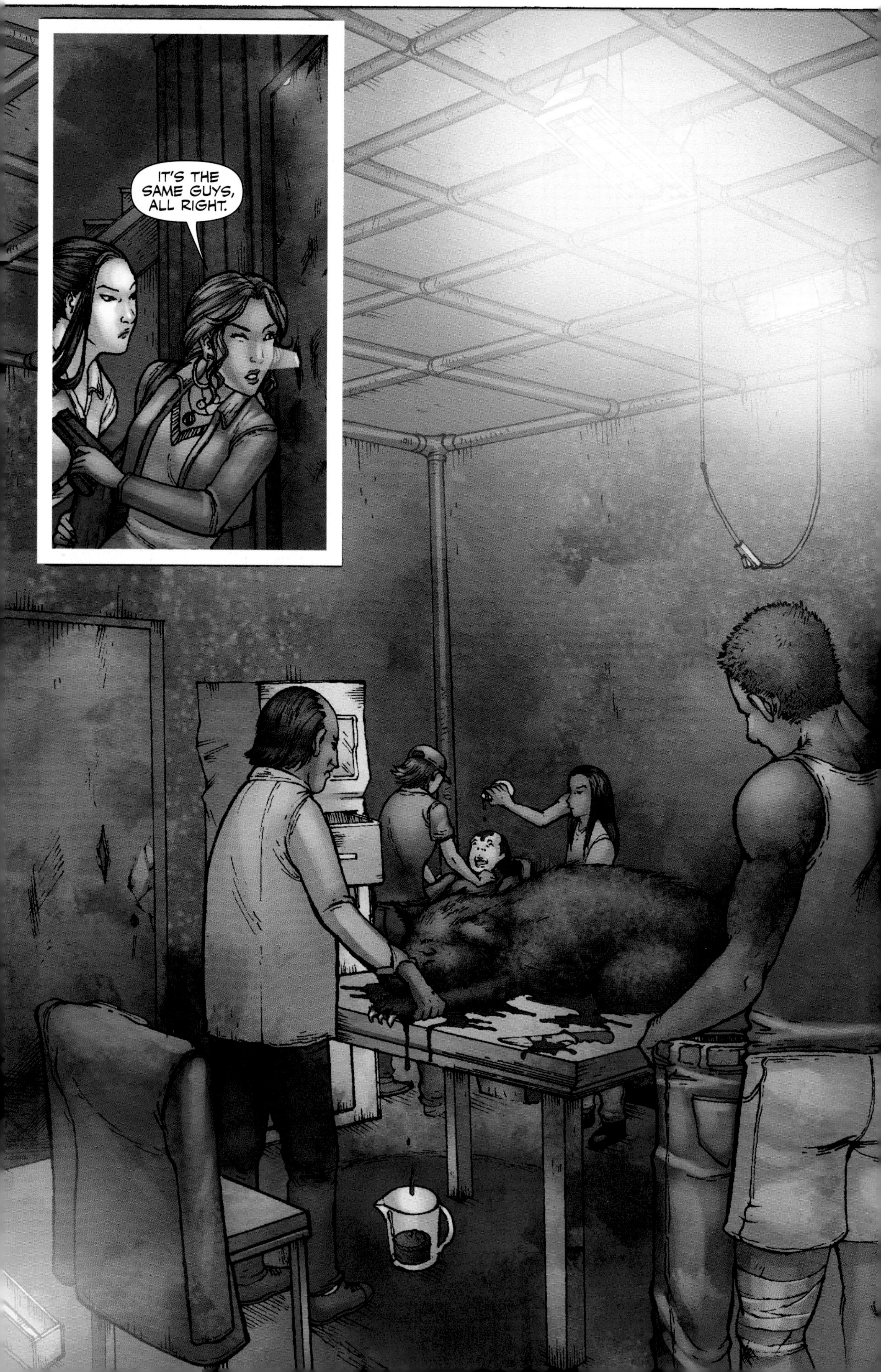
IT'S THE SAME GUYS, ALL RIGHT.

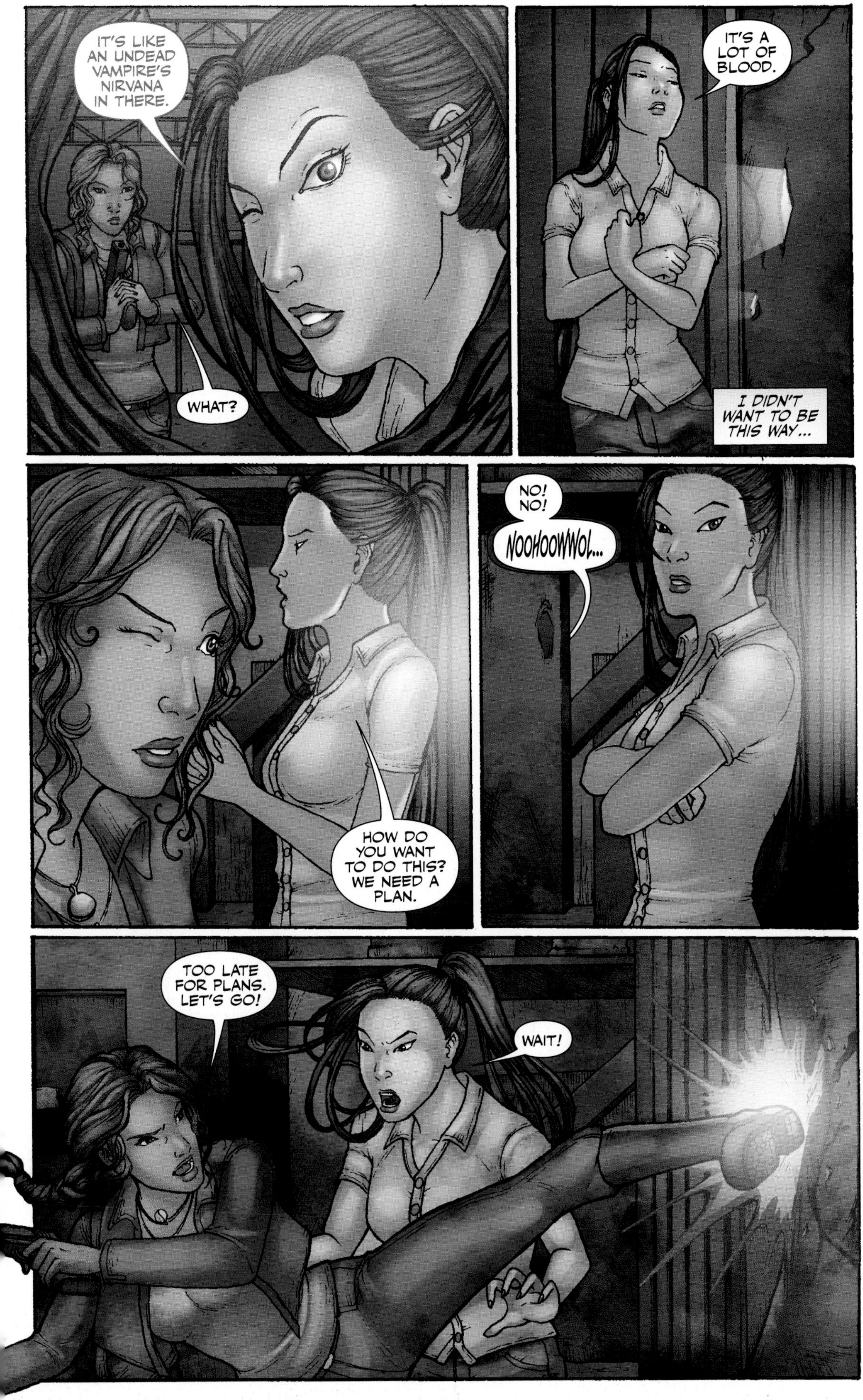
IT'S LIKE AN UNDEAD VAMPIRE'S NIRVANA IN THERE.
WHAT?
IT'S A LOT OF BLOOD.
I DIDN'T WANT TO BE THIS WAY...
HOW DO YOU WANT TO DO THIS? WE NEED A PLAN.
NO! NO!
NOOHOOWWOL...
TOO LATE FOR PLANS. LET'S GO!
WAIT!

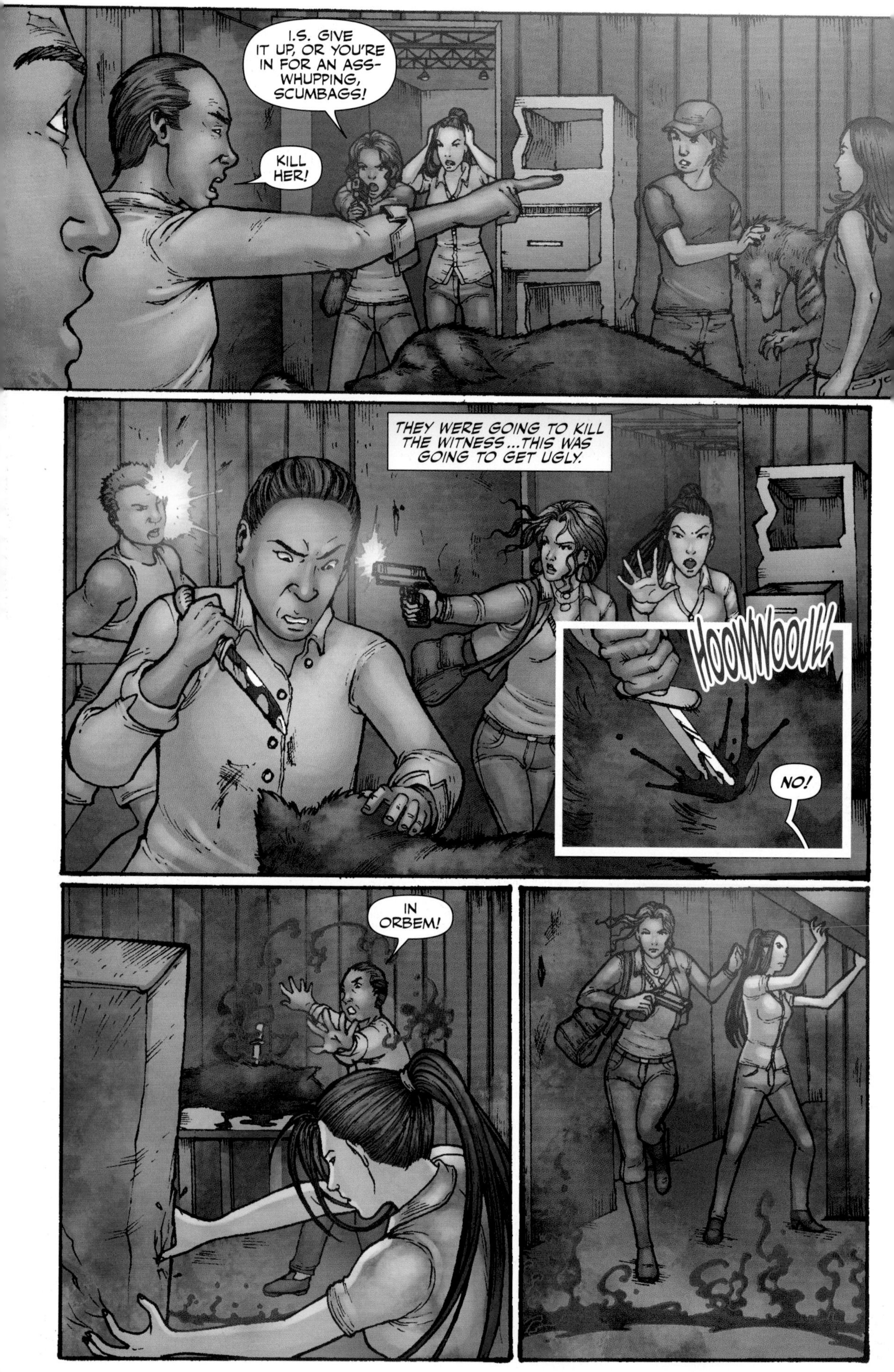
I.S. GIVE IT UP, OR YOU'RE IN FOR AN ASS-WHUPPING, SCUMBAGS!
KILL HER!
THEY WERE GOING TO KILL THE WITNESS...THIS WAS GOING TO GET UGLY.
HOOWWOOULL
NO!
IN ORBEM!

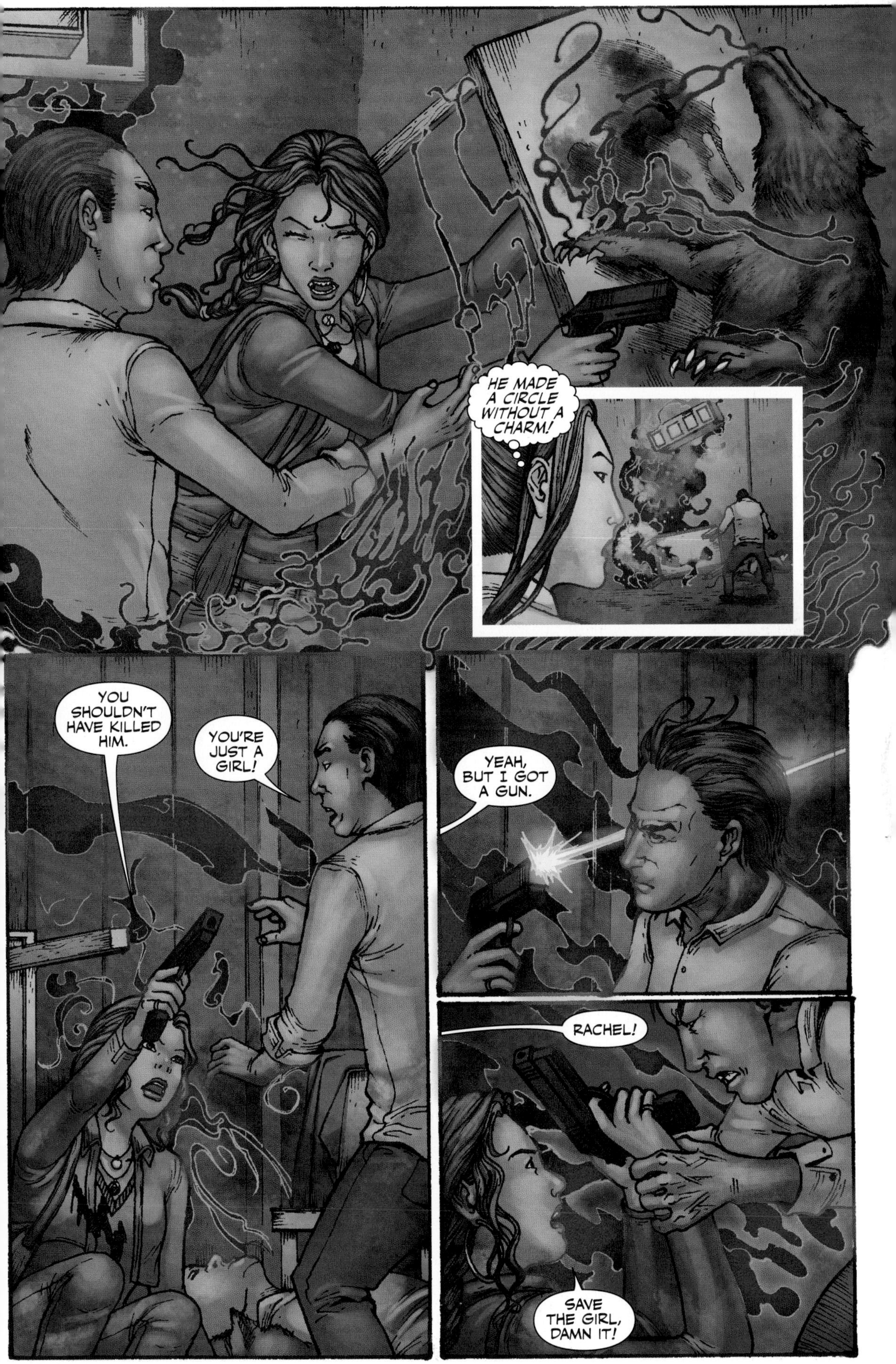
HE MADE A CIRCLE WITHOUT A CHARM!
YOU SHOULDN'T HAVE KILLED HIM.
YOU'RE JUST A GIRL!
YEAH, BUT I GOT A GUN.
RACHEL!
SAVE THE GIRL, DAMN IT!

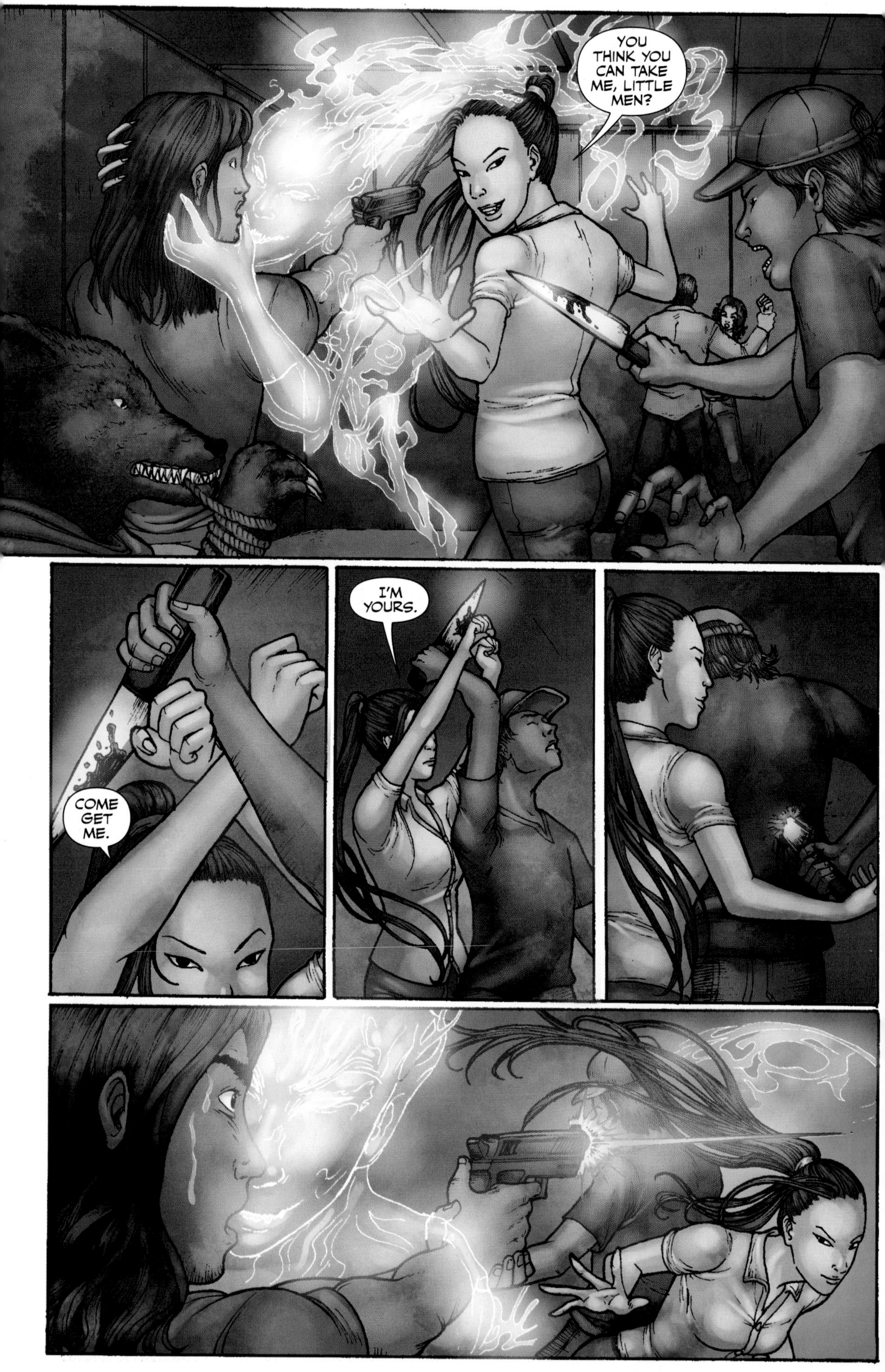
YOU THINK YOU CAN TAKE ME, LITTLE MEN?
COME GET ME.
I'M YOURS.

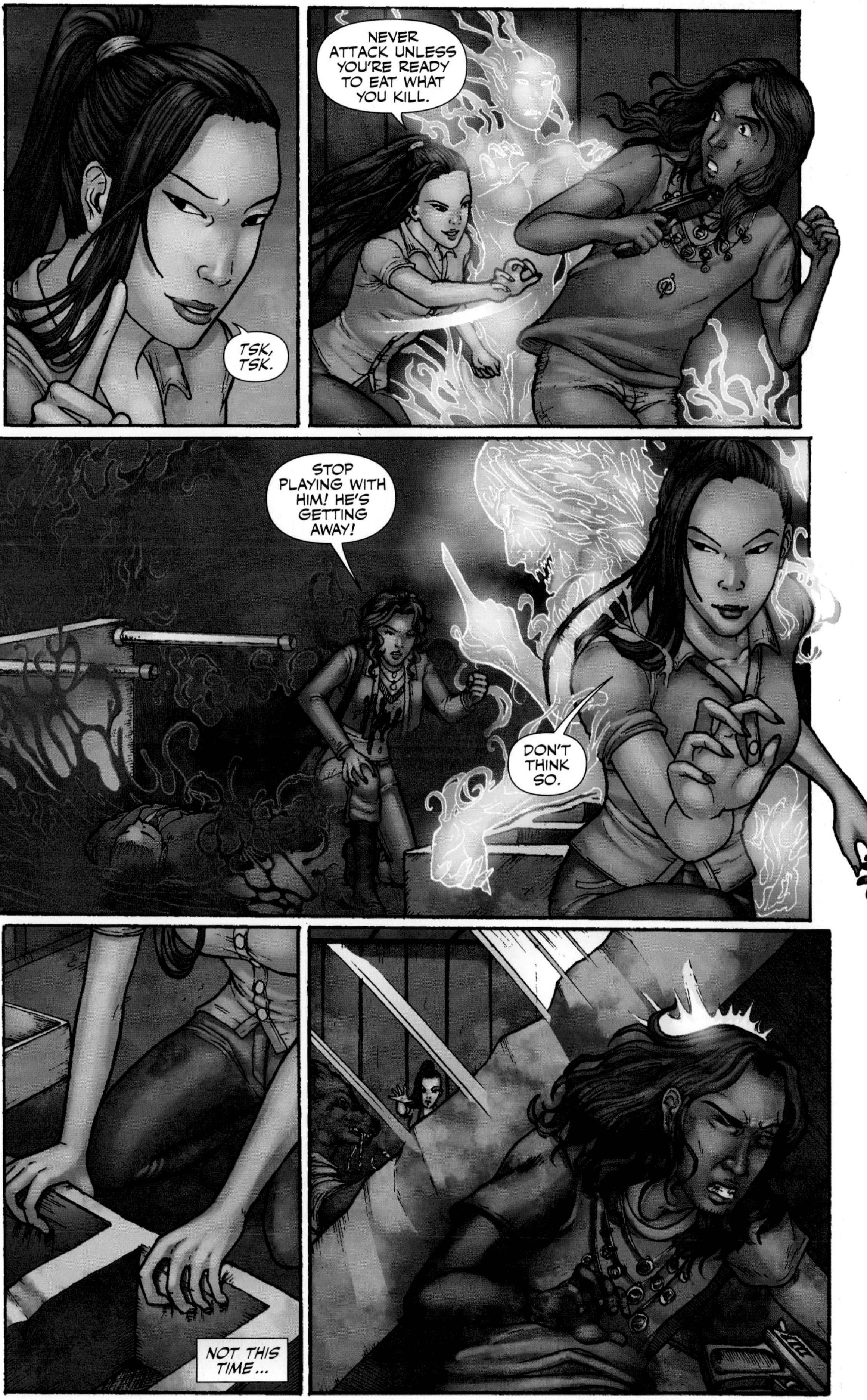
TSK, TSK.
NEVER ATTACK UNLESS YOU'RE READY TO EAT WHAT YOU KILL.
STOP PLAYING WITH HIM! HE'S GETTING AWAY!
DON'T THINK SO.
NOT THIS TIME...

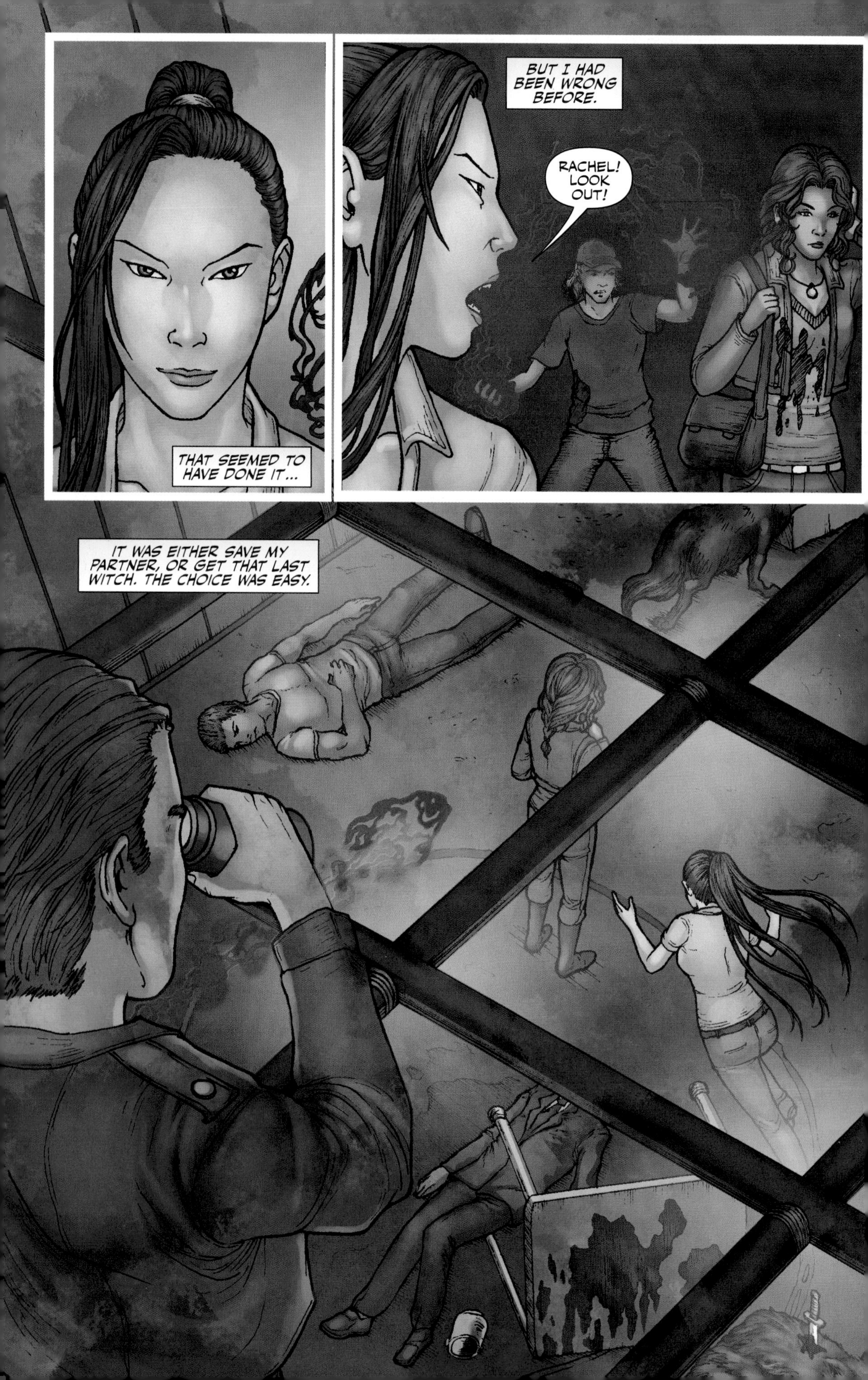
THAT SEEMED TO HAVE DONE IT...
BUT I HAD BEEN WRONG BEFORE.
RACHEL! LOOK OUT!
IT WAS EITHER SAVE MY PARTNER, OR GET THAT LAST WITCH. THE CHOICE WAS EASY.

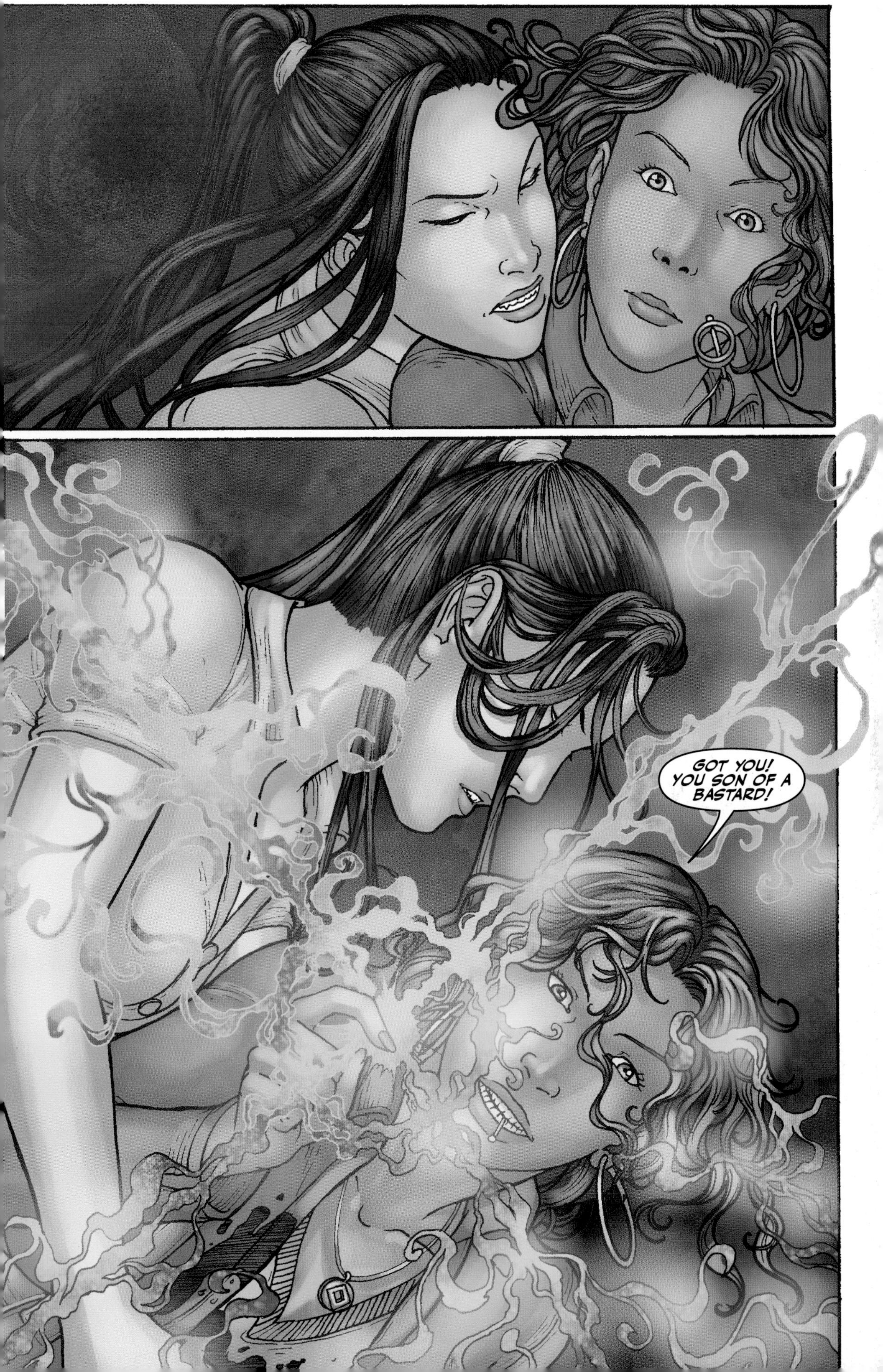
GOT YOU! YOU SON OF A BASTARD!

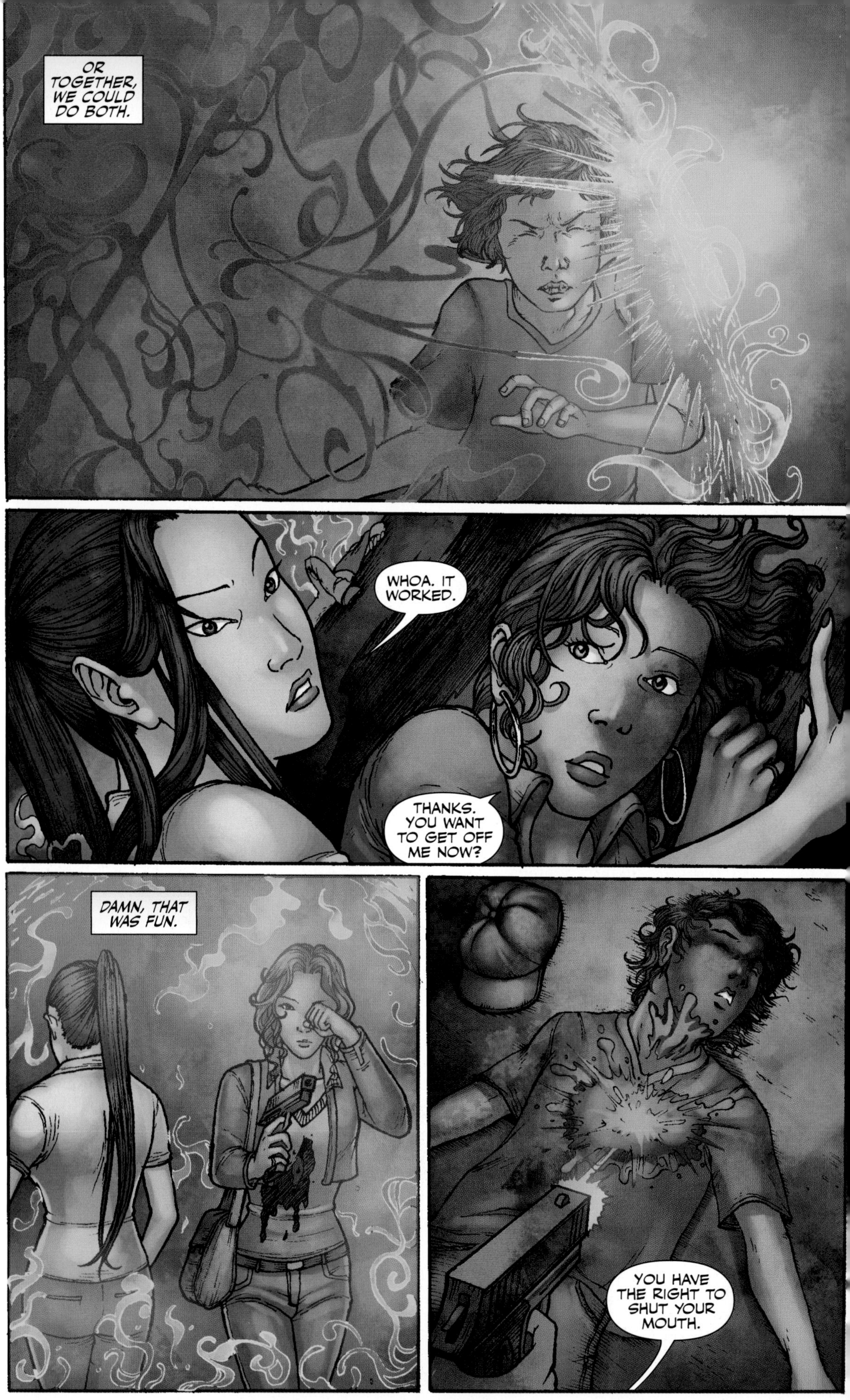
OR TOGETHER, WE COULD DO BOTH.
WHOA. IT WORKED.
THANKS. YOU WANT TO GET OFF ME NOW?
DAMN, THAT WAS FUN.
YOU HAVE THE RIGHT TO SHUT YOUR MOUTH.

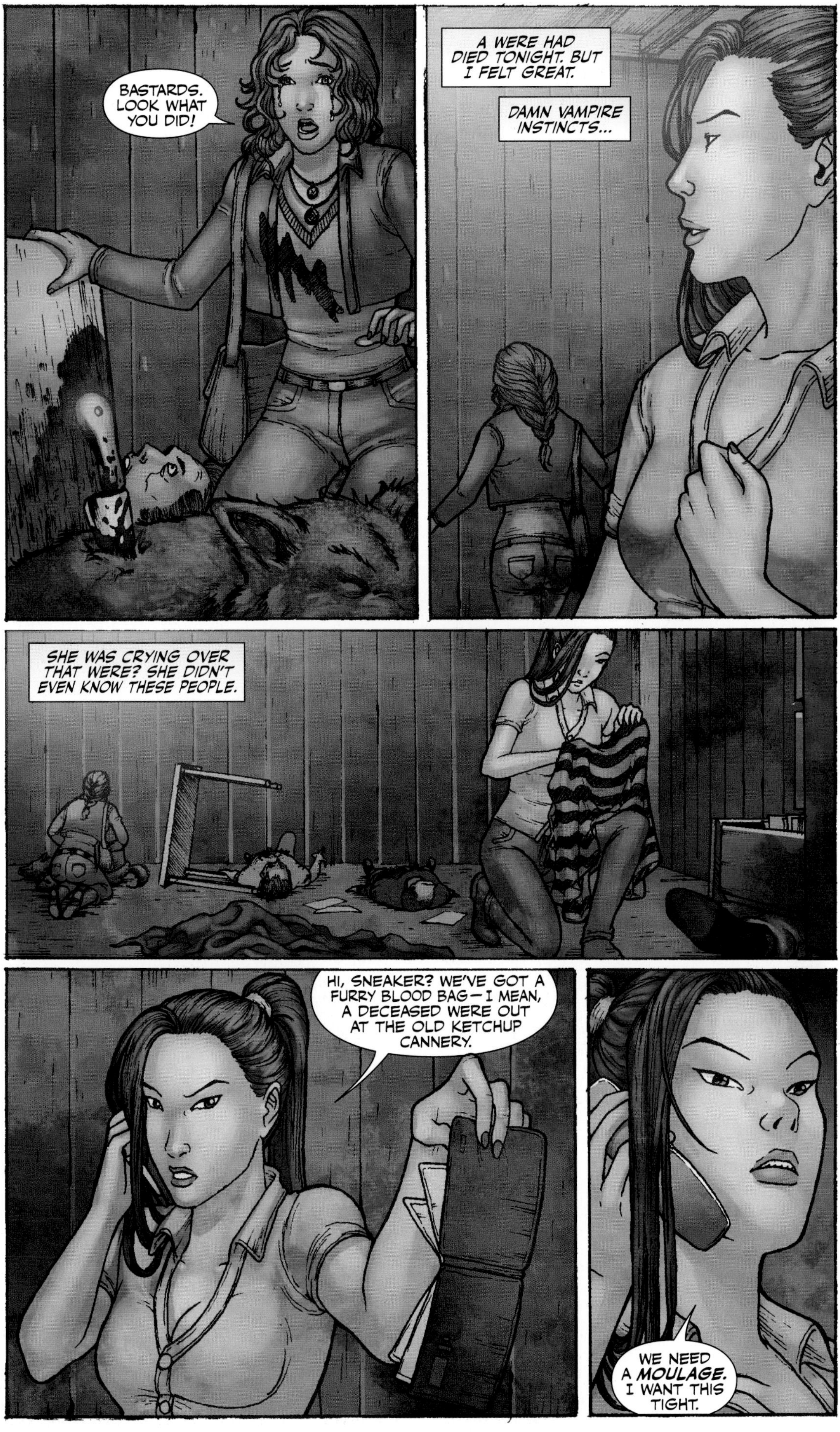
BASTARDS. LOOK WHAT YOU DID!
A WERE HAD DIED TONIGHT. BUT I FELT GREAT.
DAMN VAMPIRE INSTINCTS...
SHE WAS CRYING OVER THAT WERE? SHE DIDN'T EVEN KNOW THESE PEOPLE.
HI, SNEAKER? WE'VE GOT A FURRY BLOOD BAG—I MEAN, A DECEASED WERE OUT AT THE OLD KETCHUP CANNERY.
WE NEED A *MOULAGE.* I WANT THIS TIGHT.

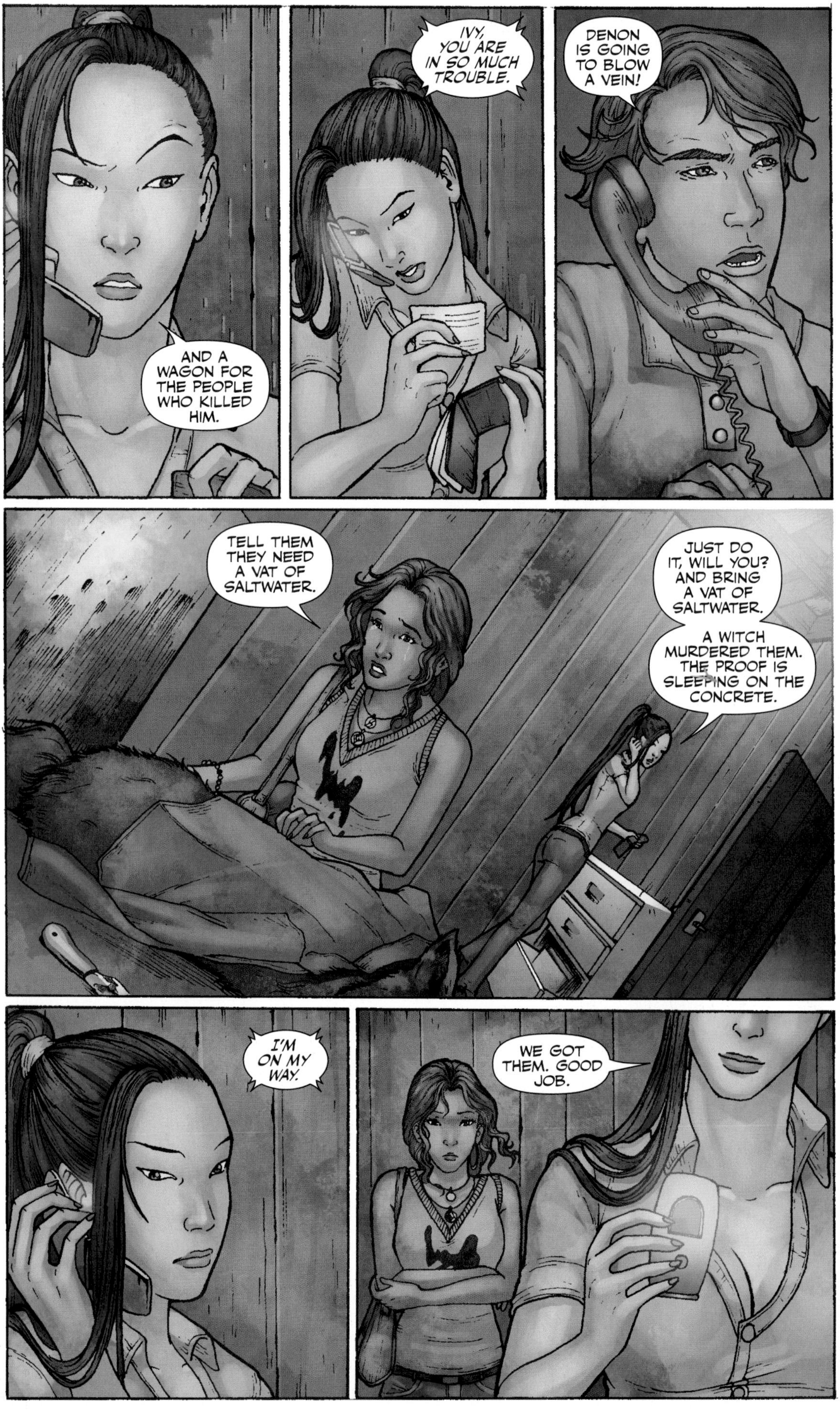
AND A WAGON FOR THE PEOPLE WHO KILLED HIM.
IVY, YOU ARE IN SO MUCH TROUBLE.
DENON IS GOING TO BLOW A VEIN!
TELL THEM THEY NEED A VAT OF SALTWATER.
JUST DO IT, WILL YOU? AND BRING A VAT OF SALTWATER.
A WITCH MURDERED THEM. THE PROOF IS SLEEPING ON THE CONCRETE.
I'M ON MY WAY.
WE GOT THEM. GOOD JOB.

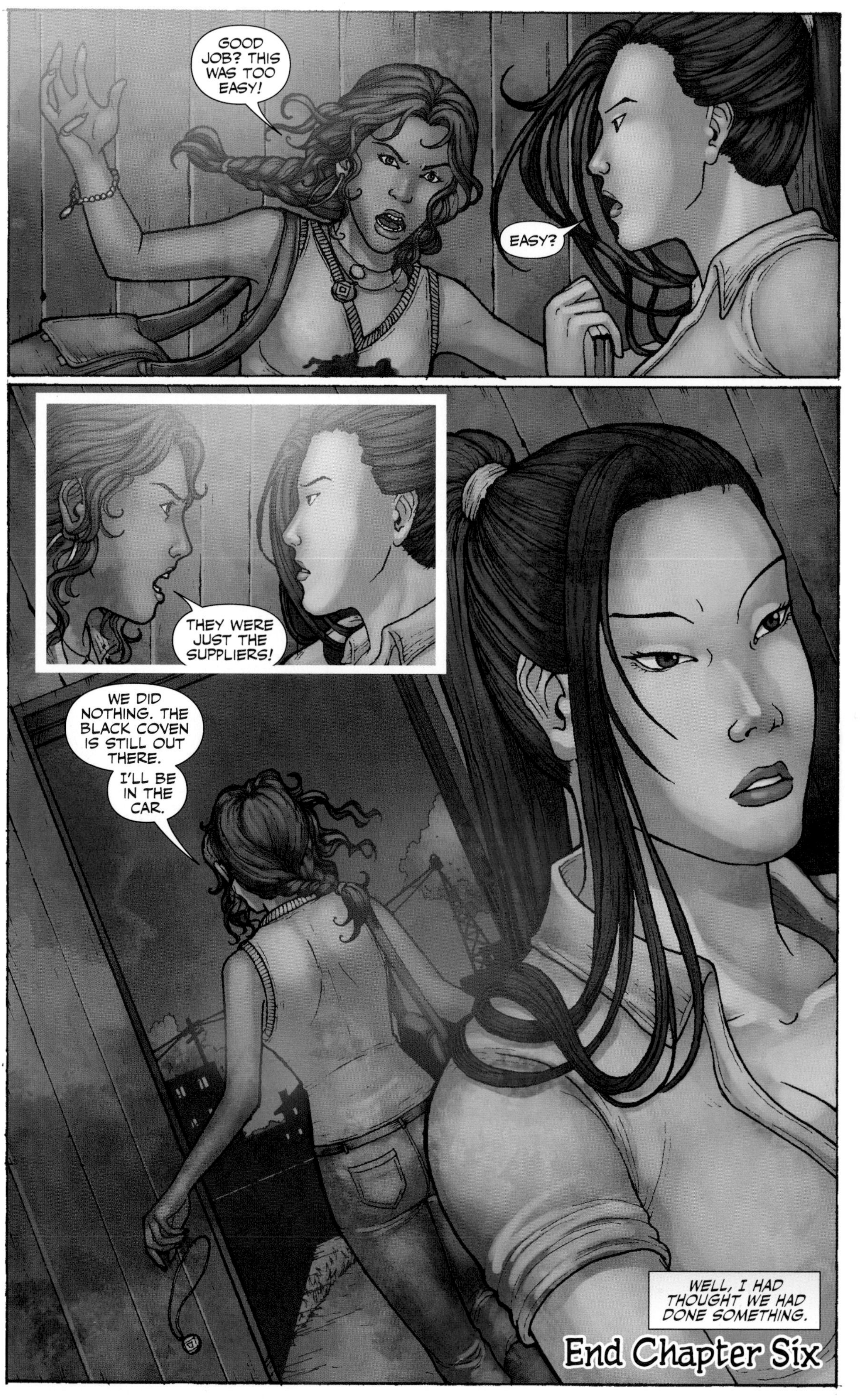
GOOD JOB? THIS WAS TOO EASY!
EASY?
THEY WERE JUST THE SUPPLIERS!
WE DID NOTHING. THE BLACK COVEN IS STILL OUT THERE.
I'LL BE IN THE CAR.
WELL, I HAD THOUGHT WE HAD DONE SOMETHING.
End Chapter Six

CHAPTER 7

WHY STILL SO TENSE? IT WASN'T A VAMPIRE WHO KILLED THEM.

I KNOW.

THEN WHAT?

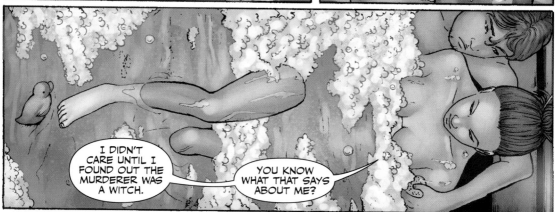

I DIDN'T CARE UNTIL I FOUND OUT THE MURDERER WAS A WITCH.

YOU KNOW WHAT THAT SAYS ABOUT ME?

WHAT?

I'M A VAMPIRE TOADY.

RACHEL IS INEPT, IMPETUOUS, AND DISORGANIZED.

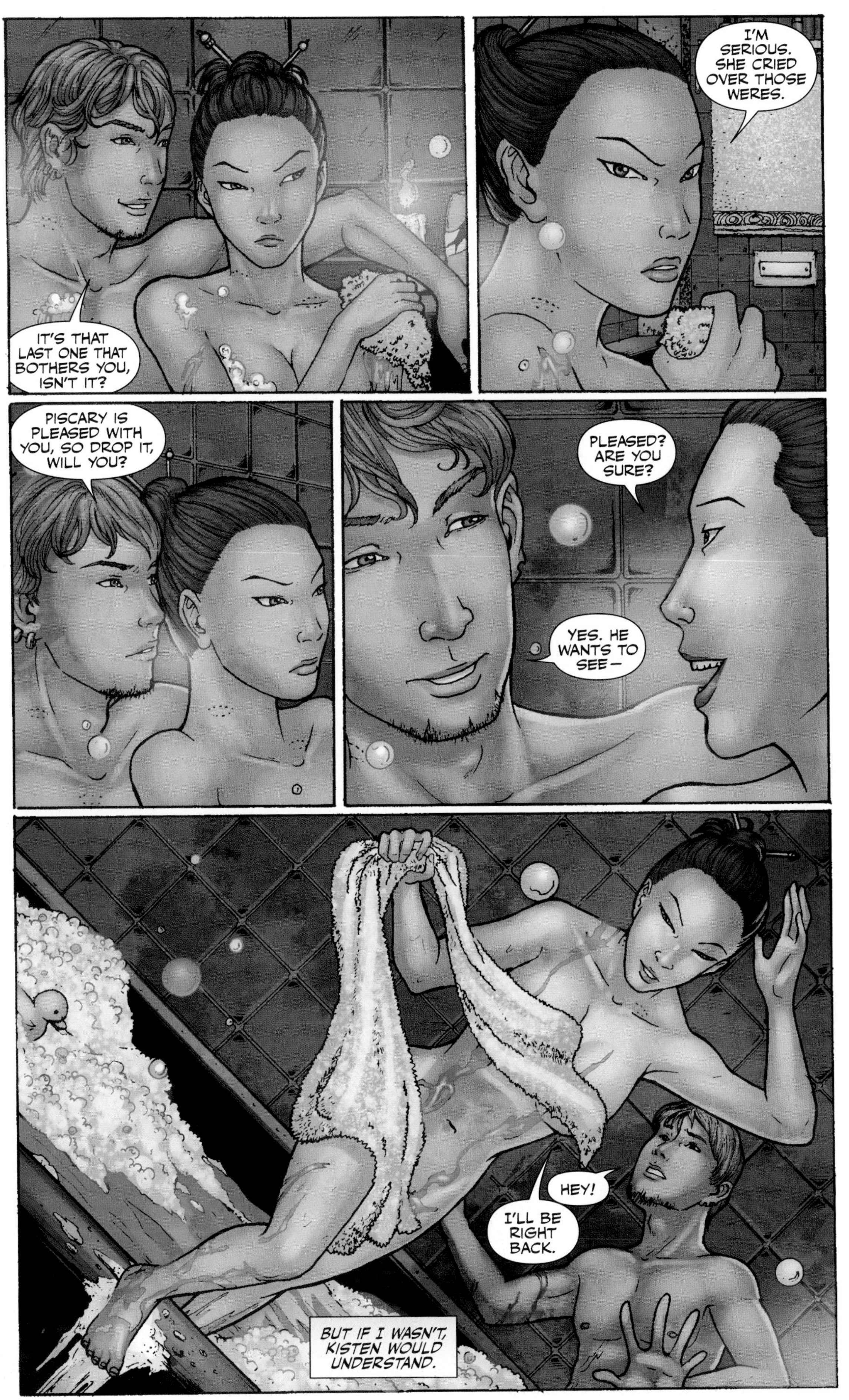
IT'S THAT LAST ONE THAT BOTHERS YOU, ISN'T IT?
I'M SERIOUS. SHE CRIED OVER THOSE WERES.
PISCARY IS PLEASED WITH YOU, SO DROP IT, WILL YOU?
PLEASED? ARE YOU SURE?
YES. HE WANTS TO SEE—
HEY!
I'LL BE RIGHT BACK.
BUT IF I WASN'T, KISTEN WOULD UNDERSTAND.

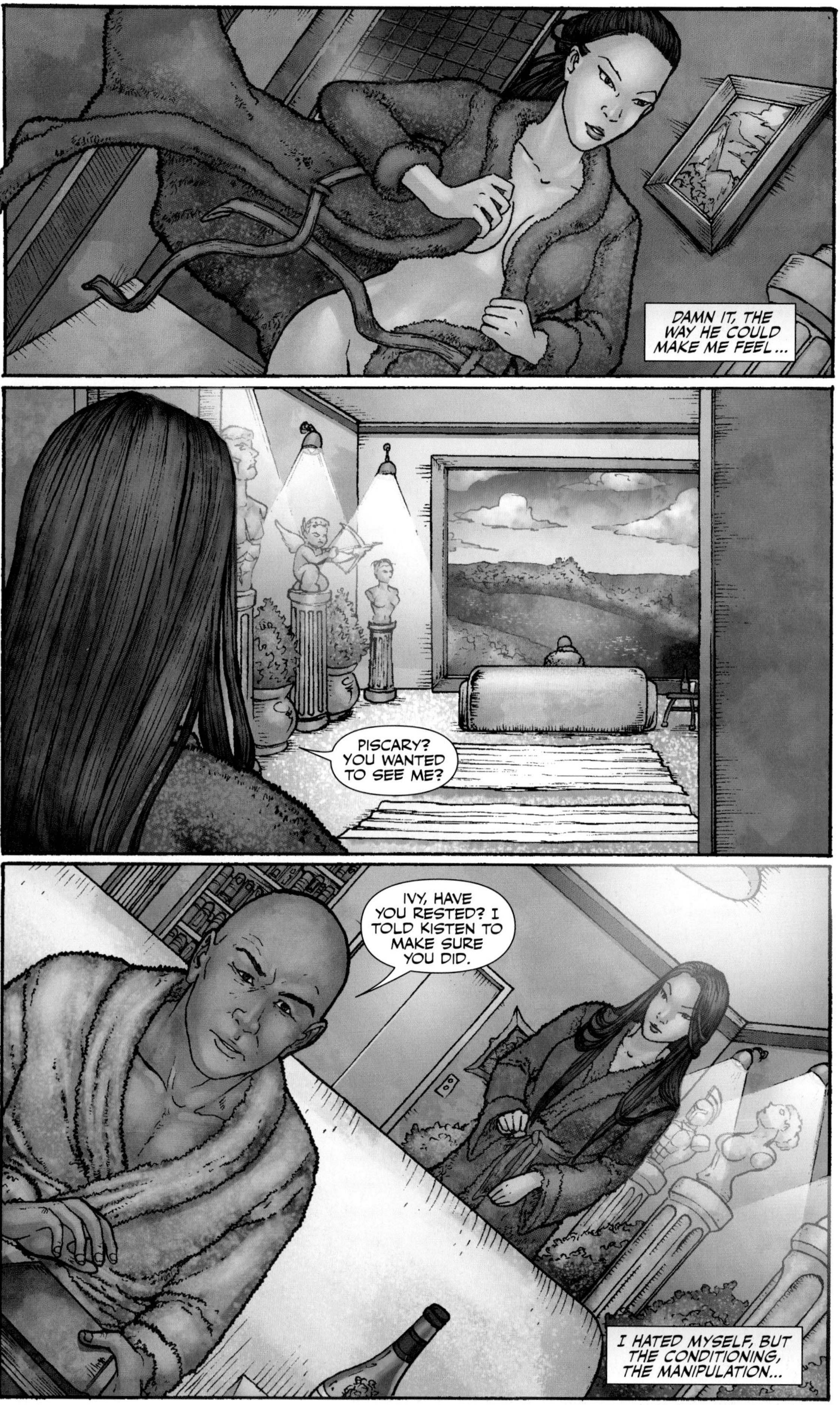
DAMN IT, THE WAY HE COULD MAKE ME FEEL...
PISCARY? YOU WANTED TO SEE ME?
IVY, HAVE YOU RESTED? I TOLD KISTEN TO MAKE SURE YOU DID.
I HATED MYSELF, BUT THE CONDITIONING, THE MANIPULATION...

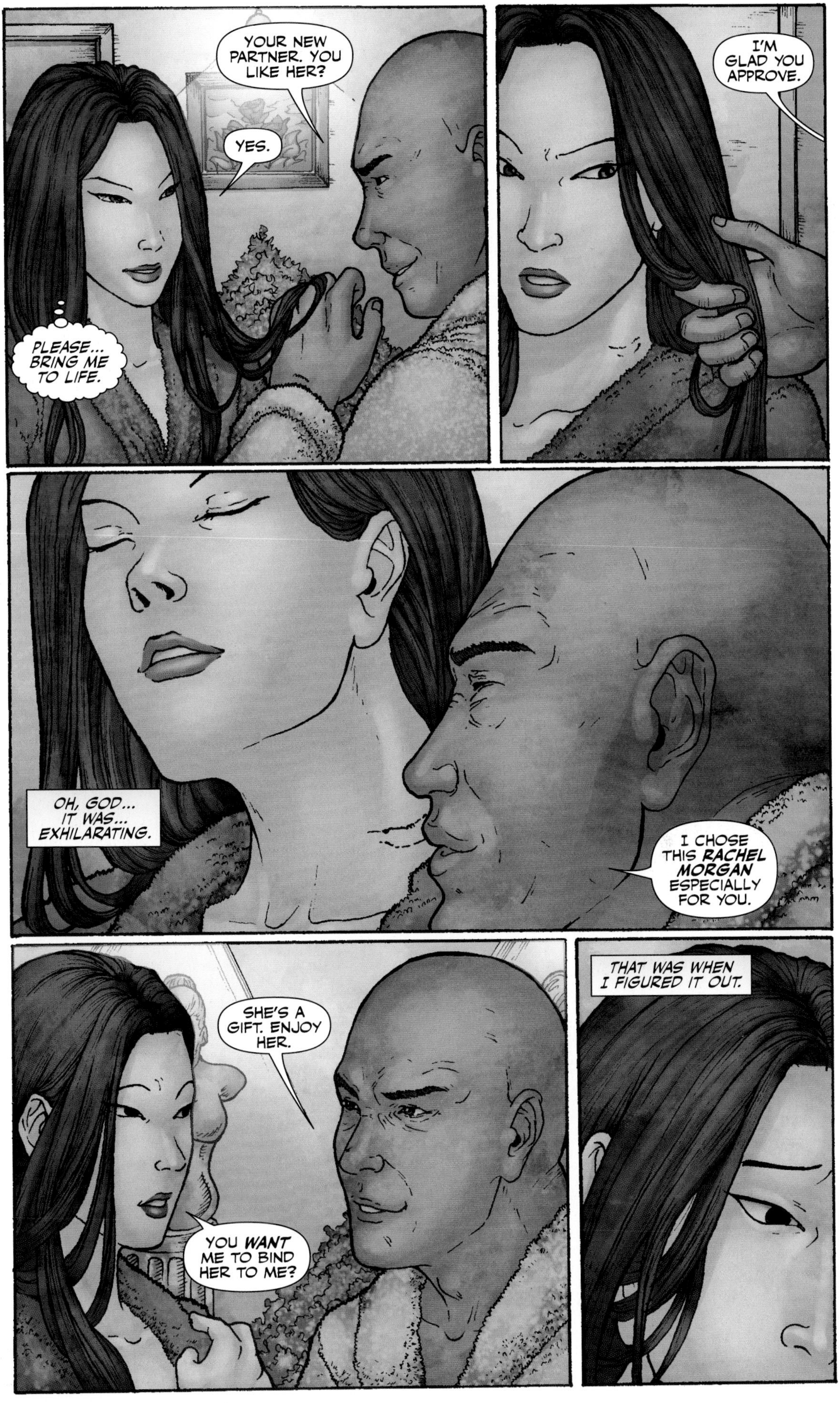
YOUR NEW PARTNER. YOU LIKE HER?
YES.
PLEASE... BRING ME TO LIFE.
I'M GLAD YOU APPROVE.
OH, GOD... IT WAS... EXHILARATING.
I CHOSE THIS **RACHEL MORGAN** ESPECIALLY FOR YOU.
SHE'S A GIFT. ENJOY HER.
YOU **WANT** ME TO BIND HER TO ME?
THAT WAS WHEN I FIGURED IT OUT.

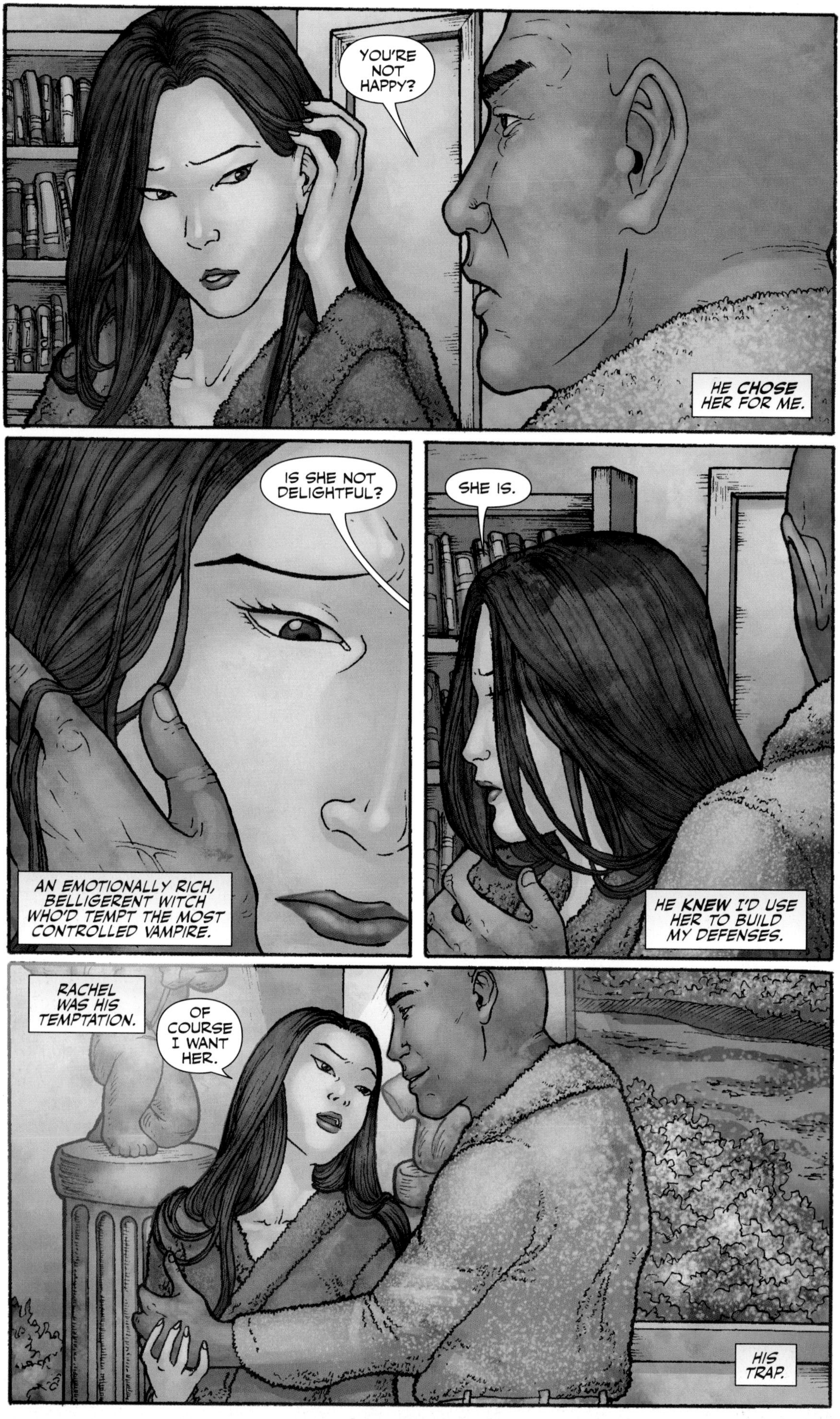
YOU'RE NOT HAPPY?
HE CHOSE HER FOR ME.
IS SHE NOT DELIGHTFUL?
AN EMOTIONALLY RICH, BELLIGERENT WITCH WHO'D TEMPT THE MOST CONTROLLED VAMPIRE.
SHE IS.
HE KNEW I'D USE HER TO BUILD MY DEFENSES.
RACHEL WAS HIS TEMPTATION.
OF COURSE I WANT HER.
HIS TRAP.

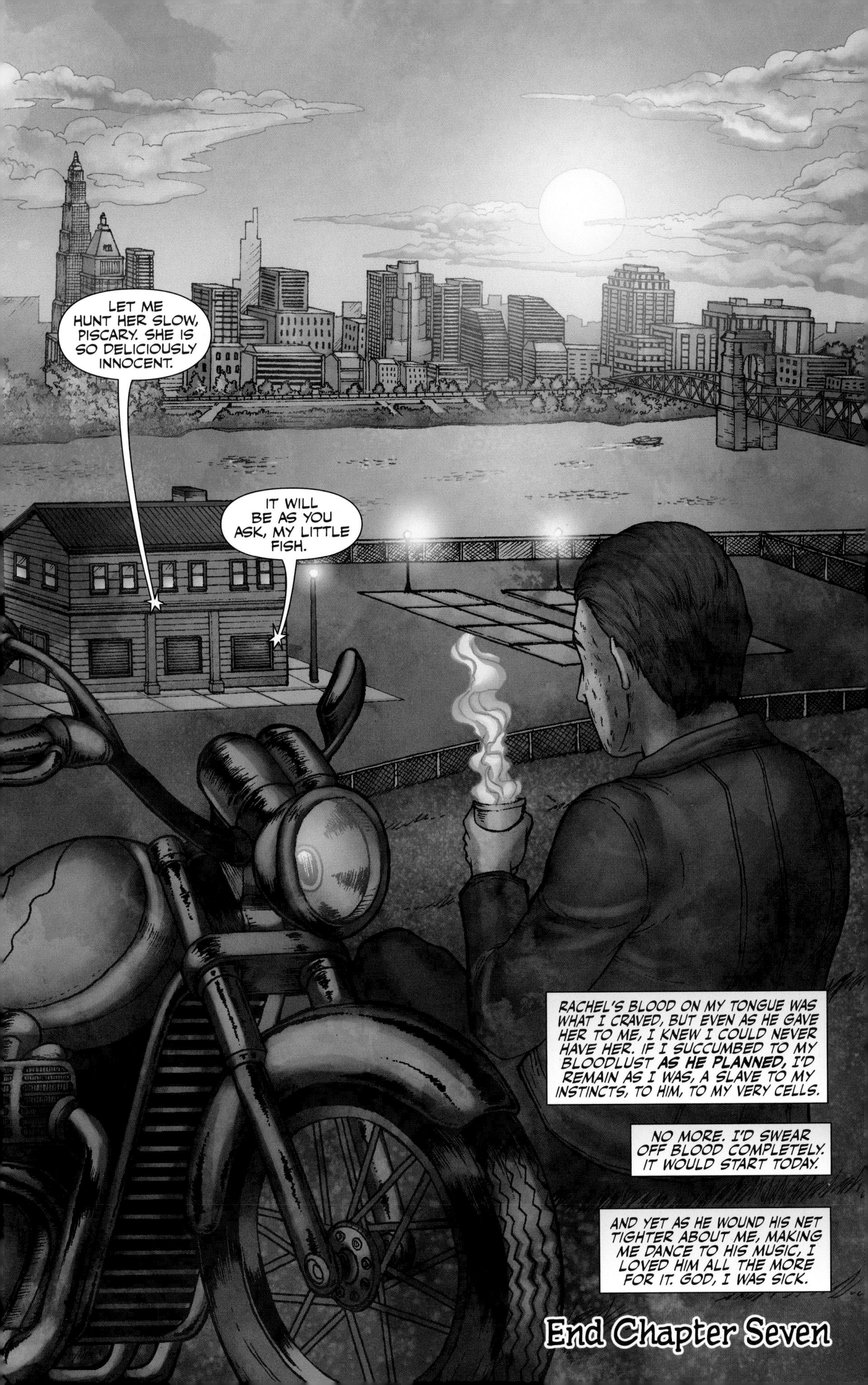
LET ME HUNT HER SLOW, PISCARY. SHE IS SO DELICIOUSLY INNOCENT.
IT WILL BE AS YOU ASK, MY LITTLE FISH.
RACHEL'S BLOOD ON MY TONGUE WAS WHAT I CRAVED, BUT EVEN AS HE GAVE HER TO ME, I KNEW I COULD NEVER HAVE HER. IF I SUCCUMBED TO MY BLOODLUST AS HE PLANNED, I'D REMAIN AS I WAS, A SLAVE TO MY INSTINCTS, TO HIM, TO MY VERY CELLS.
NO MORE. I'D SWEAR OFF BLOOD COMPLETELY. IT WOULD START TODAY.
AND YET AS HE WOUND HIS NET TIGHTER ABOUT ME, MAKING ME DANCE TO HIS MUSIC, I LOVED HIM ALL THE MORE FOR IT. GOD, I WAS SICK.
End Chapter Seven

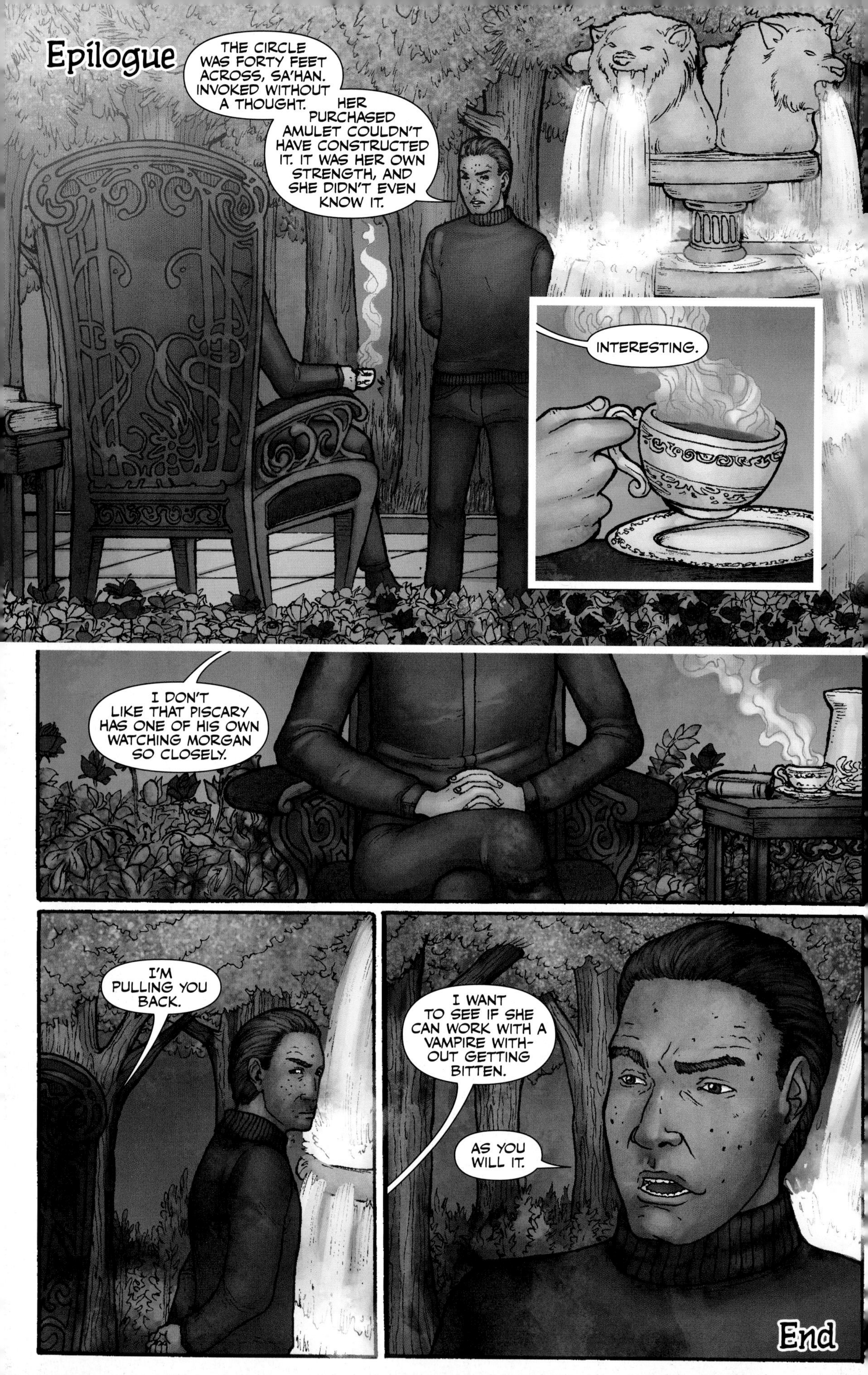
Epilogue
THE CIRCLE WAS FORTY FEET ACROSS, SA'HAN. INVOKED WITHOUT A THOUGHT.
HER PURCHASED AMULET COULDN'T HAVE CONSTRUCTED IT. IT WAS HER OWN STRENGTH, AND SHE DIDN'T EVEN KNOW IT.
INTERESTING.
I DON'T LIKE THAT PISCARY HAS ONE OF HIS OWN WATCHING MORGAN SO CLOSELY.
I'M PULLING YOU BACK.
I WANT TO SEE IF SHE CAN WORK WITH A VAMPIRE WITH-OUT GETTING BITTEN.
AS YOU WILL IT.
End

About The Creators

KIM HARRISON was born and raised in the upper Midwest. Between working on the Hollows series starring witch Rachel Morgan and living vampire Ivy Tamwood, she is writing a young adult series starring Madison Avery. She is a member of both the Romance Writers of America and the Science Fiction and Fantasy Writers of America. When not at her desk, she is most likely to be found chasing down good chocolate, exquisite sushi, or the ultimate dog chew. (For her dog.) Her bestselling novels include *Dead Witch Walking; The Good, the Bad, and the Undead; Pale Demon*; and many more.

Penciller **PEDRO MAIA** was born in 1986 and does not remember a day where drawing wasn't something important to do. He started to work with comics while still in college and is now a full-time artist. He lives in Rio de Janeiro. Penciller **GEMMA MAGNO** grew up at Morong, Rizal, Philippines. She was inspired to draw by watching anime and reading manga, and she received a Presidential Award as Artist of the Year after winning several art competitions. Inker **EMAN CASALLOS** is a native of Cavite, Philippines, who has worked on trading cards for companies such as Dynamite Entertainment. He is working on his first comics project, *Dream Police*. Inker **JAN MICHAEL T. ALDEGUER** has worked as an illustrator, designer, and comics scriptwriter for more than twelve years. He is from Manila, Philippines. Inker **JEZREEL ROJALES** lives in Antipolo, Rizal, Philippines. He studied fine arts at the University of the Philippines and has worked on various manga projects. Colorist **P. C. SIQUEIRA** was born and still lives in São Paolo, Brazil. He has worked on *Battlestar Galactica* and other projects. Colorist **MAE HAO** was born in the Philippines and has assisted in projects published by Marvel, Dark Horse, and other publishers.

Artist's Sketchbook

Penciller Pedro Maia's first task was to create character sketches that matched up—as much as possible—with the visions that Kim was seeking of her characters. Some came easily; Pedro's first drawings of Rachel and Denon were approved immediately. Others—Ivy, Piscary, and Kisten—went through several drafts. Here are examples of some of the descriptions Kim provided to Pedro and the drawings he submitted for approval.

RACHEL

PHYSICAL DESCRIPTION

Rachel is in her early twenties, about five eight, with a wild-Irish look about her. Her hair is red and curly, to the point of annoyance. It falls to her shoulders, and she braids it in one center braid when working. If it's free, she's constantly tucking it back. It never falls between her eyes. She has an amulet about the size of a wooden nickel to help tame it. Rachel has freckles, but she charms them into invisibility, so her complexion is generally very even and white. Her face is longer with a pointy chin, but still very feminine. Strong jaw line. She has narrow hips and a somewhat flat chest. A sinewy build, athletic.

Her eyes are green and widely spaced. Her nose turns up a bit at the end, and her lips are more full than Ivy's, but she doesn't look like she's taking Botox. Her eyebrows are fuller than Ivy's as well, and expressive. Her lips are her biggest tell of emotion. No tattoos. Rachel usually wears soft makeup and pays attention to her nails, keeping them cut close but painted.

MENTAL DESCRIPTION

If you're familiar with the Meyers-Briggs personality test, Rachel is an ENFP: friendly, imaginative, messy, eager to help solve problems, and sometimes makes serious errors in judgment even though she is very intuitive.

Rachel is a St. George out to kill every dragon in the shape of a bully. She usually has a cheerful outlook and wants to be taken seriously, but doesn't quite get it. Her emotions are usually curiosity, determination, belligerence, anger, laughter, and an easygoing relaxation. Her lips and body stance are her main telegraphers of mood.

TYPICAL CLOTHES

Rachel often dresses inappropriately so she can wear a new outfit. Short skirts, chemises, jeans, and bright tees, colorful hats and accessories upon occasion. She wears heels as well as boots, keeping to a low heel while on a job. Rachel likes leather, but it's of a lower quality than Ivy's and lacks the sophisticated feel. Rachel does have a short red leather jacket that she loves to wear. Rachel isn't a girly girl, but she likes her color, and her outfits reflect this.

Rachel has a wooden pinky ring on her right hand to hide her freckles, and big hoop earrings. She might wear a necklace, scarf, or flashy belt if the occasion allows. Her purse is a large fabric shoulder bag that more often than not clashes with her clothes.

RACHEL INITIAL SKETCHES

Approved without changes

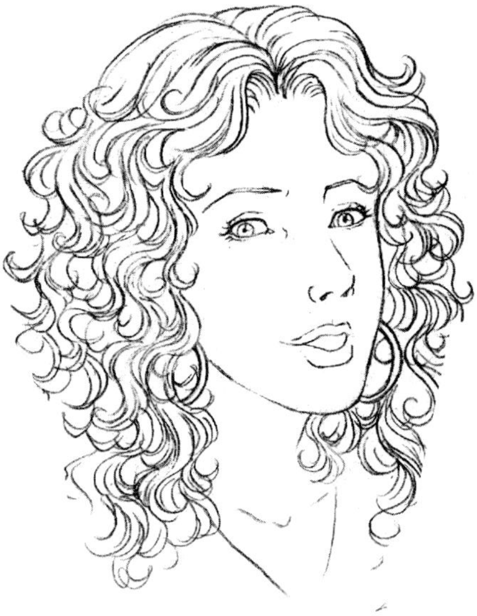

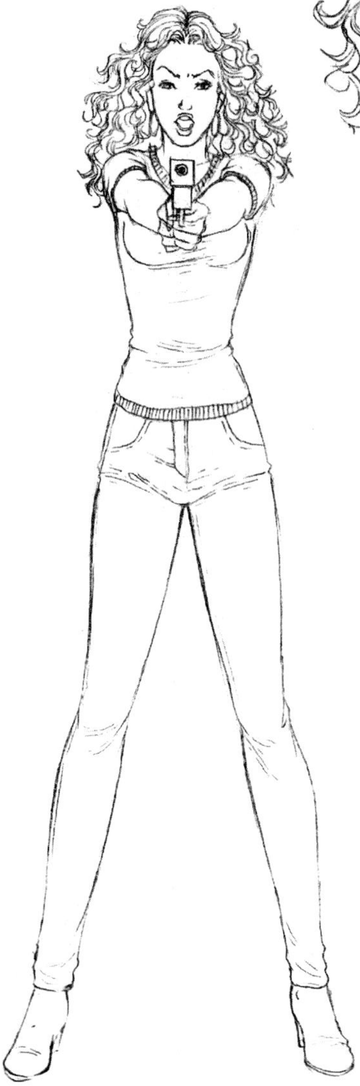

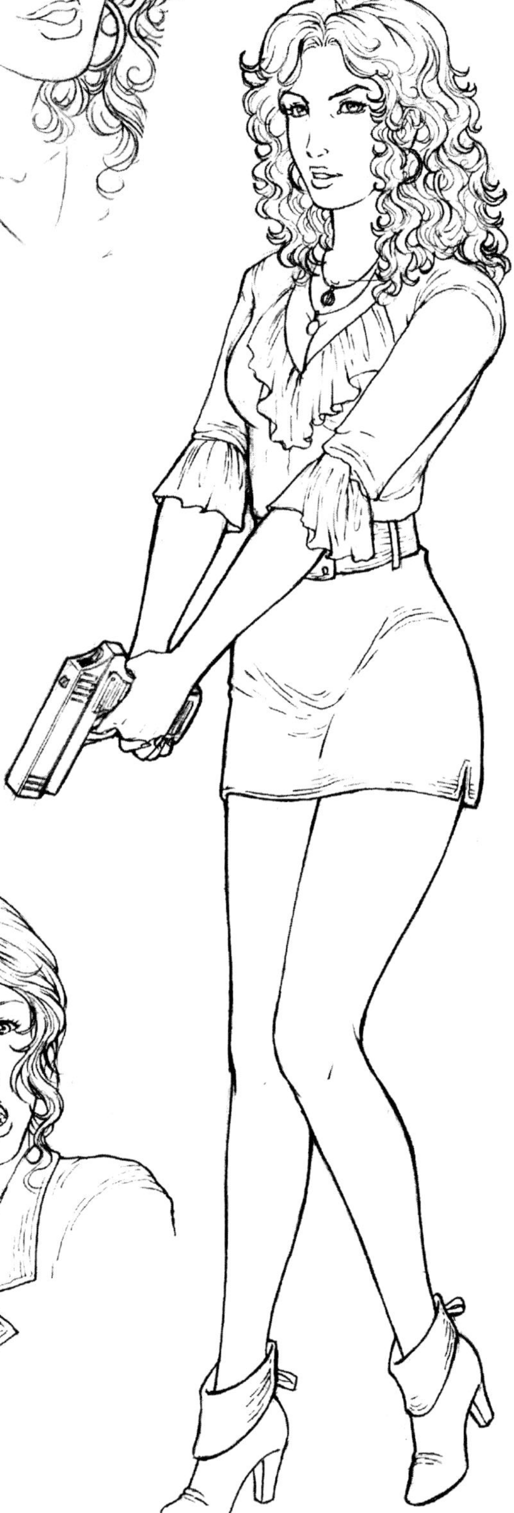

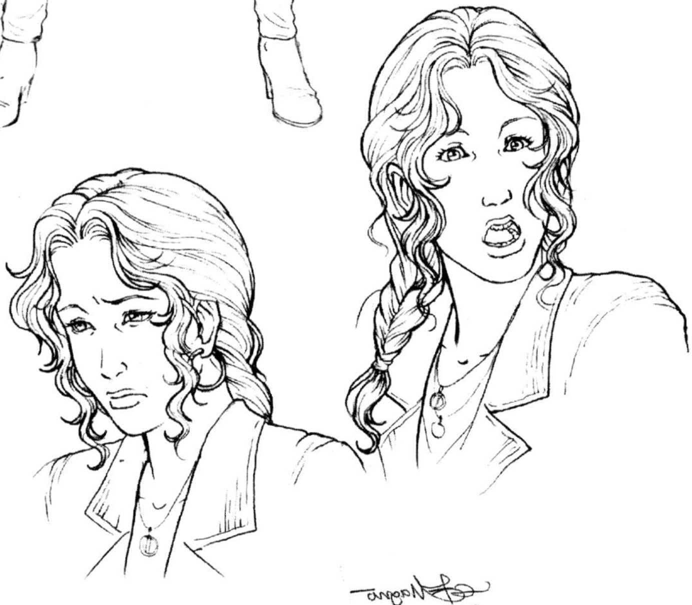

IVY

Ivy is in her early twenties, a shade under six feet tall, with a slight Asian cast to her features. Her body type is athletic and lithe without sacrificing curves. Her hair is black and very straight. It falls to her waist and is back in a ponytail most times, especially when she's working. When her hair is free, she is either relaxing or letting a vulnerable part of her psyche show. She has a long neck with one bite scar at the base on the right. It's not obvious. Her face is oval and she has a strong jaw line. Her teeth are well shaped, with the canines being more pointed than a human's and sharp. They are not especially long, just pointed. Her fingers are long and delicate.

Her eyes are brown and have a slight almond shape, but not markedly so. She has a small nose, not turned up. Thin eyebrows. Her skin is pale, with no tattoos. Ivy seldom wears makeup or nail polish.

Blood lust (vamping out) is usually accompanied by the pupils widening until her irises appear completely black and her lips pulling back to show her teeth. I'd also like to see how successful it might be to show Ivy vamping out by playing with her aura, perhaps having it show up like a second shadow that functions apart from her real one. It can touch, caress, and throttle the person triggering her blood lust. This shadow/aura is a direct expression of Ivy's id, visible to the reader when Ivy loses control of her vampire instincts. The more she loses control, the more lifelike definition the shadow has.

MENTAL DESCRIPTION

If you're familiar with the Meyers-Briggs personality test, Ivy is an ISTJ: conservative, realistic, logical, hardworking, resistant to change, and she likes organization and routine to the point of obsession. She's a rebel but can't fight, a slave to her instincts and upbringing. Jaded. Her emotions reflect this, and she usually has a stoic outlook. Her sexual orientation is bi, and she is comfortable with that.

Her typical emotional expressions are dry humor, tired acceptance, annoyance, blood lust, savage desire, anger, and on occasion, surprise. Her eyebrows are her biggest tell of her emotion.

TYPICAL CLOTHES

Ivy comes from a wealthy family, and her clothes reflect this. She dresses conservatively for a living vampire. She wears two delicate anklets of a black metal that are thin enough to wear under her boots—one on each ankle. She has a belly-button ring with a red stone, and she wears a crucifix, but otherwise, no jewelry. Ivy likes leather, but it's always tasteful and sophisticated. Her boots are functional, with a low heel. She generally wears clothes that cover the scars she received from Piscary's attentions, apart from the one on her neck.

IVY INITIAL SKETCHES

Kim's comment: Ivy needs a lot of work, but I think that making her hair black and her chest smaller to show off her athletic grace would do most of it. Her nose is thinner, smaller, and more narrow than Pedro has in most of the examples here, and she's still lacking the Asian feel that the readers will be expecting. Her clothing, also, will be dark colors, never light. A good example of Ivy might be Lucy Liu.

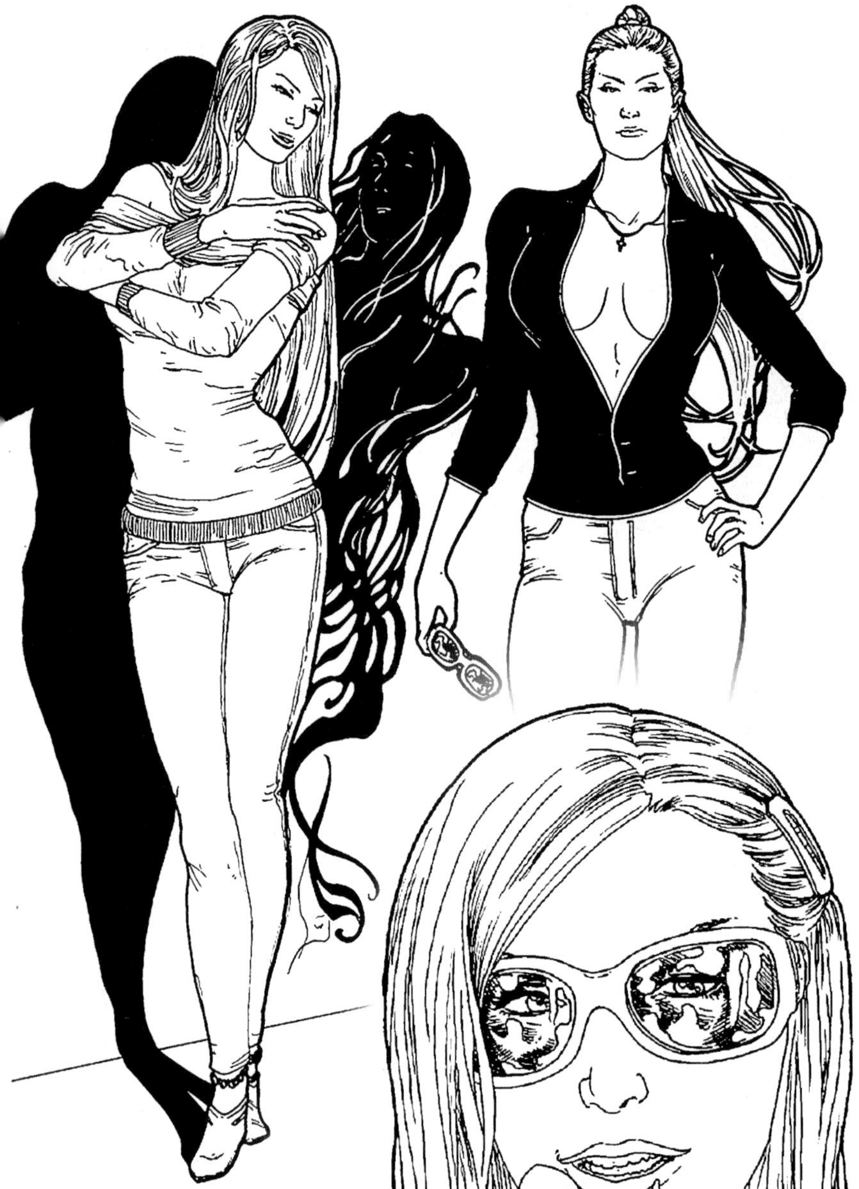

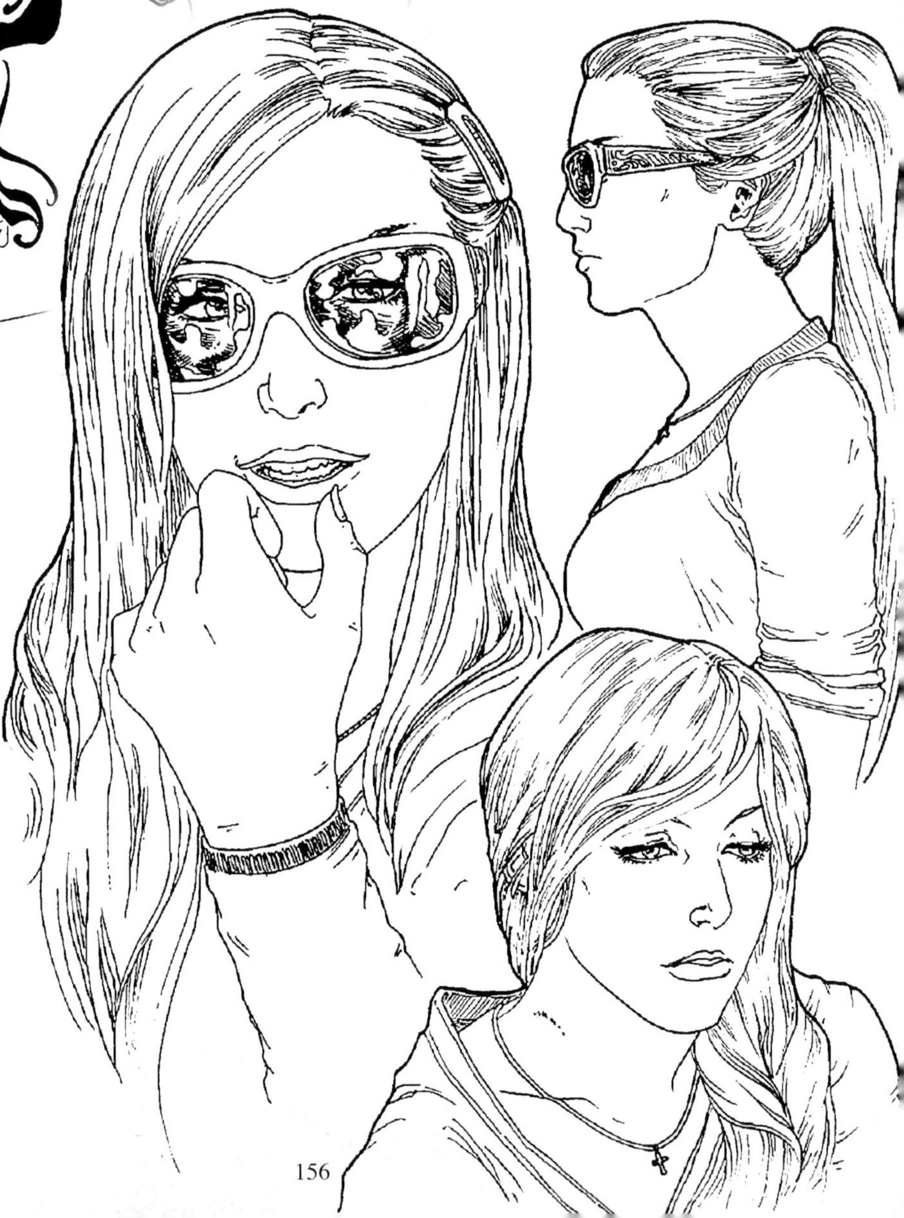

IVY REVISED

Making Ivy's hair black would be handled by the colorist.

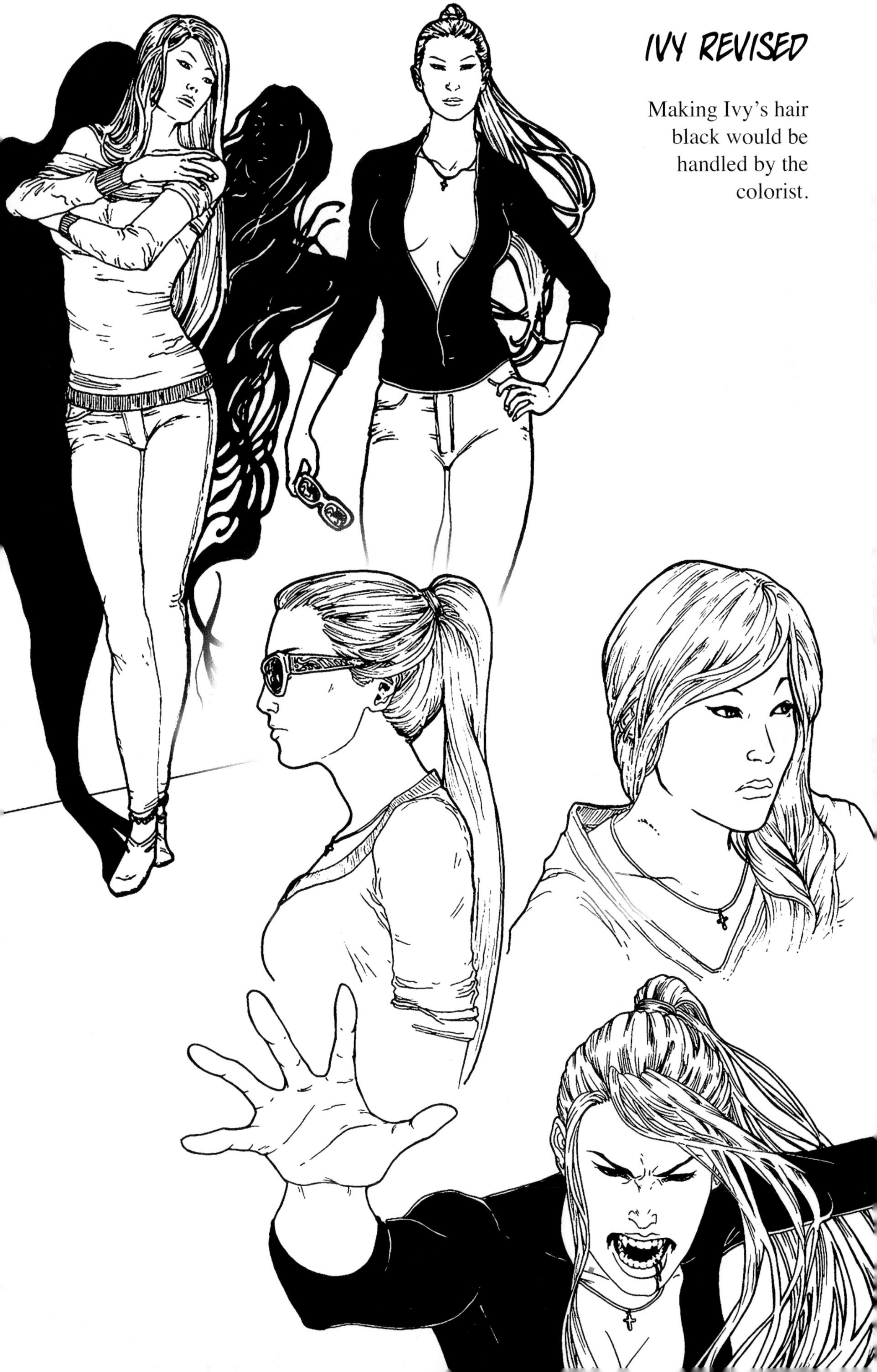

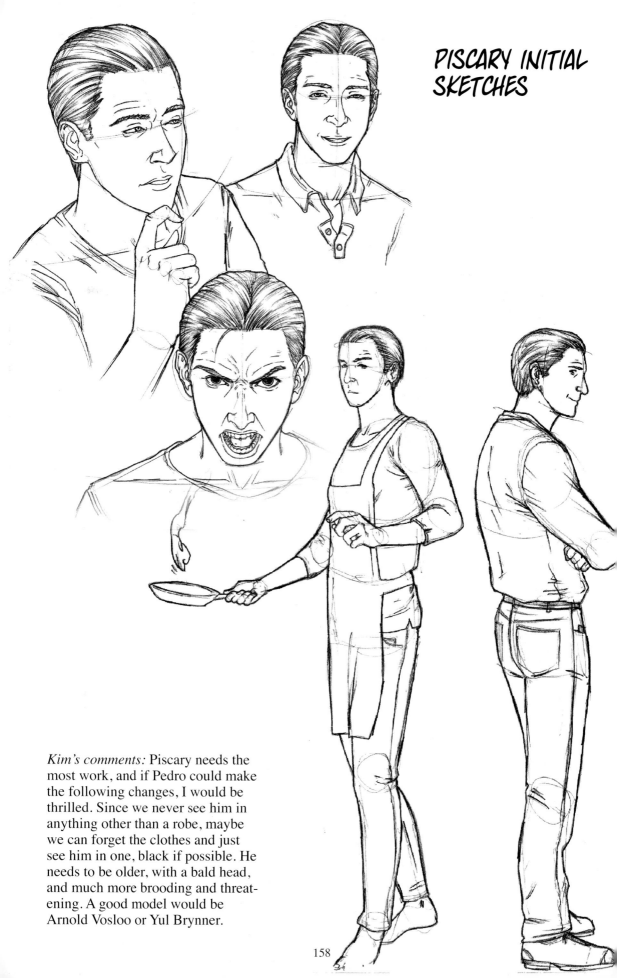

PISCARY INITIAL SKETCHES

Kim's comments: Piscary needs the most work, and if Pedro could make the following changes, I would be thrilled. Since we never see him in anything other than a robe, maybe we can forget the clothes and just see him in one, black if possible. He needs to be older, with a bald head, and much more brooding and threatening. A good model would be Arnold Vosloo or Yul Brynner.

PISCARY REVISED

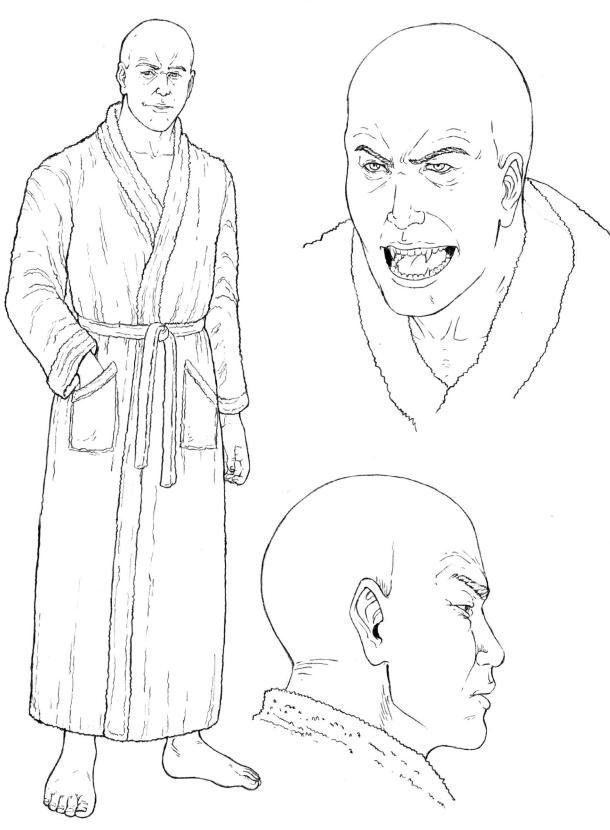

KISTEN INITIAL SKETCHES

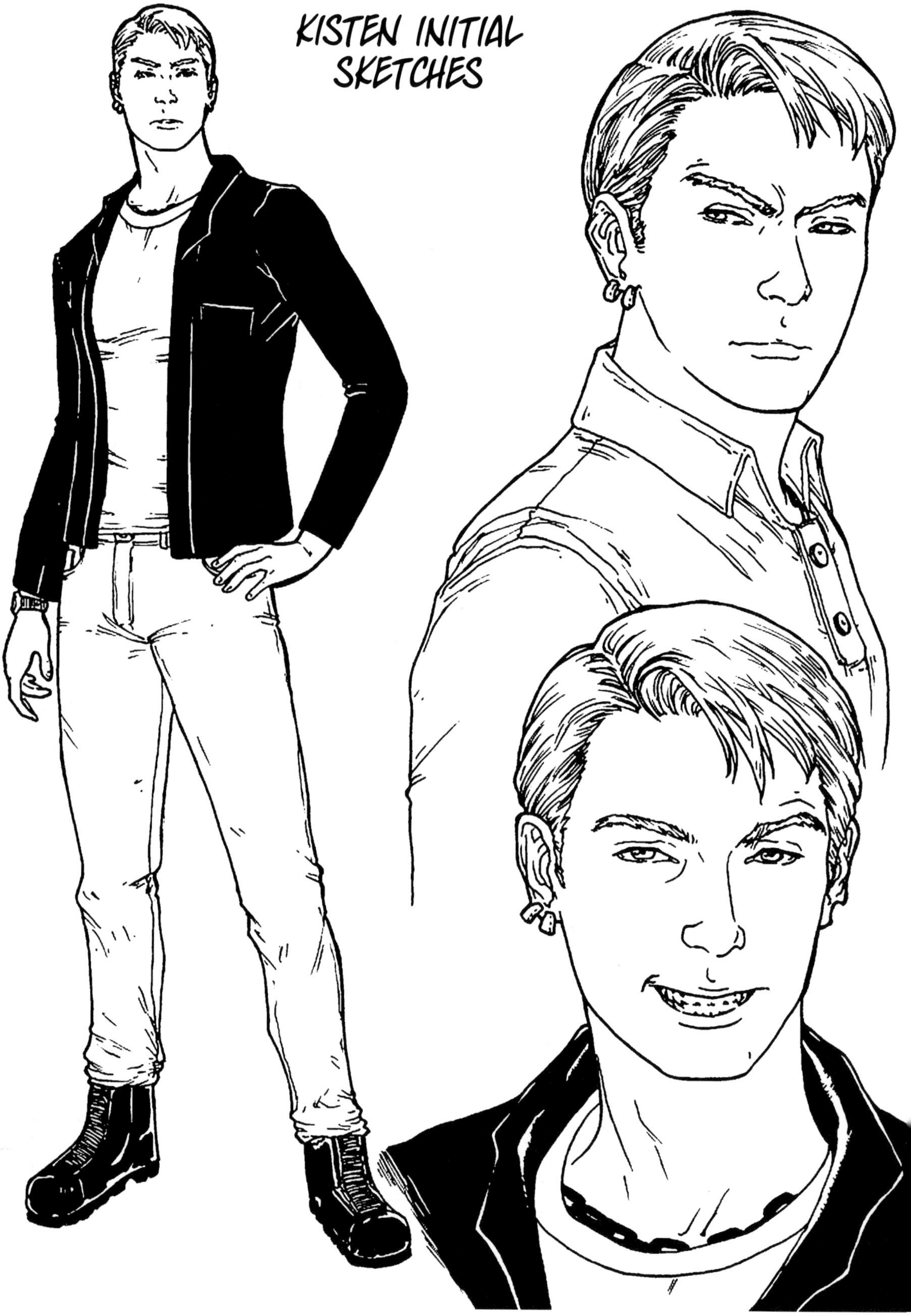

Kim's comments: Kisten looks great, but to bring out his studliness, he needs a faint beard stubble to "guy" him up. The black gold chain is excellent, but it should be a finer chain, just this side of girly. Kisten wouldn't be caught dead in a polo shirt, but a regular button-down shirt works. In the full-length shot, his chin needs to be more narrow, but I like the close-ups. Kisten is egotistical, but a nice guy. He's really close, but something in his eye is not quite there.

KISTEN REVISED

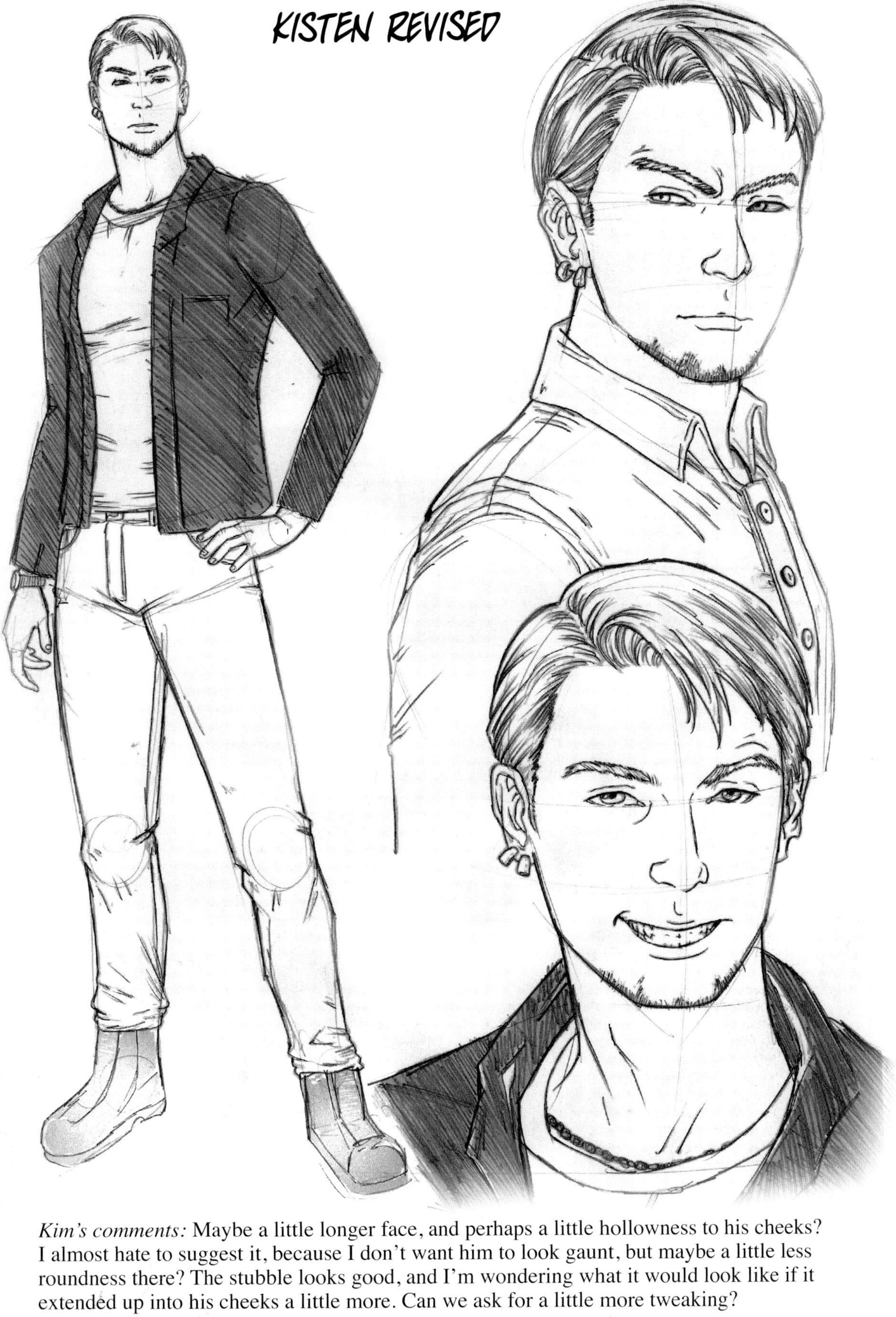

Kim's comments: Maybe a little longer face, and perhaps a little hollowness to his cheeks? I almost hate to suggest it, because I don't want him to look gaunt, but maybe a little less roundness there? The stubble looks good, and I'm wondering what it would look like if it extended up into his cheeks a little more. Can we ask for a little more tweaking?

The final version appears throughout the book.

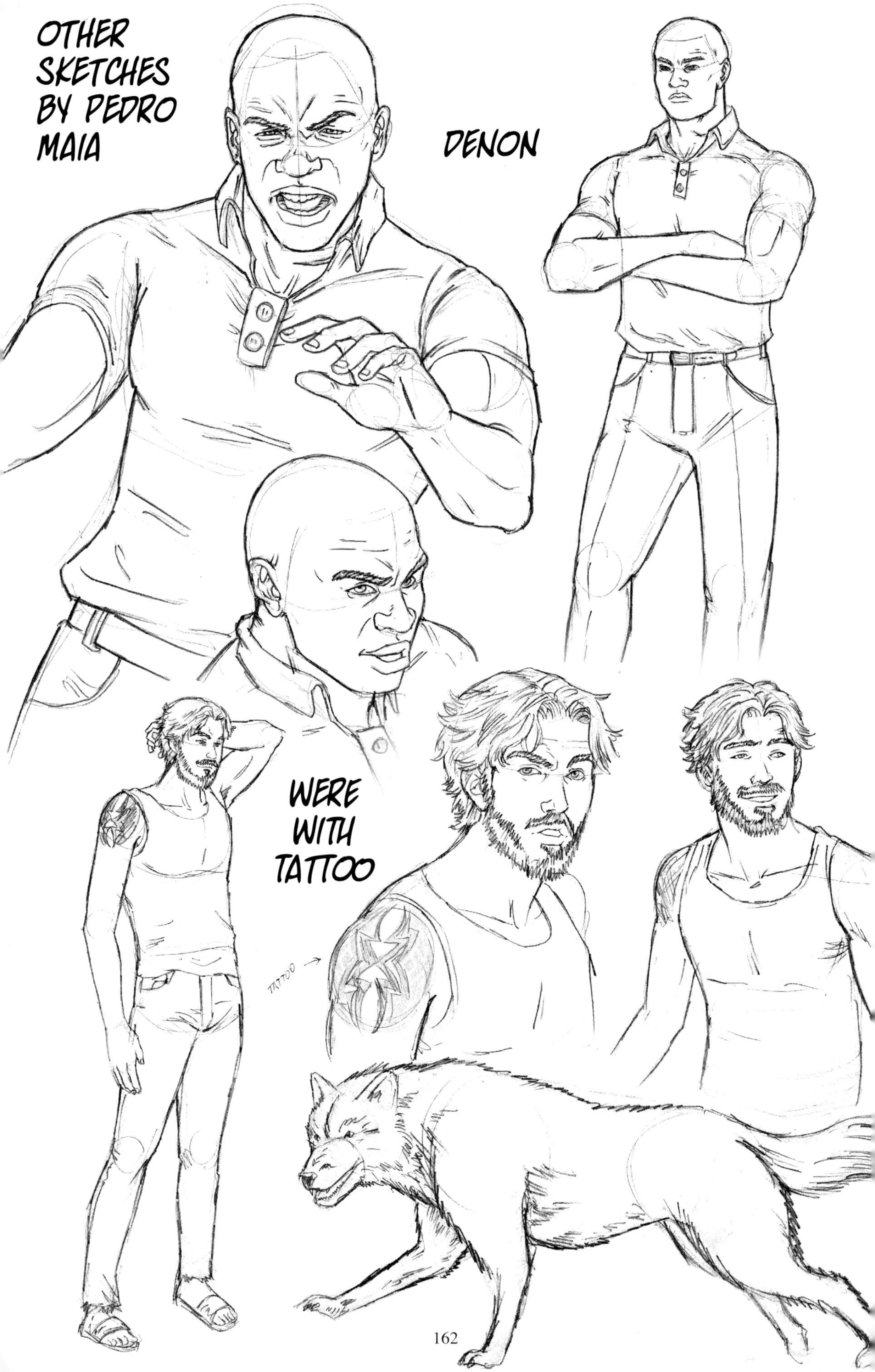
OTHER SKETCHES BY PEDRO MAIA
DENON
WERE WITH TATTOO
TATTOO

Making a Graphic Novel

A graphic novel is created in stages. Once the look of each character has been approved, the penciller translates the author's script into panel form. Here's how one panel from Kim's script went through the process.

1-23 Larger view of Ivy's office with Rachel almost to the door, her arms swinging. Ivy's eyes have gone entirely black, and she's "pulling an aura." Ivy's shadow/aura has manifested, and a dark haze with a feminine shape has its fingers around Denon's throat and its mouth on his neck, one leg around his waist. Denon feels it, and has his hand on his neck, and he's taking a step back from her desk. He's scared of her and his face shows it. Ivy's eyes are lidded, and she has a sexy posture, having stood and is now leaning over her desk toward him. She's showing her small, sharp fangs.

IVY: For you, Denon . . . I'll get creative.

First the penciller created rough page layouts following Kim's descriptions. At this point it is fairly simple to request changes in panel size, the stance of the characters, etc.

Once the pencils have been approved, an inker goes over the artwork to take it to the next step. Shadows and tones appear at this stage.

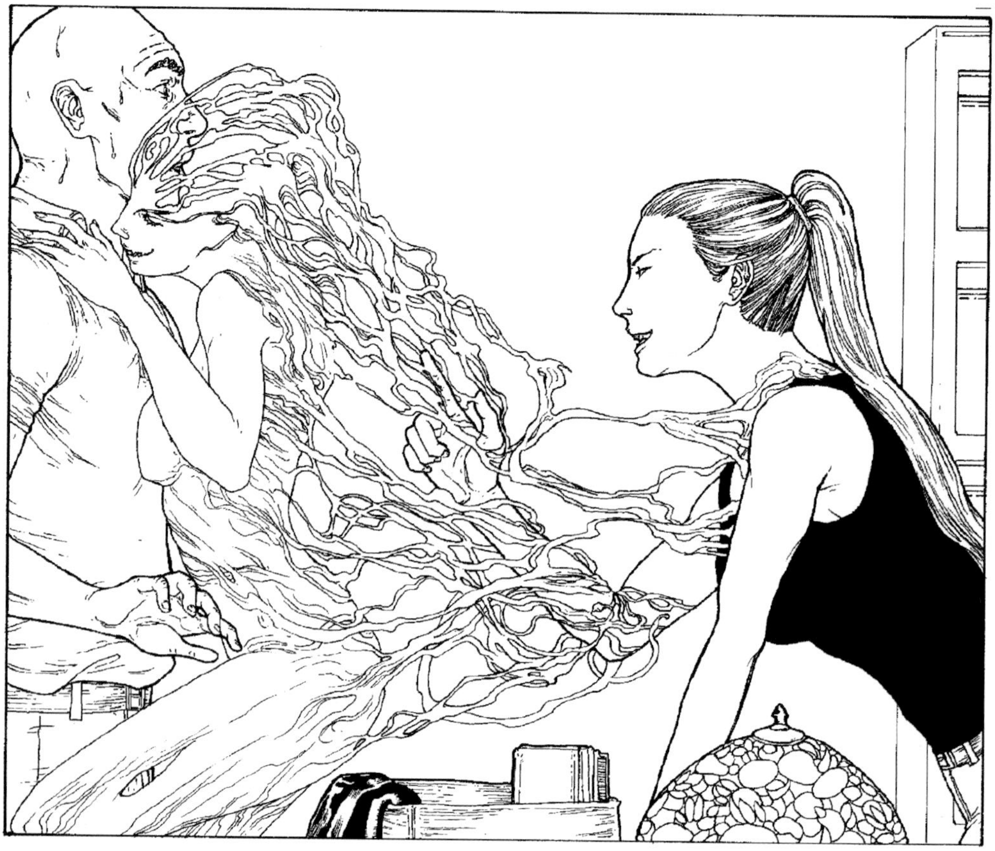

Next the colorist goes to work, following whatever specific instructions have been given regarding time of day, colors of clothing or accessories, and in the case of *Blood Work*, descriptions of magic-generated special effects.

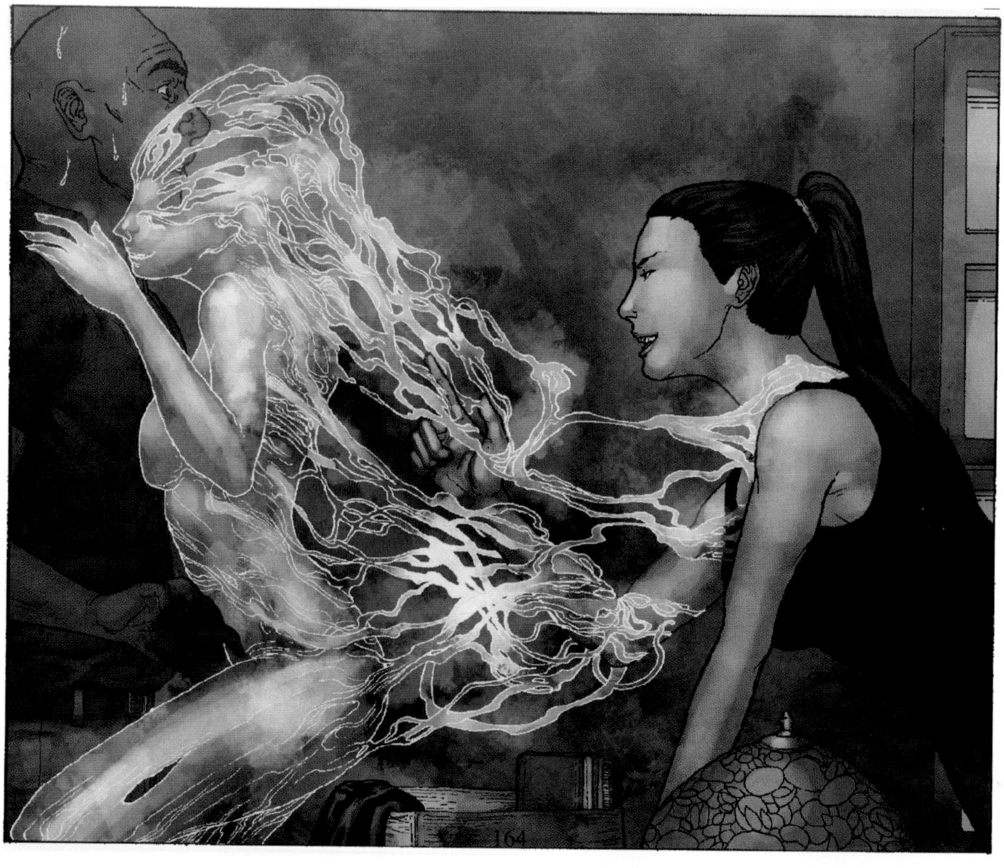

And finally the letterer inserts the script, using different type treatments to differentiate between narration and dialogue.

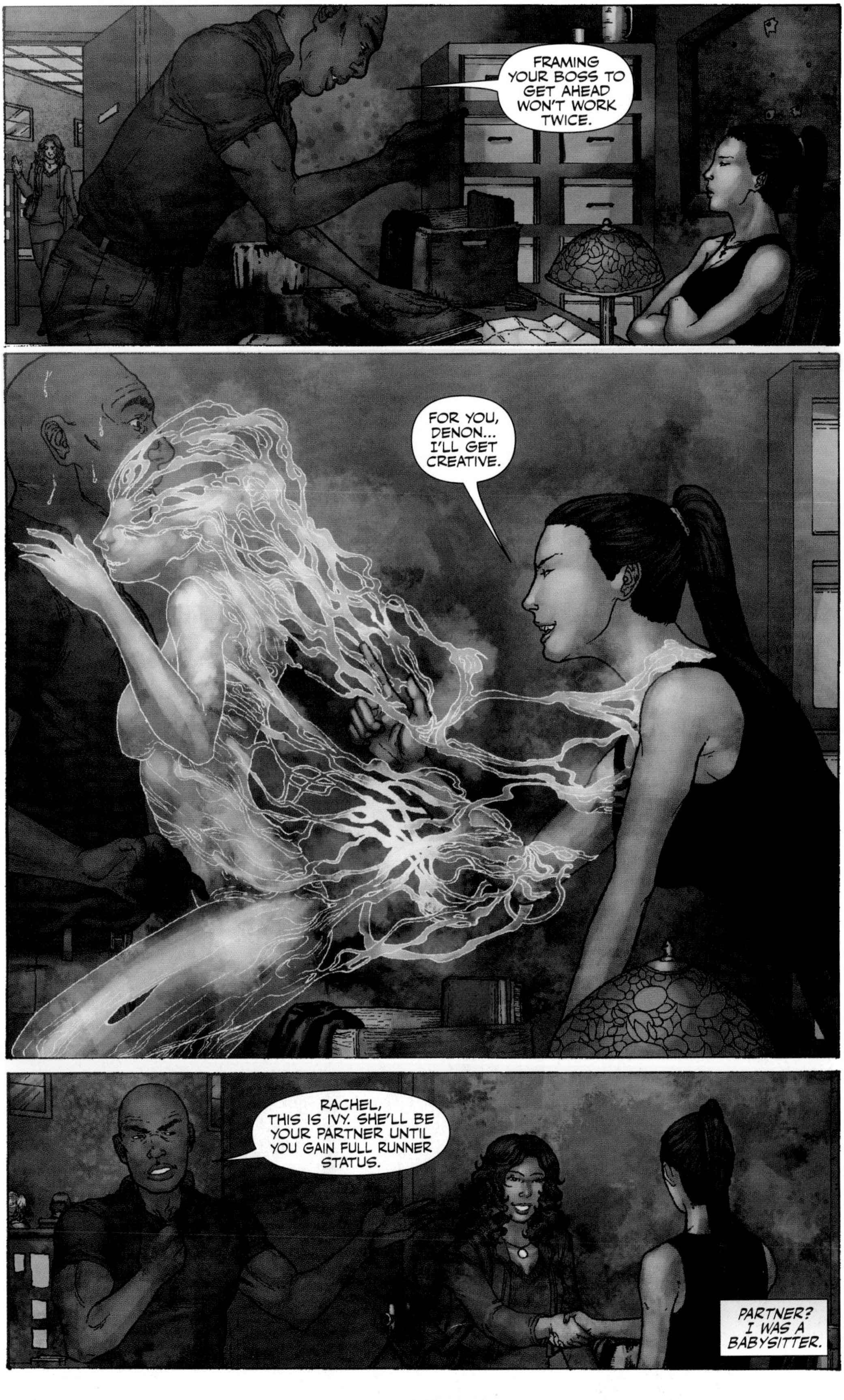
FRAMING YOUR BOSS TO GET AHEAD WON'T WORK TWICE.
FOR YOU, DENON... I'LL GET CREATIVE.
RACHEL, THIS IS IVY. SHE'LL BE YOUR PARTNER UNTIL YOU GAIN FULL RUNNER STATUS.
PARTNER? I WAS A BABYSITTER.

A Conversation with Kim Harrison

DEL REY: You say in your introduction to this book that you'd been itching for a new way to tell a story. Can you describe the creative process you went through with *Blood Work* as opposed to what you experience while writing a novel?

Scripting a graphic novel turned out to be the perfect balance for me between wanting to tell a story in a different way and yet retaining the security of familiar places and characters as I learned a new skill. It wasn't just figuring out how to make boxes in Word—the entire storytelling process that I was comfortable with had to be adjusted. Graphic novels are structured by the actions of the characters, not the thought processes of the characters, as regular novels are. You'll see a lot of captions in my GN work because I'm comfortable writing from Ivy's head. It's how I tell a story. We lost a lot of Ivy's internal dialogue between my first script and the final product, but I found there was a lot I could lose and still get my point across. I like writing sparsely, but this was akin to guerilla warfare on my usual writing style, and I found I liked it.

One of the things I most enjoyed about scripting a graphic novel was dealing with the nuts and bolts of perspective, size of pictures, and balancing that against the amount of words I could fit in without crowding the panel. I didn't want a GN that was the same pattern of boxes over and over, seeing characters facing each other talking, so I spent a lot of time trying to shake it up, bring in close-ups to show a mood without words, to drop back and show the landscape when the emotion was distant and cold. And then there was the color, adding an entirely new facet to showing emotion. I truly don't know how much of my thoughts are translating to the page, but I had fun.

Some of the odd perspectives you'll see in Blood Work *were my idea. I had a fabulous penciller, Pedro Maia, who kept me on the straight and narrow, adding in his own ideas when mine were less than effective. My editor, Betsy Mitchell, too, was great about helping me keep the word count to a reasonable level and shaping* Blood Work *into what you see here. I couldn't have done it without her, and I appreciate her patience with me.*

DR: You'd also decided you were ready to tell some new stories from Ivy's point of view. What kept you from doing that before?

Ahhhhh, Ivy. Fairly early on in the Hollows series, I wrote a novella from Ivy's point of view to show her utter dependence on Piscary, the degradation he could demand from her, the abuse he put her through—both mentally and physically—all for his enjoyment. For me, vampires have always been not the sexy, attractive model that seems to be so popular today, but rather a reflection of the abusers and users in society. They are ugly, and in trying to fit my view and the popular view together, I decided to work with living vam-pires who possess souls (the children of abusers who fight to keep from abus-ing those they love in turn) and dead vampires (the abusers themselves, who appear full of power and grace, but underneath are ugly). Putting myself into Ivy's head, the head of an abused woman struggling to not become what she both loathed and loved, was hard, and I didn't like the depth of where I had to go to portray her properly on the page. The graphic novel was a perfect opportunity for me to tell a story from her perspective and maintain a healthier distance.

DR: Your fans have been vocal about the pros and cons of coming out with a graphic novel. What are some of the concerns they've men-tioned?

Most of the concerns that I've been hearing from the readers have been about the characters not looking the way they have imagined them in their head. There's no recourse I can find to remedy the disappointment except perhaps showing the readers what we've been working with ahead of time and trying to make the jump from mental image to physical image easier.

I'll admit that some of the characters—Sharps, in particular, and even Kisten—are not the way I imagined them in my own head, but they are grow-ing on me. As I tell disappointed readers, there is NO WAY that the charac-ters can possibly look the way you expect them to. Everyone has a different filter they read the books through, and it's up to the reader to understand that going from print to visual is not an easy translation and to be kind. We didn't deviate from your mental image to make you mad. It is what it is, and if the soul of the story is the same, if the emotions pulled from you are the same, if you feel the same way when the story is done, then we have all done an excellent job.

DR: A graphic novel can be the next best thing to a film or television version. Is there anything like that in the works for Rachel and Ivy?

Not at this time. As much as it pains me to say, the Hollows might not be suitable to translate to film. Jenks would be difficult, but even when you go beyond that, the scope of the books covers so much ground, it would take a considerable investment to do it justice. The Hollows is all about shades and subtleties, and simple stories are easier to tell on the screen. Perhaps I simply lack the faith that anyone in Hollywood will ever slow down enough to see, because that's where the strength in the Hollows rests: the subtleties.

DR: How did you choose a penciller?

Choosing the penciller was probably one of the most agonizing decisions I made. The choices available were all outstanding, and though it's hard to imagine the Hollows by looking at samples of other work, there were a few key things I was looking for.

How the artist handled women's bodies was important to me. Thunder thighs and bullet boobs were not going to make it. I totally understand that they are acceptable in the graphic format, but these were women with whom I had worked for almost a decade, and I wasn't going to let them be turned into sex objects.

Another aspect that I looked for in my penciller was how he or she was able to portray city streets. Much of the draw of the Hollows is in the city itself, which almost serves as a silent character. I adored Pedro's cityscapes, and I was impressed that he could do so much in so little space with perspective and angle.

But what sold me on Pedro was his ability to take my stumbling description of Ivy's hunger shadow and make it real. He was the only artist who even tried to make my words a vision during the "what can you do with my descriptions" stage of the process, and what he came up with took my breath away, a melding of spirit and desire, Ivy's thoughts given visual depth. It's in the subtleties that the Hollows shines, showing the unique amid the everyday, and Pedro seemed to capture that.

DR: The fight scene on page 134 was the toughest one in the book for Pedro Maia to get right. Describing the movements didn't work well enough—eventually you and your son came up with a creative way to show him how to work them. Tell us about that.

I have a very dusty first-degree black belt in both tae kwon do and hap-ki-do, and I had a very clear image of what the fight scenes should look like. Scripting some of the moves became rather frustrating because of the language barrier and my stumbling attempts to block out the moves. I finally resorted to making a YouTube of me and my youngest son doing the move on page 134 where Ivy does an X-block and twists to jab the attacker's knife into his own kidney. I'm still not really happy in how it translated to the page, but only someone who practices will notice the incongruities. [wince] If you want to see the YouTube, I've got it up at the website, kimharrison.net.

DR: When you saw the scene of Ivy sniffing after the witch in the Werehouse, you exclaimed that the Were on page 78, panel 1, looked very much like your brother. We asked the colorist to give him blond hair. How is the resemblance now? Has your brother seen it yet?

Yes! Seeing the image of my brother in a Were bar was a bit of a delightful shock. I showed my brother the inked page and asked if he minded if I had the colorist tailor it a bit to match him more fully. My brother was delighted, and so his image will remain forever enshrined as the Were Ivy sniffed. I've not yet shown him the colored version, but plan on sending him Blood Work *when it's finished.*

DR: Ivy's skin tone came in for discussion as we started to receive the colored pages. At first her complexion was shown pretty much the same as Rachel's. You directed the colorist to make her paler.

It actually surprised me when the first colored pages came in and Ivy and Rachel had similar skin tones. I asked for Ivy to have a lighter tone for a couple of reasons, ignoring the logic that a woman with an Asian heritage would probably have darker skin than a woman with red hair who could burn on a cloudy day. My first thought was that the two women looked too much alike, especially when they would be sharing so much page time, and since GNs are visual, I wanted to accentuate their differences. Someone had to change, and I decided since Ivy was a vampire, it might be more logical if she was paler. The changes had the unexpected happy result of Ivy standing out more against the vividly dark color palette, making her more the center of attention. I think it works wonderfully.

DR: Author and editor had several other discussions about color issues. Here's an excerpt from the many emails that went back and forth:

Editor: You have your choice of coloration whenever blood is shown. Many full-color comics employ black instead of red for blood. We see blood on Ivy's neck in one of these pages. Let me know whether you want it red or black. And if you have any other specific requests for color, please state them now or forever hold your peace.

Kim: If you have no strong preference, I'd be happy with red for blood, as long as it's not fire-engine red. More of a dusky color. And I have no specific requests for color apart from Ivy's hunger shadow, which I'd like to see in shades of black, gray, and perhaps highlights of silver? Oh, and Ivy wears dark colors, and Rachel tends to like lighter, but not pastels.

DR: Any more graphic novels in the works?

Yes! The script for Book 2 is in the pencilling stage, and I'm looking forward to the colored pages.